Mary Jane Holmes

Gretchen

A Novel

Mary Jane Holmes

Gretchen
A Novel

ISBN/EAN: 9783337044749

Printed in Europe, USA, Canada, Australia, Japan

Cover: Foto ©Andreas Hilbeck / pixelio.de

More available books at **www.hansebooks.com**

POPULAR NOVELS.

BY

MRS. MARY J. HOLMES.

TEMPEST AND SUNSHINE.	DARKNESS AND DAYLIGHT.
ENGLISH ORPHANS.	HUGH WORTHINGTON.
HOMESTEAD ON HILLSIDE.	CAMERON PRIDE.
'LENA RIVERS.	ROSE MATHER.
MEADOW BROOK.	ETHELYN'S MISTAKE.
DORA DEANE.	MILBANK.
COUSIN MAUDE.	EDNA BROWNING.
MARIAN GREY.	WEST LAWN.
EDITH LYLE.	MILDRED.
DAISY THORNTON.	FORREST HOUSE.
CHATEAU D'OR.	MADELINE.
QUEENIE HETHERTON.	CHRISTMAS STORIES.
BESSIE'S FORTUNE.	GRETCHEN (New).

"Mrs. Holmes is a peculiarly pleasant and fascinating
writer. Her books are always entertaining, and she
has the rare faculty of enlisting the sympathy
and affections of her readers, and of holding their attention to her pages with
deep and absorbing interest."

G. W. DILLINGHAM, PUBLISHER,
SUCCESSOR TO
G. W. CARLETON & Co., New York.

A Novel.

BY

MRS. MARY J. HOLMES,

AUTHOR OF

TEMPEST AND SUNSHINE.—DARKNESS AND DAYLIGHT.—MILBANK.—
ENGLISH ORPHANS.—'LENA RIVERS.—ETHELYN'S MISTAKE.—
HUGH WORTHINGTON.—MADELINE.—WEST LAWN.—
EDNA BROWNING.—MARIAN GREY.—
BESSIE'S FORTUNE, ETC.

NEW YORK

G. W. Dillingham, Publisher,

SUCCESSOR TO G. W. CARLETON & CO.

LONDON: S. LOW, SON & CO.

MDCCCLXXXVII.

STEREOTYPED BY
SAMUEL STODDER,
42 DEY STREET, N. Y.

CONTENTS.

CHAPTER I.

THE TELEGRAM.

"BREVOORT HOUSE, NEW YORK, Oct. 6th, 18—.
"TO Mr. Frank Tracy, of Tracy Park, Shannondale.
"I arrived in the Scotia this morning, and shall take the train for Shannondale at 3 P. M. Send some one to the station to meet us.   "ARTHUR TRACY."

This was the telegram which the clerk in the Shannondale office received one October morning, and dispatched to the Hon. Frank Tracy, of Tracy Park, in the quiet town of Shannondale, where our story opens.

Mr. Frank Tracy, who, since his election to the State Legislature for two successive terms, had done nothing except to attend political meetings and make speeches on all public occasions, had an office in town, where he usually spent his mornings, smoking, reading the papers, and talking to Mr. Colvin, his business agent and l .yer, for, though born in one of the humblest New Eng' .d houses, where the slanting roof almost touched the ground in the rear, and he could scarcely stand upright in the chamber where he slept, Mr. Frank Tracy was a man of leisure now, and as he dashed along the turnpike in his handsome carriage, with his driver beside him, people looked admiringly after him, and pointed him out to strangers as the Hon. Mr. Tracy, of Tracy Park, one of the finest places in

1*

the county. It is true it did not belong to him, but he had lived there so long that he looked upon it as his, while his neighbors, too, seemed to have forgotten that there was a Mr. Arthur Tracy, who might at any time come home to claim his own and demand an account of his brother's stewardship. And it was this Arthur Tracy, whose telegram announcing his return from Europe was read by his brother with feelings of surprise and consternation.

"Not that everything isn't fair and above board, and he is welcome to look into matters as much as he likes," Frank said to himself, as he sat staring at the telegram, while the cold chills ran up and down his back and arms. "Yes, he can examine all Colvin's books; he will find them straight as a string, and didn't he tell me to take what I thought right as remuneration for looking after his property while he was gallivanting over the world ; and if he objects that I have taken too much, I can at once transfer those investments in my name to him. No, it is not that which affects me so; it is the suddenness of the thing, coming without warning, and to night of all nights, when the house will be full of carousing and champagne. What will Dolly say ? Hysterics, of course, if not a sick head-ache. I don't believe I can face her till she has had a little time to brace up. Here, boy, I want you !" and he rapped on the window at a young lad who happened to be passing with a basket on his arm. "I want you to do an errand for me," he continued, as the boy entered the office and, removing his cap, stood respectfully before him. "Take this telegram to Mrs. Tracy, and here is a dime for you."

"Thank you ; but I don't care for the money," the boy said. "I was going to the park anyway to tell Mrs. Tracy that grandma is sick and can't go there to-night."

"Sick ! What is the matter ?" Mr. Tracy asked, in dismay, feeling that here was a fresh cause of trouble and worry for his wife.

"She catched cold yesterday fixing up mother's grave," the boy replied; and, as if the mention of that grave had sent Mr. Tracy's thoughts straying backward to the past, he looked thoughtfully at the child for a moment, and then said :

"How old are you, Harold ?"

"Ten, last August," was the reply; and Mr. Tracy continued:

"You do not remember your mother?"

"No, sir; only a great crowd, and grandma crying so hard," was Harold's reply.

"You look like her," Mr. Tracy said.

"Yes, sir," Harold answered; while into his frank, open face there came an expression of regret for the mother who had died when he was three years old, and whose life had been so short and sad.

"Now, hurry off with the telegram, and mind you don't lose it. It is from my brother. He is coming to night."

"Mr. Arthur Tracy, who sent the monument for my mother—is he coming home? Oh, I am so glad!" Harold exclaimed, his face lighting up with joy, as he put the telegram in his pocket and started for Tracy Park, wondering if he should encounter Tom, and thinking that if he did, and Tom gave him any chaff, he should thresh him, or try to.

"Darn him!" he said to himself, as he recalled the many times when Tom Tracy, a boy about his own age, had laughed at him for his poverty and coarse clothes. "He ain't any better than I am, if he does wear velvet trousers and live in a big house. 'Tain't his'n; it's Mr. Arthur's, and I'm glad he is coming home. I wonder if he will bring grandma anything. I wish he'd bring me a pyramid. He's seen 'em, they say."

Meantime, Mr. Frank Tracy had resumed his seat, and, with his hands clasped over his head, was wondering what effect his brother's return would have upon him. Would he be obliged to leave the park, and the luxury he had enjoyed so long, and go back to the old life which he hated so much?

"No; Arthur will never be so mean," he said. "He has always shown himself generous, and will continue to do so. Besides that, he will want somebody to keep the house for him, unless——" And here the perspiration started from every pore as Frank Tracy thought: "What if he is married, and the *us* in his telegram means a wife, instead of a friend or servant as I imagined!"

That would indeed be a calamity, for then his reign was over at Tracy Park, and the party he and his wife were to give that night to at least three hundred people would be their last.

"Confound the party!" he thought, as he arose from his chair and began to pace the room. "Arthur won't like that as a greeting after eleven years' absence. He never fancied being cheek by jowl with Tom, Dick, and Harry; and that is just what the smash is to night. Dolly wants to please everybody, thinking to get me votes for Congress, and so she has invited all creation and his wife. There's old Peterkin, the roughest kind of a canal bummer when Arthur went away. Think of my fastidious brother shaking hands with him and Widow Shipley, who kept a low tavern on the tow path! She'll be there, in her silks and long gold chain, for she has four boys, all voters, who call me *Frank* and slap me on the shoulder. Ugh! even I hate it all;" and, in a most perturbed state of mind, the would be Congressman continued to walk the room, lamenting the party, and wondering what his aristocractic brother would say to such a crowd in his house on the night of his return.

And if there should be a Mrs. Arthur Tracy, with possibly some little Tracys! But that idea was too horrible to contemplate, and he tried to put it from his mind, and to be as calm and quiet as possible until lunch time, when, with no very great amount of alacrity and cheerfulness, he started for home.

CHAPTER II.

ARTHUR TRACY.

ALTHOUGH it was a morning in October, the grass in the park was as green as in early June, while the flowers in the beds and borders, the geraniums, the phlox, the stocks, and verbenas, were handsomer, if possible, than they had been in the summer-time; for the rain, which had fallen almost continually during the month of September, had kept them fresh and bright. Here and there the scarlet and golden tints of autumn were beginning to show on the trees; but this only added a new charm to a place which was noted for its beauty, and was the pride and admiration of the town.

And yet Mrs. Frank Tracy, who stood on the wide piazza, looking after a carriage which was moving down the avenue which lead through the park to the highway, did not seem as happy as the mistress of that house ought to have been, standing there in the clear, crisp morning, with a silken wrapper trailing behind her, a coquettish French cap on her head, and costly jewels on her short, fat hands, which once were not as white and soft as they were now. For Mrs. Frank Tracy, as Dorothy Smith, had known what hard labor and poverty meant, and slights, too, because of the poverty and labor. Her mother was a widow, sickly and lame, and Dorothy in her girlhood had worked in the cotton mills at Langley, and bound shoes for the firm of Newell & Brothers, and rebelled at the fate which had made her so poor and seemed likely to keep her so.

But there was something better in store for her than binding shoes, or working in the mills, and from the time when young Frank Tracy came to Langley as clerk in the Newell firm, Dorothy's life was changed and her star began to rise. They both sang in the choir, standing side by side, and sometimes using the same book, and once their hands met as both tried to turn the leaves together. Dorothy's were red and rough, and not nearly as delicate as those of Frank, who had been in a store all his life; and still there was a magnetism in their touch which sent a thrill through the young man's veins, and made him for the first time look critically at his companion.

She was very pretty, he thought, with bright black eyes, a healthful bloom, and a smile and blush which went straight to his heart, and made him her slave at once. In three months' time they were married and commenced housekeeping in a very unostentatious way, for Frank had nothing but his salary to depend upon. But he was well connected, and boasted some blue blood, which, in Dorothy's estimation, made amends for lack of money. The Tracys of Boston were his distant relatives, and he had a rich bachelor uncle, who spent his winters in New Orleans and his summers at Tracy Park, on which he had lavished fabulous sums of money. From this uncle Frank had expectations, though naturally the greater part of his fortune would go to his godson and namesake, Arthur Tracy, who was Frank's elder brother, and as unlike him as one brother could well be unlike another.

Arthur was scholarly in his tastes, and quiet and gentlemanly in his manners, and, though subject to moods and fits of abstraction and forgetfulness, which won for him the reputation of being a "little queer," he was exceedingly popular with everyone. Frank was very proud of his brother, and with Dorothy felt that he was honored when, six months after their marriage, he came for a day or so to visit them, and with him his intimate friend, Harold Hastings, an Englishman by birth, but so thoroughly Americanized as to pass unchallenged for a native. There was a band of crape on Arthur's hat, and his manner was like one trying to be sorry, while conscious of an inward feeling of resignation, if not content. The rich uncle had died suddenly, and the whole of his vast fortune was left to his nephew Arthur—not a farthing to Frank, not even the mention of his name in the will ; and when Dorothy heard it, she put her white apron over her face, and cried as if her heart would break. They were so poor, she and Frank, and they wanted so many things, and the man who could have helped them was dead, and had left them nothing. It was hard, and she might not have made the young heir very welcome if he had not assured her that he should do something for her husband. And he kept his word, and bought out a grocery in Langley and put Frank in it, and paid the mortgage on his house, and gave him a thousand dollars, and invited Dolly to visit him ; and then it would seem as if he forgot them entirely, for with his friend Harold, he settled himself at Tracy Park, and played the role of the grand gentleman to perfection.

Few ladies ever called at the house, for, with two or three exceptions, Arthur held himself aloof from the people of Shannondale. It was said, however, that sometimes, when he and his friend were alone, there was the sound of music in the parlor, where sweet Amy Crawford, daughter of the housekeeper, played and sang her simple ballads to the two gentlemen, who treated her with as much deference as if she had been a queen, instead of a poor young girl dependent for her bread upon her own and her mother's exertions. But beyond the singing in the twilight Amy never advanced, and so far as her mother knew, she had never for a single instant been alone with either of the gentlemen. How, then, was the household electrified one morning, when it was found that Amy had fled, and that Harold Hastings was the companion of her flight?

"I wanted to tell you," Amy wrote to her mother in the note left on her dressing-table, "I wanted to tell you and be married at home, but Mr. Hastings would not allow it. It would create trouble, he said, between himself and Mr. Tracy, who, I may confess to you in confidence, asked me twice to be his wife, and when I refused, he was so angry and behaved so strangely, and there was such a look in his eyes, that I was afraid of him, and it was this fear, I think, which made me willing to go away secretly with Harold and be married in New York. We are going to Europe; shall sail to-morrow morning at nine o'clock in the Scotia. The marriage ceremony will be performed before we go on board. I shall write as soon as we reach Liverpool. You must forgive me, mother, and I am sure you would if you knew how much I love Mr. Hastings. I know he is poor, and that I might be mistress of Tracy Park, but I love Harold best. It is ten o'clock, and the train passes at eleven, so I must say good-by.

"Yours lovingly,
"AMY."

This letter Mrs. Crawford found upon entering her daughter's room, after waiting more than an hour for her appearance at the breakfast, which they always took by themselves. To say that she was shocked and astonished would but faintly portray the state of her mind as she read that her beautiful young daughter had gone with Harold Hastings, whom she had never liked, for, though he was handsome and agreeable, and gentlemanly as a rule, she knew him to be thoroughly selfish and indolent, and she trembled for Amy's happiness when a little time had quenched the ardor of his passion. Added to this was another thought which made her brain reel for a moment. Arthur Tracy had wished to make Amy his wife, and the mistress of Tracy Park, which she would have graced so well, for in all the town there was not a fairer, sweeter girl than Amy Crawford, or one better beloved. But it was too late now. There was no turning back the wheels of fate; and forcing herself to be as calm as possible, she took the note to Arthur, who was waiting impatiently in the library for the appearance of his friend.

"Lazy dog!" Mrs. Crawford heard him say, as she approached the open door. "Does he think he has nothing to do but to sleep? We were to start by this time, and he in bed yet!"

"Are you speaking of Mr. Hastings?" Mrs. Crawford asked, as she stepped into the room.

"Yes," was his haughty reply, as if he resented the question, and her presence there.

He could be very proud and stern when he felt like it, and one of these moods was on him now, but Mrs. Crawford did not heed it, and sinking into a chair, she began:

"I came to tell you of Mr. Hastings, and—Amy. I found this note in her room. She has gone to New York with him. They took the eleven o'clock train last night. They are to be married this morning, and sail for Europe."

For a moment Arthur Tracy stood looking at her, while his face grew white as ashes, and into his dark eyes, there came a gleam like that of a madman.

"Amy gone with Harold, my friend!" he said, at last. "Gone to be married! Traitors! both of them. Curse them! If he were here I'd shoot him like a dog; and she—I believe I would kill her too."

He was walking the floor rapidly, and to Mrs. Crawford it seemed as if he really were unsettled in his mind, he talked so incoherently and acted so strangely.

"What else did she say?" he asked, suddenly, stopping and confronting her. "You have not told me all. Did she speak of me? Let me see the note," and he held his hand for it.

For a moment Mrs. Crawford hesitated, but as he grew more and more persistent she gave it to him, and then watched him as he read it, while the veins on his forehead began to swell until they stood out like a dark blue network against his otherwise pallid face.

"Yes," he said between his teeth. "I did ask her to be my wife, and she refused, and with her soft, kittenish ways made me more in love with her than ever, and more her dupe. I never suspected Harold, and when I told him of my disappointment, for I never kept a thing from him, he laughed at me for losing my heart to my housekeeper's daughter! I could have knocked him down for his sneer at Amy, and I wish now I had! He does not mean to marry your daughter, madam, but if he does not, I will kill him!"

He was certainly mad, and Mrs. Crawford shrank away from him as from something dangerous, and going to her room took her bed in a fit of frightful hysterics. This was followed by a state of nervous prostration, and for a few days she neither saw nor heard of, nor inquired for Mr. Tracy. At the end of the fourth day, however, she was told by the house-maid that he had that morning packed his valise and, without a word to any one, had taken the train for New York. A week went by, and then there came a letter from him, which was as follows:

"NEW YORK, May—, 18—.

"MRS. CRAWFORD:—I am off for Europe to-morrow, and when I shall return is a matter of uncertainty. They are married; or at least I suppose so, for I found a list of the passengers who sailed in the Scotia, and the names, Mr. and Mrs. Hastings, were in it. So that saves me from breaking the sixth commandment, as I should have done if he had played Amy false. I may not make myself known to them, but I shall follow them, and if he harms a hair of her head I shall shoot him yet. My brother Frank is to live at Tracy Park. That will suit his wife, and as you will not care to stay with her, I send you a deed of that cottage in the lane by the wood where the gardener now lives. It is a pretty little place, and Amy liked it well. We used to meet there sometimes, and more than once I have sat with her on that seat under the elm tree, and it was there I asked her to be my wife. Alas! I loved her so much, and I could have made her so happy; but that is past, and I can only watch her at a distance. When I have anything to communicate, I will write again.

"Yours truly,   "ARTHUR TRACY."

"P. S.—Take all the furniture in your room and Amy's, and whatever else you need for your house. I shall tell Colvin to give you a thousand dollars, and when you want more let him know. I shall never forget that you are Amy's mother."

This was Arthur's letter to Mrs. Crawford, while to his brother he wrote:

"DEAR FRANK:—I am going to Europe for an indefinite length of time. Why I go it matters not to you or any one. I go to suit myself, and I want you to sell out your business in Langley and live at Tracy Park, where you can see to things as if they were your own. You will find everything straight and square, for Colvin is honest and methodical. He knows all about the bonds, and mortgages, and stocks, so you cannot do better than to retain him in your service, overseeing matters yourself, of course, and drawing for your salary what you think right and necessary for your support and for keeping up the place as it ought to be kept up. I inclose a power of attorney. When I want money I shall call upon Colvin. I may be gone for years and perhaps forever.

"I shall never marry, and when I die, what I have will naturally go to you. We have not been much like brothers for the past few years, but I don't forget the old home in the mountains where we were boys together, and played, and quarreled, and slept under the roof, where the blanket's were hung to keep the snow from sifting through the rafters upon our bed.

"And, Frank, do you remember the bitter mornings, when the thermometer was below zero, and we performed our ablutions in the wood-shed, and the black eye you gave me once for telling mother that you had not washed yourself at all, it was so cold? She sent you from the table, and made you go without your breakfast, and we had ham and johnny-cake toast that morning, too. That was long ago, and our lives are different now. There are marble basins, with silver chains and stoppers, at Tracy Park, and you can have a hot bath every day if you like, in a room which would not shame Caracalla himself. And I know you will like it, and Dolly, too; but don't make fools of yourselves. Be quiet and modest, and act as if you had always lived at Tracy Park. Be kind to Mrs. Crawford, who is a lady in every sense of the word.

"And now, good-by. I shall write occasionally, but not often.

"Your brother,   "ARTHUR TRACY."

CHAPTER III.

MR. AND MRS. FRANK TRACY.

MR. FRANK, in his small grocery at Langley, was weighing out a pound of butter for the Widow Simpson, who was haggling with him about the price, when his brother's letter was brought to him by the boy who swept his store and did errands for him. But Frank was too busy just then to read it. There was a circus in the village that day, and it brought the country people into the town in larger numbers than usual. Naturally, many of them paid Frank a visit in the course of the morning, so that it was not until he went home to his dinner that he thought of the letter, which was finally brought to his mind by his wife's asking if there were any news.

Mrs. Frank was always inquiring for and expecting news, but she was not prepared for what this day brought her. Neither was her husband; and when he read his brother's letter, which he did twice to assure himself that he was not mistaken, he sat for a moment perfectly bewildered, and stared at his wife, who was putting his dinner upon the table.

"Dolly," he gasped at last, when he could speak at all —"Dolly, what do you think? Just listen. Arthur is going to Europe, to stay forever, perhaps, and has left us Tracy Park. We are going there to live, and you will be as grand a lady as Mrs. Atherton, of Brier Hill, or that young girl at Collingwood."

Dolly had a platter of ham and eggs in her hand, and she never could tell, though she often tried to do so, what prevented her from dropping the whole upon the floor. She did spill some of the fat upon her clean table-cloth, she put the dish down so suddenly, and then sinking into a chair, she demanded what her husband meant. Was he crazy, or what?

"Not a bit of it," he replied, recovering himself, and beginning to realize the good fortune which had come to him. "We are rich people, Dolly. Read for yourself;" and he passed her the letter, which she seemed to understand better than he had done.

"Why, yes," she said. "We are going to Tracy Park to live; but that doesn't make us rich. It is not ours."

"I know that," her husband replied. "But we shall enjoy it all the same, and hold our heads with the best of them. Besides, don't you see, Arthur gives me *carte blanche* as to pay for my services, and, though I shall do right, it is not in human nature that I should not feather my nest when I have a chance. Some of that money ought to have been mine. I shall sell out at once if I can find a purchaser, and if I can't, I shall rent the grocery and move out of this hole double-quick."

His ideas were growing faster than those of his wife, who was attached to Langley and its people, and shrank a little from the grand life opening before her. She had once spent a few days at Tracy Park, as Arthur's guest, and had felt great restraint even in the presence of Mrs. Crawford and Amy, whom she recognized as ladies, notwithstanding their position in the house. On that occasion she had, with her brother-in-law, been invited to dine at Brier Hill, the country-seat of Mrs. Grace Atherton, where she had been so completely overawed, that she did not know what half the dishes were, or what she was expected to do. But, by watching Arthur, and declining some things which she felt sure were beyond her comprehension, she managed tolerably well, though when the dinner was over, and she could breathe freely again, she found that the back of her new silk gown was wet with perspiration, which had oozed from every pore during the hour and a half she had sat at the table. "Such folderol!" she said to a friend, to whom she was describing the dinner. "Such folderol! Changing your plates all the time—eating peas in the winter, with nothing under the sun with them, and drinking coffee

out of a cup about as big as a thimble. Give me the good
old-fashioned way, I say, with peas and potatoes, and
meat, and things, and cups that will hold half a pint and
have some thickness that you can feel in your mouth."

And now she was to exchange the good, old-fashioned
way for what she termed "folderol," and for a time she
did not like it. But her husband was so delighted and
eager, that he succeeded in impressing her with some of
his enthusiasm, and after he had returned to his grocery,
and her dishes were washed, she removed her large
kitchen apron, and pulling down the sleeves of her dress,
went and stood before the mirror, where she examined
herself critically, and not without some degree of compla-
cency.

Her hair was black and glossy, or would be if she had
time to care for it as it ought to be cared for; her eyes
were large and bright, and perhaps in time she might
learn to use them as Mrs. Atherton used hers.

"She is older than I am," she said to herself; "there
are crow-tracks around her eyes, and her complexion is not
a bit better than mine was before I spoiled it with soap-
suds, and stove-heat, and everything else."

Then she looked at her hands, but they were red and
rough, and the nails were broken, and not at all like the
nails which an expert has polished for an hour or more.
Mrs. Atherton's diamond rings would be sadly out of place
on Dolly's fingers, but time and abstinence from work
would do much for them, she reflected, and after all it
would be nice to live in a grand house, ride in a handsome
carriage, and keep a hired girl to do the heavy work. So,
on the whole, she began to feel quite reconciled, and to
wonder how she ought to conduct herself in view of her
future position. She had intended going to the circus
that night, but she gave that up, telling her husband that
it was a second-class amusement any way, and she did not
believe that either Mrs. Atherton or the young lady at
Collingwood patronized such places. So they stayed at
home and talked together of what they should do at
Tracy Park, and wondered if it was their duty to ask all
their Langley friends to visit them. Mrs. Frank decided
that it was. She was not going to begin by being *stuck
up*, she said; and when she left Langley four weeks later,

every man, woman, and child of her familiar acquaintance
in town, had been heartily invited to call upon her at
Tracy Park, if ever they came that way.

Frank had disposed of his business at a reasonable
price, and had rented his house with all the furniture,
except such articles as his wife insisted upon taking with
her.   The bureau, and bedstead, and chairs which she and
Frank had bought together in Springfield just before their
marriage, the Boston rocker in which her old mother had
sat until the day she died, the cradle in which she had
rocked her baby boy who was lying in the Langley graveyard, were dear to the wife and mother, and though her
husband told her she could have no use for them, there
was enough of sentiment in her nature to make her cling
to them as something of the past, and so they were boxed
up and forwarded by freight to Tracy Park, whither Mr.
and Mrs. Tracy followed them a week later.

The best dressmaker in Langley had been employed
upon the wardrobe of Mrs. Frank, who, in her traveling
dress of some stuff goods of a plaided pattern, too large
and too bright to be quite in good taste, felt herself perfectly *au fait,* until she reached Springfield, where Mrs.
Grace Atherton, accompanied by a tall, elegant-looking
young lady, entered the car and took a seat in front of
her.   Neither of the ladies noticed her, but she recognized
Mrs. Atherton at once, and guessed that her companion
was the young lady from Collingwood.

Dolly scanned both the ladies very closely, noticing
every article of their costumes, from their plain linen collars and cuffs to their quiet dresses of gray, which seemed
so much more in keeping with the dusty cars than her buff
and purple plaid.

"I ain't like them, and never shall be," she said to
herself, with a bitter sense of her inferiority pressing upon
her.   "I ain't like them, and never shall be, if I live to
be a hundred.   I wish we were not going to be grand.   I
shall never get used to it," and the hot tears sprang to her
eyes as she longed to be back in the kitchen where she had
worked so hard.

But Dolly did not know how readily people can forget
the life of toil behind them, and adapt themselves to one
of luxury and ease ; and with her the adaptability com-

menced in some degree the moment Shannondale station
was reached, and she saw the handsome carriage waiting
for them. A carriage finer far and more modern than the
one from Collingwood, in which Mrs. Atherton and the
young lady took their seats, laughing and chatting so
gayly that they did not see the woman in the big plaids
who stood watching them with a rising feeling of jealousy
and resentment, because she was not noticed.

But when the Tracy carriage drew up, Grace Atherton
saw and recognized her, and whispered, in an aside to her
companion :

"For goodness' sake, Edith, look! There are the
Tracys, our new neighbors." Then she bowed to Mrs.
Tracy, and said : "Ah, I did not know you were on the
train."

"I sat right behind you," was Mrs. Tracy's rather
ungracious reply ; and then, not knowing whether she
ought to do it or not, she introduced her husband.

"Yes, Mr. Tracy—how do you do'?" was Mrs. Atherton's response ; but she did not in return introduce the
young girl, whose dark eyes were scanning the strangers so
curiously ; and this Dolly took as a slight, and inwardly
resented.

But Mrs. Atherton had spoken to her, and that was
something, and helped to keep her spirits up as she was
driven along the turnpike to the entrance of the park.

On the occasion of Mrs. Frank s first and only visit to
her brother-in-law it was winter, and everything was covered with snow. But it was summer now, the month of
roses, and fragrance, and beauty, and as the carriage
passed up the broad, smooth avenue which led to the
house, and Dolly's eye wandered over the well-kept grounds,
sweet with the scent of newly-mown grass, and filled with
every adornment which taste can devise or money procure,
she felt within her the first stirring of the pride, and satisfaction, and self-assertion which were to grow upon her so
rapidly and transform her from the plain, unpretentious
woman who had washed, and ironed, and baked, and
mended in the small house in Langley, into the arrogant,
haughty lady of fashion, who courted only the rich, and
looked down upon her less fortunate neighbors. Now,
however, she was very meek and humble, and trembled as

she alighted from the carriage before the great stone house which was to be her home.

"Isn't this grand, Dolly?" her husband said, rubbing his hands together, and looking about him complacently.

"Yes, very grand," Dolly answered him; "but somehow it makes me feel weaker than water. I suppose, though, I shall get accustomed to it."

CHAPTER IV.

GETTING ACCUSTOMED TO IT.

IN the absence of Mrs. Crawford, who for a week or more had been domesticated in the cottage which Arthur had given her, there was no one to receive the strangers except the cook and the house-maid, and as Mrs. Tracy entered the hall the two came forward, bristling with criticism, and ready to resent anything like interference in the new-comers.

The servants at the park had not been pleased with the change of administration. That Mr. Arthur was a gentleman whom it was an honor to serve, they all conceded; but with regard to the new master and mistress, they had grave doubts. Although none of them had been at the park on the occasion of Mrs. Tracy's first visit there, many rumors concerning her had reached them, and she would scarcely have recognized herself could she have heard the remarks of which she was the subject. That she had worked in a factory—which was true—was her least offense, for it was whispered that once, when the winter was unusually severe, and work scarce, she had gone to a soup-house, and even asked and procured coal from the poor-master for herself and her mother.

This was not true, and would have argued nothing against her as a woman if it had been, but the cook and the house-maid believed it, and passed sundry jokes together while preparing to meet "the pauper," as they designated her.

In this state of things their welcome could not be very cordial, but Mrs. Tracy was too tired and too much excited to observe their demeanor particularly. They were civil, and the house was in perfect order, and so much larger and handsomer than she had thought it to be, that she felt bewildered and embarrassed, and said "Yes 'em," and "No, ma'am," to Martha, and told Sarah, who was waiting at dinner, that she "might as well sit down in a chair as to stand all the time; she presumed she was tired with so many extra steps to take."

But Sarah knew her business, and persisted in standing, and inflicting upon the poor woman as much ceremony as possible, and then, in the kitchen, she repeated to the cook and the coachman, with sundry embellishments of her own, the particulars of the dinner, amid peals of laughter at the expense of the would-be lady.

It was hardly possible that mistress and maids would stay together long, especially as Mrs. Tracy, when a little more assured, and a little less in awe of her servants, began to show a disposition to know by personal observation what was going on in the kitchen, and to hint broadly that there was too much waste here and expenditure there, and quite too much company at all hours of the day.

"She didn't propose to keep a boarding-house," she said, " or to support families outside, and the old woman who came so often to the basement door with a big basket under her cloak must discontinue her calls."

Then there occurred one of those Hibernian cyclones, which sweep everything before them, and which in this instance swept Mrs. Tracy out of the kitchen for the time being, and the cook out of the house. Her self-respect, she said, would not allow her to stay with a woman who knew just how much coal was burned, how much butter was used, and how much bread was thrown away, and who objected to giving a bite now and then to a poor old woman, who, poor as she was, had never yet been helped by the poor-master, or gone to a soup-house, like my lady!

Martha's departure was followed by that of Sarah, and then Mrs. Tracy was alone, and for a few days enjoyed herself immensely, cooking her own dinner, and eating it when and where she liked—in the kitchen mostly, as that

2

kept the flies from the dining-room, and saved her many steps, for Dolly was beginning to find that there was a vast difference between keeping a house with six rooms and one with thirty or more.

Her husband urged her to try a new servant, saying there was no necessity for her to make a slave of herself; but she refused to listen. Economy was a part of her nature, and besides that she meant to show them that she was perfectly independent of the whole tribe; the *tribe* and *them* referring to the hired girls alone, for she knew no one else in town.

No one had called, and a bow from Mrs. Atherton, whom she had seen at church was all the recognition she had received from her neighbors up to the hot July morning, a week or more after the house-maid's departure, when she was busy in the kitchen canning black raspberries, of which the garden was full.

Like many housekeepers who do their own work, Dolly was not very particular with regard to her dress in the morning, and on this occasion her hair was drawn from her rather high forehead, and twisted into a hard knot at the back of her head; her calico dress hung straight down, for she was minus hoops, which in those days were very large; her sleeves were rolled above her elbows, and, as a protection against the juice of the berries, she wore an apron made of sacking. In this garb, and with no thought of being interrupted, she kept on with her work until the last kettle of fruit was boiling and bubbling on the stove, and she was just glancing at the clock to see if it were time to put over the peas for dinner, when there came a quick, decisive ring at the front door.

"Who can that be?" she said to herself, as she wiped her hands upon her apron. "Some peddler, I dare say. Why couldn't he come round to the kitchen door, I'd like to know?"

She had been frequently troubled with peddlers and feeling certain that this was one—she started for the door in no very amiable frame of mind, for peddlers were her abomination. Something ailed the key, which resisted all her efforts to turn it; and at last, putting her mouth to the keyhole, she called out, rather sharply:

"Go to the back door, I can't open this."

Then, as she caught a whiff of burnt sirup, she hurried to the kitchen, where she found that her berries had boiled over, and were hissing and sputtering on the hot stove, raising a cloud of smoke so dense that she did not see the person who stood on the threshold of the door until a voice wholly unlike that of any peddler said to her:

"Good-morning, Mrs. Tracy. I hope I am not intruding."

Then she turned, and, to her horror and surprise, saw Grace Atherton, attired in the coolest and daintiest of morning costumes, with a jaunty French bonnet set coquettishly upon her head, and a silver card-case in her hand.

For the moment Dolly's wits forsook her, and she stood looking at her visitor, who, perfectly at her ease, advanced into the room, and said:

"I hope you will excuse me, Mrs. Tracy, for this morning call. I came—"

But she did not finish the sentence, for by this time Dolly had recovered herself a little, and throwing off her apron, began nervously:

"Not at all—not at all. I supposed you were some peddler or agent when I sent you to this door. They are the plague of my life, and think I'll buy everything and give to everything because Arthur did. I am doing my own work, you see. Come into the parlor;" and she led the way into the dark drawing-room, where the chairs and sofas were shrouded in white linen, and looked like so many ghosts in the dim, uncertain light.

But Dolly opened one of the windows, and pushing back the blinds, let in a flood of sunshine, so strong and bright that she at once closed the shutters, saying, apologetically, that she did not believe in fading the carpets, if they were not her own. Then she sat down upon an ottoman and faced her visitor, who was regarding her with a mixture of amusement and wonder.

Grace Atherton was an aristocrat to her very finger-tips, and shrank from contact with anything vulgar and unsightly, and, to her mind, Mrs. Tracy represented both, and seemed sadly out of place in that handsome room, with her sleeves rolled up and the berry stains on her hands and face. Grace knew nothing by actual experience of canning

berries, or aprons made of sacking, or of bare arms, except
it were of an evening when they showed white and fair
against her satin gown, with bands of gold and precious
stones upon them, and she felt that there was an immeasur-
able distance between herself and this woman, whom she
had come to see partly on business and partly because she
thought she must call upon her for the sake of Arthur
Tracy, who was one of her friends.

Her cook, who had been with her seven years, had gone
to attend a sick mother, and had recommended as a fit
person to take her place the woman who had just left
Tracy Park.

"I do not like to take a servant without first knowing
something of her from her last employer," she said; "and,
if you don't mind, I should like to ask if Martha left you
for anything very bad."

Mrs. Tracy colored scarlet, and for a moment was
silent. She could not tell that fine lady in the white muslin dress with seas of lace and embroidery, that Martha
had called her *second classy*, and *stingy*, and *snooping*, and
mean, because she objected to the amount of coal burned,
and bread thrown away, and time consumed at the table.
All this she felt would scarcely interest a person like Mrs.
Atherton, who might sympathize with Martha more than
with herself, so she finally said:

"Martha was saucy to me, and on the whole it was better for them all to go, and so I am doing my own work."

"Doing your own work!" and Grace gave a little cry
of surprise, while her shoulders shrugged meaningly, and
made Mrs. Tracy almost as angry as she had been with
Martha when she called her mean and stingy. "It cannot be possible that you cook, and wash, and iron, and do
everything," Mrs. Atherton continued. "My dear Mrs.
Tracy, you can never stand it in a house like this, and Mr.
Arthur would not like it. Why, he kept as many as six
servants, and sometimes more. Pray let me advise you,
and commend to you a good girl, who lived with me three
years, and can do everything, from dressing my hair to
making blanc-mange. I only parted with her because she
was sick, and now that she is well, her place is filled.
Try her, and do not make a servant of yourself. It is not
fitting that you should."

Grace was fond of giving advice, and had said more than she intended saying when she began, but Mrs. Tracy, though annoyed, was not angry, and consented to receive the girl who had lived at Brier Hill three years, and who, she reflected, could be of use to her in many ways.

While sitting there in her soiled working dress talking to Mrs. Atherton, she had felt her inferiority more keenly than she had ever done before, while at the same time she was conscious that a new set of ideas and thoughts had taken possession of her, reawaking in her the germ of that ambition to be somebody which she had felt so often when a girl, and which now was to bud and blossom, and bear fruit a hundred fold She would take the girl, and from her learn the ways of the world as practiced at Brier Hill. She would no longer wear sacking aprons, and open the door herself. She would be more like Grace Atherton, whom she watched admiringly as she went down the walk to the handsome carriage waiting for her, with driver and footman in tall hats and long coats on the box.

This was the beginning of the fine lady into which Dolly finally blossomed, and when that day Frank went home to his dinner he noticed something in her manner which he could not understand until she told him of Mrs. Atherton's call, and the plight in which that lady had found her.

"Served you right," Frank said, laughing till the tears ran. "You have no business to be digging round like a slave when we are able to have what we like. Arthur said we were to keep up the place as he had done, and that does not mean that you should be a scullion. No, Dolly; have all the girls you want, and hold up your head with the best of them. Get a new silk gown, and return Mrs. Atherton's call at once, and take a card and turn down one corner or the other, I don't know which, but this girl of hers can tell you. Pump her dry as a powder horn; find out what the quality do, and then do it, and don't bother about the expense. I am going in for a good time, and don't mean to work either. I told Colvin this morning that I thought I ought to draw a salary of about four thousand a year, besides our living expenses, and though he looked at me pretty sharp over his spectacles, he said nothing. Arthur is worth a million, if he is worth a cent,

So, go it, Dolly, while you are young," and in the exuberance of his joy, Frank kissed his wife on both cheeks, and then hurried back to his office.

That day they had dined in the kitchen with a leaf of the table turned up as they had done in Langley, but the next day they had dinner in the dining-room, and were waited upon by the new girl as well as it was possible for her to do with her mistress' interference.

"Never mind ; Mr. Tracy's in a hurry. Give him his pie at once," she said, as Susan was about to clear the table preparatory to the dessert ; but she repented the speech when she saw the look of surprise which the girl gave her, and which expressed more than words could have done.

"Better let her run herself," Frank said, when Susan had left the room, "and if she wants to take every darned thing off the table and tip it over to boot, let her do it. If she has lived three years with Mrs. Atherton, she knows what is what better than we do."

"But it takes so long, and I have so much to see to in this great house," Dolly objected, and her husband replied :

"Get another girl, then ; three of them if you like. What matter how many girls we have so long as Arthur pays for them ; and he is bound to do that. He said so in his letter. You are altogether too economical. I've told you so a hundred times, and now there is no need of saving. I want to see you a lady in silks and satins like Mrs. Atherton. Pump that girl, I tell you, and find out what ladies do !"

This was Frank's advice to his wife, and as far as in her lay she acted upon it, and whatever Susan told her was done by Mrs. Atherton at Brier Hill, she tried to do at Tracy Park : except staying out of the kitchen. That, from her nature, she could not do. Consequently she was constantly changing cooks, and frequently took the helm herself, to the great disgust of her husband, who managed at last to imbue her with his own idea of things.

In course of time most of the neighbors who had any claim to society called, and among them Mrs. Crawford. But Mrs. Tracy had then reached a point from which she looked down upon one who had been housekeeper where she was now mistress, and whose daughter's good name was under a cloud, as there were some who did not believe that Harold Hastings had ever made Amy his wife. When told that Mrs. Crawford had asked for her, Mrs. Tracy sent word that she was engaged, and that if Mrs. Crawford pleased, she would give her errand to the girl.

"I have no errand. I came to call," was Mrs. Crawford's reply ; and she never crossed the threshold of her old home again until the March winds were blowing, and there was a little boy at the park.

At the last moment the expected nurse had fallen sick, and in his perplexity Mr. Tracy went to the cottage in the lane and begged Mrs. Crawford to come and care for his wife. Mrs. Crawford was very proud, but she was poor, too, and as the price per week which Frank offered her was four times as much as she could earn by sewing, she consented at last, and went as nurse to the sick woman and the baby, Tom, on whose little red face she imprinted many a kiss for the sake of her daughter, who was still abroad, and over whom the shadow of hope and fear was hanging.

Dolly Tracy's growth, after it fairly commenced, had been very rapid, and when Mrs. Crawford went to her as nurse she had three servants in her employ, besides the coachman, and was imitating Mrs. Atherton to the best of her ability ; and when, early in the following summer, they received the wedding cards of Edith Hastings, the young lady from Collingwood, who had married a Mr. St. Claire, she felt that her position was assured, and from that time her progress was onward and upward until the October morning, ten years later, when our story proper opens, and we see her standing upon the piazza of her handsome house, with every sign of wealth and luxury about her person, from the silken robe to the jewels upon her hands, which once had canned berries in her kitchen, where she received Grace Atherton with her sleeves above her elbows.

There were five servants in the house now, and they ran over and against each other, and quarreled, and gossiped, and worried her life nearly out of her, until she sometimes wished she could send them away, and do the work herself. But she was far too great a lady for that. She was thoroughly up in etiquette, and did not need Susan to tell her what to do. She knew all about visiting cards, and dinner cards, and cards of acceptance, and regret, and condolence, and she read much oftener than she did her Bible a book entitled "Habits of Good Society."

Three children played in the nursery now, Tom, and Jack, and Maude, and she strove with all her might to instill into their infant minds that they were the Tracys of Tracy Park, and entitled to due respect from their inferiors; and Tom had profited by her teaching, and was the veriest little braggart in Shannondale, boasting of his father's house, and his father's money, without a word of the Uncle Arthur wandering no one knew where, or cared particularly, for that matter.

Arthur had never been home since the day he quitted it to look after Amy Crawford, now lying in the graveyard of Shannondale, under the shadow of the tall monument which his money had bought. At first he had written frequently to Mrs. Crawford, and occasionally to his brother, and his agent, Mr. Colvin; then his letters came very irregularly, and in one he told them not to feel anxious if they did not hear from him in a long time, as in case of his death he had arranged to have the news communicated to them at once. After this letter, nothing had been heard from him until the morning when his telegram came and so greatly disturbed the mental equilibrium of both Mr. and Mrs. Frank Tracy.

CHAPTER V.

AT THE PARK.

FRANK had at first grown faster than his wife, and the change in his manner had been more perceptible; for with all her foolishness Dolly had a keener sense of right, and wrong, and justice than her husband. She had opposed him stoutly when he raised his own salary from $4,000 to $6,000 a year, on the plea that his services were worth it, and that two thousand more or less was noth-

ing to Arthur ; and when he was a candidate for the Legislature she had protested against his inviting to the house
and giving beer and cider to the men whose votes he
wanted, and for whom as men he did not care a farthing ;
but when he came up for Congress she forgot all her scru-
ples, and was as anxious as himself to please those who
could help him secure the nomination and afterward the
election. It was she who had proposed the party, to which
nearly everybody was to be invited, from old Peterkin, and
Widow Shipleigh, to Mr. and Mrs. St. Claire from Grassy
Spring, Squire Harrington from Collingwood, and Grace
Atherton from Brier Hill. Very few who could in any
way help Frank to a seat in Congress were omitted from
the list, whether Republican or Democrat; for Frank was
popular with both parties, and expected help from both.
Over three hundred cards had been issued for the party,
which was the absorbing topic of conversation in the town,
and which brought white kids and white muslins into
great requisition, while swallow-tails and non-swallow-tails
were discussed in the privacy of households, and discarded
or decided upon according to the length of the masculine
purse or the strength of the masculine resistance, for dress-
coats were not then the rule in Shannondale. Old Peterkin, however, whom Frank in his soliloquy had designated
a *canal bummer*, was resolved to show that he knew what
was *au fait* for the occasion and a new suit throughout was
in progress of making for him. " Tracy should have his
vote and that of fifty more of the boys to pay for his ticket
to the doin's," he said ; and this speech, which was reported
to Mrs. Tracy, reconciled her to the prospect of receiving
as a guest the coarsest, roughest man in town, whose only
recommendation was his money and the brute influence he
exercised over a certain class.

Dolly had scarcely slept for excitement since the party
had been decided upon, and everyting seemed to be moving on very smoothly until the morning of the day appointed
for the party, when it seemed as if every evil came at once.
First the colored boy, who was to wait in the upper hall,
was attacked with measles. Then Grace Atherton drove
round to say that it would be impossible for her to be present, as she had received news from New York which made
it necessary for her to go there by the next train. She

2*

was exceedingly sorry, she said, and for once in her life Grace was sincere. She *was* anxious to attend the party, for, as she said to Edith St. Claire in confidence, she wanted to see old Peterkin in his swallow-tail and white vest, with a shirt-front as big as a platter. There was a great deal of sarcasm and ridicule in Grace Atherton's nature, but at heart she was kind and meant to be just, and after a fashion really liked Mrs. Tracy, to whom she had been of service in various ways, helping her to fill her new position more gracefully than she could otherwise have done, and enlightening her without seeming to do so on many points which puzzled her sorely. On the whole they were good friends, and, after expressing her regret that she could not be present in the evening, Grace stood a few moments chatting familiarly and offering to send over flowers from her greenhouse, and her own maid to arrange Mrs. Tracy's hair and assist her in dressing. Then she took her leave, and it was her carriage which Mrs. Tracy was watching as it went down the avenue, when little Harold Hastings appeared around the corner of the house, and, coming up the steps, took off his cap respectfully, as he said :

"Grandma sends you her compliments, and is very sorry that she has rheumatism this morning, and can't come to-night to help you. She thinks, perhaps, you can get Mrs. Mosher."

" Your grandmother can't come, when I depended so much upon her ; and she thinks I can get Mrs. Mosher, that termagant, who would raise a mutiny in the kitchen in an hour !" Mrs. Tracy said, so sharply that a flush mounted to the handsome face of the boy, who felt as if he were in some way a culprit and being reprimanded. " She *must* come, if she does nothing but sit in the kitchen and keep order," was Mrs. Tracy's next remark.

" She can't," Harold replied ; " her foot and ankle is all swelled, and aches so she almost cries. She is awful sorry, and so am I, for I was coming with her to see the show."

This put a new idea into Mrs. Tracy's mind, and she said to the boy :

" How would you like to come any way, and stay in the upper hall, and tell the people where to go ? The boy I engaged has disappointed me. You are rather small for the place, but I guess you'll do, and I will give you fifty cents."

"I'd like it first-rate," Harold said, his face brightening at the thought of earning fifty cents and seeing the show at the same time.

Half-dollars were not very plentiful with Harold, and he was trying to save enough to buy his grandmother a pair of spectacles, for he had heard her say that she could not thread her needle as readily as she once did, and must have glasses as soon as she had the money to spare. Harold had seen a pair at the drug-store for one dollar, and without knowing at all whether they would fit his grandmother's eyes or not, had asked the druggist to keep them until he had the required amount. Fifty cents would just make it, and he promised at once that he would come; but in an instant there fell a shadow upon his face as he thought of *Tom*, his tormenter, who worried him so much.

"What is it?" Mrs. Tracy asked, as she detected in him a disposition to reconsider.

"Will Tom be up in the hall?" Harold asked.

"Of course not," Mrs. Tracy replied. "He will be in the parlors until ten o'clock, and then he will go to bed. Why do you ask?"

"Because," Harold answered, fearlessly, "if he was to be there, I could not come; he chaffs me so and twits me with being poor and living in a house his uncle gave us."

"That is very naughty in him, and I will see that he behaves better in future," Mrs. Tracy said, rather amused than otherwise at the boy's frankness.

As the mention of the uncle reminded Harold of the telegram, he took it from his pocket and handed it to her.

"Mr. Tracy said I was to bring you this. It's from Mr. Arthur, and he is coming to-night. I'm so glad, and grandma will be, too!"

If Mrs. Tracy heard the last of Harold's speech she did not heed it, for she had caught the words that Arthur was coming that night, and, for a moment, she felt giddy and faint, and her hand shook so she could scarcely open the telegram.

Arthur had been gone so long and left them in undisputed possession of the park, that she had come to feel as if it belonged to them by right, and she had grown so accustomed to a life of ease and luxury, that to give it up now and go back to Langley seemed impossible to her.

It never occurred to Dolly that they might possibly remain at the park if Arthur did come home. She felt sure they could not, for Arthur would hardly approve of his brother's stewardship when he came to realize how much it had cost him. They would have to leave, and this party she was giving would be her first and last at Tracy Park. How she wished she had never thought of it, or, having thought of it, that she had omitted from the list those who, she knew, would be obnoxious to the foreign brother, and who had only been invited for the sake of their political influence, which might now be useless, for Frank Tracy as a nobody, with very little money to spend, would not run as well, even in his own party, as Frank Tracy of Tracy Park, with thousands at his command if he chose to take them.

"It is too bad, and I wish we could give up the party," she said aloud, forgetting that Harold was still standing there. "You here yet? I thought you had gone!" she continued, as she recovered herself and met the boy's wondering eyes.

"Yes'm; but you ain't going to give the party up?" he said, afraid of losing his half dollar.

"Of course not. How can I, with all the people invited?" she asked, questioningly, and a little less sharply.

"I don't know, unless I get a pony and go round and tell 'em not to come," Harold suggested, thinking he might earn his fifty cents as easily that way as any other.

But, much as Mrs. Tracy wished the party had never been thought of, she could not now abandon it, and declining the services of Harold and the pony, she again bade him go home, with a charge that he should be on time in the evening, adding, as she surveyed him critically:

"If you have no clothes suitable, you can wear some of Tom's. You are about his size."

"Thank you; I have my meetin' clothes, and do not

want Tom's," was Harold's reply, as he walked away, thinking he would go in rags before he would wear anything which belonged to his enemy, Tom Tracy.

The rest of the morning was passed by Mrs. Frank in a most unhappy frame of mind, and she was glad when at an hour earlier than she had reason to expect him, her husband came home.

"Well, Dolly," he said, the moment they were alone, "this is awfully unlucky, the whole business. If Arthur must come home, why couldn't he have written in advance, and not take us by surprise? Looks as if he meant to spring a trap on us, don't it? And if he does, by Jove, he has caught us nicely. It will be somewhat like the prodigal son, who heard the sound of music and dancing, only I don't suppose Arthur has spent his substance in riotous living, with not over nice people; but there is no telling what he has been up to all these years that he has not written to us. Perhaps he is married. He said in his telegram, 'Send to meet *us*.' What does that mean, if not a wife?"

"A wife? Oh, Frank!" and with a great gasp Dolly sank down upon the lounge near where she was standing, and actually went into the hysterics her husband had prophesied.

In reading the telegram she had not noticed the little monosyllable "*us*," which was now affecting her powerfully. Of course it meant a wife and possibly children, and her day was surely over at Tracy Park. It was in vain that her husband tried to comfort her, saying that they knew nothing positively, except that Arthur was coming home and somebody was coming with him; it might be a friend, or, what was more likely, it might be a valet; and at all events he was not going to cross Fox River till he reached it, when he might find a bridge across it.

But Frank's reasoning did not console his wife, whose hysterical fit was succeeded by a racking headache, which by night was almost unbearable. Strong coffee, aconite, brandy, and belladonna, were all tried without effect. Nothing helped her until she commenced her toilet, when in the excitement of dressing she partly forgot her disquietude, and the pain in her head grew less. Still she was conscious of a feeling of wretchedness and regret as she sat in her handsome boudoir and felt that on the morrow another might be mistress where she had reigned so long.

It was known in the house that Arthur was expected, and some one with him, but no hint had been given of a wife, and Mrs. Tracy had ordered separate rooms prepared for the strangers, who were to arrive on the half-past ten train. How she should manage to keep up and appear natural until that time she did not know, and her face and eyes wore an anxious, frightened look, which all her finery could not hide. And still she was really very handsome and striking in her dress of peach blow satin, and lace, when at last she descended to the drawing-room and stood waiting for the first ring which would open the party.

CHAPTER VI.

THE COTTAGE IN THE LANE.

IT was so called because it stood at the end of a broad, grassy avenue or lane, which led from the park to the entrance of the grounds of Collingwood, whose chimneys and gables were distinctly visible in the winter when the trees were stripped of their foliage. At the time when Mrs. Crawford took possession of it its color was red, but the storms and rains of eleven summers and winters had washed nearly all the red away; and as Mrs. Crawford had never had the money to spare for its repainting, it would have presented a brown and dingy appearance outwardly, but for the luxurious woodbine, which she had trained with so much care and skill that it covered nearly three sides of the cottage, and made a gorgeous display in the autumn, when the leaves had turned a bright scarlet.

Thanks to the thoughtfulness of Arthur Tracy, the cottage was furnished comfortably and even prettily when Mrs. Crawford entered it, and it was from the same kind friend that her resources mostly had come up to the day when, three years after her marriage, Amy Hastings came home to die, bringing with her a little two-year-old boy,

whom she called Harold, for his father. Just where the
father was, if indeed he were living, she did not know.
He had left her in London six months before, saying he
was going to Paris for a few days, and should be back
before she had time to miss him. Just before he left her
he said to her, playfully:

"Cheer up, *petite*. I have not been quite as regular in
my habits as I ought to have been, but London is not the
place for a man of my tastes—too many temptations for a
fellow like me. When I come back we will go into the
country, where you can have a garden, with flowers and
chickens, and grow fat and pretty again. You are not
much like the girl I married. Good by." Then he kissed
her and the baby, and went whistling down the stairs. She
never saw him again, and only heard from him once. Then
he was in Pau, where he said they were having such fine
fox hunts. Weeks went by and he neither wrote nor came,
and Amy would have been utterly destitute and friendless,
but for Arthur Tracy, who, when her need was greatest,
went to her, telling her that he had never been far from
her, but had watched over her vigilantly to see that no
harm came to her. When her husband went to Paris he
knew it through a detective, and from the same source
knew when he went to Pau, where all trace of him had
been lost.

"But we are sure to find him," he said, encouragingly;
"and meantime I shall see that you do not suffer. As an
old friend of your husband, you will allow me to care for
you until he is found."

And Amy, who had no alternative, accepted his care,
and tried to seem cheerful and brave while waiting for the
husband who never came back.

At last when all hope was gone, Arthur sent her home
to the cottage in the lane, where her mother received her
gladly, thanking Heaven that she had her daughter back
again. But not for long. Poor Amy's heart was broken.
She loved her husband devotedly, and his cruel desertion
of her—for she knew now it was that—hurt her more than
years of suffering with him could have done. Occasionally
she heard from Arthur, who was still busy in search of the
delinquent, and who always sent in his letter a substantial
proof of his friendship and generosity.

And so the weeks and months went by, and then there came a letter from Arthur saying that Harold Hastings had died in Berlin, and been buried at his expense.

A few weeks later and Amy, too, lay dead in her coffin; and they buried her under the November snow, which was falling in great sheets upon the frozen ground. What Arthur felt when he heard the news no one ever knew, for he made no sign, but at once gave orders to Colvin that a costly monument should be placed at her grave, with only this inscription upon it :

AMY,
Aged 23.

Of course the low-minded people talked, and Mrs. Crawford knew they did ; but her heart was too full of sorrow to care what was said. Her beautiful daughter was dead, and she was alone with the little boy, who had inherited his mother's beauty, with all her lovely traits of character. Had Mrs. Crawford consented, Arthur would have supported him entirely ; but she was too proud for that. She would take care of him herself as long as possible, she wrote him, but if, when Harold was older, he chose to educate him, she would offer no objection.

And there the matter dropped, and Mrs. Crawford struggled on as best she could, sometimes going out to do plain sewing, sometimes taking it home, sometimes going to people's houses to superintend when they had company, and sometimes selling fruit and flowers from the garden attached to the cottage. But whatever she did, she was always the same quiet, lady-like woman, who commanded the respect of all, and who, poor as she was, was held in high esteem by the better class in Shannondale. Grace Atherton's carriage and that of Edith St. Claire stood oftener before her door than that at Tracy Park ; and though the ladies came mostly on business, they found themselves lingering after the business was over to talk with one who, in everything save money, was their equal.

Harold was a noble little fellow, full of manly instincts, and always ready to deny himself for the sake of others. That he and his grandmother were poor he knew, but he had never felt the effects of their poverty, save when Tom Tracy had jeered at him for it, and called him a pauper.

There had been one square fight between the two boys, in which Harold had come off victor, with only a torn jacket, while Tom's eye had been black for a week, and Mrs. Tracy had gone to the cottage to complain, and insist that Harold should be punished. But when she heard that Dick St. Claire had assisted in the fray, taking Harold's part, and himself dealing Tom the blow which blackened his eye, she changed her tactics, for she did not care to quarrel with Mrs. St. Claire, of Grassy Spring.

Harold and Richard St. Claire, or Dick, as he was familiarly called, were great friends, and if the latter knew there was a difference between himself and the child of poverty he never manifested it, and played far oftener with Harold than with Tom, whose domineering disposition and rough manners were distasteful to him. That Harold would one day be obliged to earn his living, Mrs. Crawford knew, but he was still too young for anything of that kind ; and when Grace Atherton, or Mrs. St. Claire offered him money for the errands he sometimes did for them, she always refused to let him take it. Had she known of Mrs. Tracy's proposition that he should be present at the party as hall-boy, she would have declined, for though she could go there herself as an employee, she shrank from suffering Harold to do so. That Mrs. Tracy was not a lady, she knew, and in her heart there was a feeling of superiority to the woman even while she served her, and she was not as sorry, perhaps, as she ought to have been, for the attack of rheumatism which would prevent her from going to the park to take charge of the kitchen during the evening.

"I am sorry to disappoint her, but I am glad not to be there," she was thinking to herself, as she sat in her bright, cheerful kitchen, waiting for Harold, when he burst in upon her, exclaiming :

"Oh, grandma, only think! I am invited to the party, and I told her I'd go, and I am to be there at half-past seven sharp, and to wear my meetin' clothes."

"Invited to the party! What do you mean? Only grown up people are to be there," Mrs. Crawford said.

"Yes, I know ; " Harold replied, "but I'm not to be with the *grown-ups*. I'm to stay in the upper hall and tell 'em where to go."

"Oh, you are to be a *waiter*," was Mrs. Crawford's rather contemptuous remark, which Harold did not heed in his excitement.

"Yes, I'm to be at the head of the stairs, and somebody else at the bottom; and they are to have fiddlin' and dancin'; I've never seen anybody dance; and ice-cream and cake, with something like plaster all over it, and oranges and cake, and, oh, everything! Dick St. Claire told me; he knows; his mother has had parties, and she's going to-night, and her gown is crimson velvet, with black and white fur on it like our cat, only they don't call it that; and—oh, I forgot—they have had a telegraph, and I took it to Mrs. Tracy, who almost cried when she read it. Mr. Arthur Tracy is coming home to-night."

Harold had talked so fast that his grandmother could hardly follow him, but she understood what he said last, and started as if he had struck her a blow.

"Arthur Tracy! Coming home to-night!" she exclaimed. "Oh, I am so glad."

"But Mrs. Tracy did not seem to be, and I guess she wanted to stop the party," Harold said, repeating as nearly as he could what had passed between him and the lady.

Harold was full of the party to which he believed he had been invited, and when in the afternoon Dick St. Claire came to the cottage to play with him, he felt a kind of patronizing pity for his friend who was not to share his honor.

"Perhaps mother will let me come over and help you," Dick said. "I know how they do it. You mustn't talk to the people as they come up the stairs, nor even say good-evening,—only:

"'Ladies will please walk this way, and gentlemen that!'"

And Dick went through with a pantomime performance for the benefit of Harold, who, when the drill was over, felt himself competent to receive the queen's guests at the head of the great staircase in Windsor Castle.

"Yes, I know," he said, "'Ladies this way, and gentleman that;' but when am I to go down and see the dancing and get some ice-cream?"

On this point Dick was doubtful. He did not believe,

he said, that waiters ever went down to see the dancing, or to get ice-cream, until the party was over, and then they ate it in the kitchen, if there was any left.

This wss not a cheerful outlook for Harold, whose thoughts were more intent upon cream and dancing than upon showing the people where to go, and it was also the second time the word waiter had been used in connection with what he was expected to do. But Harold was too young to understand that he was not of the party itself. Later on it would come to him fast enough, that he was only a part of the machinery which moved the social engine. Now, he felt like the engine itself, and long before six o'clock he was dressed, and waiting anxiously for his grandmother's permission to start."

"I'll tell you all about it," he said to her. "What they do, and what they say, and what they wear, and if I can, I'll speak to Mr. Arthur Tracy and thank him for mother's grave-stone."

By seven o'clock he was on his way to the park, walking rapidly, and occasionally saying aloud with a gesture of his hand to the right and the left, and a bow almost to the ground :

"Ladies, this way," and "gentlemen that."

When he reached the house the gas-jets had just been turned up, and every window was ablaze with light from the attic to the basement.

"My eye ! ain't it swell !" Harold said to himself, as he stood a moment, looking at the brilliantly lighted rooms. "Don't I wish I was rich and could burn all that gas, and maybe I shall be. Grandma says Mr. Arthur Tracy was once a poor boy like me ; only he had an uncle, and I haven't. I've got to earn my money, and I mean to, and sometime, maybe, I'll have a house as big as this, and just such a party, with a boy upstairs to tell 'em where to go. I wonder now if I'm expected to go into the kitchen door. Of course not. I've got on my Sunday clothes, and am invited to the party. I shall ring."

And he did ring—a sharp, loud ring, which made Mrs. Tracy, who had not yet left her room, start nervously as she wondered who had come so early.

"Old Peterkin, of course. Those whom you care for least always come first."

Peering over the banister Tom Tracy saw Harold when the door was opened, and screaming to his mother at the top of his voice, "It ain't old Peterkin, mother; it's Hal Hastings, come to the front door," he ran down the stairs, and confronting the intruder just as he was crossing the threshold, exclaimed :

"Go 'long. You hain't no business ringin' the bell as if you was a guest. Go to the kitchen door with the other servants !"

With a thrust of the hand he pushed Harold back, and was about to shut the door upon him, when, with a quick, dextrous movement, Harold darted past him into the hall, saying, as he did so :

"Darn you, Tom Tracy, I won't go to the kitchen door, and I'm not a servant, and if you call me so again I'll lick you !"

How the matter would have ended is doubtful, if Mrs. Tracy had not called from the head of the stairs :

"Thomas ! Thomas Tracy ! I am ashamed of you ! Come to me this minute ! And you, boy, go to the kitchen ; or, no—now you are here, come upstairs, and I'll tell you what you are to do."

Her directions were very much like those of Dick St. Claire, except that she laid more stress upon the fact that he was not to speak to any one familiarly, but was to be in all respects a machine. Just what she meant by that Harold did not know ; but he hung his cap on a bracket, and taking his place where she told him to stand, watched her admiringly as she went down the staircase, followed by her husband, who looked anxious and ill at ease.

Tom had disappeared, but his younger brother, Jack, who was wholly unlike him, came to Harold's side, and began telling him what quantities of good things there were in the dining-room and pantry, and that his Uncle Arthur was coming home that night, and his mother was so glad she cried ; then, with a spring he mounted upon the banister of the long staircase, and slipped swiftly to the bottom. Ascending the stairs almost as quickly as he had gone down, he bade Harold try it with him.

"It's such fun ! and mother won't care. I've done it forty times," he said, as Harold demurred ; and then, as the temptation became too strong to be resisted, two boys instead of one rode down the banister, and landed in the lower hall, and two pairs of little legs ran nimbly up the stairs just as the door opened and admitted the first arrival.

CHAPTER VII.

THE PARTY.

THE invitations had been for half-past seven, and precisely at that hour Peterkin arrived, magnificent in his swallow-tail and white shirt front, where an enormous diamond shone conspicuously. With him came Mrs. Peterkin, whose name was Mary Jane, but whom her husband always called *May* Jane. She was a frail, pale-faced little woman, who had once been Grace Atherton's maid, and had married Peterkin for his money. This was her first appearance at a grand party, and in her excitement and timidity she did not hear Harold's thrice repeated words, " Ladies go that way," but followed her husband into the gentlemen's dressing-room, where she deposited her wraps, and then, shaking in every limb, descended to the drawing-room, where Peterkin's loud voice was soon heard, as he slapped his host on the shoulder, and said :

" You see, we are here on time, though May Jane said it was too early. But I s'posed half-past seven meant half-past seven, and then I wanted a little time to talk up the ropes with you. We are going to run you in, you bet !" and again his coarse laugh thrilled every nerve in Mrs. Tracy's body, and she longed for fresh arrivals to help quiet this vulgar man.

Soon they began to come by twos, and threes, and sixes, and Harold was kept busy with his " Ladies this way, and gentlemen that."

After Mrs. Peterkin had gone down stairs, leaving her wraps in the gentlemen's room, Harold, who knew they did not belong there, had carried them to the ladies' room and deposited them upon the bed, just as the girl who was to be in attendance appeared at her post, asking

him sharply why he was in there rumma
things.

"I'm not rummaging. They are
She left them in the other room, and
here," Harold said, as he returned to the
excited, and interested in watching the
came up the stairs and went down again.
instinct of a bright, intelligent boy, he
accustomed to society and who was not, a
the banister, when not on duty, watche
entered the drawing-room and were recei
Mrs. Tracy. Unconsciously, he began t
bowing when they bowed, and saying softl

"Oh, how do you do? Good-evening
you. Pleasant, to-night. Walk in. Ye-
This was the monosyllable with wh
every sentence, and was the affirmation to
his mind that he, too, would some day
stairs and into those parlors as a guest, w
boy in the upper hall bade the ladies go tl
gentlemen that.

It was after nine when Mr. and Mrs. S
with Squire Harrington, from Collingwoc
been looking for them, anxious to see th
trimmed with ermine of which Dick had t
of the guests he had mentally criticised
Mrs. St. Clair, he knew, was genuine, and
when in passing him she smiled upon him
gracious manner, and said, pleasantly:

"Good-evening, Harold. I knew you

" Oh, Mrs. St. Claire, how handsome y
Handsomer than anybody yet, and different,
how."

Edith knew the compliment was genuine,
replied :

" Thank you, Harold ;" then, laying her ha
head and parting his soft, brown hair, she sai
noticed a look of fatigue in his eyes, " Are you
standing so long ? Why don't you bring a chair
of the rooms and sit when you can ?"

" She told me to stand," Harold replied,
toward the parlors, from which a strain of music
issued.

The dancing had commenced, and Harold's
hands beat time to the lively strains of the
violin, until he could contain himself no long
dancing he must see at all hazards, and know wl
like, and when the last guests came up the st:
was no hall-boy there to tell them, " Ladies thi:
gentlemen that," for Harold was in the thicke
crowd, standing on a chair so as to look over the
those in front of him, and see the dancers. But
poor Harold ! He was soon discovered by M
who, asking him if he did not know his place be
that, ordered him back to his post, where he wa
stay until the party was over.

Wholly unconscious of the nature of his of
very sorry that he had offended, Harold went up
wondering why he could not see the dancing,

caught a glimpse of a thin, pale face, and a pair of keen, black eyes, which seemed for an instant to take everything in ; then the head was dropped, and the two men disappeared in a room at the far end of the hall.

"I'll bet that's Mr. Arthur. How grand he is ! looks just like a pirate in that cloak and hat," was Harold's mental comment.

Before he had time for further thought, Frank Tracy came from the room, and hurried down the stairs to rejoin his guests.

Five minutes later and the door at the end of the long hall which communicated with the back staircase and the rear of the house, opened, and a man whom Harold recognized as the expressman from the station appeared with a huge trunk on his shoulder, and a large valise in his hand. These he deposited in the stranger's room, and then went back for more, until four had been carried in. But when he came with the fifth and largest of all, a hand, white and delicate as a woman's, was thrust from the door-way with an imperative gesture, and a voice with a decided foreign accent exclaimed :

"For Heaven's sake, don't bring any more boxes in here. Why, I am positively stumbling over them now. Surely there must be some place in the house for my luggage, besides my private apartment."

Then the door was shut with a bang, and Harold heard the sliding of the bolt as Arthur Tracy fastened himself into his room.

CHAPTER VIII.

ARTHUR.

ALL the time that Frank Tracy had been receiving his guests and trying to seem happy and at his ease, his thoughts had been dwelling upon his brother's telegram and the ominous words, "Send some one to meet us." How slowly the minutes dragged until it was ten o'clock, and he knew that John had started for the station to meet the dreaded *"us."* He had told everybody that he was expecting his brother, and had tried to seem glad on account of it.

"You and he were great friends, I believe," he said to Squire Harrington.

"Yes, we were friends," the latter replied ; but when he lived here my health was such that I did not mingle much in society. I met him, however, in Paris five years ago, and found him very companionable and quite Europeanized in his manner and tastes. He spoke French or German altogether, and might easily have passed for a foreigner. I shall be glad to see him."

"And so shall I," chimed in Peterkin, whose voice was like a trumpet and could be heard everywhere. "A fustrate chap, though we didn't used to hitch very well together. He was all-fired big-feelin', and them days Peterkin was nowhere ; but circumstances alter cases. He'll be glad to see me now, no doubt ;" and with a most satisfied air the millionaire put his hand, as if by accident, on his immense diamond pin, and pulling down his swallow-tail, walked away.

Frank saw the faint smile of contempt which showed itself in Squire Harrington's face, and his own grew red with shame, but paled almost instantly as the outer door was opened by some one who did not seem to think it necessary to ring ; and a stranger, in Spanish cloak and broadbrimmed hat, stepped into the hall.

Arthur had come, and was *alone.* The train had been on time, and at just half-past ten the long line of cars stopped before the Shannondale station, where John, the coachman from Tracy Park, was waiting. The night was dark, but by the light from the engine and the office John saw the foreign-looking stranger, who sprang upon the platform, and felt sure it was his man. But there was no one with him, though it seemed as if he were expecting some one to follow him from the car, for he stood for a moment waiting. Then, as the train moved on, he turned with a puzzled look upon his face to meet John, who said to him respectfully :

"Are you Mr. Arthur Tracy ?"

"Yes ; who are you ?" was the response.

"Mr. Frank Tracy sent me from the park to fetch

3

you," John replied. "I think he expected some one with
you. Are you alone?"

"Yes—no, no!" and Arthur's voice indicated growing
alarm and uneasiness as he looked around him. "Where
is she? Didn't you see her? She was with me all the
way. Surely she got off when I did. Where can she have
gone?"

He was greatly excited, and kept peering through the
darkness as he talked; while John, a good deal puzzled,
looked curiously at him, as if uncertain whether he were in
his right mind or not.

"Was there some one with you in the car?" he
asked.

"Yes, in the car, and in New York, and on the ship.
She was with me all the way," Mr. Tracy replied. "It is
strange where she is now. Did no one alight from the
train when I did?"

"No one," John answered, more puzzled than ever.
"I was looking for you, and there was no one else. She
may have fallen asleep and been carried by."

"Yes, probably that is it," Mr. Tracy said, more
cheerfully; "she was asleep and carried by. She will come
back to-morrow."

He seemed quite content with this solution of the mystery, and began to talk of his luggage, which lay upon the
platform—a pile so immense that John looked at it in
alarm, knowing that the carriage could never take it
all.

"Eight trunks, two portmanteaus, and a hat-box!" he
said, aloud, counting the pieces.

"Yes, and a nice sum those rascally agents in New
York made me pay for having them come with me,"
Arthur rejoined. "They weighed them all, and charged
me a little fortune. I might as well have sent them by
express; but I wanted them with me, and here they are.
What will you do with them? This is hers," and he designated a black trunk or box, longer and larger than two
ordinary trunks ought to be.

"I can take one of them with the box and portman-
teau, and the expressman will take the rest. He is here.
Hullo, Brown!" John said, calling to a man in the distance,
who came forward, and, on learning what was wanted,

began piling the trunks into his wagon, while Arthur followed John to the carriage, which he entered, and sinking into a seat, pulled his broad-brimmed hat over his face and eyes, and sat as motionless as if he had been a stone.

For a moment John stood looking at him, wondering what manner of man he was, and thinking of the woman who, he said, had been with him in the train. At last, remembering a message his master had given him, he began :

"If you please, sir, Mr. Tracy told me to tell you he was very sorry that he could not come himself to meet you. If he had known that you were coming sooner, he would have done different ; but he did not get your telegram till this morning, and then it was too late to stop it. We are having a great break-down to-night."

During the first of these remarks Arthur had given no sign that he heard, but when John spoke of a break-down, he lifted his head quickly, and the great black eyes flashed a looked of inquiry upon John, as he said :

"Break-down ? What's that ?"

"A party—a smasher ! Mr. Tracy is running for Congress," was John's reply.

And then over the thin face there crept a ghost of a smile, which, faint as it was, changed the expression wonderfully.

"Oh, a party !" he said. "Well, I will be a guest, too. I have my dressing-suit in some of those trunks. Frank is going to Congress, is he ? That's a good joke ! Drive on. What are you standing there for ?"

The carriage door was shut, and, mounting the box, John drove as rapidly toward Tracy Park as the darkness of the night would admit, while the passenger inside sat with his hat over his eyes, and his chin almost touching his breast, as if absorbed in thought. Once he spoke to himself, and said :

"Poor little Gretchen ! I wonder how I could have forgotten and left her in the train. What will she do alone in a strange place ? But perhaps Heaven will take care of her. She always said so. I wish I had her faith and could believe as she does."

They had turned into the park by this time, and very soon drew up before the house, from every window of which

lights were flashing, while the sound of music and dancing could be distinctly heard.

"I need not ring at my own house," Arthur thought,
as he ran up the steps, and, opening the door, stepped
into the hall ; and thus it was that the first intimation
which Frank had of his arrival was when he saw him
standing in the midst of a crowd of people, who were gazing curiously at him.

"Arthur !" he exclaimed, rushing forward and taking
his brother's hand. "Welcome home again ! I did not
hear the carriage, though I was listening for it. I am so
glad to see you ! Come with me to your room ;" and he
led the way up stairs to the apartment prepared for the
stranger.

He had seen at a glance that Arthur was alone, unless,
indeed, he had brought a servant who had gone to the side
door ; and thus relieved from a load of anxiety, he was
very cordial in his manner, and began at once to make
excuses for the party, repeating, in substance, what John
had already said.

"Yes, I know ; that fellow who drove me here told
me," Arthur replied, throwing off his coat and hat, and
beginning to lave his face, and neck, and hands in the
cold water which he turned into the bowl until it was full
to the brim, and splashed over the sides as he dashed it
upon himself.

All this time Frank had not seen his face distinctly,
nor did he have an opportunity to do so until the ablutions
were ended, and Arthur had rubbed himself with, not one
towel, but two, until it seemed as if he must have taken
off the skin in places. Then he turned, and running his
fingers through his luxuriant hair, which had a habit of
curling around his forehead as in his boyhood, looked full
at his brother, who saw that he was very pale, and that his
eyes were unnaturally large and bright, while there was
about him an indescribable something which puzzled
Frank a little. It was not altogether the air of foreign
travel and cultivation which was so perceptible, but a something else—a restlessness and nervousness of speech and
manner as he moved about the room, walking rapidly and
gesticulating as he walked.

"You are looking thin and tired. Are you not well ?" Frank asked.

"Oh, yes, perfectly well," Arthur replied ; "only this infernal heat in my blood, which keeps me up to fever pitch all the time. I shall have to bathe my face again ;" and, going a second time to the bowl, he began to throw the water over his face and hands as he had done before.

"I'd like a bath in ice-water," he said, as he began drying himself with a fresh towel. "If I remember right, there is no bath-room on this floor, but I can soon have one built. I intend to throw down the wall between this room and the next, and perhaps the next, so as to have a suite."

The second washing must have cooled him, for there came a change in his manner, and he moved more slowly and spoke with greater deliberation as he asked some questions about the people below.

"Will you come down by and by," Frank said, after having made some explanations with regard to his guests.

"No, you will have to excuse me," Authur replied. "I am too tired to encounter old acquaintances or make new. I do not believe I could stand old Peterkin, who you say is a millionaire. I suppose you want his influence ; your coachman told me you were running for Congrees," and Arthur laughed the old merry, musical laugh which Frank remembered so well ; then, suddenly changing his tone, he asked : "When does the next train from the East pass the station?"

Frank told him at seven in the morning, and he continued :

"Please send the carriage to meet it. Gretchen will probably be there. She was in the train with me, and should have gotten out when I did, but she must have been asleep and carried by."

"Gr-gr-gretchen ! Who is she ? Frank stammered, while the cold sweat began to run down his back.

Instantly into Arthur's eyes there came a look of cunning, as he replied :

"She is Gretchen. See that the carriage goes for her, will you ?"

His voice and manner indicated that he wished the conference ended, and with a great sinking at his heart

Frank left the room and returned to his guests and his wife, who had not seen the stranger when he entered the hall, and did not know of Arthur's arrival until her husband rejoined her.

" He has come," he whispered to her, while she whispered back :

" Is he alone ?"

" Yes, but somebody is coming to-morrow ; I do not know who ; Gretchen, he calls her," was Frank's reply.

" Gretchen !" Mrs. Tracy repeated, in a trembling voice. " Who is she ?"

" I don't know. He merely said she was Gretchen ; his daughter, perhaps," was Frank's answer, which sent the color from his wife's cheeks, and made her so faint and sick that she could scarcely stand, and did not know at all what her guests were saying to her.

Meantime, Arthur had changed his mind with regard to going down into the parlors, and, unlocking the trunk which held his own wardrobe, he took out an evening suit fresh from the hands of a London tailor, and, arraying himself in it, stood for a moment before the glass to see the effect. Everything was faultless, from his neck-tie to his boots ; and, opening the door, he went into the hall, which was empty, except for Harold, who was sitting near the stairs, half asleep again. Most of the guests were in the supper-room, but a few of the younger portion were dancing, and the strains of music were heard with great distinctness in the upper hall.

" Ugh !" Arthur said, with a shiver, as he stopped a moment to listen, while his quick eye took in every detail of the furniture and its arrangement in the hall. " That violinist ought to be hung—the pianist, too ! Don't they know what horrid discord they are making ? It brings that heat back. I believe, upon my soul, I shall have to bathe my face again."

Suiting the action to the word, he went back and washed his face for the third time ; then returning to the hall, he advanced toward Harold, who was now wide awake and standing up to meet him. As Arthur met the clear brown eyes fixed so curiously upon him, he stopped suddenly, and put his hand to his head as if trying to recall something ; then going nearer to Harold, he said :

"Well, my little boy, what are you doing up here?"

"Telling the folks which way to go," was Harold's answer.

"Who are you?" Arthur continued. "What is your name?"

"Harold Hastings," was the reply; and instantly there came over the white face, and into the large, bright eyes, an expression which made the boy stand back as the tall man came up to him and, laying a hand on his shoulder, said excitedly:

"Harold Hastings! He was once my friend, or I thought he was; but I hate him now. And he was your father, and Amy Crawford was your mother? *N'est-ce pas?* Answer me!"

"Yes, sir—yes sir; but I don't know what you mean by '*na-se par*,'" Harold said, in a frightened voice; and Arthur continued, as he tightened his grasp on his shoulder:

"I hated your father, and I hate you, and I am going to throw you over the stair railing!" and seizing Harold's coat collar, he swung him over the banister as if he had been a feather, while the boy struggled and fought, and held on to the rails, until help appeared in the person of Frank Tracy, who came swiftly up the stairs, demanding the cause of what he saw.

He had been standing near the drawing-room door, and had caught the sound of his brother's voice and Harold's as if in altercation. Excusing himself from those around him, he hastened to the scene of action in time to save Harold from a broken limb, if not a broken neck.

"What is it? What have you been doing?" he asked the boy, who replied amid his tears:

"I hain't been doing anything, only minding my business, and he came and asked me who I was, and when I told him, he was going to chuck me over the railing—darn him! I wish I was big; I'd lick him!"

Harold's cheeks were flushed, and the great tears glittered in his eyes, as he stood up, brave, and defiant, and resentful of the injustice done him.

"Arthur, are you mad?" Frank said.

And whether it was the tone of his voice, or his words, something produced a wonderful effect upon his brother, whose mood changed at once, and who advanced towards Harold with outstretched hand, saying to him:

"Forgive me, my little man, I think I must have been mad for the instant; there is such a heat in my head, and the crash of that music almost drives me wild. Shall it be peace between us, my boy?"

It was next to impossible to resist the influence of Arthur Tracy's smile, and Harold took the offered hand and said, between a sob and a laugh:

"I don't know now why you wanted to throw me down stairs."

"Nor I, and I will make it up to you some time," was Arthur's reply, as he took his brother's arm and said: "Now introduce me to your guests."

The moment the gentlemen disappeared from view Harold's resolution was taken. It was nearly midnight. He was very tired and sleepy, and his head was aching terribly. He could not see the dancing. He had had nothing to eat; he had stood until his legs were ready to drop off, and to crown all a lunatic had tried to throw him over the banister.

"I won't stay here another minute," he said.

And leaving the hall by the rear entrance, and slipping down a back stairway, he was soon in the open air, and running swiftly through the park toward the cottage in the lane.

Meanwhile, the two brothers had descended to the drawing-room, where Arthur was soon surrounded by his old acquaintances, whom he greeted with that cordiality and friendliness of manner which had made him so popular with those who knew him best. Every trace of excitement had disappeared, and had he been master of ceremonies himself, he could not have been more gracious or affable. Even old Peterkin was treated with a consideration which put that worthy man at his ease, and set his tongue in motion. At first he had felt a little overawed by Arthur's elegant appearance, and had whispered to his neighbor:

"That's a swell, and no mistake. I s'pose that's what you call foreign get up. Well, me and ma is goin' to Europe some time, and hang me if I don't put on style when I come home. I'd kind of like to speak to the feller.

I wonder if he remembers that I was runnin' a boat when he went away?"

If Arthur did remember it he showed no sign when Peterkin at last pressed up to him, claiming his attention, as "Captain Peterkin, of the 'Liza Ann, the fastest boat on the canal, and by George, the all-firedest meanest, too, I guess," he said; "but them days is past, and the old captain is past with them. I dabbled a little in ile, and if I do say it, I could about buy up the whole canal, if I wanted to; but I ain't an atom proud, and I don't forget the old boatin' days, and I've got the 'Liza Ann hauled up inter my back yard as a relict. The children use it for a play-house, but to me it is a—a—what do you call it? a—gol darn it, what is it?"

"Souvenir," suggested Arthur, vastly amused at this tirade, which had assumed the form of a speech, and drawn a crowd around Peterkin.

"Wall, yes; I s'pose that's it, though 'tain't exactly what I was trying to think of," he said. "It's a reminder, and keeps down my pride, for when I get to feelin' pretty big, after hearin' myself pointed out as Peterkin, the millionaire, I go out to that old boat in the back yard, and says I, 'Liza Ann,' says I, 'you and me has took many a trip up and down the canal, with about the wust crew, and the wust hosses, and the wust boys that was ever created, and though you've got a new coat of paint onto you, and can set still all day and do nothin', while I can wear the finest of broadcloth and set still, too, it won't do for us to forget the pit from which we was dug, and I don't forget it neither, no more than I forgit favors shown when I was not just cut.' You, sir, rode on the 'Liza Ann with that crony of yours—Hastings was his name—and you paid me han'some, though I didn't ask nothin'; and there's your brother—Frank, I call him. I don't forgit that he used to speak to me civil when I was nobody, and now, though I'm a Dimocrat, as everybody who knows me knows, and everybody most does know me, for Shannondale allus was my native town, I'm goin' to run him into Congress, if it takes my bottom dollar, and anybody, Republican or Dimocrat, who don't vote for him ain't my friend, and must expect to feel the full heft of my—my—"

3*

"Powerful disapprobation," Arthur said, softly, and Peterkin continued :

"Thank you, sir, that's the word—powerful, sir, powerful," and he glowered threatingly at two or three young men in white kids and high shirt collars, who were known to prefer the opposing candidate.

Peterkin had finished his harangue, and was wiping his wet face with his hankerchief, when Arthur, who had listened to him with well-bred attention, said :

"I thank you, Captain Peterkin, for your interest in my brother, who, if he succeeds, will I am sure, owe his success to your influence, and be grateful in proportion. Perhaps you have a bill you would like him to bring before the house ?"

"No," Peterkin said, with a shake of the head. "My Bill is a little shaver, eight or nine years old ; too young to go from home, but "—and he lowered his voice a little—" I don't mind saying that if there should be a chance, I'd like the post-office fust rate. It would be a kind of hist, you know, to see my name in print, Captian Joseph Peterkin, P. M."

Here the conversation ended, and this aspirant for the post-office stepped aside and gave place to others who were anxious to renew their acquaintance with Arthur.

It was between one and two o'clock in the morning when the party finally broke up, and, as the Peterkins had been the first to arrive, so they were the last to leave, and Mrs. Peterkin found herself again in the gentlemen's dressing-room looking for her wraps. But they were not there, and after a vain and anxious search she said to her husband :

"Joe, somebody has stole my things, and 'twas my Indian shawl, too, and gold-headed pin, with the little diamond."

Mrs. Tracy was at once summoned to the scene, and the missing wraps were found in the ladies-room, where Harold had carried them, but the gold-headed shawl-pin was gone and could not be found.

Lucy, the girl in attendance, said, when questioned, that she knew nothing of the pin or Mrs. Peterkin's wraps either, except that on first going up after the lady's arrival she had found Harold Hastings fumbling them over, and

that she sent him out with a sharp reprimand. Harold
was then looked for and could not be found, for he had
been at home and in bed for a good two hours. Clearly,
then, he knew something of the pin ; and Peterkin and his
wife said good night resolving to see the boy the first thing
in the morning and demand their property.

When the Peterkins were gone Arthur started at once
for his room, but stopped at the foot of the stairs and said
to his brother :

"Don't forget to have the carriage at the station at
seven o'clock. Gretchen is sure to be there."

"All right," was Frank's reply.

While Mrs. Tracy asked :

"Who is Gretchen ?"

If Arthur heard her he made no reply, but kept on up
the stairs to his room, where they heard him for a long
time walking about, opening and shutting windows, looking and unlocking trunks, and occasionally splashing water
over his face and hands.

"Your brother is a very elegant-looking man," Mrs.
Tracy said to her husband, as she was preparing to retire.
"Quite like a foreigner ; but how bright his eyes are, and
how they look at you sometimes. They almost make me
afraid of him.

Frank made no direct reply. In his heart there was
an undefined fear which he could not then put into words,
and with the remark that he was very tired, he stepped into
bed, and was just falling into a quiet sleep when there
came a knock upon his door loud enough. it seemed to him,
to waken the dead. Starting up he demanded who was
there, and what was wanted.

"It is I," Arthur said. "I thought I smelled gas and
I have been hunting round for it. There is nothing worse
to breathe than gas whether from the furnace or the drain.
I hope that is all right."

"Yes," Frank answered, a little crossly. "Had a
new one put in two weeks ago."

"If there's gas in the main sewer it will come up just
the same, and I am sure I smell it," Arthur said. "I think
I shall have all the waste-pipes which connect with the
drain cut off. Good-night. Am sorry I disturbed you."

They heard him as he went across the hall to his room,

and Frank was settling down again to sleep when there
came a second knock, and Arthur said, in a whisper :

"I hope I do not trouble you, but I have decided to go
myself to the station to meet Gretchen. She is very timid,
and does not speak much English. Good-night, once
more, and pleasant dreams."

To sleep now was impossible, and both husband and
wife turned restlessly on their pillows, Frank wondering
what ailed his brother, and Dolly wondering who Gretchen
was, and how her coming would affect them.

CHAPTER IX.

WHO IS GRETCHEN?

THIS was the question which Mr. and Mrs. Tracy asked
each other many times during the hours which inter-
vened between their retiring and rising. But speculate as
they might, they could reach no satisfactory conclusion,
and were obliged to wait for what the morning and the
train might bring. The party had been a success, and
Frank felt that his election to Congress was almost certain ; but of what avail would that be if he lost his foot-
hold at Tracy Park, as he was sure to do if a woman
appeared upon the scene. Both he and his wife had out-
grown the life of eleven years ago, and could not go back
to it without a struggle, and it is not strange if both wished
that the troublesome brother had remained abroad instead
of coming home so suddenly and disturbing all their plans.
They heard him moving in his room before the clock
struck six, and knew he was getting himself in readiness
to meet the dreaded Gretchen. Then, long before the carriage came round they heard him in the hall opening the
windows and admitting a gust of wind which blew their
door open, and when Frank arose to shut it, he saw the
top of Arthur's broad-brimmed hat disappearing down the
stairs.

"I believe he is going to walk to the station ; he certainly is crazy," Frank said to his wife, as they dressed

themselves, and waited with feverish impatience for the return of the carriage.

Arthur did walk to the station, which he reached just as the ticket agent was unlocking the door, and there, with his Spanish cloak wrapped around him, he stalked up and down the long platform for more than an hour, for the train was late, and it was nearer eight than seven when it finally came in sight.

Standing side by side, Arthur and John looked anxiously for some one to alight, but nobody appeared, and the expression of Arthur's face was pitiable as he turned it to John, and said :

"Gretchen did not come. Where do you suppose she is ?"

"I am sure I don't know. On the next train, may be," was John's reply, at which Arthur caught eagerly.

"Yes, the next train, most likely. We will come and meet it ; and now drive home as fast as you can. This disappointment has brought that heat to my head, and I must have a bath. But stop a bit ; who is the best carpenter in town ?"

John told him that Belknap was the best, and Burchard the highest priced.

"I'll see them both," Arthur said. "Take me to their houses ;" and in the course of half an hour he had interviewed both Burchard and Belknap, and made an appointment with both for the afternoon.

Then he was driven back to Tracy Park, where breakfast had been waiting until it was spoiled, and the cook's temper was spoiled, too, and when Frank and Dolly met him at the door, both asked in the same breath :

"Where is she ?"

"She was not on this train. She will come on the next. We must go and meet her," was Arthur's reply, as he passed up the stairs, while Frank and his wife looked wonderingly at each other.

The spoiled breakfast was eaten by Mr. and Mrs. Tracy alone, for the children had had theirs and gone to their lessons, and Arthur had said that he never took anything in the morning except a cup of coffee and a roll, and these he wished sent to his room, together with a time-table.

After breakfast Mrs. Tracy, who was suffering from a

sick headache, declared her inability to sit up a moment
longer and returned to her bed, leaving her husband and
the servants to bring what order they could out of the confusion reigning everywhere, and nowhere to a greater
extent than in Arthur's room, or rather the rooms which
he had appropriated to himself, and into which he had all
his boxes and trunks brought, so that he could open them
at his leisure.   There were more coming, he said, boxes
which were still in the custom-house, and which contained
many valuable things, such as pictures, and statuary, and
rugs, and inlaid tables, and china.

The house, which was very large, had two wings, while
the main building was divided by a wide hall, with three
rooms on each side, the middle one being a little smaller
than the other two, with each of which it communicated
by a door.   And it was into this middle room on the
second floor Arthur had been put, and which he found
quite too small for his use.   So he ordered both the doors
to be opened and took possession of the suite, pacing them
several times, and then measuring their length, and
breadth, and height, and the distance between the windows.   Then he inspected the wing on that side of the
house, and, going into the yard, looked the building over
from all points, occasionally marking a few lines on the
paper he held in his hand.   Before noon every room in the
house, except the one where Dolly lay sick with a headache, had been visited and examined minutely, while Frank
watched him nervously, wondering if he would think they
had injured anything, or had expended too much money
on furniture.   But Arthur was thinking of none of these
things, and found fault with nothing except the drain and
the gas-fixtures, all of which he declared bad, saying that
the latter must be changed at once, and that ten pounds
of copperas must be bought immediately and put kown the
drain, and that quantities of chloride of lime and carbolic
acid must be placed where there was the least danger of
vegetable decomposition.

"I am very sensitive to smells, and afraid of them, too,
for they breed malaria and disease of all kinds," he said to
the cook, whose nose and chin both were high in the air,
not on account of any obnoxious odor, but because of this
meddling with what she considered her own affairs.   If

things were to go on in this way, she said to the house-
maid, and if that man was going to put his nose into
drains, and gas-pipes, and kerosene lamps, and bowls of
sour milk which she might have forgotten, she should give
notice to quit.

But when, half an hour later, some boxes and trunks
which had come by express were deposited in the back hall,
and Arthur, who was superintending them, said to her, as
he pointed to a large black trunk, "I think this has the
dress patterns and shawls I brought for you girls ; for
though I did not know you personally, I knew that women
were always pleased with anything from Paris," her feelings underwent a radical change, and Arthur was free to
smell the drain and the gas-fixtures as much as he liked.

He was very busy, and, though always pleasant, and
even familiar at times, there was in all he said and did an
air, as if he had assumed the mastership. And he had.
Everything was his, and he knew it, and Frank knew it,
too, and gave no sign of rebelling when the reins were
taken from him by one who seemed to be driving at a
break-neck speed.

At lunch, while the brothers were together, Arthur
declared his intentions in part, but not until Frank, who
was anxious to get it off his mind, said to him :

"By the way, I suppose you will be going to the office
this afternoon, to see Colvin and look over the books.   I
believe you will find them straight, and hope you will not
think I have spent too much, or drawn too large a salary.
If you do, I will——"

"Nonsense !" was Arthur's reply, with a graceful
shrug of his shoulders.   "Don't bother about that ; there
is money enough for us both.   What I invested in Europe
has trebled itself, and more too, and would make me a
rich man if I had nothing else.   I am always lucky.   I
played but once at Monte Carlo, just before I came home,
and won ten thousand dollars, which I invested in—— But
no matter; that is a surprise—something for your wife and
Gretchen. I have come home to stay. I do not think I am
quite what I used to be. I was sick all that time when you
heard from me so seldom, and I am not strong yet.   I need
quiet and rest.   I have seen the world, and am tired of it,
and now I want a house for Gretchen and myself, and you,

too. I expect you to stay with me as long as we pull together pleasantly, and you do not interfere with my plans. I am going to take the three south rooms on the second floor for my own. I shall put folding-doors, or rather a wide arch between two of them, making them seem almost like one, and these I shall fit up to suit my own taste. In the smaller and middle room, where I slept last night, I shall have a large bow window, with shelves for books in the spaces between, and beneath, and by the sides of the windows. I got the idea in a villa a little way out of Florence. Opposite this bow window, on the other side of the room, I shall have niches in the wall and corners for statuary, with shelves for books above and below. I have some beautiful pieces of marble from Florence and Rome. The Venus de Milo, Apollo Belvidere, Nydia and Psehye, and Ruth at the Well. But the crowning glory of this room will be the upper half of the middle window of the bow. This is to be of stained glass, bright but soft colors which harmonize perfectly, two rows on the four sides, and in the center a lovely picture of Gretchen, also of cathedral glass, and so like her that it seems to speak to me in her soft German tongue. I had it made from a photograph I have of her, and it is very natural—the same sad, sweet smile around the lips which never said an unkind word to any one—the same bright, wavy hair, and eyes of blue, innocent as a child—and Gretchen is little more than that. She is only twenty-one—poor little Gretchen!" and, leaning back in his chair, Arthur seemed to be lost in recollections of the past.

Not pleasant, all of them, it would seem, for there was a moisture in his eyes when he at last looked up in response to his brother's question

"Who did you say Gretchen was?"

Instantly the expression of the eyes changed to one of wariness and caution, as Arthur replied:

"I did not say who she was, but you will soon know. I saw by the time-table that the train which passes here at eleven does not stop, but the three o'clock does, and you will please see that John goes with the carriage. I may be occupied with the carpenters, Burchard and Belknap, who are coming to talk with me about the changes I purpose to make, and which I wish commenced immediately. It is a rule of mine, when I am to do a thing, to do it at once. So I shall employ at least twenty men, and before Christmas everything will be finished, and I will show you rooms worthy of a palace. It is of Gretchen I am thinking, more than of myself. Poor Gretchen!"

Arthur's voice was inexpressibly sad and pitiful as he said "Poor Gretchen," while his eyes again grew soft and tender, with a far-away look in them, as if they were seeing things in the past rather than in the future.

There was not a particle of sentiment in Frank's nature, and Gretchen was to him an object of dread rather than of romance. So far as he could judge his brother had no intention of routing him ; but a woman in the field would be different, and he should at once lose his vantage-ground.

"You seem to be very fond of Gretchen," he said, at last.

"Fond!" Arthur replied. "I should say I am, though the poor child has not much cause to think so. But I am going to atone, and this suite of rooms is for her. I mean to make her a very queen, and dress her in satin and diamonds every day. She has the diamonds. I sent them to her when I wrote her to join me in Liverpool."

"And she did join you, I suppose?" Frank said, determined by adroit questioning to learn something of the mysterious Gretchen.

"Yes, she joined me," was the reply.

"Was she very sea-sick?" Frank continued.

"Not a minute. She sat by me all the time while I lay in my berth, but she would not let me hold her hand, and if I tried to touch even her hair, she always moved away to the other side of the state-room, where she sat looking at me reproachfully with those soft blue eyes of hers."

"And she was with you at the Brevoort in New York?" Frank said.

"Yes, with me at the Brevoort."

"And in the train?"

"Yes, and in the train."

"And you left her there?"

"No ; she left herself. She did not follow me out. She went on by mistake, but is sure to come back this afternoon," Arthur replied, rather excitedly, just as a

sharp ring at the bell announced the arrival of Burchard
and Belknap, the leading carpenters of the town, with
whom he was closeted for the next two hours, and both of
whom he finally hired in order to expedite the work he
had in hand.

At precisely three o'clock the carriage from Tracy
Park drew up before the station, awaiting the arrival of
the train and Gretchen. But though the former came,
the latter did not, and John returned alone, mentally vowing to himself that he would not be sent on a fool's errand
a third time ; but five o'clock found him there again, with
the same result. Gretchen did not come, and Arthur's
face wore a sad, troubled expression, and looked pale and
worn, notwithstanding the many times he bathed it in the
coldest water, and rubbed it with the coarsest towels.

He had unpacked several of his trunks and boxes, and
made friends of all the servants by the presents, curious
and rare, which he gave them, while Dolly's headache had
been wholly cured at sight of the exquisite diamonds which
her husband brought to her room and told her were the
gift of Arthur, who had bought them in Paris, and who
begged her to accept them with his love.

The box itself, which was of tortoise shell, lined with
blue velvet, was a marvel of beauty, while the pin was a
cluster of five diamonds, but the ear-rings were solitaires,
large and brilliant, and Dolly's delight knew no bounds as
she took the dazzling stones in her hands and examined
them carefully. Diamonds were the jewels of all others
which she coveted, but which Frank had never felt warranted in buying, and now they were hers, and for a time
she forgot even Gretchen, whose arrival, or rather non-
arrival, troubled her as much as it did her brother-in-law.

Arthur had been very quiet and gentle all the afternoon, showing no sign of the temper he had exhibited the
previous night at sight of Harold, until about six o'clock,
when Tom, his nephew came rushing into the library, followed by Peterkin, very hot and very red in the face, which
he mopped with his yellow silk handkerchief.

" Oh, mother," Tom began, " what do you think Harold Hastings has done ? He stole Mrs. Peterkin's gold pin
last night. It was stuck in her shawl, and she could not
find it, and Lucy saw him fumbling with the things, and

he denies it up hill and down, and Mr. Peterkin is going to
arrest him. I guess Dick St. Clair won't think him the
nicest boy in town now. The thief! I'd like"—

But what he would like was never known, for with a
spring Arthur bounded towards him, and seizing him by
the coat collar, shook him vigorously, while he exclaimed :

"Coward and liar ! Harold Hastings is not a thief !
No child of Amy Crawford could ever be a thief, and if
you say that again, or even insinuate it to any living being,
I'll break every bone in your body. Do you understand ?"

"Yes, sir ; no, sir. I won't ; I won't," Tom gasped, as
well as he could, with his head bobbing forward and back
so rapidly that his teeth cut into his under lip.

"But *I* shall," Peterkin roared. "I'll have the young
dog arrested, too, if he don't own up and give up."

There was a wicked look in Arthur's black eyes which
were fastened upon Peterkin, as he said :

"What does it all mean, sir ? Will you please
explain ?"

"Yes, in double quick time," Peterkin replied, a little
nettled by Arthur's manner, which he could not understand. "You see me and May Jane was early to the doin's ;
fust ones, in fact, for when your invite says half past seven
it means it, I take it. Wall, we was here on time, and
May Jane has been on a tear ever since, and says Miss St.
Claire nor none of the big bugs didn't come till nine, which
I take as imperlite, don't you ?"

"Never mind ; we are not discussing etiquette. Go on
with the pin and the boy," Arthur said, haughtily.

"May Jane," Peterkin continued, "had a gold-headed
shawl-pin, with a small diamond in the head—real, too, for
I don't b'lieve in shams, and hain't sence the day I quit
boatin' and hauled the 'Liza Ann up inter my back yard.
Wall, she left this pin stickin' in her shawl, and no one was
up there but this boy of that Crawford gal's and nobody
knows who else."

Something in Arthur's face and manner made Frank
think of a tiger about to pounce upon its prey, and he felt
himself growing cold with suspense and dread as he
watched his brother, while Peterkin continued :

"When May Jane came to go home, her things wa'n't
there, and the pin was missin' ; and Lucy, the girl, said

she found the boy pullin' them over by himself, when he had no call to be in there; and, sir, there ain't a lawyer in the United States that would refuse a writ on that evidence, and I'll get one of St. Claire afore to-morrow night. I told 'em so, the widder and the boy, who was as brassy as you please, and faced me down and said he never seen the pin, nor knowed there was one; while she—wall, I swow, if she didn't start round lively for a woman with her leg bandaged up in vinegar and flannel. When I called the brat a thief and said I'd have him arrested, she made for the door and ordered me out—me, Joel Peterkin, of the 'Liza Ann! I'll make her smart, though, wus than the rheumatiz. I'll make her feel the heft"—

He did not have time to finish the sentence, for the tiger in Arthur was fully roused, and with a spring toward Peterkin he opened the door, and, in a voice which seemed to fill the room, although it was only a whisper, he said:

"Clown! loafer! puff-ball! Leave my house instantly, and never enter it again until you have apologized to Mrs. Crawford and her grandson for the insult offered them by your vile accusations. If it were not for soiling my hands, I would throw you down the steps," he continued, as he stood holding the door open, and looking, with his flashing eyes and dilated nostrils, as if he were fully equal to anything.

Like most men of the boasting sort, Peterkin was a coward, and though he probably had twice the strength of Arthur, he went through the door-way out upon the piazza, where he stopped, and, with a flourish of his fist, denounced the whole Tracy tribe, declaring them a race of upstarts no better than he was, and saying he would yet be even with them, and make them feel the heft of his powerful disapprobation. Whatever else he said was not heard, for Arthur shut the door upon him, and returning to the library, where his brother stood, pale, trembling, and anxious for the votes he felt he had lost, he became on tha instant as quiet and gentle as a child, and, consulting his watch, said, in his natural tone:

"Quarter of seven, and the train is due at half-past. Please tell John to have the carriage ready. I am going myself this time."

Frank opened his lips to protest against it, but something in his brother's manner kept him quiet and submissive. He was no longer master there—unless—unless— he scarcely dared whisper to himself what; but when the carriage went for the fourth time to the station after Gretchen and returned without her, he said to his wife:

"I think Arthur is crazy, and we may have to shut him up."

"Oh, I wish you would," was Dolly's reply, in a tone of relief, for, thus far, Arthur's presence in the house had not added to her comfort. "Of course he is crazy, and ought to be taken care of before he tears the house down over our heads, or does some dreadful thing."

"That's so, and I'll see St. Claire to-morrow and find out the proper steps to be taken," said Frank.

That night he dreamed of windows with iron bars across them, and strait-jackets, into which he was putting his brother, while a face, the loveliest he had ever seen, looked reproachfully at him, with tears in the soft blue eyes, and a pleading pathos in the voice which said words he could not understand, for the language was a strange one to him.

With a start Frank awoke, and found his wife sitting up in bed, listening intently to sounds which came from the hall, where some one was evidently moving around.

Going to the door and looking out he saw his brother, wrapped in a long dressing-gown, with a candle in his hand, opening one window after another until the hall was filled with the cold night wind, which swept down the long corridor, banging a door at the farther end and setting all the rest to rattling.

"Oh, Frank, is that you?" Arthur said. "I am sorry I woke you, but I smelled an awful smell somewhere, and traced it to the hall, which you see I am airing; better shut the door or you will take cold. The house is full of malaria."

There could be no doubt of his insanity, and next morning, when Mr. St. Claire entered his office, he found Frank Tracy waiting there to consult him with regard to the legal steps necessary to procure his brother's incarceration in a lunatic asylum.

Arthur St. Claire's face wore a troubled look as he listened, for he remembered a time, years before, when he,

too, had been interested in the lunatic asylum at Worces-
ter, where a beautiful young girl, his wife, had been confined. She was dead now, and the Florida roses were
growing over her grave, but there were many sad, regret-
ful memories connected with her short life, and not the
least sad of these were those of the asylum.

"If it were to do over again I would not put her there,
unless she became dangerous," he had often said to himself, and he said much the same thing to Frank Tracy
with regard to his brother.

"Keep him at home, if possible. Do not place him
with a lot of lunatics if you can help it. No proof he is
crazy because he smells everything. My wife does the
same. And as to this Gretchen, it is possible there was
some woman with him on the ship, or in New York, and
he may be a little muddled there. You can inquire at the
hotel where he stopped."

This was Mr. St. Claire's advice, and Frank acted upon
it, and took immediate steps to ascertain if there had been
a lady in company with his brother at the Brevoort House,
where he had stopped, or if there had been any one in his
company on the ship, which was still lying in the dock at
New York. But Arthur Tracy alone was registered
among the list of passengers, and only Arthur Tracy was
on the books at the hotel. He had come alone, and been
alone on the sea and at the hotel.

Gretchen was a myth, or at least a mystery, though he
still insisted that she would arrive with every train from
Boston ; and for nearly a week the carriage was sent to
meet her, until at last there seemed to dawn upon his
mind the possibility of a mistake, and when the carriage
had made its twentieth trip for nothing, and Mr. St.
Claire, who was standing by him on the platform when the
train came up and brought no Gretchen, said to him,
"She did not come," he answered, sadly, "No ; there has
been some mistake. She will never come." Then, after
a moment he added, "But there *is* a Gretchen, and I
wrote to her to join me in Liverpool, and I thought she
did, and was with me on the ship and in the train, but
sometimes, when my head is so hot, I get things mixed,
and am not sure; but—" and he looked wistfully in his
companion's face, while his voice trembled a little.

"Don't let them shut me up; it will do no good. I was in an asylum three years or more near Vienna; went of my own accord, because of that heat in my head."

"Been in an asylum?" Mr. St. Claire said, wonderingly.

"Yes," Arthur continued, "I was only out three months before I sailed for home. I wrote occasionally to Frank and Gretchen, but did not tell them where I was. They called it a *maison de sante*, and treated me well because I paid well, but the sight of so many crazy people made me worse, and if I had staid I should have been mad as the maddest of them.

"Mine was a curious case, they said, and one not often met with in mental diseases. I was all right in everything except my memory which played me the wildest tricks—why I actually forgot my name, and fancied myself an Austrian. Strangest of all I forgot where Gretchen lived and forget her, too, a part of the time, and I don't know now how long it was before I went to that place that I saw her last. As soon as I came out I was better, and in Paris things came back to me, and when I reached Liverpool I wrote to Gretchen to join me. That is all I know. I can see that I am in Frank's way and he would like to shut me up. But stand by me St. Claire—don't let him do it."

Assuring him of his support against any steps which might be taken to prove him mad enough for the asylum, Mr. St. Claire continued: "I wouldn't come for Gretchen any more. Who is she?"

"That is my little secret, my surprise which will be like a bomb-shell in the camp when she comes," Arthur replied, as he walked towards the carriage, while Mr. St. Claire looked curiously after him, and said to himself:

"That fellow is not right, but he is not a subject for a mad-house, and I should oppose his being sent there. I do not believe, however, that they will try it on."

CHAPTER X.

ARTHUR SETTLES HIMSELF.

THEY did try it on, but not until after the November election, at which Frank was defeated by a large majority, for Peterkin worked against him and brought all the "heft of his powerful disapprobation" to bear upon him. Although Frank had had no part in turning him from the door that morning after the party, he had not tried to prevent it by a word, and this the low, brutal man resented, and declared his intention to defeat Frank if it cost him half his fortune to do so. And it did cost him at least two thousand dollars, for Frank Tracy was popular with both parties; many of the Democrats voted for him, but those who could be bought on both sides, went against him, even to the Widow Shipley's four sons; and when all was over, Frank found himself defeated by just as many votes as old Peterkin had paid for, not only in Shannondale, but in the adjoining towns, where his money carried "heft," as he expressed it.

It was a terrible disappointment to Frank and his wife, who had looked forward to a winter in Washington, where they intended to take a house and enjoy all society had to offer them in the National Metropolis. Particularly were they anxious for the change now that Arthur had come home, for it was not altogether pleasant to be ruled where they had so long been rulers, and to see the house turned upside down without the right to protest.

"I can't stand it, and I won't," Frank said to his wife, in the first flush of his bitter disappointment. "Ever since he came home he has raised Cain, generally, with his carpenters, and masons, and painters, and stewing about water-pipes, and sewer-gas, and smells. He's mad as a March hare, and if I can't get rid of him by going to Washington, I'll do it in some other way. You know he is crazy, and so do I, and I'll swear to it on a stack of Bibles as high as the house."

And Frank did swear to it, before two or three physicians and **Mr. St. Claire**, who, at his solicitation, came to Tracy Park, and were closeted with him for an hour or more, while he related his grievances, asserting finally that he considered his brother dangerous, and did not think his family safe with him, citing as proof, that he had on one occasion threatened to kill his son Tom for accusing Harold Hastings of theft.

How the matter would have terminated is doubtful, if Arthur himself had not appeared upon the scene, calm, dignified, and courtly in his manner, which insensibly won upon his hearers, as, in a few well-chosen and eloquent words, he proceeded to prove that though he might be peculiar in some respects, he was not mad, and that a man might repair his own house, and cut off his own water pipes, and take up his sewer, and detect a bad smell, and still not be a subject for a lunatic asylum.

"And," he continued, addressing his brother, "it ill becomes you to take this course against me—you, who have enriched yourself at my expense, while I have held my peace. Suppose I require you to give an account of all the money which you have considered necessary for your support and salary? Would the world consider you strictly honorable? But I have no wish to harm you. I have money enough, and cannot forget that you are my brother. But molest me, and I shall molest you. If I go to the asylum, you will leave Tracy Park. If I am allowed to stay here in peace, you can do so, too. Good-morning, gentlemen!" and he bowed himself from the room, leaving Frank covered with confusion and shame as he felt that he was beaten.

The physicians did not think it a case in which they were warranted to interfere. Neither could conscientiously sign a certificate which should declare Arthur a lunatic, and their advice to Frank was that he should suffer his brother to have his own way in his own house, and when he felt that he could not bear with his idiosyncracies he could go elsewhere. But it was this going elsewhere which Frank did not fancy; and, after a consultation with his wife, he decided to let matters take their course for a time at least.

Arthur's allusion to the sums of money his brother had appropriated to his own use had warned Frank that he was

4

not quite so indifferent to or ignorant of his business affairs as he had seemed ; and this, of itself, served to keep him quiet and patient during the confusion which ensued, as walls were torn down, and doors and windows cut, while the house was filled with workmen, and the sound of the hammer and saw was heard from morning till night.

It was the middle of October when Arthur commenced his repairs, but so many men did he employ, and so rapidly was the work pushed on, that the first of January found everything finished and Arthur installed in his suite of rooms, which a prince might have envied, so richly and tastefully were they fitted up. Beautiful pictures and rich tapestry covered the walls in the first room, where the floor was inlaid with colored woods, and the center was covered with a costly Oriental rug, which Arthur had bought at a fabulous price in Paris. But the gem of the suite was the library, where the statuary stood in the niches, and where, from the large bow-window at the south, a young girl's face looked upon the scene with an expression of shy surprise and half regret in the blue eyes, as if their owner wondered how she came there, and was always thinking of the fields and forests of far-away Germany. For it was decidedly a German face of the higher type, and such as is seldom found among the lower or even middle classes. And yet you instinctively felt that it belonged to the latter, notwithstanding the richness of the dress, from the pearl-embroidered cap set jauntily on the reddish golden hair to the velvet bodice and the satin peasant waist. The hands, small and dimpled like those of a child, were clasped around a prayer-book and a bunch of wild flowers which had evidently just been gathered. It was a marvelously beautiful face, pure and sweet as that of a Madonna, and the workmen involuntarily bowed their heads before it, wondering who she was, or where, if living, she was now, and what relation she bore to the strange man who often stood before her whispering to himself :

" Poor little Gretchen ! Will you never come ? "

If he were expecting her now he no longer asked that the carriage be sent to meet her. That had been one of the proofs of his insanity as alleged by his brother, and Arthur was sane enough to avoid a repetition of that offense, but he often went himself to the station, when the

New York trains were due, as it was from the west rather than the east that he was now looking for her.

Frank, who watched him nervously, with all his senses sharpened, guessed what had caused the change and grew more nervous and morbid on the subject of Gretchen than ever. At first his brother, who was greatly averse to going out, had asked him to post his letters; business letters they seemed to be, for they were addressed to business firms in New York, London and Paris, with all of which Arthur had relations. But one morning when Frank went as usual to his brother's room asking if there was any mail to be taken to the office, Arthur, who was just finishing a letter, replied :

" No, thank you, I will post this myself. I have been writing to Gretchen."

" Yes, to Gretchen? " Frank said, quickly, as he advanced nearer to the writing-desk, hoping to see the address on the envelope.

But Arthur must have suspected his motive, for he at once turned over the envelope and kept his hand upon it, while Frank said to him :

" Is she in London now? "

" No; she was never in London," was the curt reply, and then, turning suddenly, Arthur faced his brother and said : " Why are you so curious about Gretchen? It is enough for you to know that she is the sweetest, truest little girl that ever lived. When she comes I shall tell you everything, but not before. You have tried to prove me crazy: have said I was full of cranks; perhaps I am, and Gretchen is one of them, but it does not harm you, so leave me in peace, if you wish for peace yourself."

There was a menacing look in Arthur's eyes which Frank did not like, and he resolved to say no more to him of Gretchen, whose arrival he again began to look for and dread. But she did not come, or any tidings of her, and Christmas came and went, and the lovely bracelets which Arthur brought from the trunk he said was hers, and into which no one had ever looked but himself, remained unclaimed, as did the costly inlaid work-box and the cut-glass bottles with the golden stoppers, while Arthur seemed to be settling into a state of great depression, caring nothing for the outside world, but spending all his time

in the rooms he had prepared for himself and one who
never came.

As far as possible he continued his foreign habits, having his coffee and rolls at eight in the morning, his breakfast, as he called it, at half-past twelve, and his dinner at
half-past six. All these meals were served in his room as
elaborately and with as much ceremony as if lords and
ladies sat at the table instead of one lone man, who required
the utmost attention and care in the waiting. The finest
of linen, and china, and glass, and silver adorned his
table, with a profusion of flowers—roses mostly, if he
could get them, for Gretchen, he said, was fond of these,
and, as she might surprise him at any moment, he wished
to be ready for her and show that he was expecting her.

Opposite him, at the end of the table, was always an
empty plate with its surroundings, and the curiously
carved chair, which had seen the lion at Lucerne. But
no one ever sat in it. No one ever used the decorated
plate, or the glass mug at its side, with its twisted handle
and the letter "G." on the silver cover. Just what this
mug was for, none of the household knew, until Grace
Atherton, who had traveled in Europe, and to whom Mrs.
Tracy showed it one day when Arthur was out, said :

"Why, it is a beer-mug, such as is used in Germany,
though more particularly among the Bavarian Alps and in
the Tyrol. This Gretchen is probably a tippler, with a
red nose and double chin. I wish to goodness she would
come and satisfy our curiosity."

But Gretchen did not come, and as the days went by
Arthur became more and more depressed and remained
altogether in his room, seeing no one and holding no intercourse with the outside world. He had returned no calls,
and had been but once to see Mrs. Crawford. That interview had been a long and sad one, and when they talked
of Amy, whose grave Arthur had visited on his way to the
cottage, both had cried together, and Gretchen seemed for
the time forgotten. They talked of Amy's husband, and
then Arthur spoke of Amy's son, who was not present, and
whom he seemed to have forgotten, for when Mrs. Crawford said to him, "You saw him on the night of your
return home," he looked at her in a perplexed kind of way,
as if trying to remember something which had gone almost

entirely from his mind. It was this utter forgetfulness of
people and events which was a marked feature of his insanity, if insane he were, and he knew it and struggled
against it ; and when Mrs. Crawford told him he had seen
Harold he tried to recall him, and could not until the boy
came in, flushed and excited from a race with Dick St.
Claire through the crisp November wind which had
brought a bright color to his cheek and a sparkle to his
eye. Then Arthur remembered everything, and something of his old prejudice came back to him, and his manner was a little constrained as he talked to the boy, whose
only fault was that Harold Hastings had been his father.

He did not stay long after Harold came in, but said
good-morning to Mrs. Crawford and walked slowly away,
going again to Amy's grave, and taking from it a few
leaves of the ivy which was growing around the monument. And this was all the intercourse he held with Mrs.
Crawford, except to send her at Christmas a hundred dollars, which he said was for the boy Harold, to whom he
had done an injustice.

After this he seldom went out, but settled down into
the life of a recluse, talking occasionally to himself, with
some unseen person, who must have spoken in a foreign
tongue or tongues, for sometimes it was French, sometimes
Italian, and oftener German in which he addressed his
fancied guest, and neither Frank nor Dolly could understand a word of the strange jargon. On the whole, however, he was very quiet and undemonstrative, and if he
were still expecting Gretchen, he gave no sign of it, and
Frank was beginning to breathe freely, and to look upon
his presence in the house as not altogether unbearable,
when an event occurred which excited all Shannondale,
and for a time made Frank almost as crazy as his brother.

CHAPTER XI.

THE STORM.

THE winter since Christmas had been unusually severe, and the oldest inhabitants, of whom there are always many in every town, pronounced the days, as they came and went, the coldest they had ever known. Ten, twelve, and even fourteen degrees below zero the thermometers marked more than once, while old Peterkin's which was hung inside the 'Lizy Ann and always took the lead, went down one morning to seventeen, and all the water-pipes and pumps in town either froze or burst, and Arthur Tracy, who never forgot the poor, sent tons and tons of coal to them, and whispered to himself :

"Poor Gretchen ! It is hard for her if she is on the sea in such weather as this. Heaven protect her, poor little Gretchen !"

The next day there was a change for the better, and the next, and the next, until when the last day of February dawned people began to look more cheerful, while the sun tried to break through the grey clouds which shrouded the wintry sky. But this was only temporary, for before noon the mercury fell again to eight below, the wind began to rise, and when the New York train came panting to the station at half-past six, clouds of snow so dense and dark were driving over the hills and along the line of the track that nothing could be distinctly seen at a distance.

It was not until the train had moved on that the station-master, who was gathering up the mail-bag, which had been unceremoniously dropped, saw across the track at a little distance from him the figure of a woman, who seemed to be trying to examine a paper she held in her hand, while clinging to her skirts and crying piteously was a child, but whether boy or girl, he could not tell.

"Can I do anything for you ?" he said, advancing toward the stranger, who caught up the child in her arms, and without a word of answer, hurried away in the storm and rapidly increasing darkness.

"Curis ! She must have got off t'other side of the car.

I wonder who she is and where she is goin'. Not fur, I hope, such a night as this. Ugh! the wind is like so many screech owls and almost takes a feller off his feet," the agent said to himself, as he went back to the light and warmth of his office, where he soon forgot the woman, who, with the child held closely in her arms, walked swiftly on, her eyes strained to their utmost tension as they peered through the darkness until she reached a gate open‐ing into a grassy road which led through the fields in a straight line to Tracy Park and Collingwood beyond.

Carriages seldom traversed this road, but in the sum‐mer the people from Collingwood and Tracy Park fre‐quently walked that way, as it was a much nearer route to town. Here the woman stopped, and looking up at the tall arch over the gate, said aloud, as if repeating a lesson learned by heart.

"Leave the car on your right hand; take the road to the right, as I have drawn it on paper; go straight on for a quarter of a mile or more until you come to a wide iron gate with a tall arch over it. This gate is also at your right. You cannot mistake it."

" No," she continued, " I cannot mistake it. This is the place. We are almost there," and putting down the child, she tugged with all her strengh at the gate, which she at last succeeded in opening, and resuming her burden, passed through into the field where the snow lay on the ground in great white drifts, while the blinding flakes and cutting sleet from the leaden clouds above beat pitilessly upon her as she struggled on her wearisome way.

And while she toiled on, fighting bravely with the storm, and occasionally speaking a word of encouragement to the little child nestled in her bosom, Arthur Tracy stood at one of the windows in his library, with his face pressed against the pane, as he looked anxiously out into darkness, shuddering involuntarily as the wind came screaming round a corner of the house, bending the tall evergreens until their slender tops almost touched the ground, and then rushing on down the carriage-drive with a shriek like so many demons let loose from the ice-caves of the north, where the winds are supposed to hold high carnival.

They were surely holding a carnival to-night, and as

Arthur listened to the roar of the tempest he whispered to
himself :

"A wild, wild night for Gretchen to arrive, and her
dear little feet and hands will be so cold; but there is
warmth and comfort here, and love such as she never
dreamed of, poor Gretchen ! I will hold her in my arms
and chafe her cold fingers and kiss her tired face until
she feels that her home-coming is a happy one. It must
be almost time," and he glanced at a small clock which
stood upon the mantle.

In the adjoining room the dinner table was laid for
two, and one could see that more care than usual had been
given to its arrangement, while the roses in the center
were the largest and finest of their kind. In the grate a
bright fire was burning, and Arthur placed a large easy-
chair before it and then brought from the library a footstool, with a delicate covering of blue and gold. No foot
had ever yet profaned this stool with a touch, for it was
one of Arthur's specialties, bought at a great price in
Algiers ; but he brought it now for Gretchen and saw in
fancy resting upon it the cold little feet his hands were to
rub and warm and caress until life came back to them,
while Gretchen's blue eyes smiled upon him and Gretchen's
sweet voice said :

"Thank you, Arthur. It is pleasant coming home."

For the last two or three weeks Arthur had been very
quiet and taciturn, but on the morning of this day he had
seemed restless and nervous, and his nervousness and
excitability increased until a violent headache came on,
and Charles, the servant who attended him, reported to
Mrs. Tracy that his lunch had been untouched, and that
he really seemed quite ill. Then Frank went to him, and
sitting down beside him as he lay upon a couch in the
room with Gretchen's picture, said to him, not unkindly :

"Are you sick to-day?"

For a few moments Arthur made no reply, but lay
with his eyes closed as if he had not heard. Then suddenly rousing himself, he burst out, vehemently :

"Frank, you think me crazy, and you have based that
belief in part, on the fact that I am always expecting
Gretchen. And so for a long time I have suppressed all
mention of her, though I have never ceased to look for her

arrival, since—since—well, I may as well tell you the truth. I know now that she could not have been with me on the ship and in the train, although I thought she was. I wrote her to join me in Liverpool, and fancied she did. But my brain must have been a little mixed. She did not come with me, and when I made up my mind to that, as I did a few weeks ago, I wrote again telling her to come at once, and giving her directions how to find the park if she should arrive at the station and no one there to meet her. She has had more than time to get here, but I have said nothing about sending the carriage for her, as that seems to annoy you. But Frank—" and Arthur's voice trembled as he went on—"I dreamed of her last night ; such strange dreams, and to-day she seems so near to me that more than once I have put out my hand to touch her. Frank, it is not insanity—this presentiment that she is near me—that she is coming to me, or tidings of her; it is mind acting upon mind ; her thoughts of me reaching forward and fastening upon my thoughts of her, making a mental bridge on which I see her coming to me. And you will send for her. You will let John go again. Think if she should arrive in this terrible storm and no one there to meet her. You will send this once, and if she is not there I will not trouble you again."

There was something in Arthur's face which Frank could not resist, and he promised that John should go.

" Oh, Frank," Arthur exclaimed, his face brightening at once, " you have made me so happy ! My headache is quite gone ;" and then he began to plan the dinner, which was to be more elaborate than usual, and served an hour later, so as to give plenty of time for Gretchen to rest and dress herself if she wished to do so.

" And she will when she sees the lovely dress I have for her," he thought, and after his brother left him he went to the large closet where he kept the trunk which he called Gretchen's, and into which Dolly's curious eyes had never looked, although she longed to know its contents.

This Arthur now opened, and had Dolly been there she would have held her breath in wonder at the many beautiful things which it contained. Folded in one of the trays, as only a French packer accustomed to the business could have arranged it, was an exquisite dinner-dress of

4*

salmon-colored satin, with a brocaded front and jacket of blue and gold, and here and there a knot of duchess lace, which gave it a more airy effect. This Arthur took out carefully and laid upon the bed in his sleeping-apartment, together with every article of the toilet necessary to such a dress, from a lace pocket-handkerchief to a pair of pale-blue silk hose, which he kissed reverently as he whispered :

"Dear little feet, which are so cold now in the wretched car ; but they will never be cold again when once I have them here."

He was talking in German, as he always did when Gretchen was the subject of his thoughts, and so Dolly, who came to say that some things which he had ordered for dinner were impossible now, could not understand him, but she caught a glimpse of the dress upon the bed, and advanced quickly toward the open door, exclaiming :

"Oh, Arthur, what a lovely gown ! Whose—"

But before she completed her question Arthur was upon the threshold and had closed the door, saying as he did so :

"It is Gretchen's. I had it made at Worth's. She is coming to-night, you know."

Dolly had heard from her husband of Arthur's fancy, and though she had no faith in it, she replied :

"Yes, Frank told me you were expecting her, and I came to say that we cannot get the fish you ordered, for no one can go to town in this storm, and I doubt if we could find it if we did. You will have to skip the fish."

"All right; all right. Gretchen will be too much excited to care," Arthur replied, standing with his hand upon the door-knob until Dolly left the room and went to the kitchen, where Frank was interviewing the coachman.

He had found that important personage before the fire, bending nearly double, and complaining bitterly of a fall he had just had on his way from the stable to the house. According to his statement, the wind had taken him up bodily, and carrying him a dozen rods or so, had set him down upon a stone flower-pot which was left outside, nearly breaking his back, as he declared. This did not look very promising for the drive to the station, and Frank opened the business hesitatingly, and asked John what he thought of it.

"I think I would not go out in such a storm as this with my back if Queen Victoria was to be there," John answered, gruffly. "And what would be the use?" he continued. "I have been to meet that woman, if she is a woman, with the outlandish name, more than fifty times, I'll bet. He don't know what he is talking about when he gets on her track. And s'posin' she does come. She can find somebody to fetch her. She ain't going to walk."

This seemed reasonable; and as Frank's sympathies were with his coachman and horses rather than with Gretchen and his brother, he decided with John that he need not go, and then returned to the library, resolving not to see his brother again until after train time, but to let him think that John had gone to the station.

At half-past five, however, Arthur sent for him, and said :

"Has he gone ? It must be time."

"Not quite ; it is only half-past five. The train does not come until half-past six, and is likely to be late," was Frank's reply.

"Yes, I know," Arthur continued ; "but he should be there on time. Tell him to start at once, and take an extra robe with him, and say to Charles that I will have sherry to-night, and champagne, too, and Hamburgh grapes, and——"

The remainder of his speech was lost on Frank, who was hurrying down the stairs, with a guilty feeling in his heart, although he felt that the end justified the means, and that under the circumstances he was warranted in deceiving his half-crazy brother. Still he was ill at ease. He had no faith in Arthur's presentiments, and no idea that any one bound for Tracy Park would be on the train that night, but he could not shake off a feeling of anxiety, amounting almost to a dread of some impending calamity, which possibly the sending of John to the station might have averted, and going to a window in the library, he, too, stood looking out into the night, trying not to believe that he was watching for some possible arrival, when, above the storm, he heard the shrill scream of the locomotive as it stopped for a moment, and then dashed on into the white snow clouds ; trying to believe, too, that he was not glad, as the minutes became a quarter, the quarter a half, and the half three-quarters of an hour, until at last he heard the clock strike the half-hour past seven, and nobody had come.

"I shall have to tell Arthur," he thought, and, with something like hesitancy, he started for his brother's room.

Arthur was standing before the fire, with his arm thrown caressingly across the chair where Gretchen was to sit, when Frank opened the door and advanced a step or two across the threshold.

"Has she come? I did not see the carriage. Where is she?" Arthur cried, springing swiftly forward, while his bright, eager eyes darted past his brother to the open doorway and out into the hall.

"No, she has not come. I knew she wouldn't; and it was nonsense to send the horses out such a night as this," Frank said, sternly, with a mistaken notion that he must speak sharply to the unfortunate man, who, if rightly managed, was gentle as a child.

"Not come! There must be some mistake!" Arthur said, all the brightness fading from his face, which grew pinched and pallid as he continued: "Not come! Oh, Frank! did John say so? Was no one there? Let me go and question him—there must be a mistake."

He was hurrying toward the door, when Frank caught his arm and detained him, while he said, decidedly:

"No use to see John. Can't you believe me when I tell you no one was there—and I knew there would not be. It was folly to send."

For a moment Arthur's pale, haggard face, which looked still more haggard and pale with the fire-light flickering over it, confronted Frank steadily; then the lips began to quiver and the eyelids to twitch, while great tears gathered in his eyes, until at last, covering his face with his hands, he staggered to the couch, and throwing himself upon it, sobbed convulsively.

"Oh, Gretchen, my darling!" he said "I was so sure, and now everything is swept away, and I am left so desolate."

Frank had never seen grief just like this, and with his conscience pricking him for the deception he had practiced, he found himself pitying his brother as he had never done before; and when at last the latter cried out loud, he went to him, and laying his hand gently upon his bowed head, said to him soothingly :

"Don't Arthur; it is terrible to see a man cry as you are crying."

"No, no ; let me cry," Arthur replied. "The tears do me good, and my brain would burst without them. It is all on fire, and my head is aching so hard again."

At this moment Charles appeared, asking if his master would have dinner served. But Arthur could not eat, and the table which had been arranged with so much care for Gretchen was cleared away, while Gretchen's chair was moved back from the fire and Gretchen's footstool put in its place, and nothing remained to show that she had been expected except the pretty dress, with its accessories, which lay upon Arthur's bed. These he took care of himself, folding them with trembling hands and tear-wet eyes, as a fond mother folds the clothes her dead child has worn, sorrowing most over the half worn shoes, so like the dear little feet which will never wear them again. So Arthur sorrowed over the high-heeled slippers, with the blue rosettes and pointed toes, fashionable in Paris at that time. Gretchen had never worn them, it is true, but they seemed so much like her, that his tears fell fast as he held them in his hands, and dropping upon the pure white satin, left a stain upon it.

When everything was put away and the long trunk locked again, Arthur went back to the couch and said to his brother, who was still in the room :

"Don't leave me, Frank, till I am more composed. My nerves are dreadfully shaken to-night, and I feel afraid of something, I don't know what. How the wind howls and moans! I never heard it like that but once before and that was years ago, among the Alps in Switzerland. Then it blew off the roof of the chalet where I was staying, and I heard afterward that Amy died that night. You remember Amy, the girl I loved so well, though not as I love Gretchen. If she had come, I should have told you all about her, but now it does not matter who she is, or where I saw her first, knitting in the sunshine, with the halo on her hair, and the blue of the summer skies reflected in her eyes. Oh, Gretchen, my love, my love !"

He was talking more to himself than to Frank, who sat

beside him until far into the night, while the wild storm raged on and shook the solid house to its very foundations. A tall tree in the yard was uprooted, and a chimney-top came crushing down with a force which threatened to break through the roof. For a moment there was a lull in the tempest, and, raising himself upon his elbow, Arthur listened intently, and then, in a whisper, which made Frank's blood curdle in his veins, he said :

"Hark ! there's more abroad to-night than the storm ! Something is happening which affects me. I have heard voices in the wind all the evening—Gretchen calling me from far away. Frank, Frank, *did* you hear that ? It was a woman's cry ; her voice—Gretchen's. Yes, Gretchen, I am coming."

With a bound he was at the window, which he opened, and leaning far out of it, listened to hear repeated a sound which Frank, too, had heard—a cry like the voice of one in mortal peril calling for help.

It might have been the wind which swept round the corner in a great gust, driving the snow and sleet into Arthur's face, and making him draw in his body, nearly half of which was leaning from the window as he waited for the cry to be repeated. But it did not come again, though Frank, whose nerves were strung to almost as high a tension as his brother's, thought he heard it once more above the roar of the tempest, and a feeling of disquiet took possession of him as he sat for an hour longer talking to his brother, and listening to the noise without.

Gradually the storm subsided, and when the clock struck one the wind had gone down, the snow had ceased to fall, and the moon was struggling feebly through a rift of dark clouds in the west. After persuading his brother to go to bed, Frank retired to his own room, and was soon asleep, unmindful of the tragedy which was being enacted not very far away, where a little child was smiling in its dreams, while the woman beside it was praying for life until her mission should be accomplished.

CHAPTER XII.

THE TRAMP HOUSE.

ABOUT midway between the entrance to the park and
the Collingwood grounds, and twenty rods or more
from the cross-road which the strange woman had taken on
the night of the storm, stood a small stone building, which
had been used as a school-house until the Shannondale
turnpike was built and the cross-road abandoned. After
that it was occupied by one poor family after another, until
the property of which it was a part came into the hands of
the elder Mr. Tracy, who, with his English ideas, thought
to make it a lodge and bring the gates of his park down to
it. But this he did not do, and the house was left to the
mercy of the winds, and the storms, and the boys, until
Arthur became master, and with his artistic taste thought
to beautify it a little and turn it to some use.

"I would tear it down," he said to Mr. St. Claire, who
stood with him one day looking at it, "I would tear it
down, and have once or twice given orders to that effect,
but as often countermanded them. I do not know that I
am superstitious, but I am subject to fancies, or presentiments, or whatever you choose to call those moods which
take possession of you and which you cannot shake off, and,
singularly enough, one of these fancies is connected with
this old hut, and as often as I decide to remove it something tells me not to ; and once I actually dreamed that a
dead woman's hand clutched me by the arm and bade me
leave it alone. A case of 'Woodman spare that tree,' you
see."

And Arthur laughed lightly at his own morbid fancies,
but he left the house and planted around it quantities of
woodbine, which soon crept up its sides to the chimney-top
and made it look like the ivy-covered cottages so common
in Ireland. It was the nicest kind of rendezvous for lovers,
who frequently availed themselves of its seclusion to whisper their secrets to each other, and it was sometimes used
as a dining-room by the people of Shannondale, when in

summer they held picnics in the pretty pine grove not far
away.   But during Arthur's absence it had been suffered
to go to decay, for Frank cared little for lovers or picnics,
and less for the tramps who often slept there at night, and
for whom it came at last to be called the Tramp House.
So the winds, and the storms, and the boys did their work
upon it unmolested, and when Arthur came home, the
door hung upon one hinge, and there was scarcely a whole
light of glass in the six windows.

"Better tear the old rookery down.   It is of no earthly
use except to harbor rats and tramps.   I've known two or
three to spend the night in it at a time, and once a lot of
gipsies quartered themselves here for a week and nearly
scared Dolly to death," Frank said to his brother as they
were walking past it, and Arthur was commenting upon its
dilapidated appearance.

"Oh, the tramps sleep here, do they?" Arthur said.
"Well, let them.   If any poor, homeless wretches want to
stay here nights they are very welcome, I am sure, and I
will see that the door is re-hung and glass put in the windows.   May as well make them comfortable."

"Do as you like," Frank replied, and there, so far as
he was concerned, the matter ended.

But while the carpenters were at work at the Park,
Arthur sent one of them to the old stone house and had
the door fixed and glass put in two of the windows, while
rude but close shutters were nailed before the others, and
then Arthur went himself into the room and pushed a long
table, which the picnic people had used for their refreshments and the tramps for a bed, into a corner, where one
sleeping upon it would be more sheltered from the draught.
All this seemed nonsense to Frank, who laughingly suggested that Arthur should place in it a stove and a ton of coal
for the benefit of his lodgers.   But Arthur cared little for
his brother's jokes.   His natural kindness of heart, which
was always seeking another's good, had prompted him to
this care for the Tramp House, in which he felt a strange
interest, never dreaming that what he was doing would
reach forward to the future and influence not only his life
but that of many others.

The storm which had raged so fiercely around the house
in the park had not spared the cottage in the lane, which

rocked like a cradle, as gust after gust of wind struck it with a force which made every timber quiver, and sent Harold close to his grandmother's side, as he asked, tremblingly :

" Do you think we shall be blown away?"

The rheumatism from which Mrs. Crawford had been suffering in the fall had troubled her more or less during the entire winter, and now, aggravated by a cold, it was worse than it had ever been before, and on the night of the storm she was suffering intense pain, which was only relieved by the hot poultices which Harold made under her direction and applied to the swollen limb. This kept him up later than usual, and the clock was striking eleven when his grandmother declared herself easier, and bade him go to bed.

It was at this hour that Arthur Tracy had fancied he heard the cry for help, and the snow was sweeping past the cottage in great billows of white when Harold went to the window and looked out into the night. In the summer when the leaves were upon the trees the old stone house could not be seen from the cottage, from which it was distant a quarter of a mile or more, but in the winter when the trees were stripped of their foliage it was plainly discernible, and as Harold glanced that way a gleam of light appeared suddenly, as if the door had been opened and the flickering rays of a candle had for a moment shone out into the darkness. Then it disappeared, but not until Harold had cried out :

" Oh, grandma, there's a light in the Tramp House ; I saw it plain as day. Somebody is in there."

" God pity them," was Mrs. Crawford's reply, though she did not quite credit Harold's statement, or think of it again that night.

It was late next morning when Harold awoke to find the sun shining into the room, and all traces of the terrible storm gone except the snow, which lay in great piles everywhere and came almost to the window's edge. But Harold was not afraid of snow, and soon had the walks cleared around the cottage, and when, after breakfast, which he prepared himself, for his grandmother could not step, he was told that a doctor must be had and he must go for him, he commenced his preparations at once for the long and wearisome walk.

"Better go through the park," his grandmother said to him, as he was tying his warm comforter about his ears and putting on his mittens. "It is a little farther that way, but somebody has broken a path by this time, and the cross-road, which is nearer, must be impassable."

Harold made no reply, but remembering the light he had seen in the Tramp House, resolved to take the cross-road and investigate the mystery. Bidding his grandmother good-bye, and telling her he should be back before she had time to miss him, he started on his journey, and was soon plunging through the snow, which, in some places, was up to his armpits, so that his progress was very slow, but by kicking with his feet and throwing out his arms like the paddles of a boat, he managed to get on until he was opposite the Tramp House, which looked like an immense snow-heap, so completely was it covered. Only the chimney and the slanting roof showed any semblance to a house as Harold made his way toward it, still beating the snow with his arms, and thinking it was not quite the fun he had fancied it might be.

He was close to the house at last, and stood for a moment looking at it, while a faint thrill of fear stirred in his veins as he remembered to have heard that burglars and thieves sometimes made it their rendezvous after a night's marauding. What if they were there now, and should rush upon him if he ventured to disturb them?

"I don't believe I will try it," he thought, as he glanced nervously at the door, which was blockaded by a great bank of snow ; and he was about to retrace his steps, when a sound met his ear which made him stand still and listen until it was repeated a second time.

Then, forgeting both burglar and thief, he started forward quickly, and was soon at the door, from which he dug away the snow with a desperate energy, as if working for his life. For the sound was the cry of a little child, frightened and pleading.

"Ma-ma! ma-ma!" it seemed to say; and Harold answered, cheerily :

"I am coming as fast as I can."

Then the crying ceased, and all was still inside, while

Harold worked on until enough snow was cleared away to allow of his opening the door about a foot, and through this narrow opening he forced his way into the cold, damp room, where for a moment he could see nothing distinctly, for the sunlight outside had blinded him, and there was but little light inside, owing to the barred and snow-bound windows.

Gradually, however, as he became accustomed to the place, he saw upon the long table in the corner where Arthur Tracy had moved it months before, what looked like a human form stretched at full length and lying upon its back, with its white, stony face upturned to the rafters above, and no sound or motion to tell that it still lived.

With an exclamation of surprise, Harold sprang forward and laid his hand upon the pale forehead of the woman, but started back quickly with a cry of horror, for by the touch of the ice-cold flesh he knew the woman was dead.

"Frozen to death!" he whispered, with ashen lips; and then, as something stirred under the gray cloak which partly covered the woman, he conquered his terror and went forward again to the table, over which he bent curiously.

Again the cry, which was more like "mah-nee," now than "mamma" met his ear, and, stooping lower, he saw a curly head nestled close to the bosom of the woman, while a little fat white hand was clasping the neck, as if for warmth and protection.

At this sight all Harold's fear vanished, and, bending down so that his lips almost touched the bright, wavy hair, he said:

"Poor little girl!"—he felt instinctively that it was a girl—"poor little girl! come with me away from this dreadful place;" and he tried to lift up her head, but she drew it away from him, and repeated the piteous cry of "Mah-nee, mah-nee!"

At last, however, as Harold continued to talk to her, the cries ceased, and, cautiously lifting her head, she turned toward him a chubby face, and a pair of soft, blue eyes, in which the great tears were standing. Then her lips began to quiver in a grieved kind of way, as if the horror of the previous night had stamped itself upon her tender mind and she were asking for sympathy.

"Mah-nee!" she said again, placing one hand on the cold, dead face, and stretching the other toward Harold, who put out his arm to take her.

But something resisted all his efforts, and a closer inspection showed him a long, old-fashioned carpet-bag, which enveloped her body from her neck to her feet, and into which she had evidently been put to protect her from the cold.

"Not a bad idea either," Harold said, as he comprehended the situation; "and your poor mother gave you the most of her cloak, too, and her shawl," he continued, as he saw how carefully the child had been wrapped, while the mother, if it were her mother, had paid for her unselfishness with her life.

"What is your name, little girl?" he asked.

The child, who had been staring at him while he talked as if he were a lunatic, made no reply until he had her in his arms, when she, too, began to talk in a half-frightened way. Then he looked at her as if she were the lunatic, for never had he heard such speech as hers.

"I do believe you are a Dutchman," he said, as he wrapped both shawl and cloak around her and started for the door, which he kicked against some time in order to make an opening wide enough to allow of his egress with his burden.

When at last they emerged from the cold, dark room into the bright sunshine, the child gave a great cry of delight, and the blue eyes fairly danced with joy as they fell upon the dazzling snow. Then she put both arms around Harold's neck, and, nestling her face close to his, kissed him as fondly as if she had known him all her life, while the boy paid her back kiss after kiss as he proceeded slowly toward home.

The child was heavy, and the bag and shawl made such an unwieldy bundle that his progress was very slow, and he stopped more than once to rest and take breath, and as often as he stopped the blue eyes would look up inquiringly at him with an expression which made his boyish heart beat faster as he thought what pretty eyes they were, and wondered who she was. Once he fell down, and bag and baby rolled in the snow; but only the vigorous kicking of a pair of little legs inside the bag showed that the child disapproved of the proceeding, for she made no sound, and when he picked her up she brushed the snow from his hair, and laughed as if the thing had been done for fun.

He reached the cottage at last, and bursting into the room where his grandmother was sitting with her foot in a chair, exclaimed, as he put down the child, who, as she was still enveloped in the bag, stood with difficulty:

"Oh, grandma, what do you think ? I did see a light in the Tramp House, and there is somebody there—a woman—dead—frozen to death, with nothing over her, for she had given her cloak and shawl to her little girl. I went there. I found her, and brought the baby home in the carpet-bag, and now I must go back to the woman. Oh, it was dreadful to see her white face, and it is so cold there and dark ;" and as if the horror of what he had seen had just impressed itself upon him, the boy turned pale and faint, and, staggering to a chair, burst into tears.

Too much astonished to utter a word, Mrs. Crawford stared at him a moment in a bewildered kind of way, and then, when the child, seeing him cry, began also to cry for "Mah-nee," and struggle in the bag, she forgot her lame foot, on which she had not stepped for a week, and going to the little girl, released her, and taking her upon her lap, began to untie the soft woolen cloak, and to chafe the cold fingers, while she questioned her grandson.

Having recovered himself somewhat, Harold repeated his story, and asked, with a shudder :

"Must I go for her alone ? I can't, I can't. I was not afraid with the baby there, but it is so awful, and I never saw any one dead before."

"Go back alone ! Of course not !" his grandmother replied. "But you must go to the park at once and tell them ; go as fast as you can. She may not be dead."

"Yes, she is," Harold answered, decidedly. "I touched her face, and nothing alive could feel like that."

He was buttoning his overcoat preparatory to a fresh start, but before he went he kissed the little girl, who was sitting on his grandmother's lap, and who, as she saw him leaving her, began to cry for him, and to utter curious sounds unintelligible to them both. But Harold brought her a piece of bread, which she began to devour ravenously, and then he stepped quietly out and was soon breaking through the drifts which lay between the cottage and the park.

CHAPTER XIII.

THE WOMAN.

THEY had slept later than usual at the park house that morning, and Frank and his family were just sitting down to breakfast, when John, with a white, scared face, looked in and said :

"Excuse me, Mr. Tracy,—but something dreadful has happened. There's a woman frozen to death in the Tramp House, with a baby, and Harold Hastings found them ; he is here, sir ; he will tell you himself ;" and he went for the boy, who soon entered the room, followed by every servant in the house.

Harold had came upon John in the stable, and sinking down exhausted upon the hay, had told his story, while the man listened terror-stricken and open-mouthed. Then, seeing how weak and tired Harold seemed, and how he sank back upon the hay when he attempted to rise, he took him in his arms, and carrying him to the kitchen, left him there while he went with the news to his master.

"A woman dead in the Tramp House, and a baby !" Frank exclaimed, and for an instant he felt as if he were dying, for there flashed over him a conviction that the woman had come in the train the previous night, and that it was her cry for help which had been borne to him on the winds, and to which he had paid no heed.

"Are you sick ? Are you going to faint ?" his wife said to him, as she saw how white he grew, as Harold related the particulars of his finding the woman and the child.

"I am not going to faint ; but it makes me sick and shaky to think of a woman freezing to death so near us that if she had cried for help we might perhaps have heard her," Frank replied.

Then, turning to Harold, he continued :

"How did she look ? Was she young ? Was she pretty ? Was she dark or fair ?"

He almost gasped the last word, as if it choked him, and

no one guessed how anxiously he waited for Harold's
answer.

"I don't know; it was so dark in there, and cold, and I
was afraid some of the time, and in a hurry. I only know
that her nose was long and large, for I touched it when I
was trying to get at the little girl, and it was so cold—oh,
oh!"

And Harold shuddered as if he still felt the icy touch of
the dead.

"A long nose and a large one," Frank said, involuntarily, while a sigh of relief escaped him as he remembered
that the nose of the picture in his brother's room was
neither long nor large.

Still Harold might be mistaken, and though he had no
good cause for believing that the woman lying dead in the
Tramp House was Gretchen, there was a horrible feeling in
his heart, while a lump came into his throat and affected
his speech, which was thick and indistinct, as he rose from
his chair at last and said to John:

"We have no time to lose. Hitch the horses to the
long sleigh as quick as you can. We must go to the Tramp
House after the woman, and send to the village for a doctor,
and telegraph to Springfield for the coroner. I suppose
there must be an inquest; and, Dolly, see that a room is
prepared for the body."

"Oh, Frank, must it come here? Why not take it to
the cottage? The child is there." Mrs. Tracy said.

"I tell you that woman must come here," was Frank's
decided reply, as he began to make himself ready for the
ride.

"Don't tell Arthur yet," he said, as he left the house
and took his seat in the sleigh, which was soon plowing its
way through the snow banks in the direction of the Tramp
House.

It was Harold who acted as master of ceremonies, for
John was nervous and hung back from the half opened
door, while Frank was too much unstrung to know just
what he was doing or saying, as he squeezed through the
narrow space and then stood for a moment, snow-blind and
dizzy, in the cheerless room.

Harold was not afraid now. He had been there before,
had seen and touched the white face of the corpse, and he

went fearlessly up to it, followed by Frank, who could
scarcely stand, and who laid his hand for support on Harold's shoulder, and then turned curiously and eagerly
toward the woman.

John had lingered outside, shoveling the snow from the
door, which he succeeded in opening wide, so that the full,
broad sunlight fell upon the face, which was neither young,
nor pretty, nor fair, while the hair was black as night.

Frank noted all these points at a glance, and could
have shouted aloud for joy, so great was the revulsion of
his feelings. It was not Gretchen lying there before him,
and he was not a murderer, as he had accused himself of
being, for this woman did not come by the train; she had
no connection with Tracy Park; she was going somewhere
else—to Collingwood, perhaps—when overcome by the
storm and the cold, she had sought shelter for the night in
this wretched place.

"I suppose the proper thing to do is to leave her here
till the coroner can see her," he said to John; "but no
train can get through from Springfield to-day, I am sure,
and I shall have her taken to the park. Bring me the
blankets from the sleigh."

He was very collected now, for a great load was lifted
from his mind.

"Had she nothing with her? nothing to cover her?" he
asked, as they proceeded to wrap her in the warm blankets,
which, had they sooner come, would have saved her life.

Harold told him again of the carpet-bag, and the cloak,
and the shawl, which had covered the child, and added:
"That's all; there don't seem to be anything else. Oh,
what's this?" and stooping down, he picked up some hard
substance which he had kicked against the table.

It proved to be one of those olive-wood candle sticks, so
convenient in traveling, as when not in use, they can be
made into a small round box or ball, and take but little
room. It contained the remains of a wax candle, which
had burned down into the socket and then gone out. Near
by, upon the floor, was a tiny box of matches, with two or
three charred ones among them.

"The poor woman must have had a light for at least
a portion of the time," Frank said, as he picked up the
box.

"She had, I know she had," Harold cried, excitedly ; "for I saw it and told grandma so. It was like she had opened the door and let out a big blaze, and then everything was dark, as if the door was shut or the wind had blown the candle out."

"What time was that, do you think?" Frank asked.

"It must have been about eleven," Harold replied, "for I remember hearing the clock strike and grandma's saying I must go to bed, it was so late. I was up with her because her foot was so bad, and I warmed the poultices."

Frank groaned aloud, unmindful of the boy looking so curiously at him, for that was the time when he had heard the sound like a human voice in distress. He had thought it a fancy then communicated to him by his brother's nervousness, but now he was certain it must have been the stranger calling through the storm, in the vain hope that somebody would hear and come. Somebody had heard, but no one had come ; and so in the cold and the darkness, with the snow sifting through every crevice and blowing down the wide chimney to the hearth, where it made a drift like a grave, she had battled for her own life and that of the child beside her, saving the latter, but losing her own.

"If I had only believed it was a cry," Frank thought, and as he wrapped the body in the blankets and buffalo robe as tenderly and reverently as if the stiffened limbs had belonged to his mother, he saw as distinctly before him as if painted upon canvas, the angry sky, the half-open door, through which the sleet was driving, the light behind, and the frantic, freezing woman, screaming for help, while only the winds made answer, and the pitiless storm raged on.

This was the picture which Frank was destined to see in his dreams for many and many a night, until the mystery was solved concerning the woman whom they carried to the sleigh, which was driven to the park house, where, within fifteen or twenty minutes, a crowd of anxious, curious people gathered. The messenger sent to town had done his work rapidly and thoroughly, and half the villagers who heard of the tragedy enacted at their very doors, started at once for Tracy Park. The boy had stopped at the station and told his story there, making the baggage-master feel as if he, too, were a murderer, or at least an accessory.

"If I had only gone after that woman," he said, as he told of the stranger who had come on the train and gotten off on the side of the car farthest from the depot—"if I had gone after her and made her take a conveyance to where she was going, this would not have happened ; but it was so all-fired cold, and the wind was yelling so, and she walked off so fast, as if she knew her own business. So I just minded mine, or rather I didn't, for I never even see the box, or trunk, which was pitched out helter-skelter, and which I found this morning, all covered up with snow. It is hers, of course, and I shall send it right over there, as it may tell who the poor critter was."

This trunk, which was little more than a strong wooden box, with two double locks upon it, was still further secured by a bit of rope wound twice around it, and tied in a hard knot. There was nothing upon it to tell whose it was, or whence it came, except the name of a German steamer, on which its owner had probably crossed the ocean, and the significant word "Hold," showing that it had not been used in the state-room. It had been checked at the Grand Central depot in New York for Shannondale, and the check was still attached to the iron handle when it was put down in the kitchen at Tracy Park, where the utmost excitement prevailed, the servants huddling together with scared faces, and talking in whispers of the terrible thing which had happened, while Mrs. Tracy and the housekeeper, scarcely less excited than the servants, gave their attention to the dead.

At the end of the rear hall was a small room, where Frank sometimes received business calls when at home, and there they laid the body, after the physician, who had arrived, declared that life had been extinct for many hours.

Seen in the full daylight, she seemed to be at least thirty-five years of age, and her features, though not un-pleasing, were coarse and large, especially the nose. Her hair was black, her complexion dark, and the hands, which lay folded upon her bosom, showed marks of toil, for they were rough and unshapely. Her woolen dress of grayish blue was short and scant ; her knit stockings were black and thick, and her leather shoes were designed for use rather than ornament. A wide white apron was tied around her waist, and she wore a small black and white plaided shawl pinned about her neck.

And there she lay, helpless and defenseless against the curious eyes bent upon her and the remarks concerning her, as one after another of the villagers came in to look at her and speculate as to who she was, or how she came in the Tramp House.

Among the crowd was Mr. St. Claire, who gave it as his opinion that she was a Frenchwoman of the lower class, and asked if nothing had been found with her except the clothes she wore. Harold told him of the shawl, and cloak, and carpet-bag which he had carried with the child to the cottage.

"Yes, there is something more—her trunk," chimed in the baggage-master, who had just entered the room, trembling and breathless.

"Her trunk! Then she did come in the cars?" Frank said, his hands dropping helplessly at his side, and his lips growing pale, as the man replied:

"Yes; last night, on the quarter-past-six from New York; and, what is curi's, she got out on the side away from the depot. and I never seen her till the cars went on, when she was lookin' at a paper, and the child cryin' at her feet. I spoke to her, but she didn't answer, and snatching up the child, she hurried off, almost on a run. It was storming so I didn't see her trunk till this mornin', when I found it on the platform. I wish I had gone after her and made her take a sleigh. If I had she wouldn't now have been dead, and, I swow, I feel as if I had killed her. I wonder why under the sun she turned into the lots, unless she was going to Collingwood——"

"Or Tracy Park," Frank said, involuntarily.

"Were you expecting any one?" Mr. St. Claire asked; and sinking into a chair, Frank replied:

"No, I was not; but Arthur, who has been worse than usual for a few days, has again a fancy that Gretchen is coming. He says now that she was not in the ship with him, but that he has written her to join him here, and yesterday he took it into his head that she would be here last night, and insisted that the carriage be sent to meet her;

but John had hurt his back, and as I had no faith in her coming, he didn't go. I wish he had ; it might have saved this woman's life, although she is not Gretchen."

Frank had made his confession, except so far as deceiving his brother was concerned, and he felt his mind eased a little, though there was still a lump in his throat, and a feeling of disquiet in his heart, with a wish that the dead woman had never crossed his path, and a conviction that he had not yet seen the worst of it.

Mr. St. Claire looked at him thoughtfully a moment, and then said :

"I should not accuse myself too much. You couldn't know that any one would be there, and this woman certainly is not the Gretchen of whom your brother talks so much. Has he seen her ? Does he know of the accident ?"

"I have not told him yet. He is not feeling well to-day. Charles says he is still in bed," was Frank's reply.

"We may find something in her trunk," Mr. St. Claire continued, "which will give us a clew to her history. Where do you suppose she kept her key ?"

No one volunteered an answer, until Harold suggested that if she had a pocket it was probably there, when half a dozen hands or more at once felt for the pocket, which was found at last, and proved to be one of great capacity, and to contain a heterogeneous mass of contents : A purse, in which were two or three small German coins, an English sovereign, and a five-dollar greenback ; two handkerchiefs, one soiled and coarse, bearing in German text the initials "N. B.," the other small and fine, bearing the initial "J.," also in German text ; a pair of scissors, a thimble, a small needle-case, a child's toy, a worn picture-book, printed in Leipsic, a box of pills, some peanuts, some cloves, a piece of candy, a seed cake, a pocket comb, half a biscuit ; and, at the very bottom, the brass check whose number corresponded with that upon the trunk ; also a ring to which were attached three keys, one belonging to the trunk, another evidently to the carpet-bag, while the third, which was very small and straight, must have been used for fastening some box or dressing-case.

It was Mr. St. Claire who opened the trunk, from which one of the servants had removed the rope, while Frank sat near, watching anxiously as article after article was taken out and examined, but afforded no satisfaction whatever or gave any sign by which the stranger might be traced.

There was a black alpaca dress and a few garments, which must have belonged to the woman. Some of them bore the initials "N. B.," some were without a mark, and all were cheap and plain, like the clothes of a servant. The child's dresses were of a better quality, and one embroidered petticoat bore the name "Jerrine," while the letter "J." was upon them all, except a towel of the finest linen, on one corner of which was the letter "M." worked with colored floss.

"Jerrine!" Mr. St. Claire repeated. "That is a French name, and a pretty one. It is the child's, of course."

To this no one replied, and he continued his examination of the trunk until it was quite empty.

"That is all," he said in a tone of disappointment; and Frank, who had been sitting by and holding some of the things in his lap as they were taken from the trunk, answered, faintly:

"No, here is a book. It was in a handkerchief," and he held up what proved to be a German Bible; but he did not tell of the photograph he had found, and thrust into his pocket when no one was looking at him.

It had slipped from the leaves of the Bible, and at sight of the face, of which he only had a glimpse, every drop of blood seemed to leave his heart and come surging to his brain, making him so giddy and wild that he did not realize what he was doing when he hid away the picture until he could examine it by himself. Once in his pocket he dared not take it out, although he raised his hand two or three times to do so, but was as often deterred by the thought that everybody would think that he had intended to hide it and suspect his motive. So he kept quiet and saw them examine the book, the blank page of which had been torn half off, leaving only the last three letters of what must have been the owner's name, "——ich"—that was all, and might as well not have been there, for any light it shed upon the matter.

Opening the book by chance at 1st Corinthians, 2d chapter, Mr. St. Claire, who could read German much

better than he could speak it, saw pencil-marks around the
9th verse, and read aloud :

"Eye hath not seen nor ear heard, neither have entered
into the heart of man the things which God hath prepared
for them that love him."

On the margin opposite this verse was written in a girl-
ish hand :   .

"Think of me as there when you read this, and do not
be sorry."

A lock of soft, golden hair, which might have been cut
from a baby's head, and a few faded flowers were tied with
a bit of thread, and lying between the leaves. And except
that the book was full of marked passages, chiefly comfort-
ing and consolatory, there was nothing more to indicate the
character of the owner.

"If this Bible were hers, she was a good woman," Mr.
St. Claire said, laying his hand reverently upon the forehead of the dead, while Frank, who saw another meaning
between the lines, shook like one in an ague fit, for he did
not believe that those hands, so pulseless and cold, had ever
traced the words "Think of me as there when you read this
and do not be sorry." She who wrote them might be and
probably was dead, but her grave was far away, and the
fact did not at all change the duty which he owed to her
and him for whom the message was intended.

"What shall I say to Arthur, and how shall I tell him,"
he was wondering to himself, when Mr. St. Claire roused
him by saying :

"You seem greatly unstrung by what has happened. I
never saw you look so ill."

"Yes, I feel as if I had murdered her by not sending John
to the station," Frank stammered, glad to offer this as an
excuse for his manner, which he knew was strange and
unnatural.

"You are too sensitive altogether. John might not
have seen her, she hurried off so fast, and you had no particular reason to think she was coming here," Mr. St. Claire
said, adding : "We'd better leave her now. We can do

nothing more until the coroner comes, which will hardly be to-day. I hear the roads are all blocked and impassable. Let everything remain in the trunk where he can see them."

Mechanically Mrs. Tracy, who was present, put the different articles into the trunk, leaving the Bible on the top, and then followed her husband from the room. She knew there was more affecting him than the fact that a dead woman was in the house, or that he had not sent John to the station. But what it was she could not guess, unless, and she, too, felt faint and giddy for a moment as a new idea entered her head.

"Frank," she said to him when they were alone for a few moments, "Arthur had a fancy that Gretchen was coming last night. You do not think this woman is she?"

"Gretchen? No. Don't be a fool, Dolly. Gretchen is fair and young, and the woman is old and black as the ace of spades. Gretchen! No, indeed!"

Just then Charles came to the room and said that his master was very much excited and wished to know the reason for so much commotion in the house, and why so many people were coming and going down and up the avenue.

"I thought it better that you should tell him," Charles added, and with a sinking heart Frank started for his brother's room.

He had not seen him before that day, and now as he looked at him it seemed to him that he had grown older since the previous night, for there were lines about his mouth, and his face was very thin and pale. But his eyes were unusually bright, and his voice rang out clear as a bell as he said:

"What is it, Frank? What has happened that so many people are coming here, banging doors and talking so loud that I heard them here in my room, but could not distinguish what they said. What's the matter? Any one hurt or dead?"

He put the question direct, and Frank gave a direct reply.

"Yes, a woman was found frozen to death in the Tramp House this morning, and was brought here. She is lying in the office at the end of the back hall."

"A woman frozen to death in the Tramp House!"

Arthur repeated. " Then I did hear a cry. Oh, Frank, who is she? Where did she come from?"

" We do not know who she is, or where she came from!" Frank replied. Mr. St. Claire thinks she is French. There is nothing about her person to identify her, but I would like you to see her, and—and"—

" I see her! Why should I see her, and shock my nerves more than they are already shocked?" Arthur said, with a decided shake of his head.

" But you must see her," Frank continued. " Perhaps you know her. She came last night. She"—

Before he could utter another word Arthur was at his side, and seizing him by the shoulder with the grip of a giant, demanded, fiercely:

" What do you mean by her coming last night? How did she come ? Not by train, for John was there. Frank, there is something you are keeping back. I know it by your face. Tell me the truth. Is it Gretchen dead in this house ?"

" No," Frank answered, huskily. " It is not Gretchen, if that picture is like her, for this woman is very dark and old, and besides that, has Gretchen a child?"

For an instant Arthur stood looking at him, or rather at the space beyond him, as if trying to recall something too distant or too shadowy to assume any tangible form ; then bursting into a laugh, he said :

"Gretchen a child! That is the best joke I have heard. How should Gretchen have a child? She is little more than one herself, or was when I saw her last. No, Gretchen has no child. Why do you ask ?"

"Because " Frank replied, " there was a little girl found in the Tramp House with this woman. She is at the cottage where Harold carried her. He found the woman this morning. Will you see her now ?"

Arthur answered "no," decidedly, and then Frank, who knew that he should never again know peace of mind if his brother did not see her, summoned all his courage, and said :

" Arthur you must. I have not told you all. This woman did come by train from New York."

" Then why did not John see her?" interrupted Arthur.

"He was not there," Frank replied. "Forgive me, Arthur. I did not send him as you thought. It was so cold and stormy, and I had no faith in your presentiments, and so—so"—

"And so you lied to me, and I will never trust you again as long as I live, and if this had been Gretchen, I would kill you, where you stand!" Arthur hissed in a whisper, more terrible to hear than louder tones would have been. "Yes, I will see this woman whose death lies at your door," he continued, with a gesture that Frank should precede him.

Arthur was very calm, and collected, and stern, as he followed to the office where the body lay, covered now from view, but showing terribly distinct through the linen sheet folded over it.

"Remove the covering," he said, in the tone of a master to his slave, and Frank obeyed.

Then bending close to the stiffened form, Arthur examined the face minutely, while Frank looked on alternating between hope and dread, the former of which triumphed as his brother said, quietly:

"Yes, she is French; but I do not know her. I never saw her before. Had she nothing with her to tell who she was?"

His mood had passed, and Frank did not fear him now.

"She had a trunk," he replied. "Here it is, with her clothes, and the child's, and—a Bible."

He said the last slowly, and, taking up the book, opened it as far as possible from the writing on the margin, which might or might not be dangerous.

"It is a German Bible," he continued, and then Arthur took it quickly from him as if it had been a long-lost friend, turning the worn pages rapidly, but failing to discover the marked passage and the message for some one.

The lock of hair and the faded flowers caught his attention, and his breath came hard and pantingly, as for a moment he held the little golden tress in his hand.

"This must be her child's hair. You know I told you there was a little girl found with her. Would you like to see her?" Frank said.

"No, no!" Arthur answered hastily. "Let her stay

5*

where she is, I don't like children, as a rule. You know I
can't abide the noise yours sometimes make."

He was leaving the room with the Bible in his hand,
but Frank could not suffer that, and he said :

"I suppose all these things must stay here till the
coronor sees them ; so I will put the Bible where I found
it."

Arthur gave it up readily enough, and then as he
reached the door, looked back, and said :

"If forty coroners and undertakers come on this business, don't bother me any more. My head buzzes like a
bee-hive. See that everything is done decently for the poor
woman, and don't let the town bury her. Do it yourself,
and send the bill to me. There is room enough in the
Tracy lot ; put her in a corner."

"Yes," Frank answered, standing in the open door and
watching him as he went slowly down the long hall, and
until he heard him going up stairs.

Then locking the door, which shut him in with the
dead, he took the photograph from his pocket and examined
it minutely, feeling no shadow of doubt in his heart that it
was Gretchen—if the picture in the window was like her.
It was the same face, the same sweet mouth and sunny blue
eyes, with curls of reddish-golden hair shading the low
brow. The dress was different and more in accordance
with that of a girl who belonged to the middle class, but
this counted for nothing, and Frank felt himself a thief,
and a liar, and a murderer as he stood looking at the lovely
face and debating what he should do.

Turning it over he saw on the back a word traced in
English letters, in a very uncertain, scrawling hand, as if
it were the writer's first attempt at English. Spelling it
letter by letter he made out "Wiesbaden," and knew it was
some German town. Did Gretchen live there, he wondered,
and how could he find out, and what should he do ? He had
not yet seen the child at the cottage, but from some things
Harold said, he knew she was more like this picture than
like the dead woman, and he felt sure that he ought to
show Arthur the photograph, and tell him his suspicions.

Frank was not a bad man, nor a hard-hearted man, but
he was ambitious and weak. He had enjoyed money, and
ease, and position long enough to make him unwilling to

part with them now, while for his children he was more
ambitious than for himself. To see Tom master of Tracy
Park was the great desire of his life, and this could not be,
if what he feared were proved true.

"I will see the child before I decide what to do," he
thought. "I can never know anything for certain, and I
should be a fool to give up all my children's interests for an
idea which may have no foundation. Arthur does not
know half the time what he is saying, and might not tell
the truth about Gretchen. She may not have been his
wife. On the whole, I do not believe she was. He would
never have left her if she had been, and if so, this child, if
she is Gretchen's, has no right to come between me and
mine.. No, I shall wait a little while and think, though in
the end I mean to do right."

With these specious arguments Frank tried to quiet his
conscience, but he could not help feeling that Satan had
possession of him, and as he hurried through the hall he
said aloud, as if speaking to some one :

"Go away—go away! I shall do right, if I only know
what right is."

He did not see his brother again that day, or go to the
cottage either, but as he was dressing himself next morning
he said to his wife :

"That little girl ought to see her mother before she is
buried. I shall send for her to-day. The coroner will be
here, too. Did I tell you I had a telegram last night ? He
is coming on the early train."

Mrs. Tracy passed the allusion to the coroner in silence,
but of the little girl she said :

"I suppose the child must come to the funeral, but you
surely do not mean to keep her ? We are not bound to do
that because her mother froze to death on our premises."

"Would you let her go to the poor-house ?" Frank
asked, but Dolly did not reply, and as the breakfast-bell just
then rang, no more was said of the little waif until the
sleigh was brought to the door, and Frank announced his
intention of stopping for the child on his way back from
the station, where he was going to meet the coroner.

CHAPTER XIV.

LITTLE JERRY.

IT was nearly noon when Harold left Tracy Park the previous day and started for home, eager and anxious with regard to the child whom he claimed as his own. He had found her. She was his, and he should keep her, he said to himself, and then he wondered how his grandmother had managed with her, and if she had cried for him or her mother, and as he reached the house he stood still a moment to listen. But the sounds which met his ear were peals of laughter, mingled with mild, and, as it would seem, unavailing expostulations from his grandmother.

Opening the door suddenly, he found the child seated at the table in the high chair he used to occupy. Standing before her was a dish of bread and milk, of which she had evidently eaten enough, for she was playing with it, and amusing herself by striking the spoon into the milk, which was splashed over the table, while three or four drops of it were standing on the forehead and nose of the distressed woman, who was vainly trying to take the spoon from the little hand clenching it so firmly.

Mrs. Crawford had had a busy and exciting day with her charge, who, active, and restless, and playful, kept her on the alert and made her forget in part how lame she was. As she could not put her foot to the floor without great pain, and as she must move about, she had adopted the expedient of placing her knee on a chair to the back of which she held, while she hobbled around the room, followed by the child, who, delighted with this novel method of locomotion, put her knee in a low chair, and, holding to Mrs. Crawford's skirts, limped after her, imitating her perfectly, even to the groans she sometimes uttered when a twinge sharper than usual ran up her swollen limb. It was fun for the child, but almost death to the woman, who, when she could endure it no longer, sank into a chair, and tried, by speaking sharply, to make the little girl understand that she must be quiet. But when she scolded, baby scolded back, in a language wholly unintelligible, shaking her curly head, and sometimes stamping her foot by way of emphasizing her words.

When Mrs. Crawford laughed the child laughed, and when once a pang severer than usual wrung the tears from her eyes, baby looked at her compassionately a moment, while her little face puckered itself into wrinkles as if she, too, were going to cry; then, putting up her hand, she wiped the tears from Mrs. Crawford's cheeks, and, climbing into her lap, became as quiet as a kitten. But a touch sufficed to start her up, for she was full of fun and frolic, and her laughing blue eyes, which were of that wide-open kind which see every thing, were brimming over with mischief. Once or twice she called for " Mah-nee," and, going to the window, stood on tip-toe, looking out to see if she were coming. But on the whole she seemed happy and content, exploring every nook and corner of the kitchen, and examining curiously every article of furniture as if it were quite new to her.

Once when Mrs. Crawford was talking earnestly to her, trying to make her understand, she stood for a moment watching and imitating the motion of the lady's lips and the expression of her face; then going up to her, she began to examine her mouth and her teeth, as if she would know what manner of machinery it was which produced sounds so new and strange to her. She was a remarkable child for her age, though Mrs. Crawford was puzzled to know just what that was. She was very small, and, judging from her size, one would have said she was not more than four years old; but the expression of her face was so mature, and she saw things so quickly and understood so readily, that she must have been older. She was certainly very precocious, and Mrs. Crawford felt herself greatly interested in her as she watched her active movements and listened to the musical prattle she could not understand.

She had examined the carpet-bag, in which she found the articles necessary for an ocean voyage, and little else. Most of these were soiled from use, but there was among them a little clean, white apron, and this Mrs. Crawford put upon the child, after having washed her face and hands and brushed her hair, which had a trick of coiling itself into soft, fluffy curls all over her head.

The bread and milk had been given her about twelve o'clock, and the laugh she gave when she saw it showed her appreciation of it quite as much as the eagerness with which she ate it. Her appetite appeased, however, she began to play with it, and throw the milk over the table and into Mrs. Crawford's face, just as Harold came in, full of what he had seen at the park, and anxious to see his baby, as he called her.

Taking her on his lap and kissing her rosy cheeks, he began to narrate to his grandmother all that had been done, and told her that Mr. St. Claire had said that the woman was French.

"And if so," he continued, "baby must be French, too, though she does not look a bit like her mother, who is very dark and not—well, not at all like you or Mrs. St. Claire."

Then he told of the trunk which the baggage-master had taken to the park, and of what it contained.

"The woman's clothes were marked 'N. B.'" he said, "and some of the baby's—such a funny name. Mr. St. Claire said it was French, and pronounced 'Jerreen,' though it is spelled 'Jerrine.'"

"That is the name on the child's things in the bag," Mrs. Crawford said.

"Of course it is baby's, then," Harold replied; "but I shall call her Jerry for short, even if it is a boy's name, and so, my little lady, I christen you Jerry;" and kissing the forehead, the eyes, the nose, and the chin, he marked the shape of the cross upon the face upturned to his, and named his baby "Jerry," and when he called her that she laughed and nodded as if the sound were not new to her. She was a beautiful child, with complexion as pure as wax, and eyes which might have borrowed their color from the blue lakes of Italy, or from the skies of England when they are at their brightest.

"I wish she could talk to me. I suppose she must speak French," he said, as he was trying in vain to make her understand him. "Don't you know a word I say?" he asked her, and her reply was what sounded to him like "We, we."

"That's English," he cried, delighted with her progress, but when he spoke to her again, her answer was "Yah, yah," which seemed to him so nonsensical that after

.

a few attemps to make her say "yes," and to teach her
what it meant, he gave up his lesson for the remainder of
the day and talked to her by signs and gestures which she
seemed to understand.

Whatever he did she did, and he saw her more than
once imitating his grandmother's motions as well as his
own, to the life.

Late in the afternoon Mr. St. Claire came to the cottage, curious to see the child, who, at sight of him,
retreated behind Harold, and then peered shyly up at him,
with a look in her great blue eyes which puzzled him on
the instant, as one is frequently puzzled with a likeness to
something or somebody he tries in vain to recall. In this
instance it was hardly the eyes themselves, but rather the
way they looked at him, and the sweep of the long lashes,
together with a firm shutting together of the lips, which
struck Mr. St. Claire as familiar, and when, with a swift
movement of her little hand, she swept the mass of golden
hair back from her forehead, he would have sworn that he
had seen that trick a thousand times, and yet he could not
place it. That she was the child of the dead woman he
believed, and as the mother was French, so also was she.
He had once passed two years in France, and was master
of the language; so he spoke to her in French, but she
made no reply, until he said to her :

"Where is your mother, little one ?"

Then she answered, promptly, "Dead," but the language was German, not French.

"Ho-ho ! You are a little Dutchman," Mr. St. Claire
said, with some surprise in his voice.

Then, as he noted the purity of her complexion, her
fair hair and blue eyes, he said to himself :

"Her father was a German, and probably they lived in
Germany, but the mother was certainly French."

He could speak German a little, and turning again to
the child, he managed to say :

"What is your name ?"

"Der-ree," was the reply, and Harold exclaimed :

"That's it; she means Jerry; that's short for the name
on her clothes, which you said was Jerreen. I have christened her Jerry, and she is my little girl, ain't you,
Jerry ?"

"Yah—oui—'ess," was the answer, and there was a gleam of triumph in the blue eyes which flashed up to Harold for approbation.

She had not, of course, understood a word he said, except, indeed, her name, but the tone of his voice was interrogatory and seemed to expect an affirmative answer, which she gave in three languages, emphasizing ' 'ess' with a nod of her head, as if greatly pleased with herself.

"Bravo!" Harold shouted. "She can say yes. I taught her, and I shall have her talking English in a few days as well as I do, sha'n't I, Jerry?"

"Yah—'ess," was the reply.

Then Mr. St. Claire tried to question her further with regard to herself and her home, but no satisfactory result was reached beyond the fact that her mother was dead, that her name was Jerry, or Derree, as she called it, and that she had been on a ship with Mah-nee, who did *so*—and she imitated perfectly the motions and contortions of one who was deathly sea-sick.

"I suppose she means her mother by Mah-nee," Mr. St. Claire said; and when he asked her if it were not so, she answered "yah," and " 'ess," as she did to everything, adopting finally the latter word altogether because she saw it pleased Harold.

No matter what was the question put to her, her reply was " 'ess," which she repeated quickly, in a lisping tone, with a prolonged sound on the "s."

When at last Mr. St. Claire took his leave, it was with a strange feeling of interest for the child, whose antecedents must always be shrouded in mystery, and whose future he could not predict.

It seemed impossible for Mrs. Crawford to keep her, poor as she was, and as he had no idea that the Tracys would take her, there was no alternative but the poor-house, unless he took her himself and brought her up with his own little five-year-old Nina. He would wait until after the funeral and see, he decided, as he went back to his home at Brier Hill, where his children, Dick and Nina, were eager to hear all he had to tell them of the little girl whose mother had been frozen to death.

The next morning the sleigh from Tracy Park stopped before the cottage door, and Frank, who had been to meet the coroner, alighted from it. He was pale and haggard as he entered the room where Jerry was playing on the floor with Harold's Maltese kitten. As he came in she looked up at him, and, lifting her hand, swept the hair back from her forehead just as she had done the day before when Mr. St. Claire was there. The motion had struck the latter as something familiar, though he could not define it; but Frank did, and his knees shook so he could hardly stand as he talked with Mrs. Crawford and told her he had come for the child, who ought to be where her mother was until after the funeral.

"Then she will come back again. You will not keep her. She is mine, ain't you, Jerry?" Harold exclaimed, eagerly; while Jerry, who, with a child's instinct, scented danger from Harold's manner, and associated that danger with the strange man looking so curiously at her, sprang to her feet, which she stamped vigorously, while she cried, "'Ess, 'ess, 'ess," with her blue eyes anything but soft and sunny, as they usually were.

In this mood she was not much like Gretchen in the picture, but she was like some one else whom Frank had seen in excited moods, and he grew faint and sick as he watched her, and saw the varying expression of her face and eyes. The way she shook her head at him and flourished her hands was a way he had seen many times, and he felt as if his heart would leap from his throat as he tried to speak to her. A turn of the head, a gesture of the hands, a curve of the eyelashes, a tone in the voice, seemed slight actions on which to base a certainty; but Frank did feel certain, and his brain reeled for an instant as his thoughts leaped forward years and years until he was an old man, and he wondered if he could bear it and make no sign.

Then, just as he had decided that he could not, the tempter suggested to him a plan which seemed so feasible and fair that the future, with a secret to guard, did not look so formidable, and to himself, he said:

"It is not likely I can ever be positive; and so long as there is a doubt, however small, it would be preposterous to give up what otherwise must come to my children, if not to me; but I will not wrong her more than I can help."

"Come, little girl," he said, in his kindest tones, as he

advanced toward her, while Harold went for her cloak and hood.

Jerry knew then that she was expected to go with the stranger, and without Harold, and resisted with all her might. Standing behind him as if safe there, and clinging to his coat, she sobbed piteously, intermingling her sobs with "'Ess, 'ess, 'ess," the only English word she knew, and which she seemed to think would avail in every emergency.

And it did help her now, for Harold asked that he might go, too; and when Jerry saw him with his coat and hat, and understood that he was to be her escort, she allowed herself to be made ready, and was soon in the sleigh, and on her way to Tracy Park.

CHAPTER XV.

JERRY AT THE PARK.

" A ND so this is the little girl. We'll take her right to the kitchen, where she can get warm," Mrs. Tracy said as she met her husband in the hall, with Harold, and the mite of a creature wrapped in the foreign looking cloak and hood.

"No Dolly!" and Frank spoke very decidedly. "She is going to the nursery, with the other children, and when they have their dinner she will have hers with them."

"'Ess, 'ess, 'ess!" Jerry said, as if she comprehended that there was a difference of opinion between the man and woman, and that she was on the affirmative side.

"Take her to the nursery! Oh, Frank! she may have something about her which the children will catch," Mrs. Tracy said, blocking the way as she spoke.

But Jerry, who through the half-open door had caught sight of the pretty sitting-room, with its warm carpet and curtains, and cheerful fire, shook her head defiantly at the lady, and brushing past her, went boldly into the room whose brightness had attracted her.

Marching up to the fire, she stood upon the rug and looked about her with evident satisfaction; then glancing at Harold, she nodded complacently, and said, "'Ess, 'ess," while she held her little cold hands to the fire.

"Acts as if she belonged here, doesn't she?" Frank said to his wife, who did not reply, so intent was she upon watching the strange child, who deliberately took off her cloak and hood, and tossing them upon the floor, drew a chair to the fire, and climbing into it, sat down as composedly as if she were mistress there instead of an intruder.

"Take her to the nursery now. I must see to that coroner," Frank continued, "and Harold must go too, or there will be the Old Harry to pay."

"'Ess, 'ess," came very decidedly from the child, who went willingly with Harold, and was soon ushered into the large upper room, which was used as both nursery and school-room, for Mrs. Tracy would not allow her two sons, Tom and Jack, to come in contact with the boys at school : so she kept a governess, who, glad of a home and the liberal compensation, sat all day in the nursery and bore patiently with Tom's freaks and Jack's dullness, to say nothing of the trouble it was to have Maude toddling about and interfering with everything.

"Hallo !" Tom cried, as his mother came in, followed by Harold and Jerry. "Hallo, what's up ?" And throwing aside the slate on which he had been trying to master the difficulties of a sum in long division, he went toward them, and said : "Has the coroner come, and can't I go and see the inquest ? You said maybe I could if I behaved, and I do, don't I Miss Howard ?"

Just then he caught sight of Jerry, and stopping short, exclaimed :

"By Jingo ! ain't she pretty ? I mean to kiss her."

And he made a movement toward the little girl who looked up so shyly at him. But his mother caught his arm and held him back, as she said, sharply :

"Don't touch her, there is no telling what you may catch. I wanted her to go to the kitchen, the proper place for her, but your father insisted that she should be brought here. I hope, Miss Howard, you will see that she does not go near the children."

"Yes, madam," Miss Howard replied ; "but I am sure there can be no danger. She looks as clean and sweet as a rose."

Miss Howard was fond of children, and she held out her hand to the little girl, who seemed to have a most wonderful faculty for discriminating between friends and enemies, and who went to her readily; and leaning against her arm, looked curiously at the group of children—Tom, and Jack, and Maude—the latter of whom wished to go to her, but was restrained by the nurse. The moment the door closed upon Mrs. Tracy, Tom walked up to the child, and said: "I wonder who you are anyway, and how you will like the poor-house?"

"Who said she was going to the poor-house?" Harold exclaimed, indignantly.

"Mother said so," Tom replied. "I heard her talking to the cook. Where would she go if she didn't go to the poor-house? Who would take care of her?"

"I shall take care of her," Harold answered. She will live with grandmother and me. I found her, and she is mine."

"'Ess, 'ess," came from Jerry, as she swung one little foot back and forth and looked confidingly at her champion.

"*You* take care of her!" Tom sneered, with that supercilious air he always assumed toward those he considered his inferiors. "Why, you and your grandmother can't take care of yourselves, or you couldn't if it wasn't for Uncle Arthur. You wouldn't have any house to live in if he hadn't give it to you."

Harold's arms were unfolded now and the doubled fists were in his pockets, clenching themselves tighter and tighter as he advanced to Tom, who began to back toward the nurse for safety.

"It's a lie, Tom Tracy," Harold said. "Mr. Arthur does not take care of us. We do it ourselves, and have for ever so long. He did give us the house, but it ain't for you to twit me of that. Whose house is this, I'd like to know? It isn't yours, nor your father's, and there isn't a thing in it yours. It is all Mr. Arthur's."

"Well, we are to be his heirs—Jack, and Maude, and me. Mother says so," Tom stammered out, while Jerry, who had been looking intently, first at one boy, and then at the other, called out:

"Nein, nein," and struck her hand toward Tom.

" What does she mean by her 'Nine, nine,'" he asked
of Miss Howard, who replied that she thought it was the
German for ' No, no,' and that the child probably did not
approve of him.

Tom knew she did not, and though she was only a
baby, he felt chagrined and irritable. Had he dared, he
would have struck Harold, but he was afraid of Miss Howard, and remembering it must be time for the inquest, he
slipped from the room, whispering to Harold as he passed
him:

" I'll thrash you yet."

" Let me know when you are ready," was Harold's
taunting reply, as the door closed upon the discomfited
Tom.

. . . . .

The inquest was a mere matter of form, for there was
no doubt in any one's mind that the woman had been
frozen to death, and she had no friends to complain that
due attention had not been paid her. So after a few questions put to Mr. Tracy, and more to Harold, who was summoned from the nursery to tell what he knew, a verdict
was rendered of " Frozen to death."

Then came the question where should she be buried,
and at whose expense. Quite a number of people had
assembled, and the little room was full. Conspicuous
among them was Peterkin, who, having been elected to an
office, which necessitated a care for the expenditures of the
village, was swelling with importance, and dying for a
chance to be heard.

When Harold came into the room Jerry was with him.
She had refused to let him leave her, and he led her by
the hand into the midst of the men, who grew as silent and
respectful the moment she appeared as if she had been a
woman instead of a little child, who could speak no word
of their language, or understand what was said to her. It
was her mother lying there dead, and they made way for
her as, catching sight of the white face, she uttered a cry
of joy, and running up to the body, patted the cold cheeks,
while she kept calling " Mah-nee, Mah-nee," and saying
words unintelligible to all, but full of pathos and love, and
child-like coaxing for the inanimate form to rouse itself,
and speak to her again.

"Poor little thing," was said by more than one, and hands went up to eyes unused to tears, for the sight was a touching one—that lovely child bending over the dead face, and imprinting kisses upon it.

Harold took her away from the body, and lifting her into a chair, kept by her as with her arm around his neck she stood watching, and sometimes imitating the gestures of the men around her.

It was Peterkin who spoke first; standing back so straight that his immense stomach, with the heavy gold watch-chain hanging across it, seemed to fill the room, he gave his opinion before any one else had a chance to express theirs.

It was the first time he had been in the house since the morning after the party, when Arthur had turned him from the door. He had vowed vengeance against the Tracys and kept this vow by spending two thousand dollars in order to defeat Frank as member of Congress and to get himself elected as one of the village trustees, and now he had come, partly out of curiosity to see the woman and partly to oppose her being buried by the town, if such a thing were suggested.

"Let them Traceys bury their own dead," he said to his wife before he left home, and he said it again in substance now, as with a tremendous "ahem!" he commenced his speech, standing close to little Jerry, who watched him with a face which varied in its expression with every variation in his voice and manner, and reached its climax when he said : "I don't b'lieve in saddlin' the town with a debt we don't orto pay. Let the Tracys bury their own dead, I say ! "

"'Ess, 'ess," Jerry chimed in, with an emphatic nod of her head with each "'ess," and a flourish of her hand more threatening than approving toward the speaker, who glanced at her and went on :

"Don't you see, gentlemen of the jury, who this cub looks like. I do ! and so can you with half an eye. She looks like Arthur Tracy ! "

Just then Jerry swept back her golden hair, and, opening her eyes very wide flashed them around the room until they rested by accident upon Frank, who, pale and faint, and terrified, was leaning against the door-way trying to

seem only amused at the tirade which was concluded as
follows :

"Yes, Arthur Tracy ! Not her skin, perhaps, nor
hair, nor her eyes, leastwise not the color, but something I
can't describe ; and this woman, her mother, you say is a
furriner ; that may be, but he's been in furren parts too.
I don't say nothin', nor insincrate nothin', but I won't
consent to have the town pay what belongs to the Tracys.
Let 'm run their own canoes and funerals, too, I say ; and
as for this young one with the yaller hair—though where
she got that the lord only knows ; 'tain't her's," pointing
to the corpse ; "nor 'tain't his'n," pointing in the direction of Arthur's rooms ; "as for her, I'm opposed to
sendin' to the poor-house another pauper."

"She is not a pauper, and she is not going to the poor-
house either," Harold exclaimed, while Jerry came in with
her "*nien, nien,*" which made the bystanders laugh, as
Peterkin went on, addressing himself to Harold :

"You are her champion, hey, and intend to take care of
her. Mighty fine, I'm sure, but hadn't you better fetch
back May Jane's pin that you took at the party."

"It is false," Harold cried. "I never saw the pin,
never !" and the hot tears sprang to his eyes at this
unmanly assault.

By this time Peterkin, who felt that everybody was
against him, was swelling with rage, and seizing Harold by
the collar, roared out :

"Do you tell me I lie ! You rascal ! I'll teach you
what belongs to manners !" and he would have struck
the boy but for Jerry, who had been watching him as a
cat watches a mouse, and who, raising her war-cry of
"*nien, nien,*" sprang at him like a little tiger, and by the
fierceness of her gestures and the volubility of her German
jargon actually compelled him to retreat step by step until
she had him outside the door, which she barred with her
diminutive person. No one could help laughing at the discomfited giant and the mite of a child facing him so bravely,
while she scolded at the top of her voice.

Peterkin saw that he was beaten and left the house,
while Frank, who had recovered his composure during the
ludicrous scene, said to those present :

"I would not explain to that brute, but it is not my

intention to trouble the town. I have no more idea who this woman is than you have, and I'll swear that Peterkin's vile insinuations with regard to her are false. My brother says he never saw her, and he speaks the truth. She has every appearance of a foreigner, and her child "— here Frank's tongue felt a little thick, but he cleared his throat and went on—" her child speaks a foreign language—German, they tell me. This poor woman died on my — or rather my brother's premises. I have consulted with him, and he thinks as I do, that she should be cared for at our expense. He says, further, that as there is room in the Tracy lot, she is to be buried there. I shall attend to it at once, and the funeral will take place to-morrow morning at ten o'clock from this house. What disposition will be made of the child I have not yet decided, but she will *not* go to the poor-house."

"Oh, Mr. Tracy," Harold burst out, "she is mine. She is to live with grandma and me. You will not take her from me—say you will not?"

"*Vill not*," Jerry reiterated, imitating as well as she could Harold's last words.

For a moment Mr. Tracy looked fixedly at the boy, pleading for a burden which would necessitate toil, and self-denial, and patience of no ordinary kind, and never had he despised himself more than he did when, believing what he did believe, he said at last:

"I will talk with your grandmother, and see what arrangements we can make. I rather think you have the best right to her. But she must stay here until after the funeral, when she can go with you, if you like."

To this Harold did not object, and, as Jerry seemed very happy and content, he left her, while she was exploring the long drawing-room, and examining the different articles of furniture. As she did not seem disposed to touch anything she was allowed to go where she liked, although Mrs. Frank remonstrated against her roaming all over the house as if she belonged there, and suggested again that she be sent to the kitchen. But Frank said "no," and Jerry was left to herself, except as the nurse-girl and Charles looked after her a little.

And so it came about that toward evening she found herself in the upper hall, and after making the tour of the rooms whose doors were open, she came to one whose door was shut—nor could she turn the knob, although she tried with all her might. Doubling her tiny fist, she knocked upon the door, and then, as no one came, kicked against it with her foot, but still with no result.

Inside the room Arthur sat in his dressing-gown, very nervous, and a little inclined to be irritable and captious. He knew there had been an inquest, and that many people had come and gone that day, for he had seen them from his window, and had seen, too, the sleigh, with Frank, and the coroner, and Harold, and a blue hood, drive into the yard. But to the blue hood he never gave a thought, as he was only intent upon the dead woman, whose presence in the house made him so nervous and restless.

" I shall be glad when she is buried. I have been so cold and shaky ever since they brought her here," he said to Charles, as, with a shiver, he drew his chair nearer to the fire, and leaning back wearily in it, fixed his eyes upon Gretchen's picture smiling at him from the window. " Dear little Gretchen," he said in a whisper, "you seem so near to me now that I can almost hear your feet at the door, and your voice asking to come in. Hush !" and he started suddenly, as Jerry's kicks made themselves heard even in the room where he sat. Hush ! Who is that banging at the door ? Surely not Maude ! They would not let her come up here. Go and see, and send her away."

He had forgotten that he was listening for Gretchen, and when Charles, who had opened the door cautiously and descried the intruder, said to him, " It is that woman's child. Shall I let her in ? She is a pretty little thing," he replied, " Let her in ? No ; why should you ? and why is she allowed to prowl about the house ? Tell her to go away."

So Jerry was sent away with a troubled, disappointed look in her little face, and as the chill night came on, and the dark shadows crept into the room, and Gretchen's picture gradually faded from sight in the gathering gloom, until it seemed only a confused mixture of lead and glass, Arthur felt colder, and drearier, and more wretched than he had ever felt before. It was a genuine case of home-sickness, if one can be homesick in his own house, sur-

6

rounded by every possible comfort and luxury. He was tired, and sick, and disappointed, and his head was aching terribly, while thoughts of the past were crowding his brain where the light of reason seemed struggling to rein-state itself. He was thinking of Gretchen, and longing for her so intensely, that once he groaned aloud and whispered to himself :

"Poor Gretchen ! I am so sorry for it all. I can see it clearer now, how I left her and did not write, and I don't know where she is, or if she will ever come ; and yet I feel as if she had come, or tidings of her. Perhaps my letter reached her. Perhaps she is on her way. God grant it, and forgive me, for all I have made her suffer."

It was very still in the room where Arthur sat, for Charles had gone out, and only the occasional crackling of the coal in the grate and the ticking of the clock broke the silence which reigned around him ; and at last, soothed into quiet, he fell asleep and dreamed that on his door he heard again the thud of baby feet, while Gretchen's voice was calling to him to let the baby in.

CHAPTER XVI.

THE FUNERAL, AND AFTER.

LONG before ten o'clock, the hour appointed for the funeral, the people began to gather at the Park House, and the avenue seemed full of them. The news that an unknown woman had been frozen to death in the Tramp House, had spread far and wide, awakening in many a curiosity to see the stranger, and discover, if possible, a likeness to some one they might have known.

It was strange how many reminiscences were brought to mind by this circumstance, of girls who had disappeared years before and were supposed to be dead—or worse. And this woman might be one of them ; and they came in crowds to see her, and to see, as well, the inside of the handsome house, of which they had heard so much, especially since Mr. Arthur's return. But in this they were disappointed, for all the front rooms were locked against them, and only the large dining-room, the break-fast-room, the servants' hall, and the little back office were thrown open to the public. In the first of these the corpse was lying in a handsome coffin, for Frank would have no other ; and when the undertaker suggested to him that a cheaper one would answer just as well, he said :

"I mean to bury her decently. Give me this one, and send the bill to me, not to Arthur."

It was *his* funeral, and, judging from his face, he was burying all his friends, instead of a poor, unknown woman, whose large, coarse features and plain woolen dress looked out of place in that handsome black coffin, with its silver-plated trimmings. Frank had suggested that she should have a white merino shroud, but his wife had overruled him. It was *not* her funeral, and she had no interest in it, except that it should be over as soon as possible, and the house cleansed from the atmosphere of death. So when her husband asked if the child ought not to have a mourning-dress, she scoffed at him for the sug-gestion, saying she did not like to see children in black, and even if she died herself, she should not wish hers to wear it.

"I cannot imagine," she continued, "why you have taken so unaccountable a fancy to and interest in these people, especially the child. One would think she be-longed to royalty, the fuss you make over her. What are we to do with her to-night ? Where is she to sleep ?"

"In the nursery," was his reply, and he saw his wishes carried out and ordered in a crib, which used to be Jack's, and bade the nurse see that she was comfortable.

So Jerry was put to bed in the nursery and slept very quietly until about ten o'clock when she awoke and cried piteously for both "Mah-nee" and "Ha-roll." Frank who was sitting alone in the library, heard the cry, and knew it was not Maude's. Had it been he would not have minded it, for he knew that she would be cared for without his interference. But something in the crying of this little foreign girl stirred him strangely, and after listening to it a few moments he arose and going softly to the door of the nursery stood listening until a sharp hush from the nurse girl decided him to enter, and going to the crib he bent over the sobbing child and tried to comfort her. She could not understand him, but the tone of his voice was kind, and when he put his hand on her hot head she took it in hers and held it fast, as if she recognized in him a friend. And Frank, as he felt the clasp of the soft, warm fingers, and saw the confiding look in the wide-open eyes, grew faint and cold, and asked himself again, as he had many times that day, *if he could do it.*

Jerry was asleep at last, but she sobbed occasionally in her sleep, and there were great tears on her eye-lashes, while her fingers clutched Frank's hand tightly as if fearing to let it go. But he managed to disengage it and stealing cautiously from the room went back to the library where he sat late into the night, facing the future and wondering if he could meet it.

He had Jerry at the table next morning and saw that she was helped to everything she wanted without any regard to its suitability for her, and when his wife said rather curtly that she never supposed he was so fond of children, he answered her :

"I am only doing as I would wish some one to do to Maude if she were like this poor little girl."

When, at last, the hour for the funeral arrived he placed her upon a high chair close to the coffin, where she sat through the short service, conspicuous in her gray cloak and blue hood, with her hair falling on her neck and piled in wavy masses on her forehead, while her bright eyes scanned the crowd eagerly as if asking why they were there and why they were all looking so intently at her. More than one kind-hearted woman went up and kissed her, and when, at the close of the services, Mr. Tracy held her in his arms for a last look at her mother, their tears fell fast for the child, so unconscious of the meaning of what was passing around her.

"Is'nt she beautiful ! Such lovely hair, and eyes, and dazzling complexion !" was said by more than one ; and then they speculated as to her future.

"Would she go to the poor-house ? Would Frank Tracy keep her, or was it true as they had heard, that Mr. Arthur Tracy was to adopt her as his own ? And where was Mr. Arthur ? He might at least, have shown enough respect for the dead woman to come into the room," they said.

But Arthur was sick in bed, suffering alternately from chills and a raging fever, which set his brain on fire and made him wilder than usual. He had not slept well during the night. Indeed, he said, he had not slept at all. But this was a common assertion of his, and one to which Charles paid little heed.

"A man can't snore and not sleep," was the unanswerable argument with which he refuted the sleepless nights of his master.

On this occasion, however, he had heard no snoring, and Arthur's face, seen by the morning light, was a sufficient proof of the wakeful hours he had passed. He, too, had heard the distant crying, and felt instinctively that it was not Maude's. Starting up in bed to listen, he said :

"What's that ? Is that child here yet ?"

" Yes, sir : she is to stay till after the funeral," was Charles's reply, and Arthur continued :

" Bring me some cotton for my ears. I never can stand that noise. It is a peculiar cry."

The cotton was brought. A window in the hall which had a habit of rattling with every breath of wind was made fast with a bit of shingle whittled out for that purpose, and then Arthur became tolerably quiet until morning, when he began to talk to himself in the German language, which Charles could not understand. But he caught the name Gretchen, and knew she was the subject of the sick man's thoughts. Suddenly turning to his attendant, to whom he always spoke in English, Arthur said :

" The funeral is to-day ?"

" Yes, sir, at ten o'clock."

" Well, lock every door leading up this way, and shut out the gossiping blockheads who will come by hundreds, and, if we would let them, swarm into my room as thick as the frogs were in the houses of the Egyptians. Shut the doors, Charles, and keep them out."

So the doors were shut and bolted, and then Arthur lay listening with that intensity which so quickens one's hearing, that the faintest sounds are distinct at great distances. He heard the trampling footsteps as the people came crowding in, and the tread of horses' feet as sleigh after sleigh drove up the avenue, and once, with a shudder, he said :

"That is the hearse. I am sure of it."

Then all was still, and listen as he might he could not distinguish the faintest sound until the services were over, and the people began to leave the house.

"There," he said, with a sigh of relief; "it will soon be over. Bring me my clothes, Charles. I am going to get up and see the last of this poor woman. God help her, whoever she was."

He was beginning to feel a great pity for the woman whose coffin they were putting in the hearse, which moved off a few rods, and then stopped until the open sleigh came up, the sleigh in which Frank Tracy sat, muffled in his heavy overcoat, for the day, though bright and sunny, was cold, and a chill wind was blowing. Dolly had taken refuge in a headache which had prevented her from being present at the funeral, and kept her from going to the grave, as her husband had wished her to do. So only Harold and Jerry occupied the sleigh with Frank, and these sat opposite him, with their backs to the horses, Jerry in her gray cloak and blue hood showing conspicuously as she came into full view of the window where Arthur stood looking at the procession, with a feeling at his heart as if in some way he were interested in the sad funeral, where there was no mourner, no one who had ever seen or known the deceased, except the little helpless girl, looking around her in perfect unconcern, save as she rather liked the stir and all that was going on.

They had tied a thin vail over her head to shield her from the cold, and thus her face was not visible to Arthur. But he saw the blue hood and the golden hair on the old gray cloak, and the sight of it moved him mightily, making him hold fast to the window-casing for support, while he stood watching it. Just as far as he could see it his eye followed that hood, and when it disappeared from view, he turned from the window, deathly sick, and tottering back to his bedroom, vomited from sheer nervous excitement.

"Thank Heaven it is over and the rabble gone," he said, when he became easier. "Go now and open all the doors and windows to let out the smell they are sure to have left. Ugh! I get a whiff of it now. Burn some of that aromatic paper, but open the hall windows first."

Charles did as he was ordered, and the wind was soon sweeping through the wide hall, while Arthur's rooms were filled with an odor like the sweet incense burned in the old cathedrals.

"I am very giddy and faint," Arthur said, when Charles came back to him after his ventilating operation. "I have looked at the bright snow too long, and there are a thousand rings of fire dancing before my eyes, and in every ring I see a blue hood and vail, with waves of hair like Gretchen's. Wheel me out there, Charles, where I can see her."

Charles obeyed, and moved the light bed-lounge into the library, where his master could feast his eyes upon the sweet face which knew no change, but which always, night and day, smiled upon him the same. The picture had a soothing effect upon Arthur, and he gazed at it now until it began to fade away and lose itself in the blue hood and vail he had seen in the sleigh far down the avenue; and when, a few minutes later, Charles came in to look at him, he found him fast asleep.

Meantime the funeral train had reached the cemetery, where the snow was piled in great drifts, and where, in a corner of the Tracy lot, they buried the stranger, with no tear to hallow her grave, and no pang of regret save that she had ever come there, with the mystery and the doubt which must always cling to her memory. Frank Tracy's face was very pale and stern as he held little Jerry in his arms during the committal of the body to the grave, and then bade her take one last look at the box which held her mother. But Jerry, who was growing cold and tired, began to cry, and so Frank took her back to the sleigh, which was driven to the cottage in the lane. Here she felt at home and was soon supremely happy devouring the ginger cookie which Mrs. Crawford had given her, and in trying to pronounce English words under Harold's teaching.

While the children were thus employed, Mr. Tracy was divulging to Mrs. Crawford the object of his visit. He could hardly explain, he said, why he was so deeply interested in the child, except it were that her mother had died on his premises.

"I can't see her go to the poor-house," he continued, with a trembling in his voice which made Mrs. Crawford wonder a little, as she had never credited him with much sympathy for anything outside his own family. "I can't see her go to the poor-house, and I can't well take her into my family, as we have three children of our own. But I have made up my mind to care for her, and I have come to ask if, for a compensation, you will keep her here?"

"Yes, grandma—say yes!" Harold cried; while Jerry, with her mouth full of cookie, repeated, "'ay 'ess."

"You see the children plead for me," Mr. Tracy said. "While she is young—say, until she is ten years old—I will pay you three dollars a week, and after that more, if necessary. I know you will be kind to her, and that she will be happy here and well brought up. Is it a bargain?"

Mrs. Crawford had never seen him so interested in anything, and felt somewhat surprised and puzzled, but she expressed her willingness to take the child and do what she could for her.

And so Jerry's future was settled, and counting out twelve dollars, Frank handed them to Mrs. Crawford saying:

"I will pay you for four weeks in advance, as you may need the money, and—and—perhaps—" His face grew very red as he stammered on, "perhaps it may be as well not to tell how much I pay you. People—or rather—well, Mrs. Tracy might think it strange, and not understand why I feel such an interest in the child. I don't understand it myself."

But he did understand, and all the way from the cottage to the park, he kept trying to reassure himself by saying:

"I know nothing for sure. Arthur is expecting Gretchen, whoever she may be. He says he has written to her, and he has one of his presentiments that she was coming on the night when this woman arrived, who is no more like the Gretchen he raves about than I am. This woman has a child. He says Gretchen has none, and that he never saw this woman. And yet I find among the things a photograph exactly like the picture in the window, while the child certainly bears a resemblance to my brother, though no one else, perhaps, would see it. Now, sir," and he appeared to be addressing some unseen person, from whom he shrank, for he drew himself as far as was possible to his side of the sleigh and shivered as he went on : "Now, sir, is that sufficient proof to warrant me in turning everything topsy-turvy, and making Arthur crazier than he is?"

"Certainly not," he heard in reply, either from within or without, he hardly knew which, and he went on :

"I shall try to find out who the woman was, of course, and where she came from; but how am I to do it ? Arthur will not tell me a word about Gretchen, or what she is to him. Still, I mean to do right by the child. Arthur cannot live many years. His nerves will wear him out, if nothing else, and when he dies, his money will naturally come to me."

"Naturally," his spectral companion replied, and he continued :

"Well, what I intend doing is this. I shall make my will, in which Jerry will share with my children, and I shall further draw up a written request that in case I die before my brother, any money which may fall to my children from him shall be shared equally with her. I shall, out of my own private funds, provide for her support and education until she comes of age, or marries. Can anything more be required of me ?"

"Nothing," was the consoling reply ; and, as the sleigh just then drew up before his door, Frank alighted from it, and said to himself as he ran up the steps :

"I believe I have been riding with the devil, and have made a league with him !"

He found the house thoroughly aired and cleansed from all signs of the recent funeral ; and when, at one o'clock, he sat down to lunch in the handsome dining room, and sipped his favorite claret, and ate his foreign preserves, and thought how much comfort and luxury money could buy, he was sure he had done well for himself and his children after him. But Frank Tracy never knew real peace of mind again, until years after, when, with his sin confessed, he was freed from the shadow which followed him day and night, walking by him when he walked, sitting by him when he sat, and watching by him when he slept, until life seemed at times unbearable.

He made his will as he had said he would, but he went to Springfield to have it drawn up, for he knew that Col-

vin, or any lawyer whom he might employ in Shannondale, would wonder at it. He also wrote out what he
called his dying request to his children, in case he should
die before his brother. In this he stated emphatically his
wish that Jerry should have her share of whatever might
come to them from the Tracy estate, the same as if she
were his own child.

"I have a good and sufficient reason for this," he
wrote in conclusion, "and I enjoin it upon you to carry
out my wishes as readily as you would were I to speak to
you from my grave."

This done, Frank felt better, and the shadow at his
side was not quite as real as it had been. He put his will
and his dying request in a private drawer with Gretchen's
photograph and testament. He had kept this last back
when the stranger's trunk was sent to the cottage, thinking that if it were missed and inquired for, he could easily
produce it as having been mislaid. At the suggestion of
Mr. St. Claire he went to New York, to the office of the
German line of steamers, and made inquiries with regard
to the passengers who had come on a certain ship at such
a time. But nothing could be learned of any woman with
a child, and after inserting in several of the New York
papers a description of the woman, with a request for any
information concerning her which could be given, he
returned home, with a feeling that he had done all that
could be required of him.

He was very kind and even tender to his brother, who
for several weeks suffered from low nervous depression,
which kept him altogether in his room, to which he refused
to admit any one except his attendant and Frank. He
had ceased for the time being to talk of Gretchen, and
never inquired for the child. Once Frank spoke of her to
him and told him where she was, and that she was learning to speak English very rapidly, and growing prettier
every day. But Arthur did not seem at all interested and
only said ·

"How can Mrs. Crawford afford to keep her?"

Others than Arthur asked that question, and among
them Dolly, who, with a woman's quick wit, sharpened by
something she accidentally saw, divined the truth, which
she wrung at last from her husband. There was a fierce

quarrel—almost their first,—a sick headache which lasted three days, and a month or more of coldness between the married pair, and then, finding she could accomplish nothing, for Frank was as firm as a rock, Dolly gave up the contest, and tried by economizing in various ways, to save the money which she felt was taken from her children by the little girl, who had become so dear to Mrs. Crawford, that she would not have parted with her had nothing been paid for her keeping.

CHAPTER XVII.

"MR. CRAZYMAN, DO YOU WANT SOME CHERRIES?"

MORE than two years had passed away since the terrible March night when the strange woman was frozen to death in the Tramp House, and her history was still shrouded in mystery. Not a word had been heard concerning her, and her story was gradually being forgotten by the people of Shannondale. Her grave, however, was tolerably well kept, and every Saturday afternoon, in summer-time, a few flowers were put upon it by Harold. Not so much for the sake of the dead as for the beautiful child who always accompanied him, laughing, and frolicking, and sometimes dancing around the grave where he told her her mother was buried.

As there had been no date on which to fix Jerry's birth, they had called the first day of March her birthday, so that when more than two years later we introduce her to our readers on a hot July morning, she was said to be six years and four months old. In some respects, however, she seemed older, for there was about her a precocity only found in children who have always associated with people much older than themselves, or into whose lives strange experiences had come. In stature she was very short, though round and plump as a partridge. "Dutchy," Mrs. Tracy called her, for Mrs. Tracy did not like her, and took no pains to conceal her dislike, though it was based upon nothing except the money which she knew was paid regularly to Mrs. Crawford for the child's maintenance.

There could be no reason, she said to her husband, why he should support the child of a tramp, and the woman had been little better, judging from appearances, unless, indeed —and then she told what old Peterkin had said more than once, to the effect that Jerry Crawford, as she was called, was growing to be the image of the Tracys, especially Arthur.

"And if so," she added, "you'd better let Arthur take care of her, and save your money for your own children."

To this Frank never replied. He knew better than old Peterkin that Jerry was like his brother, and that it was not so much in the features as in the expression and certain movements of the head and hands, and tones of the voice when she was in earnest. She could speak English very well now, and sometimes, when Frank, who was a frequent visitor at the cottage, sat watching her at her play, and listening to her as she talked to herself, as was her constant habit, he could have shut his eyes and sworn it was his brother's voice calling to him from the hay-loft or apple tree where they had played together when boys.

Jerry's favorite amusement was to make believe that either herself, or a figure she had made out of a shawl, was a sick woman, lying on a settee which she converted into a bed. Sometimes she was the nurse and took care of the sick woman, to whom she always spoke in German, bending fondly over her, and occasionally holding up before her a doll which Mrs. St. Claire had given her, and which she played was the woman's baby. Then she would be the sick woman herself, and tying on the broad frilled cap which had been found in the trunk, would slip under the covering, and, laying her head upon the pillow, go through with all the actions of some one very sick, occasionally hugging and kissing the doll.

Sometimes she enacted the pantomime of dying. Folding her hands together and closing her eyes, her lips moved, as if in prayer, for a moment, then stretching out her feet she lay perfectly motionless, with a set expression on the little face which looked so comical under the broad frilled cap. Then, as if it had occurred to her that action was necessary from some one, she exchanged places with the lay figure, and tying the cap upon its head, tucked it carefully in the bed, by which she knelt, and covering her face with her hands, imitated perfectly the sobs and moans of a middle-aged person, mingled occasionally with the clearer, softer notes of a child's crying.

The first time Frank witnessed this piece of acting Jerry had been at the cottage a year, and he had come to pay his weekly due. Both Mrs. Crawford and Harold were gone, but knowing they would soon return, as it was not their habit to leave Jerry long alone, he sat down to wait, while she went back to the corner in the kitchen, which she used as her play-house.

"Somebody is sick and I am taking care of her," she said to Mr. Tracy, who watched her through the pantomime of the death scene with a feeling, when it was over, that he had seen Gretchen die.

There was not a shadow of doubt in his mind that the sick woman was Gretchen, the nurse the stranger found in the Tramp House, and the doll baby the little girl upon whose memory that scene had been indelibly stamped, and who, with her wonderful powers of imitation, could rehearse it in every particular. Calling her to him after her play was over he took her in his lap, and kissed the little grave face where the shadow of the scene she had been enacting had left its impress.

"Jerry," he said, "that lady who just died in the bed with the cap on was your mamma, was it not?"

"'Ess," was Jerry's reply, for she still adhered to her first pronunciation of the word.

"And the other was the nurse?"

"'Ess," Jerry said again; "Mah-nee."

This was puzzling, for he had always supposed that by "mah-nee" the child meant "mam-ma;" but he went on:

"Try to understand me, Jerry; try to think away back before you came in the ship."

"'Ess, I vill," she said, with a very wise look on her face, while Mr. Tracy continued:

"Had you a papa? Was he there with you?"

"*Nein*," was the prompt reply, and Mr. Tracy continued:

"Where did your mamma live? Was it in Wiesbaden?"

He knew he did not pronounce the word right, and was surprised at the sudden lighting up of the child's eyes as she tried to repeat the name. "Oo-oo-ee," she began, with a tremendous effort, but the W mastered her, and she gave it up with a shake of her head.

"I not say dat oo-oo-ee," she said, and he put the question in another form:

"Where did your mamma die?"

"Tamp House; foze to deff," was the ready answer, and a natural one, too, for she had been taught by Harold that such was the case, and had often gone with him to the house, which was now shunned alike by tramps and boys.

No one picnicked there now, for the place was said to be haunted, and the superstitious ones told each other that on stormy nights, when the wild winds were abroad, lights had been seen in the Tramp House, where a pale-faced woman, with her long, black hair streaming down her back, stood in the door-way, shrieking for help, while the cry of a child mingled with her call. But Harold shared none of these fancies. He was not afraid of the building, and often went there with Jerry, and sitting with her on the table, told her again and again how he had found her mother that wintry morning, and how funny she herself had looked in the old carpet-bag, and so it is not strange that when Mr. Tracy asked her where her mother died, she should answer, "In the Tramp House," although she had acted a pantomime whose reality must have taken place under very different circumstances.

"Of course she died in the Tramp House, and I have nothing with which to reproach myself. I am altogether too morbid on the subject," Frank said, and he had decided that he was a pretty good sort of fellow, after all, when at last Mrs. Crawford came in, and he paid her for Jerry's board.

In some respects he was doing his duty by the child, who, as time went on learned to love him better than any one else except Harold and Mrs. Crawford, whom she called grandma. She always ran to meet him when he came and sometimes when he went away accompanied him down the lane, holding his hand and asking him about Tracy Park and Maude and the *crazy man*.

This was Harold's designation of Mr. Arthur, and perhaps of all the things at Tracy Park, Jerry was most desirous to see him and his rooms. Harold, who, on one of the rare occasions when Arthur was out to dine, had been sent to the house on an errand, had gone with Jack into these rooms, which he described minutely to his grandmother and Jerry, dwelling longest upon the beautiful picture in the window. "Gretchen, he calls it," he said; and then Jerry, who was listening intently, gave a sudden upward and side-wise turn to her head, just as she had done when Mr. Tracy spoke to her of Wiesbaden.

"Detchen," she repeated, with a little hesitancy. "Vat the name was? Say again."

He said it again, and over the child's face there came a puzzled expression, as if she were trying to recall something which baffled all her efforts, and that evening Mrs. Crawford heard her saying to herself, "Detchen, Detchen, who am she?"

Jerry had seen Maude Tracy many times, and had admired her greatly, with her pretty white dresses and costly embroideries; and once, at church, when Maude passed near where she was standing, she stood back as far as possible and held her plain gingham dress aside, as if neither it nor herself had any right to come in contact with so superior a being. Of Maude's home she knew nothing, except that it was a place to be admired and gazed at breathlessly at a respectful distance. But she was going there at last with Harold, who had permission to gather cherries for his grandmother from some of the many trees which grew upon the place.

It was a hot morning in July, and the air seemed thunderous and heavy when she set off on what to her was as important an expedition as is a trip to Europe to an older person. She wanted to wear her pink gingham dress, the one kept sacred for Sunday, and had even hoped that she might be allowed to display her best straw hat with the blue ribbons and cluster of apple blossoms. She had no doubt that she should go into the house and see the crazy man, and Mrs. Tracy, who she heard wore silk stockings every day, and she wished to be suitably attired for the occasion.

But Mrs. Crawford dispelled her air-castles by telling her that she was only to go into the side yard where the cherry trees were, and that she must be very quiet, so as not to disturb Mr. Arthur, whose windows looked that way. To wear her pink dress was impossible, as she would get it stained with the juice of the cherries, while the best hat was not for a moment to be thought of.

So Jerry submitted to the dark calico frock and high-necked, long-sleeved apron which Mrs. Crawford thought safe and proper for her to wear on a cherry expedition. A clean, white sun-bonnet with a wide cape covered her head when she started from the cottage, with her tin pail on her arm; but no sooner was she in the path which led to the park than the obnoxious bonnet was removed and was swinging on her arm, while she was admiring the shadow which her long bright curls made in the sunshine as she shook her head from side to side.

To tell the truth, our little Jerry was rather vain. Passionately fond of pictures and flowers, and quick to detect everything beautiful both in art and nature, she knew that the little face she sometimes saw in Mrs. Craw-ford's old-fashioned mirror was pretty, and after the day when Dick St. Claire told her that her hair was "awful handsome," ' she had felt a pride in it, and in herself, which all Mrs. Crawford's asseverations that "Handsome is that handsome does" could not destroy. Maude Tracy's hair was black and straight, and here she felt she had the advantage over her.

"I do hope we shall see her," she said to Harold, as she danced along. "Do you think we shall ?"

Harold thought it doubtful, and, even if they did, it was not likely she would speak to them, he said.

"Why not ?" Jerry asked, and he replied :

"Oh, I suppose they feel big because they are rich and we are poor."

"But why ain't I rich, too ? Why don't I live at the park like Maude, and wear low-necked aprons instead of this old high one ?" Jerry asked; but Harold could not tell, and only said :

"Would you rather live at the park than with me ?"

"No," Jerry answered, promptly, stopping short and digging her heel into the soft loam of the path. "I would not stay anywhere without you ; and when I live at the

park you will live there too, and have codfish and tatoe
every day."

This was Harold's favorite dish, and, as it was not his
grandmother's, his taste was not gratified in that respect
as often as he would have liked ; hence Jerry's promise of
the luxury.

Just then, at a sudden turn in the path, they came
upon Jack and Maude Tracy playing on a bench under a
tree, while the nurse was at a distance either reading or
asleep. Harold would have passed them at once, as he
knew his grandmother was in a hurry for the cherries, but
Jerry had no such intention.

Stopping in front of Maude, she inspected her carefully,
from her white dress and bright plaid sash, to the string of
amber beads around her neck ; while, side by side with
this picture, she saw herself in her dark calico frock and
high-necked apron, with her sun-bonnet and tin pail on
her arm. Jerry did not like the contrast, and a lump
began to swell in her throat. Then, as a happy thought
struck her, she said, with something like exultation in her
tone :

"My hair curls and yours don't."

"No," Maude answered, slowly—"no, it don't curl,
but it's black, and yours is yaller."

This was a set-back to Jerry, who hated everything
yellow, and who had never dreamed of applying that color
to her hair. She only knew that Dick St. Claire had
called it pretty, but in this new light thrown upon it all
her pride vanished, for she recognized like a flash that it
might be " yaller," and stood there silent and vanquished,
until Maude, who in turn had been regarding her atten-
tively, said to her :

"Ain't you Jerry Crawford ?"

That broke the ice of reserve, and the two little girls
were soon talking together familiarly, and Jerry was asking Maude if she wore beads and her best clothes every
day.

"Pooh ! These ain't my best clothes. I have one gown
all brawdery and lace," was Maude's reply, while Jack,
who was standing near, chimed in :

"My father's got lots of money, and so has Uncle

Arthur, and when he dies we are going to have it ; Tom says so."

Slowly the shadows gathered on Jerry's brow as she said, sadly :

"I wish I had an Uncle Arthur, and could wear beads and a sash every day." Then, as she looked at Harold, her face brightened immediately and she exclaimed, "But I have Harold and a grandma, and you hain't," and running up to Harold, she threw her arms around his neck and kissed him lovingly, as if to make amends for the momentary repining.

"We must go now," Harold said, and taking her hand he led her away toward the house, which impressed her with so much awe that as she drew near to it, she held her breath and walked on tiptoe, as if afraid that any sound from her would be sacrilege in that aristocratic atmosphere.

"Oh, isn't it grand, Harold ? Isn't it grand ?" she kept repeating, with her mouth full of cherries, after they had reached the trees on which the ripe, red fruit hung so thickly. "Do you s'pose we shall see the crazyman ?" she asked, and Harold replied :

"I guess not, unless he comes to the window. Those are his rooms, and that window which looks so ugly outside, is the one with the picture in it," and he pointed to the south wing, most of the windows of which were open, while against one a long ladder was standing.

It had been left there by a workman who had been up to fix the hinge of a blind, and who had gone to the village in quest of something he needed. Jerry saw the ladder and its close proximity to the open window, and she thought to herself,

"I mean to fill my pail with cherries, and go up that ladder and take them to him. I wonder if he will bite me ?"

Suiting the action to the word she stopped eating, and began to pick from the lower limbs as rapidly as possible until her pail was full.

"Pour them into the basket," Harold called to her from the top of the tree, but Jerry did not heed him. She had seen the tall figure of a man pass before the window, and a pale, thin face had for a moment looked out, apparently to discover whence the talking came.

"I'm going to take the crazyman some cherries," she cried, and before Harold could protest, she was half way up the ladder, which she climbed with the agility of a little cat.

"Jerry, Jerry! What are you doing?" Harold exclaimed, "Come back this minute. He doesn't like children; he tried to throw me over the banister once; he will knock you off the ladder; oh, Jerry!" and Harold's voice was almost a sob as he watched the girl going up round after round until the top was reached, and she stood with her flushed, eager face, just on a level with the window, so that by standing on tiptoe, she could look into the room.

It was Arthur's bedroom, and there was no one in it, but she heard the sound of footsteps in the adjoining apartment, and raising herself as far as possible, and holding up her pail, she called out in a clear, shrill voice:

"Mr. Crazyman, Mr. Crazyman, don't you want some cherries?"

CHAPTER XVIII.

ARTHUR AND JERRY.

ARTHUR had passed a restless night. Thoughts of Gretchen had troubled him and two or three times he had started up to listen, thinking that he heard her calling to him from a distance. He had dreamed also of the blue hood seen that day of the funeral, and of the child who had come knocking at his door whom he had refused to admit. He had never seen her since, and had never mentioned her of his own accord.

Even Mrs. Crawford seemed to have passed completely from his mind. He never went to the cottage, or near it. He never went anywhere, in fact, but lived the life of a recluse, growing thinner, and paler, and more reticent every day, talking now but seldom of Gretchen, though he never arose in the morning or retired at night without

kissing her picture and whispering to it some words of
tenderness in German.

He had measured the length of his three rooms and
dressing-room, and found it to be nearly one hundred
feet, so that by passing back and forth twenty-five times
he would walk almost a mile.

Regularly each morning, when it was not too cold or
stormy, he would throw open his windows and take his
daily exercise, which was but a poor substitute for what
he might have had in the fresh air outside, but was nevertheless much better than nothing.

On this particular morning, when Harold and Jerry
were at the park, he was taking his walk as usual, though
very slowly, for he felt weak and sick, and, so inexpressibly lonely and desolate that it seemed to him he would
gladly lie down and die.

"If I knew Gretchen was dead, nothing would seem so
desirable to me as the grave," he was saying to himself,
when the sound of voices outside attracted his attention,
and going to the window, he saw the children, Harold in
the top of the tree, and Jerry at the foot, with her white
sun-bonnet shading her face.

Recognizing Harold, he guessed who the little girl was,
and a strange feeling of interest stirred in his heart for her,
as he said :

" Poor little waif ! I wonder where she came from, or
what will become of her ?"

Then, resuming his walk, he forgot all about the little
waif, until startled by a voice which rang, clear and bell-
like, through the rooms :

" Mr. Crazyman ! Mr. Crazyman ! don't you want
some cherries ?"

It was not so much the words as something in the tone,
the foreign accent, the ring like a voice he never could forget, and which the previous night had called to him in his
dreams. And now it was calling again from the adjoining
room, which no one could enter without his knowledge.

Mentally weak as he was, and apt to be superstitious,
his limbs shook, and his heart beat faster than its wont, as
he went toward his sleeping-apartment, from which the
voice came louder and more peremptory :

"Mr Crazyman! where are you? I've brought you some cherries."

He had reached the door by this time, and saw the pail on the broad window-ledge where Jerry had put it, and to which she was clinging, with her white sun-bonnet just in view.

"Oh, Gretchen! how did you get here?" he said, bounding across the floor, with no thought of Jerry in his mind, no thought of any one but Gretchen, whom he was constantly expecting to come, though not exactly in this way.

"I climbed the ladder to fetch you some cherries, and I'm standing on the toppest stick," Jerry said, craning her neck until her bonnet fell back, disclosing to view her beautiful face flushed with excitement, and her bright wavy hair, which, moist with perspiration, clung in masses of round curls to her head and forehead.

"Great Heaven!" Arthur exclaimed, as he stood staring at the wide-open blue eyes confronting him so steadily. "Who are you, and where did you come from?"

"I'm Jerry, and I comed from the carpet-bag in the Tramp House. Take me in, won't you?" Jerry said ; and, mechanically leaning from the window, Arthur took her in, while Harold from below looked on, horror-stricken with fear as to what the result might be if Jerry were left alone with a madman who did not like children.

"He may kill her; I must tell the folks," he said; and, going round to the side door, he entered, without knocking, and asked for Mrs. Tracy.

But she was not at home, and so he told the servants of Jerry's danger, and begged them to go to her rescue.

"Pshaw! he won't hurt her. Charles will come pretty soon, and I'll send him up. Don't look so scared; he is harmless," the cook said to Harold, who, in a wild state of nervous fear, went back to the cherry trees, where he could listen and hear the first scream which should proclaim Jerry's danger.

But none came, and could he have looked into the room where Jerry stood, he would have been amazed.

As Arthur lifted Jerry through the window, and put her down upon the floor, he said to her:

"Take off that bonnet and let me look at you."

She obeyed, and stood before him with an eager, questioning expression in her blue eyes, which looked at him
so fearlessly. Arthur knew perfectly well who she was,
but something about her so dazed and bewildered him that
for a moment he could not speak, but regarded her with
the hungry, wistful look of one longing for something just
within his reach, but still unattainable.

" Do you like me?" Jerry asked, at last.

" Like you ?" he replied. " Yes. Why did you not
come to me sooner?"

And, stooping, he kissed the cherry-stained mouth as
he had never kissed a child before.

Sitting down upon the lounge, he took her in his lap
and said to her again:

" Who are you, and where did you come from ? I
know your name is Jerry, which is a strange one for a
girl, and I know you live with Mrs. Crawford, but before
that night where did you live? Where did you come
from?"

" Out of the carpet-bag in the Tramp House. I told
you that once," Jerry said. " Harold found me. I am his
little girl. He is out in the cherry tree, and said I must
not come up, because you were crazy and would hurt me.
You won't hurt me, will you ? And be you crazy ?"

" Hurt you ? No," he answered, as he parted the rings
of hair from her brow. " I don't know whether I am crazy
or not. They say so, and perhaps I am, when my head is
full of bumble-bees."

" Oh-h !" Jerry gasped, drawing back from him. " Can
they get out ? And will they sting ?"

Arthur burst into a merry laugh, the first he had
known since he came back to Shannondale. Jerry was
doing him good. There was something very soothing in
the touch of the little warm hands he held in his, and something puzzling and fascinating, too, in the face of the
child. He did not think of a likeness to any one ; he only
knew that he felt drawn toward her in a most unaccountable manner, and found himself wondering greatly who she
was.

" Harold told me there were pictures and marble folks
up here with nothing on, and everything, and that's why I

comed—that and to bring you some cherries. I like pictures. Can I see them ?" Jerry said.

"Yes, you shall see them," Arthur replied ; and he led her into the room where Gretchen's picture looked at them from the window.

"Oh, my !" Jerry exclaimed, with bated breath. "Ain't she lovely ! Is she God's sister ?" and folding her hands together, she stood before the picture as reverently as a devout Catholic stands before a Madonna.

It was some time since Jerry had spoken a word of German, but as she stood before Gretchen's picture old memories seemed to revive, and with them the German word for *pretty*, which she involuntarily spoke aloud.

Low as was the utterance, it caught Arthur's ear, and grasping her shoulder, he said :

"What was that ! What did you say, and where did you learn it ?"

His manner frightened her ; perhaps the bumble-bees were coming out, and she drew back from him, forgetting entirely what she had said.

"It was a German word," he continued, "and the accent is German, too. Can you speak it ?"

Unconsciously, as he talked, he dropped into that language, while Jerry listened, with a strained look on her face, as if trying to recall something which came and went, but went more than it came, if that could be.

"I talked that once," she said, "when I lived with mamma ; but she is dead. Harold found her, and I put flowers on her grave."

Half the time she was speaking in German, or trying to, and Arthur listened in amazement, while his interest in her deepened every moment, as he took her through the rooms and showed her "the marble people with nothing on them," and the beautiful pictures which adorned his walls.

"How would you like to come and be my little girl ?" he asked her at last, when, remembering Harold and the cherries, she told him she must go, and started toward the window, as if she would make her egress as she had come in.

"Can Harold come, too ? I can't leave Harold," she said. Then, as she caught sight of him still standing at a distance, gazing curiously up at the window through which she had disappeared, she called out : "Yes, Harold, I'm coming. I've seen him and everything, and he did not hurt me. Good-by!" and she turned toward Arthur with a little nod.

Then, before he could stop her, she sprang out upon the ladder, and went down faster than she had come up, leaving the pail of cherries, and leaving, too, in Arthur's breast a tumult of emotions which he could not define.

That night, when Frank, who had heard of Jerry's visit to his brother, went up to see him, he found him more cheerful and natural than he had seen him in weeks. As Frank expected, his first words were of the little girl who had come to him through the window and left him the cherries, of which he said he had eaten so many that he feared they might make him sick. What did Frank know of the child? What had he learned of her history? Of course he had made inquiries everywhere?

It was just in the twilight, before the gas was lighted, and so Arthur did not see how his brother's face flushed at first, and then grew white as he recapitulated what the reader already knows, dwelling at length upon the inquiries he had made in New York, all of which had been fruitless. There was the name Jerrine on the child's clothing, he said, and the initials "N. B." on that of her mother, who was evidently French, although she must have come from Germany.

"Yes," Arthur replied, "the child is a German, and interests me greatly. Her face has haunted me all the afternoon. Was there nothing in that trunk or the carpet-bag which would be a clew?"

"Nothing," Frank replied. "There were articles of clothing, all very plain, and a picture book printed at Leipsic. I can get that for you if you like, though it tells nothing, unless it be that the mother lived in Leipsic."

Frank talked very rapidly, and laid so much stress on Leipsic, that Arthur got an idea that Jerry had actually come from there, just as his brother meant he should, and he began to speak of the town and recall all he knew of it.

"I was never there but once," he said "for although I spent a great deal of time in Germany, it was mostly in Heidelberg and Wiesbaden. Oh, that is lovely —Wies-

baden—and nights now, when I cannot sleep, I fancy
that I am there again, in the lovely park, and hear the
music of the band, and see the crowds of people strolling
through the grounds, and I am there with them, though
apart from the rest, just where a narrow path turns off
from a bridge, and a seat is half hidden from view behind
the thick shubberies. There I sit again with Gretchen,
and feel her hand in mine, and her dear head on my arm.
Oh, Gretchen—"

There was a sob now in his voice, and he seemed to be
talking to himself rather than to his brother, who said to
him,

"Gretchen lived in Wiesbaden then ?"

"Yes; but for Heaven's sake pronounce it with a V,
and not a W, and in three syllables instead of four," Arthur
answered, pettishly, his ear offended as it always was with
a discordant sound or mispronunciation.

"Veesbaden then," Frank repeated, understanding now
why Jerry had stumbled over the name when he once spoke
it to her.

Clearly she had come from Wiesbaden, where Gretchen
had lived, and where he believed she had died, though he
did not tell Arthur so ; he merely said :

"Gretchen was your sweetheart, I suppose ?"

But Arthur did not reply ; he never replied to direct
questions as to who Gretchen was; but after a moment's
silence he said :

"You speak of her as something past. Do you believe
she is dead ?"

"Yes, I do," was Frank's decided answer. "You have
never told me who she was, though I have my own opinion
on the subject, and I know you loved her very much, and if
she loved you as much—"

"She did—she did ; she loved me more—far more than
I deserved," was Arthur's vehement interruption.

"Well then," Frank continued, "If she did, and were
living, she would have come to you, or answered your letters, or sent you some message."

Frank's voice trembled here, and he seemed to see again
the cold, still face of the dead woman, whose lips, could
they have spoken, might have unlocked the mystery and
brought a message from Gretchen.

7

"True, true," Arthur replied. "She would have come or written. How long is it since I came home?"

"Four years next October," Frank said.

"Four years;" Arthur went on, "is it so long as that? and it was then years since I had seen her. Every thing was blotted out from my mind from the time I entered that accursed *Maison de Sante* until I found myself in Paris. I am afraid she is dead."

Just then Charles came in with lights, and the chocolate his master always took before retiring, and so Frank said good-night, and went out upon the broad piazza, hoping the night air would cool his heated brow, or that the laughter and prattle of Jack and Maude, who were frolicing on the gravel walk, would drown the voice which said to him:

"Frank Tracy, you are the biggest rascal living, but you have gone too far now to go back. People would never respect you again. And then there is Maude. You cannot disgrace her."

No, he could not disgrace his darling Maude, who, as if guessing that he was thinking of her, came up the steps to his side, and seating herself upon his lap, pushed the hair from his forehead and kissed him lovingly.

"My beautiful Maude," he thought, for he knew she would be beautiful, with her black hair, and starry eyes, and brilliant complexion, and he loved her with all the strength of his nature. To see her grow into womanhood, admired and sought after by every one, was the desire of his heart, and as he believed that money was necessary to the perfect fulfilment of his desire, for her sake he would carry his secret to the grave.

"Are you sick, papa?" Maude asked, looking into his face, on which the moon shone brightly,

"No, pet," he answered her; "only tired. I am thinking of little Jerry Crawford. She was here this afternoon."

"Yes, I saw her in the park with Harold. Isn't he handsome, papa? and such a nice boy! so different from Tom," Maude said, and then she went on: "Jerry is pretty, too; prettier than I am; her hair curls and mine doesn't, but her dress is so ugly—that old high apron and calico gown. What makes her so poor and me so rich ?"

Mr. Tracy groaned, as he replied :

"You are not rich, my child."

"Oh, yes I am," Maude said. "I heard mamma tell Mrs. Brinsmade so. She said Uncle Arthur was worth millions and when he died we should have it all, because he could not make a will if he wanted to, and he had no children of his own."

Maude had heard so much from her mother and others of their prospective wealth, that she understood the situation far better than she ought, and was already counting on the thousands waiting for her when her uncle died. And yet Maude Tracy had in her nature qualities which were to ripen into a noble womanhood. Truthful and generous, her instincts of right and wrong were very keen, and young as she was, she had no respect for anything like deception or trickery This her father knew, and his bitterest pang of remorse came from the thought, "What would Maude say if she knew ?" And it was more for her sake he was sinning than for his own or that of any other. She was so pretty, or would be, when grown to young ladyhood, and the adornments which money could bring would so well become her.

"Maude," he said at last, "how would you like to change places with Jerry ? That is, let her come here and live, while we go away and be poor ; not quite as she is, but like many people."

"And not wear a sash, and beads, and buttoned boots every day ?" Maude interrupted him quickly. "I should not like it at all. Why, Jerry dresses herself, and wipes the dishes, and wears those big aprons all the time. No, I don't want to be poor ;" and as if something in her father's mind had communicated itself to her, she raised her head from his shoulder and looked beseechingly at him.

"Nor shall you be poor if I can help it," he said ; "but you must be very kind to Jerry, and never let her feel that you are richer than she. Do you understand ?"

"I think I do," Maude answered, adding as she kissed him fondly : "And now I s'pose I must go, for there is Hetty come for me ; so, good-night, you dearest, best papa in the world."

He knew she believed in him fully ; and he could not undeceive her. He would bear the burden he said to himself. There should be no more repining or looking back. Maude must never know ; and so Jerry's chance was lost.

The next morning Arthur awoke with a racking headache. He was accustomed to it, it is true ; but this one was particularly severe.

"It's the cherries ; no wonder ; a quart of those sour things would turn upside down any stomach," Charles said, as he glanced at the empty tin pail which was adorning an inlaid table, and then suggested a dose of ipecac as a means of dislodging the offending cherries.

But Arthur declined the medicine. His stomach was well enough, he said. It was his head which ached, and nothing would help that but the cool little hands he had held in his the previous day. Charles must go for Jerry, for he wanted her, and, as when Arthur wanted a thing he wanted it immediately, Charles was soon on his way to the cottage in the lane, where he found the little girl under a tall lilac bush, busy with the mud pies she was making, and talking to herself, partly in English and partly in broken German, which she had resumed since her visit to the park.

"Seemed like something I had dreamed, when he talked like that, and I could almost do it myself," she said to Harold when describing the particulars of her interview with Mr. Tracy, and her tongue fell naturally into the language of her babyhood.

On hearing Charles' errand, her delight was unbounded.

"'Ess. You'll let me go," she cried, as she stood before Mrs. Crawford, with the mud-spots on her hands and face ; "and you'll let me wear my best gown now, and my white apron with the shoulder-straps, and my morocco shoes, because this is visiting."

As Mrs. Crawford could see no objection to the plan, Jerry was soon dressed, and on her way to the Park, tripping along airily, with an air of dignity and importance very amusing.

Mrs. Tracy, who seldom troubled herself with her brother-in-law's affairs, knew nothing of his having sent for Jerry, and was surprised when she saw her coming up the walk with Charles, whose manner indicated that he knew perfectly what he was about. She had heard of Jerry's visit on the previous day, and had wondered what Arthur could find in that child to interest him, when he would never allow Maude in his room. She did not like Jerry, because of the three dollars a week, which she felt was so much taken from herself, and why they should be burdened with the support of the child, just because her mother happened to be found dead upon their premises, she could not understand. Only that morning she had spoken to her husband on the subject, and asked him how long he proposed to support her.

"Just as long as I have a dollar of my own, and she needs it," was his reply, as he left the room, slamming the door behind him, and leaving her to think him almost as crazy as his brother.

Thus it was not in a very quiet frame of mind that she went out upon the piazza, and, taking one of the large willow chairs standing there, began to rock back and forth and wonder what had so changed her husband, making him silent and absent-minded, and even irritable at times, as he had been that morning. Was there insanity in his veins as well as in his brother's, and would her children inherit it—her darling Maude, of whom she was so proud, and who, she hoped, would some day be the richest heiress in the county and marry Dick St. Claire, if, indeed, she did not look higher?

It was at this point in her soliloquy that she saw Jerry coming up the walk, her face glowing with excitement and her manner one of freedom and assurance.

Ascending the steps, Jerry nodded and smiled at the lady, whose expression was not very inviting, and who, to the child's remark, "I've comed again," answered, icily:

"I see you have. Seems to me you come pretty often."

Turning to Charles, Mrs. Tracy continued:

"Why is she here again so soon? What does she want?"

Quick to interpret the meaning of the tones of a voice, and hearing disapprobation in Mrs. Tracy's, Jerry's face was shadowed at once, and she looked up entreatingly at Charles, who said:

"Mr. Tracy sent me for her. She was with him yesterday, and he will have her again to-day."

" Then Jerry's face brightened, and she chimed in:

" I'm visiting. I'm invited, and I'm going to stay to eat."

Mrs. Tracy dared not interfere with Arthur, even if he took Jerry to live there altogether, and, with a bend of her head, she signified to Charles that the conference was ended.

"Come, Jerry," Charles said ; but Jerry held back a moment, and asked:

" Where's Maude ?"

If Mrs. Tracy heard, she did not reply, and Jerry followed on after Charles through the hall and up the broad staircase to the darkened room where Arthur lay, suffering intense pain in his head, and moaning occasionally. But he heard the patter of the little feet, for he was listening for it, and when Jerry entered his room he raised himself upon his elbow, and reaching the other hand toward her, said :

"So you have come again, little Jerry ; or, perhaps I should call you little *Cherry*, considering how you first came to me. Would you like that name ?"

" 'Ess," was Jerry's reply, in the quick, half-lisping way which made the monosyllable so attractive.

" Well, then, Cherry," Arthur continued, "take off that bonnet, and open the blind behind me. Then bring that stool and sit where I can look at you while you rub my head with your hands. It aches enough to split, and I believe the bumble-bees are swarming ; but they can't get out, and if they could, they are the white-faced kind, which never sting."

Jerry knew all about white-faced bumble-bees, for Harold had caught them for her, and with this fear removed, she did as Arthur bade her, and was soon seated at his side, rubbing his forehead, where the blue veins were standing out full and round, and smoothing his hair caressingly with her fingers, which seemed to have in them a healing power, for the pain and heat grew less under their touch, and, after awhile, Arthur fell into a quiet sleep.

When he awoke, after half an hour or so, it was with a delicious sense of rest and freedom from pain. Jerry had dropped the shades to shut out the sunlight, and was walking on tiptoe round the room, arranging the furniture and talking to herself in whispers, as she usually did when playing alone.

"Jerry," Arthur said to her, and she was at his side in a moment, "you are an enchantress. The ache is all gone from my head, charmed away by your hands. Now, come and sit by me again, and tell me all you know of yourself before Harold found you. Where did you live? What was your mother's name? Try and recall all you can."

Jerry, however, could tell him very little besides the Tramp House, and the carpet-bag, and Harold letting her fall in the snow. Of the cold and the suffering she could recall nothing, or of the journey from New York in the cars. She did remember something about the ship, and her mother's seasickness, but where she lived before she went to the ship, she could not tell. It was a big town, she thought, and there was music there, and a garden, and somebody sick. That was all. Everything else was gone entirely, except now and then when vague glimpses of something in the past bewildered and perplexed her. Her pantomime of the dying woman and the child had not been repeated for more than a year, for now her acting always took the form of the tragedy in the Tramp House, with herself in the carpet-bag, and a lay figure dead beside her. But gradually, as Arthur questioned her, the old memories began to come back and shape themselves in her mind, and she said at last:

"It was like this—play you was a sick lady and I was your nurse. I can't think of her name. I guess I'll call her Manny. And there must be a baby; that's me, only I can't think of my name."

"Call it Jerry, then," Arthur suggested, both interested and amused, though he did not quite understand what she meant.

But he was passive in her hands, and submitted to have a big handkerchief put over his head for a cap, and to hold on his arm the baby she improvised from a sofa-cushion of costly plush, around which she arranged as a dress an expensive table-spread, tied with the rich cord and tassel of his dressing-gown.

"You must cry a great deal," she said, "and pray a

great deal, and kiss the baby a great deal, and I must scold you some for crying so much, and shake the baby some in the kitchen for making a noise, because, you know, the baby can walk and talk, and is me, only I can't be both at a time."

She was not very clear in her explanations, but Arthur began to have a dim perception of her meaning, and did what she bade him do, and rather enjoyed having his face and hands washed with a wet rag, and his hair brushed and *turled*, as she called it, even though the fingers which *turled* it sometimes made suspicious journeys to her mouth. He cried when she told him to cry; he coughed when she told him to cough; he kissed the baby when she told him to kiss it; he took medicine from the tin pail in the form of the cherry juice left there, and did not have to make believe that it sickened him, as she said he must, for that was a reality. But when she told him he must *die*, but pray first, he demurred, and asked what he should say. Jerry hesitated a little. She knew that her prayers were, "Our Father," and "Now I lay me," but it seemed to her that a person dying should say something else, and at last she replied:

"I can't think what she did say, only a lot about *him*. There was a *him* somewhere, and I guess he was naughty, so pray for *him*, and the baby—that's me—and tell Manny she must take me to Mecky."

"To whom?" Arthur asked, and she replied:

"To Mecky, where he was, don't you know?"

Arthur did not know, but he prayed for *him*, saying what she bade him say — a mixture half English, half German.

"There, now, you are dead," she said, at last, as she closed his eyes and folded his hands upon his chest. "You are dead, and musn't stir nor breathe, no matter how awful we cry, Manny and I."

Kneeling down beside him, she began a cry so like that of two persons that if Arthur had not known to the contrary, he would have sworn there were two beside him, a woman and a child, the voice of one shrill, and clear, and young, and frightened, the other older, and harsher, and stronger, and both blending together in a most astonishing manner.

"With a little practice she would make a wonderful ventriloquist," Arthur thought, as he watched her flitting about the room, talking to unseen people and giving orders with regard to himself.

Once Frank had witnessed a pantomine very similar to this, only then the play had ended with the death, while now there was the burial, and when Arthur moved a little and asked if he might get up, she laid her hand quickly on his mouth, with a peremptory, "Hush! you are dead, and we must bury you."

But here Jerry's memory failed her, and the funeral which followed was an imitation of the one which had left the Park House three years before, and which Arthur had watched from his window. Frank was there, and his wife, and Peterkin, and Jerry imitated the voices of them all, and when some one bade her kiss her mother she stooped and kissed Arthur's forehead, and said:

"Good-by, mamma;" then, throwing a thin tidy over his face, she continued, "Now I am going to shut the coffin;" and as she worked at the corners, as if driving down the screws, Arthur felt as if he were actually being shut out from life, and light, and the world.

To one of his superstitious tendencies the whole was terribly real, and when at last she told him he was buried, and the folks had come back, and he could get up, the sweat was standing upon his face and hands in great drops, and he felt that he had in very truth been present at the obsequies of some one whose death had made an impression so strong upon Jerry's mind that time had not erased it. There was in his heart no thought of Gretchen, as there had been in Frank's when he was a spectator at the play. He had no cause for suspicion, and thought only of the child whose restlessness and activity were something appalling to him.

"Now, what shall we play next?" she asked, as he sat white and trembling in his chair.

"Oh, nothing, nothing," he groaned. "I cannot stand any more now."

"Well, then, you sit still and I'll clean house; it needs it badly. Such mud as that boy brings in I never see, and I'm so lame, too!" Jerry responded, and Arthur now recognized Mrs. Crawford, whose tidiness and cleanliness

7*

were proverbial, and for the next half-hour he watched
the little actress as she limped around the room exactly as
Mrs. Crawford limped with her rheumatism, sweeping,
dusting, and scolding, both to Harold and Jerry, the latter of whom once retorted :

"I wouldn't be so cross as that if I had forty rheuma-
tisses in my laigs, would you, Harold?"

But Harold only answered, softly:

"Hush, Jerry! You should not speak so to grandma,
and she so good to us both, when we haven't any mother."

Arthur would have laughed, so perfect was the imitation of voice and gesture, but at the mention of Harold's
mother there came into his mind a vision of sweet Amy
Crawford, who had been his first love, and for whose son
he had really done so little.

"Jerry," he said, "I guess you have cleaned house
long enough. Wash your hands and come to me."

She obeyed him, and, looking into his face, said:

"Now, what? Can you play cat's cradle, or casino ?"

"No; I want to talk to you of Harold. You love him
very much?"

"Oh, a hundred bushels—him and grandma, too."

"And he is very kind to you?"

"Yes, I guess he is. He never talks back, and I am
awful sometimes, and once I spit at him, and struck him ;
but I was so sorry, and cried all night, and offered to give
him my best doll 'cause it was the plaything I loved most,
and I went without my piece of pie so he could have two
pieces if he wanted," Jerry said, her voice trembling as
she made this confession, which gave Arthur a better
insight into her real character than he had had before.

Hasty, impulsive, repentant, generous, and very affectionate, he felt sure she was, and he continued:

"Does Harold go to school ?"

"Yes ; and I, too—to the district ; but I hate it !" Jerry
replied.

"Why hate it ?" Arthur asked. "What is the matter
with the district school ?"

"Oh, it smells awful there sometimes when it is hot,"
Jerry replied, with an upward turn to her nose. "And
the boys are so mean, some of them. Bill Peterkin goes
there, and I can't bear him, he plagues me so. Wants to

kiss me. A-a-h, and says I am to be his wife, and he's got
warts on his thumb !"

"Jerry's face was sufficiently indicative of the disgust
she felt for Bill Peterkin with his warts, and, leaning back
in his chair, Arthur laughed heartily, as he said:

"And so you don't like Bill Peterkin ? Well, what
boy's do you like ?"

"Harold and Dick St. Claire," was the prompt response,
and Arthur continued :

"What would you have in place of the district school ?"

"A governess," was Jerry's answer. "Nina St. Claire
has one, and Ann Eliza Peterkin has one, and Maude Tracy
has one."

Here Jerry stopped suddenly, as if struck with a new
idea.

"Why Maude is your little girl isn't she ? You are her
rich uncle, and she is to have all your money when you die.
I wish I was your little girl."

She spoke the last very sadly, and something in the
expression of her face brought Gretchen to Arthur's mind,
and his voice was choked as he said to her :

"I'd give half my fortune if you were my little girl."

Then, laying his hand on her bright hair, he questioned her adroitly of her life at the cottage, finding that
it was a very happy one, and that she had never known
want, although Mrs. Crawford was unable to work as she
once had done, and was largely dependent upon the price
for Jerry's board, which Frank paid regularly. Of this,
however, Jerry did not speak. She only said :

"Harold works in the furnace, and in folks' gardens, and
does lots of things for everybody, and once Bill Peterkin
twitted him because he goes to Mrs. Baker's sometimes
after stuff for the pig, and Harold cried, and I got up early
the next morning and went after it myself, and drew the cart
home. After that grandma wouldn't let Harold go for any
more, and so I s'pose the pig will not weigh as much. I'm
sorry, for I like sausage, don't you ?"

Arthur hated it, but he did not tell her so, and she went
on :

"Harold studies awful hard, and wants to go to college. He is trying to learn latin, and recites to Dick St.
Claire ; but grandma says its up-hill business. Oh, if I's

only rich I'd give it all to Harold, and he should get learning like Dick. Maybe I can work some time and earn
some money. I wish I could."

Arthur did not speak for a long time, but sat looking
at the child whose face now wore an old and troubled look.
In his mind he was revolving a plan which, with his usual
precipitancy, he resolved to carry into effect at once. But
he said nothing of it to Jerry, whose attention was diverted
by the entrance of Charles and the preparations for
luncheon, which, on the little girl's account, was served
with more care than usual.

Jerry who had a great liking for everything luxurious,
had taken tea once or twice at Grassy Spring with Nina St.
Claire, and had been greatly impressed with the appointments of the table, prizing them more even than the
dainties for her to eat. But what she had seen there
seemed as nothing compared to this round Swiss table,
with its colored glass and rare china, no two pieces of
which were alike.

"Oh, it is just like a dream!" she cried, as she watched
Charles' movement and saw that there were two places
laid. "Am I to sit down with you?" she said, in an awestruck voice, "and in that lovely chair? I am glad I
wore my best gown. It won't dirty the chair a bit."

But she took her pocket-handkerchief and covered it
over the satin cushion before she dared seat herself in the
chair, which had once been brought out for Gretchen, and
in which she now sat down, dropping her head and shutting her eyes a moment. Then, as she heard no sound,
she looked up wonderingly, and asked :

"Ain't you going to say 'for Christ's sake,' grandma
does ?"

Arthur's face was a study with its mixed expression of
surprise, amusement and self-reproach. He never prayed,
except it were in some ejaculatory sentences wrung from
him in his sore need, and the thought of asking a blessing
on his food had never occurred to him. But Jerry was
persistent.

"You must say 'for Christ's sake,'" she continued, and
with his weak brain all in a muddle. Arthur began what
he meant to be a brief thanksgiving, but which stretched
itself into a lengthy prayer, full of the past and of

Gretchen, whom he seemed to be addressing rather than his Maker.

For a while Jerry listened reverently; then she looked up and moved uneasily in the chair, and at last when the prayer had continued for at least five minutes she burst out impulsively:

"Oh, dear, do say 'amen.' I am so hungry!"

That broke the spell, and with a start Arthur came to himself, and said:

"Thank you, Jerry. Praying is a new business for me, and I do believe I should have gone on forever if you had not stopped me. Now what will you have?"

He helped her to whatever she liked best, but could eat scarcely anything himself. It was sufficient for him to watch Jerry sitting there in Gretchen's chair and using Gretchen's plate which every day for so many years had been laid for her. Gretchen had not come. She would never come, he feared, but with Jerry he did not feel half as desolate as when alone, with only his morbid fancies for company. And he must have her there, at least a portion of the time. His mind was made up on that point, and when about four o'clock, Jerry said to him:

"I want to go now. Grandma said I was to be home by five," he replied:

"Yes, I am going with you. I wish to see your grandmother. I am going to drive you in the phaeton. How would you like that?"

Her dancing eyes told him how she would like it, and Charles was sent to the stable with an order to have the little pony phaeton brought round as soon as possible as he was going for a drive.

CHAPTER XIX.

ARTHUR'S PLAN.

"WHY, the madam is going to drive, too, and I've come to harness; there'll be a row somewhere," John said.

"Can't help it," Charles replied. "Mr. Arthur wants the phaeton, and will have it for all of madam."

"Yes, I s'p'o' so. Wall, I'll go and tell her," was John's rejoinder, as he started for the house, where Mrs. Tracy was just drawing on her long driving gloves and admiring her new hat and feather before the glass.

Dolly looked almost as young, and far prettier, than when she came to the park, years before. A life of luxury suited her. She had learned to take things easily, and the old woman with the basket might now come every day to her kitchen door without her knowing it. She aped Mrs. Atherton, of Brier Hill, in everything, and had the satisfaction of knowing that she was on all occasions quite as stylish-looking and well-dressed as that aristocratic lady whom she called her intimate friend. She had also grown very proud and very exclusive in her ideas, and when poor Mrs. Peterkin, who was growing, too, with *her* million, ventured to call at the park, the call was returned with a card which Dolly's coachman left at the door. Since the night of her party, and the election which followed, when Frank was defeated, she had ignored the Peterkins, and laughed at what she called their vulgar imitation of people above them, and when she heard that Mary Jane had hired a governess for her two children, Bill and Ann Eliza, she scoffed at the airs assumed by *come-up* people, and wondered if Mrs. Peterkin had forgotten that she was one of Grace Atherton's hired girls. Dolly had certainly forgotten the Langley life, and was to all intents and purposes the great lady of the park, who held herself aloof from the common herd, and taught her children to do the same.

She had seen Jerry enter the house that morning with a feeling of disapprobation, which had not diminished as the day wore on and still the child staid, and what was worse, Maude was not sent for to join her.

"Not that I would have allowed it, if she had been," she said to herself, for she did not wish her daughter intimate with one of whose antecedents nothing was known, but Arthur might at least have invited her. He had never noticed her children much, and this she deeply resented. Maude, who knew of Jerry's presence in the house, had cried to go and play with her, but Mrs. Tracy had refused, and promised as an equivalent a drive in the phaeton around the town. And it was for this drive Dolly was preparing herself, when John came with the message that she could not have the phaeton, as Mr. Arthur was going to take Jerry home in it.

Usually Arthur's slightest wish was a law in the household, for that was Frank's order; but on this occasion Dolly felt herself justified in rebelling.

"Not have the phaeton! That's smart I must say," she exclaimed. "Can't that child walk home, I'd like to know? Tell Mr. Tracy Maude has had the promise of a drive all day, and I am ready, with my things on. Ask him to take the Victoria; he never drives."

All this in substance was repeated to Arthur, who answered, quietly:

"Let Mrs. Tracy take the Victoria. I prefer the phaeton myself."

That settled it, and in a few moments Jerry was seated at Arthur's side, and skimming along through the park, and out upon the highway which skirted the river for miles.

"This is not going home, and grandma will scold," Jerry said.

"Never mind grandma—I will make it right with her. I am going to show you the country," Arthur replied, as he chirruped to the fleet pony who seemed to fly along the smooth road.

No one who saw the tall, elegant-looking man, who sat so erect, and handled the reins so skillfully, would have suspected him of insanity, and more than one stopped to look after him and the little girl whose face looked out from the white sun bonnet with so joyous an expression.

On the homeward route they met the Victoria, with John upon the box, and Mrs. Tracy and Maude inside.

"There's Maude! Hallo, Maude — see me! I'm riding!" Jerry called out, cheerily, while Maude answered back:

"Hallo, Jerry!"

But Mrs. Tracy gave no sign of recognition, and only rebuked her daughter for her vulgarity in saying "Hallo," which was second class and low.

"Then Nina St. Claire is second class and low, for she says 'Hallo,'" was Maude's reply, to which her mother had no answer.

Meanwhile the phaeton was going swiftly on toward the cottage, which it reached a few minutes after the furnace whistle blew for six, and Harold, who had been working there, came up the lane. There were soiled spots on his hands, and on his face, and his clothes showed marks of toil, all of which Arthur noticed, while he was explaining to Mrs. Crawford that he had taken Jerry for a drive, and kept her beyond the prescribed hour. Then, turning to Harold, he said:

"And so you work in the furnace?"

"Yes, sir, during vacation, when I can get a job there," Harold answered, and Mr. Tracy continued:

"How much do you get a day?"

"Fifty cents in dull times," was the reply, and Arthur went on:

"Fifty cents from seven in the morning to six at night, and board yourself. A magnificent sum, truly. Pray, how do you manage to spend so much? You must be getting rich."

The words were sarcastic, but the tone belied the words, and Harold was about to speak, when his grandmother interrupted him, and said:

"What he does not spend for us he puts aside. He is trying to save enough to go to the High School, but it's slow work. I can do but little myself, and it all falls upon Harold."

"But I like it, grandma. I like to work for you and Jerry, and I have almost twenty dollars saved," Harold said, "and in a year or two I can go away to school, and work somewhere for my board. Lots of boys do that."

Arthur was hitching his pony to the fence, while a new idea was dawning in his mind.

"Fifty cents a day," he said to himself, "and he has twenty dollars saved, and thinks himself rich. Why, I've spent more than that on one bottle of wine, and here is this boy, Amy's son, wanting on education, and working to support his grandmother like a common laborer. I believe I *am* crazy."

He was in the cottage by this time—in the clean, cool kitchen where the supper table was laid with its plain fare, wholly unlike the costly viands which daily loaded his board.

"Don't wait for me, Harold must be hungry," he said, adding quickly: "Or stay if you will permit me, I will take a cup of tea with you. The drive has given me an appetite, and your tea smells very inviting."

It was a great honor to have Arthur Tracy at her table, and Mrs. Crawford felt it as such, and was very sorry, too, that she had nothing better to offer him than bread and butter and radishes, with milk, and a dish of cold beans, and chopped beets, and a piece of apple pie saved for Harold from dinner. But she made him welcome, and Jerry, delighted to return the hospitality she had received, brought him a clean plate and cup and saucer, and asked if she might get the best sugar-bowl and the white sugar. Then, remembering the beautiful flowers which had adorned the table at Tracy Park, she ran out, and gathering a bunch of June pinks, put them in a little glass by his plate.

When all was ready and they had taken their seats at the table, Mrs. Crawford closed her eyes reverently and asked the accustomed blessing which in that house preceded every meal. Jerry's amen was a good deal louder and more emphatic than usual, while she nodded her head to Arthur, with an expression which he understood to mean, "You know now what you ought to say, instead of that long prayer," and he nodded back that he did so understand it.

Arthur enjoyed the supper immensely, or pretended that he did. He ate three slices of bread and butter; he drank three cups of tea; he even tried the beans and the beets, but declined the radishes, which, he said, would give him nightmare.

When supper was over and the table cleared away, he

still showed no signs of going, but asking Mrs. Crawford
to take a seat near him, he plunged at once into the business which had brought him there, and which, since he
had seen Harold in his working-dress and heard what he
was trying to do, had grown to be of a two-fold nature.
He was very lonely, he said, and the little taste he had
had of Jerry's society had made him wish for more, and he
must have her with him a part at least of every day.

"In short," he said, "I should like to undertake her
education myself until she is older, when I will see that she
has the proper finishing. She tells me she hates the district school, with Bill Peterkin and his warts—"

"Trying to kiss me," Jerry interrupted, as, open-eyed
and open-mouthed, she stood, with her hand on his shoulder, listening to him.

"Yes, trying to kiss you, though I do not blame him
much for that," Arthur said, with a smile, and then continued : "She is ambitious enough to want a governess like
Ann Eliza Peterkin and my brother's daughter, but I am
better than a dozen governesses. I can teach her all the
rudiments of an English education, with French and German, and Latin, too, if she likes ; and my plan is, that she
shall come to me every day, except Saturdays and Sundays,
at ten in the morning, get her lessons and her lunch with
me, and return home at four in the afternoon. Would you
like it, Cherry ?"

"Oh-h-oh !" was all the answer Jerry could make for a
moment, but her cheeks were scarlet, and tears of joy
stood in her eyes, until she glanced at Harold ; then all the
brightness faded from her face, for how could she accept
this great good and leave him to drudge and toil alone ?

"What is it, Cherry ?" Mr. Tracy asked ; and, with a
half sob, she replied :

"I can't go without Harold. If I get learning, he must
get learning, too," and leaving Arthur, she crossed over
to the boy, and putting her arm around him, looked up at
him with a look which in after years he would have given
half his life to win.

"I shall not forget Harold," Arthur hastened to say,
"and I have something better in store for him than recit-
ing his lessons to me. When the High School opens in
September, he is going there, and if he does well he shall

go to Andover in time, and perhaps to Harvard. It will all depend upon himself, and how he improves his opportunities. What! crying? Don't you like it?" Arthur asked, as he saw the tears gathering in Harold's eyes and rolling down his cheeks.

"Yes, oh, yes; but it don't seem real, and—and—I guess it makes me kind of sick," Harold gasped, as, freeing himself from Jerry's encircling arm, he hurried from the room, to think over this great and unexpected joy which had come so suddenly to him.

With his naturally refined tastes and instincts the dirty furnace work was not pleasant to him, neither were the many menial duties he was obliged to perform for the sake of those he loved. How to get an education was the problem he was earnestly trying to solve, and lo! it was solved for him. For a moment the suddenness of the thing overcame him, and he sat down upon a block of wood in the yard, faint and bewildered, while Arthur made his plan clear to Mrs. Crawford, saying that what he meant to do was partly for Jerry's sake and partly for the sake of the young girl who had been his early love.

"I always intended to take care of you," he said; "but things go from my mind, and I forget the past as completely as if it had never been. But this will stay by me, for I shall have Cherry as a reminder, and if I am in danger of forgetting she will jog my memory."

For a moment Mrs. Crawford could not speak, so great was her surprise and joy that the good she had thought unattainable was to be Harold's at last. And yet something in her proud, sensitive nature rebelled against receiving so much from a stranger, even if that stranger were Arthur Tracy. It seemed like charity, she said. But Arthur overruled her with that persuasive way he had of converting people to his views; and when at last he left the cottage it was with the understanding that Jerry should commence her lessons with him the first week in September, and that Harold should enter the High School in Shannondale when it opened in the autumn,

CHAPTER XX.

THE WORKING OF ARTHUR'S PLAN.

AS Arthur was wholly uncommunicative with regard to his affairs, and as Mrs. Crawford kept her own counsel, and bade Harold and Jerry do the same, the Tracy's knew nothing whatever of the plan until the September morning when Jerry presented herself at the park house, and was met in the door-way by Mrs. Frank, who was just going out. Very few could have resisted the bright little face, so full of childish happiness, or the clear, assured voice, which said so cheerily:

"Good-morning, Mrs. Tracy. I'm come to school."

But, prejudiced as she was against the girl, Mrs. Tracy could resist any thing, and she answered, haughtily:

"Come to school! What do you mean! This is not a school-house, and if you have any errand here, go round to the other door. Only company come in here."

"But I'm company. I'm going to get learning; he told me to come," Jerry answered, flushed and eager, and altogether sure of her right to be there.

Before Mrs. Frank could reply, a voice, distinct and authoritative, and to which she always yielded, called from the top of the stairway inside:

"Mrs. Tracy, if that is Jerry to whom you are talking, send her up at once. I am waiting for her."

Jerry did not mean the nod she gave the lady as she passed her to be disrespectful, but Mrs. Frank felt it as such, and went to her own room in a most perturbed state of mind, for which she could find no vent until her husband came in, when she stated the case to him, and asked if he knew what it meant.

But Frank was as ignorant as herself, and could not enlighten her until that night, after he had seen his brother, and heard from him what he was intending to do.

"God bless you, Arthur. You don't know how happy you have made me," Frank said, feeling on the instant that a great burden was lifted from his mind.

Jerry was to be educated and cared for, and would probably receive all that the world would naturally concede to her if the truth were known. He believed, or thought he did, that Gretchen had never been his brother's wife, though to believe so seemed an insult to the original of the sweet face which looked at him from the window every time he entered his brother's room. Jerry was a great trouble to him, and he would not have liked to confess to any one how constantly she was in his mind, or how many plans he had devised in order to atone for the wrong he knew he was doing her. And now his brother had taken her off his hands, and she was to be cared for and receive the education which would fit her to earn her own livelihood, and make her future life respectable. No particular harm was done her after all, and he might now enjoy himself, and cast his morbid fancies to the winds, he reflected, as he went whistling to his wife's apartment, and told her what he heard.

For a moment Dolly was speechless with astonishment, and when at last she opened her lips, her husband silenced her with that voice and manner of which she was beginning to be afraid.

It was none of their business, he said, what Arthur did in his own house, provided, they were not molested, and if he chose to turn schoolmaster, he had a right to do so. For his part, he was glad of it, as it saved him the expense of Jerry's education, for if Arthur had not taken it in hand, he should, and Dolly was to keep quiet and let the child come and go in peace.

After delivering himself of these sentiments, Frank went away, leaving his wife to wonder, as she had done more than once, if he, too, were not a little crazy, like his brother. But she said no more about Jerry's coming there, except to suggest that she might at least come in at the side door instead of the front, especially on muddy days when she was liable to soil the costly carpets. And Jerry, who cared but little how she entered the house, if she only got in, came through the kitchen after the second day, and wiped her feet upon the mat ; and once, when her shoes were worse than usual, took them off, lest they should leave a track.

It is not our intention to linger over the first few

months of Jerry's school days at Tracy Park, but rather to hasten on to the summer four years after her introduction to Tracy Park as Arthur's pupil. During all that time he had never once seemed to be weary of the task he had imposed upon himself, but, on the contrary, his interest had deepened in the child who developed so rapidly under his training that he sometimes looked at her in astonishment, marveling more and more who she was, and from whom she had inherited her wonderful memory and power to grasp points which are usually far beyond the comprehension of a child of ten, or even twelve, and which Maude Tracy could no more have mastered than her brother, the stupid Jack, whose intellect had not grown with his body.

There was a tutor now at Tracy Park for Jack, but Maude had been transferred to Arthur's care. This was wholly due to Jerry, who alone could have induced him to let Maude share her instruction. Arthur did not care for Maude. She was dull, he said, and would never have her lessons. But Jerry coaxed so hard that Arthur consented at last, and when Jerry had been with him about three years, Maude became his pupil, and that of Jerry as well, for nearly every day when the lessons were over, the two little girls might have been seen sitting together under the trees in the park, or in some corner of the house, Maude puzzled, and perplexed, and worried, and Jerry anxious, decided, and peremptory, as she went over and over again with what was so clear to her and so hazy to her friend.

"Oh, dear me, suz, what does ail you?" she said one day, with a stamp of her foot, after she had tried in vain to make Maude see through a simple sum in long division. "Can't you remember first to divide, second multiply, third subtract, and fourth bring down?"

"No, I can't. I can't remember anything, and if I could, how do I know what to divide or what to bring down? I am stupid, and shall never know anything," was Maude's sobbing reply, as she covered her face with her slate.

Maude's tears always moved Jerry, who tried to comfort her with the assurance that if she tried very hard, she might some time know enough to teach a district school. This was the height of Jerry's ambition, to teach a district school and board around; but Maude's aspirations were different. She was rich. She was to be a belle and wear diamonds and satins like her mother ; and it did not matter so much whether she understood long division or not, though it did hurt her a little to be so far outstripped by Jerry, who was younger than herself.

To Arthur, Jerry was a constant delight and surprise, and nothing astonished or pleased him more than the avidity with which she took up German. This language was like play to her, and by the time she was ten years old she spoke, and read, and wrote it almost as well as Arthur himself.

" It takes me back somewhere, I can't tell where," she said to him ; " and I seem to be somebody else than Jerry Crawford, and I hear music and see people, and a pale face is close to me, and my head gets all confused trying to remember things which come and go."

Only once after her first day at the park had she enacted the pantomime of the sick woman and the nurse, and then she had done it at Arthur's request. But it was not quite as thrilling as at first ; the *him* for whom the dying woman had prayed was omitted, and the whole was mixed with the Tramp House, and the carpet-bag, and Harold, who was now a youth of seventeen, and a student at the high-school in Shannondale, where he was making as rapid progress in his studies as Jerry was at the park,

But Harold's life was not as serene and happy as Jerry's, for it was not pleasant for him to hear, as he often did, that he was a charity student, supported by Arthur Tracy. Such remarks were very galling to the high-spirited boy, and he was constantly revolving all manner of schemes by which he could earn money and cease to be dependent. All through the long summer vacations, he worked at whatever he could find to do, sometimes in people's gardens, sometimes on their lawns, but oftener in the hay-fields, where he earned the most, Here Jerry was not unfrequently his companion. She liked to rake hay, she said ; it came natural to her, and she had no doubt she inherited the taste from her mother, who had probably worked in the fields in Germany.

One afternoon, when Jerold knew that Harold was busy in one of Mr. Tracy's meadows, she started to join him, for he had complained of a headache at noon, and had expressed a fear that he might not be able to finish the task he had imposed upon himself. The road to the field was by the Tramp House, which looked so cool and quiet, with its thick covering of woodbine and ivy over it, that Jerry turned aside for a moment to look into the room which had so great a fascination for her, and where she spent so much time. Indeed, she seldom passed near it without going in for a moment and standing by the old table which had once held her and her dead mother. Things came back to her there, she said, and she could almost give a name to the pale-faced woman who haunted her so often.

As she entered the damp, dark place now, she started with an exclamation of surprise, which was echoed by another, as Frank Tracy sprang up and confronted her. It was not often that he visited the Tramp House, and he would not have confessed to any one his superstitious dread of it, or that, when he was in it, he always had a feeling that the dead woman found there years ago would start up to accuse him of his deceit and hypocrisy. Could he have had his way he would have pulled the building down ; but it was not his, and when he suggested it to Arthur, as he sometimes did, the latter opposed it, saying latterly, since Jerry had been so much to him;

" No, Frank ; let it stand. I like it, because, but for it, Jerry might have perished with her mother, and I should not have had her with me."

So the Tramp House stood, and grew damper and mustier each year, as the moss and ivy gathered on the walls outside, and the dust and cobwebs gathered on the walls within. These, however, Jerry was careful to brush away, for she had a play-house in one corner, and a little work-bench and chair, and she often sat there alone and talked to herself, and the woman dead so long ago, and to others whose faces were dim and shadowy, but whom she felt sure she had known. Very frequently she went through the process of cleaning up, as she called it, and her object in stopping there now was, in part, to see if it did not need her care again.

"Oh, Mr. Tracy ! are you here ? How you scared me ! I thought it was a tramp !" she said, as he came toward her.

"Do you come here often ?" he asked, as he offered her his hand.

" Yes, pretty often. I like it, because mother died here, and sometimes I feel as if she would make it known to me here who she was. I talk to her and ask her to tell me, but she never has. Oh, don't you wish she would ?"

Frank shuddered involuntarily, for to have Jerry told who she really was, was the last thing he could desire, but as a criminal is said always to talk about the crime he has committed and is hiding, so Frank, when with Jerry, felt impelled to talk with her of the past and what she could remember of it. Seating himself upon the bench with her at his side, he said :

" And you really believe the woman found here was your mother ?"

" Why, yes. Don't you ? Who was my mother, if she wasn't ?" and Jerry's eyes opened wide as they looked at him.

" I don't know, I am sure. Does my brother talk of Gretchen now ?" was the abrupt reply.

" Yes, at times," Jerry answered ; " and yesterday, after I sang him a little German song, which he taught me, he had them pretty bad—the bees in his head, I mean ; that is what he calls it when things are mixed ; and he says he is going to write to her, or her friends."

" Write to her ! I thought he had given that up. I thought he—— Did he say, ' Write to her friends ?'" Frank gasped, as he felt himself grow cold and sick with this threatened danger.

Arthur had seemed so quiet and happy with Jerry, and had said so little of Gretchen, that Frank had grown quite easy in his mind, and the black shadow of fear did not trouble him as much as formerly. But now it was over him again, and grew in intensity as he questioned the child.

" Have you ever tried to find out who Gretchen is ?" he asked, at last.

" No," she replied, " but I guess she is his wife."

" Yes," Frank said, falteringly, " his wife ; and where do you think she lived ?"

" Oh, I know that. In Wiesbaden. He told me so once, and it seems as if I had been there, too, when he talked about it, and I hear the music and see the flowers, and a white-faced woman is with me, not at all like mother, who, they say, was ugly and dark ; black as a

8

nigger, Tom told me once, when he was mad. Was she black ?"

Mr. Tracy made no reply to this, but said, suddenly :

" Jerry, do you like me well enough to do me a great favor ?"

" Why, yes, I guess I do. I like you very much, though not as well as I do Harold and Mr. Arthur. What do you want ?" was Jerry's answer.

After hesitating a moment, Mr. Tracy began

"'There are certain reasons why I ought to know if my brother writes to Gretchen, or her friends, or any one in Germany, especially Wiesbaden. A letter of that kind might do me a great deal of harm ; if he should write to any one in Germany, you would, perhaps, be asked to post the letter, as he never goes to town ?"

He said this interrogatively, and Jerry answered him, promptly :

" I think he would give it to me, as I post nearly all his letters."

" Yes, well ; Jerry, can you keep a secret, and never tell any one what I am saying to you ?" was Frank's next remark, to which Jerry responded :

"I think I should tell · Harold, and, perhaps, Mr. Arthur."

" No, no, Jerry, never !" and Frank laid his hand half menacingly upon the little girl's shoulder. " I have been kind to you, have paid for your board to Mrs. Crawford ever since you have been there "—

He felt how mean it was to say this, and did not at all resent Jerry's quick reply :

" Yes, but Mrs. Peterkin says you do not pay enough."

" Perhaps not," he continued ; "but if Mrs. Crawford is satisfied, it matters little what Mrs. Peterkin thinks. Jerry, you *must* do this for me," he went on rapidly, as his fears kept growing. " You must never tell any one of our conversation, and if my brother writes that letter soon, or at any time, you must bring it to me. Will you do it ? Great harm would come if it were sent—harm to me, and harm to Maude, and "—

" To Maude !" Jerry repeated. " I would do anything for Maude. Yes, I will bring the letter to you if he writes one. You are sure it would be right for me to do so ?"

Frank had touched the right chord when he mentioned his daughter's name, for during the years of close companionship the two little girls had learned to love each other devotedly, though naturally Jerry's was the stronger and less selfish attachment of the two. To her Maude was a queen who had a right to tyrannize over and command her if she pleased ; and as the tyranny was never very severe, and was usually followed by some generous act of contrition, she did not mind it at all, and was always ready to make up and be friends whenever it suited the capricious little lady.

"Yes, I will do it for Maude," she said again ; but there was a troubled look on her face, and a feeling in her heart as if, in some way, she was false to Arthur in thus consenting to his brother's wishes.

But, she reflected, Arthur was crazy, so people said, and she herself knew better than any one else of his many fanciful vagaries, which, at times, took the form of actual insanity. For weeks he would seem perfectly rational, and then suddenly his mood would change, and he would talk strange things to himself and the child, who was now so necessary to him, and who alone had a soothing influence over him. Only the day before, he had been unusually excited, after listening to a simple air which he had taught her, and which, at his request, she sang to him after Maude had gone out and left them alone.

"I could swear you were Gretchen, singing to me in the twilight, and across the meadow comes the tinkle of the bells where the cows and goats are feeding," he said to her, as he paced up and down the room.

Then, stopping suddenly, he went up to her, and pushing her hair from her forehead, looked long and earnestly into her face.

"Cherry," he said at last, using the pet name he often gave her, "you *are* some like Gretchen as she must have been when of your age. Oh, if you only were hers and mine ! But there was no child ; and yet—and yet—"

He seemed to be thinking intently for a moment, and then, going to a drawer in his writing-desk which Jerry had never seen open before, he took out a worn, yellow letter, and ran his eye rapidly over it until he found a certain paragraph, which he bade Jerry read.

The paragraph was as follows:

"I have something to tell you when you come, which I am sure will make you as glad as I am."

Jerry read it aloud slowly, for the handwriting was cramped and irregular, and then looked up questioningly to Arthur, who said to her:

"What do you think she meant by the something which would make me glad as she was?"

"I don't know," Jerry answered him. "Who wrote it? Gretchen?"

"Yes, Gretchen. It is her last letter to me, and I never went back to see what she meant, for the bees were bad in my head and I forgot everything, even Gretchen herself. Poor little Gretchen! What was the idea which came to me like a flash of lightning, in regard to this letter, when I heard you sing? It is gone, and I cannot recall it."

There was a worried, anxious look on his face as he put the letter away, and went on talking to himself of Gretchen, saying he was going to write her again, or her friends, and find out what she meant.

The next day Jerry met Frank in the Tramp House, as we have described, and gave him the promise to bring him any letter directed to Germany which Arthur might entrust to her. But the promise weighed heavily upon her as she walked slowly on toward the field where Harold was at work, and where she found him resting for a moment under the shadow of a wide-spreading butternut. He looked tired and pale, and there was an expression on his face which Jerry did not understand.

Harold was not in a very happy frame of mind. Naturally cheerful and hopeful, it was not often that he gave way to fits of despondency, or repining at his humble lot, so different from that of the boys of his own age, with whom he came in daily contact, both at school and in the town.

Dick St. Claire, his most intimate friend, always treated him as if he were fully his equal, and often stood between him and the remarks which boys make thoughtlessly, and which, while they mean so little, wound to the quick such sensitive natures as Harold's. But not even Dick St. Claire could keep Tom Tracy in check. With each suc-

ceeding year he grew more and more supercillious and
unbearable, pluming himself upon his position as a Tracy
of Tracy Park, and the wealth he was to inherit from his
Uncle Arthur. For the last year he had been at Andover,
where he had formed a new set of acquaintances, one of
whom was spending the vacation with him. This was
young Fred Raymond, whose home was at Red Stone Hall,
in Kentucky, and whose parents were in Europe. Between
the two youths there was but little similarity of taste or
disposition, for young Raymond represented all that was
noble and true, and though proud of his State and proud
of his name, he never assumed the slightest superiority over
those whom the world considered his inferiors. He was
Tom's room-mate, and hence the intimacy between them
which had resulted in Fred's accepting the invitation to
Tracy Park. If anything had been wanting to complete
Tom's estimate of his own importance this visit of the Kentuckian would have done it. All his former friends were
cut except Dick St. Claire, while Harold was as much
ignored as if he had never existed. Tom did not even see
him or recognize him with so much as a look, but passed
him by as he would any common day laborer whom he
might chance to meet. All through the summer days,
while Harold was working until every bone in his body
ached, Tom and his friend were enjoying themselves in
hunting, fishing, driving, or rowing, or lounging under the
trees in the shady lawns.

That afternoon, when Jerry joined him in the hayfield,
Tom and the Kentuckian had passed him in their fanciful
hunting-suits, with their dogs and guns, but though Harold
was within a few yards of them, Tom affected not to see
him, and kept his head turned the other way, as if intent
upon some object in the distance.

Leaning upon his rake, Harold watched them out of
sight, with a choking sensation in his throat, as he wondered
if it would always be thus with him, and if the day would
never come when he, too, could know what leisure meant,
with no thought for the morrow's bread.

"I am Tom's superior in everything but money, and yet
he treats me like a dog," he said, as he seated himself upon
the grass, where he sat fanning himself with his straw
hat.

When Jerry appeared in view he brightened at once, for in all the world there was nothing half so sweet and lovely to him as the little blue-eyed girl who sat down beside him, and, nestling close to him, laid her curly head upon his arm.

"I've come to help you rake the hay," she said, "for grandma told me you had a headache at noon, and could'nt eat your huckleberry pie. I am awfully sorry, Harold, but I ate it myself, it looked so good, instead of saving it for your supper. It was nasty and mean in me, and I hope it will make me sick."

But Harold told her he did not care for the pie, and was glad that she ate it if she liked it. Then he questioned her of the park house and of Arthur, asking if the bees were often in his head now, or had she driven them out.

"No, I guess I haven't. They were awful yesterday," Jerry replied. "He was talking of Gretchen all the time. I wonder who she was. Sometimes I look at her until it seems to me I have seen her or something like her, a paler face with sadder eyes. How he must have loved her, better than you or I could ever love anybody ; don't you think so ?"

Harold hesitated a moment, and then replied :

"I don't know, but it seems to me I love you as much as one could ever love another."

"Phoo ! Of course you do ; but that's boy love ; that isn't like when you are old enough to have a beau !" and Jerry laughed merrily, as she sprang up, and, taking Harold's rake, began to toss the hay about rapidly, bidding him sit still and see how fast she could work in his place.

Harold was very tired, and his head was aching badly, so for a time he sat still, watching the graceful movements of the beautiful child, who, it seemed to him, was slipping away from him. Constant intercourse with a polished man like Arthur Tracy had not been without its effect upon her, and there was about her an air which with strangers would have placed her at once above the ordinary level of simple country girls. This Harold had been the first to detect, and though he rejoiced at Jerry's good fortune, there was always with him a dread lest she should grow beyond him, and that he should lose the girl he loved so much.

" What if she should think me a clown and a clodhopper, as Tom Tracy does ?" he said to himself, as he watched her raking up the hay faster, and quite as well as he could have done himself. " I believe I should die."

It was impossible that Jerry should have guessed the nature of Harold's thoughts, but once, as she passed near him, she dropped her rake, and going up to him, wiped his forehead with her apron, and, kissing him fondly, said to him :

" Poor, tired boy, is your head awful ? You look as if you wanted to vomit ? Do you ?"

" No, Jerry," Harold answered, laughingly. " I am not as bad as that. I was only wishing that I were rich and could give you and grandma a home as handsome as Tracy Park. How would you like it ?"

" First-rate, if you were there," Jerry replied ; " but if you were not I shouldn't like it at all. I never mean to live anywhere without you ; because, you know I am your little girl, the one you found in the carpet-bag, and I love you more than all the world, and will love and stand by you forever and ever, amen !"

She said the last so abruptly, and it sounded so oddly, that Harold burst into a laugh, and taking up the rake she had dropped, began his work again, declaring that the headache was gone, and that he was a great deal better.

CHAPTER XXI.

MRS. TRACY'S DIAMONDS.

MRS. TRACY was going to have a party—not a general one, like that which she gave when our readers first knew her, and Harold Hastings stood at the head of the stairs and bade " the ladies go this way and the gentlemen that." Since she had become a leader of fashion, she had ignored general parties and limited her invitations to a select few, which, on this occasion, numbered about sixty or seventy. But the entertainment was prepared as elaborately as if hundreds had been expected, and the hostess was radiant in satin, and lace, and diamonds, as she received her guests and did the honors of the occasion.

The September night was soft and warm, and the grounds were lighted up, while quite a crowd collected near the house to hear the music and watch the proceedings.

Mrs. Tracy would have liked to have Jerry in the upper hall, where Harold had once stood.

"It would help to keep the child in her place," she thought.

But her husband promptly vetoed the proposition, saying that when Jerry Crawford came to the park house to an entertainment it would be as a guest, and not as a waiter. So a colored boy stood in the upper hall, and a colored boy stood in the lower hall, and there were colored waiters everywhere, and Dolly had never been happier or prouder in her life; for Governor Markham and his wife, from Iowa, were there, and a judge's wife from Springfield —all guests of Grace Atherton, and, in consequence, bidden to the party.

Another remarkable feature of the evening was the presence of Arthur in the parlors. He had known both Governor Markham and his wife, Ethelyn Grant, and had been present at their wedding, and it was mostly on their account that he had consented to join in the festivities. Jerry, it is true, had done a great deal toward persuading him to go down, repeating, in her own peculiar way, what she had heard people say with regard to his seclusion from society.

"You just make a hermit of yourself," she said, "cooped up here all the time. I don't wonder folks say you are crazy. It is enough to make anybody crazy, to stay in one or two rooms and see nobody but Charles and me. Just dress yourself in your best clothes and go down and be somebody, and don't talk of Gretchen all the time! I am tired of it, and so is everybody. Give her a rest for one evening, and show the people how nice you can be if you only have a mind to."

Jerry delivered this speech with her hands on her hips, and with all the air of a woman of fifty; while Arthur laughed immoderately, and promised her to do his best not to disgrace her.

Jerry's anxiety was something like that of a mother for a child whose ability she doubts; and, after her supper was over, she took her way to the park house to see that Arthur was dressed properly for the occasion.

"It would be like him to go without his neck-tie and wear his every-day boots," she thought.

But she found him as faultlessly gotten up as he well could be in his old-fashioned evening dress, which sat rather loosely upon him, for he had grown thinner with each succeeding year.

Jerry thought him splendid, and watched him admiringly as he left the room and started for the parlors, with her last injunction ringing in his ears:

"Not a word out of your head about Gretchen, but try and act as if you were not crazy."

"I'll do it, Cherry. Don't you worry," he said to her, with a little reassuring nod, as he descended the stairs.

And he kept his promise well. There was no word out of his head about Gretchen, and no one ignorant of the fact would ever have suspected that his mind was unsettled as he moved among the guests, talking to one and another with that pleasant, courtly manner so natural to him. A very-close observer, however, might have seen his eyes dilate and even flash with some sudden emotion when his brother's wife passed him and her brilliant diamonds sparkled in the bright gas-light. The setting was rather peculiar, but Mrs. Tracy liked it for the peculiarity, and had never had it changed. She was very proud of her diamonds, they were so large and clear, and she had the satisfaction of knowing that there were no finer, if as fine, in town. She seemed to know, too, just in what light to place herself in order to show them to the best advantage, and at times the gleams of fire from them were wonderful, and once Arthur put his hand before his eyes as she passed him, and muttering something to himself moved quickly to another part of the room. This was late in the evening, and soon after he excused himself to those around him, saying it was not often that he dissipated like this, and as he was growing tired he must say good-night.

The next morning Charles found him looking very pale and worn, with a bad pain in his head. He had not slept at all, he said, and would have his coffee in bed, after

which Charles was to leave him alone and not come back
until he rang for him, as he might possibly fall asleep.

It was very late that morning when the family break-
fasted, and as they lingered around the table, discussing
the events of the previous night, it was after eleven o'clock
when at last Mrs. Tracy went up to her room.

As she ascended the stairs, she caught a glimpse of Harold disappearing through a door at the lower end of the
hall, evidently with the intention of going down the back
stairway and making his exit from the house by the rear
door, rather than the front. Mrs. Tracy knew that he was
sometimes sent by his grandmother on some errand to
Arthur, and giving no further thought to the matter went
on to her own room, which her maid had put in order.
All the paraphernalia of last night's toilet was put away,
diamonds and all. Contrary to her usual custom, for she
was very careful of her diamonds, and very much afraid
they would be stolen, she had left them in the box on her
dressing bureau. But they were not there now. Sarah,
who knew where she kept them, had put them away, of
course, and she gave them no more thought until three
days later, when she received an invitation to a lunch party
at Brier Hill.

"I shall wear my dark blue satin and diamonds," she
said to her maid, who was dressing her hair, but the diamonds, when looked for, were not in their usual place.

Sarah had not put them away, nor in fact had she seen
them at all, for they were not upon the bureau when she
went to arrange her mistress' room the morning after the
party. The diamonds were gone, nor could any amount of
searching bring them to light, and Mrs. Tracy grew cold,
and sick, and faint, and finally broke down in a fit of crying, as she explained to her husband that her beautiful
diamonds were stolen. She called it that, now, and the
whole household was roused and questioned as to when and
where each had last seen the missing jewels. But no one
had seen them since they were in the lady's ears, and she
knew she had left them upon her bureau when she went
down to breakfast. She was positive of that. No one had
been in the room, or that part of the house, except Tom,
Fred Raymond, Charles, and Sarah. Of these the first two
were not to be thought of for a moment, while the last two

had been in the family for years, and were above suspicion. Clearly, then, it was some one from outside, who had watched his or her opportunity and come in.

"Had any one been seen about the house at that hour?" Frank asked, and Charles remembered having met Harold Hastings coming out of the rear door ; "but," he added, "I would sooner suspect myself than him."

And this was the verdict of all except Mrs. Tracy, who now recalled the fact that she, too, had seen Harold "sneaking through the door as if he did not wish to be seen."

That was the way she expressed herself, and her manner had in it more meaning even than her words.

"What was Harold doing in the house ? What was his errand? Does any one know?" she asked, but no one volunteered any information until Charles suggested that he probably came on some errand to Mr. Arthur ; he would inquire, he said, and he went at once to his master's room.

Arthur was sitting by his writing desk, busy with a letter, and did not turn his head when Charles asked if he remembered whether Harold Hastings had been to his room the morning after the party.

"No, I have not seen him for more than a week," was the reply.

"But he must have been here that morning," Charles continued. "Try and think."

"I tell you no one was here. I am not quite demented yet. Now go. Don't you see you are interrupting me ?" was Arthur's rather savage response, and without having gained any satisfactory information, Charles returned to the group anxiously awaiting him.

"Well?" was Mrs. Tracy's sharp interrogatory, to which Charles responded :

"He does not remember what happened that morning ; but that is not strange. He was very tired and unusually excited after the party, and when he is that way he does not remember anything. Harold might have been there a dozen times and he would forget it."

"Bring the boy, then. He will know what he was doing here," was Mrs. Tracy's next peremptory remark, and her husband said to her, reproachfully :

" Surely you do not intend to charge him with the theft ?"

" I charge no one with the theft until it is proven against him ; but I must see the boy and know what he was doing here. I never liked this free running in and out by those people in the lane. I always knew something would come of it," Mrs. Tracy said, and Charles was dispatched for Harold.

He found him mowing the lawn for a gentleman whose premises joined Tracy Park, and without any explanation told him that he was wanted immediately at the park house.

" But it is noon," Harold said, glancing up at the sun. " And there is Jerry coming to call me to dinner."

" Better come at once. Jerry can go with you, if she likes," Charles said, feeling intuitively that in the little girl Harold would find a champion.

Harold left his lawn mower, and explaining to Jerry that he had been summoned to the park house, whither she could accompany him if she chose, he started with her and Charles, whom he questioned as to what was wanted with him.

" Were you in the park house the morning after the party ? That would be Tuesday," Charles asked.

" Yes, I went to see Mr. Arthur Tracy, but could get no answer to my knock," Harold promptly replied, while his face flushed scarlet, and he seemed annoyed at something.

He could not explain to Charles his motive in going to see Arthur, as, now that the first burst of indignation was over, he felt half ashamed of it himself. On the afternoon of the day of the party he had been at Grassy Spring, helping Mrs. St. Claire with her flowers, and after his work was done he had gone with Dick into the billiard-room, where they found Tom Tracy and his friend, young Raymond. They had come over for a game, and the four boys were soon busily engaged in the contest. Harold, who had often played with Dick, and was something of an expert, proved himself the most skillful of them all, greatly to the chagrin of Tom, who had not recognized him even by a nod. Dick, on the contrary, had introduced him to Fred Raymond with as much ceremony as if he had been the

Governor's son, instead of the boy who sometimes worked in his mother's flower garden. And the Kentuckian had taken him by the hand and greeted him cordially, with a familiar :

" How d'ye, Hastings ? Glad to make your acquaintance."

There was nothing snobbish about Fred Raymond, whose every instinct was gentlemanly and kind, and Harold felt at ease with him at once, and all through the game appeared at his best, and quite as well bred as either of his companions.

When the play was over Dick excused himself a moment, as he wished to speak with his father, who was about driving to town. As he staid away longer than he had intended doing, Tom grew restless and angry, too, that Fred should treat Harold Hastings as an equal, for the two had at once entered into conversation, comparing notes with regard to their standing in school, and discussing the merits of Cicero and Virgil, the latter of which Harold had just commenced.

" We can't wait here all day for Dick," Tom said. " Let us go out and look at the pictures."

So they went down the stairs to a long hall, in which many pictures were hanging—some family portraits and others copies of the old masters which Mr. St. Claire had brought from abroad. Near one of the portraits Fred lingered a long time, commenting upon its beauty, and the resemblance he saw in it to little Nina St. Claire, the daughter of the house, and whose aunt the original had been. The portrait was not far from the stairway which led to the billiard-room, and Harold, who had remained behind, and was listlessly knocking the balls, could not help hearing all that was said :

" By the way, who is that Hastings ? I don't think I have seen him before ; he is a right clever chap," Fred Raymond said, and Tom replied, in that sneering, contemptuous tone which Harold knew so well, and which always made his blood boil and his fingers tingle with a desire to knock the speaker down :

" Oh, that's Hal Hastings, a poor boy, who does chores for us and the St. Claires. His grandmother used to work

at the park house, and so Uncle Arthur pays for his school-
ing, and Hal allows it, which I think right small in him.
I wouldn't be a charity student, anyway, if I never knew
anything. Besides that, what's the use of education to
chaps like him. Better stay as he was born. I don't believe in educating the masses, do you?"

Of himself, Tom could never have thought of all this,
but he had heard it from his mother, who frequently used
the expression "not to elevate the masses," forgetting that
she was once herself a part of the mass which she would
not have elevated.

Just what Fred said in reply Harold did not hear.
There was a ringing in his ears, and he felt as if every drop
of blood in his body was rushing to his head as he sat down,
smarting cruelly under the wound he had received. He
had more than once been taunted with his poverty and
dependence upon Mr. Tracy, but the taunts had never hurt
him so before, and he could have cried out in his pain as
he thought of Tom's words, and knew that in himself there
was the making of a far nobler manhood than Tom Tracy
would ever know.

Was poverty, which one could not help, so terrible a
disgrace, an insuperable barrier to elevation, and was it
mean and small in him to accept his education from a man
on whom he had no claim? Possibly ; and if so, the state
of things should not continue. He would go to Arthur
Tracy, thank him for all he had done, and tell him he
could receive no more from him ; that if he had an education, he must get it himself by the work of his own hands,
and thus be beholden to no one.

Full of this resolution, he went down the stairs and out
into the open air, which cooled his hot head a little, though
it was still throbbing terribly as he went through the leafy
woods toward home.

In the lane he saw Jerry coming toward him, with her
sun-bonnet hanging down her back. The moment she saw
him she knew something was the matter, and, hastening
her steps to a run, asked him what had happened, and why
he looked so white and angry.

Harold was sure of sympathy from Jerry, and he told
her his story, which roused her to a high pitch of indignation.

"The miserable, nasty, sneaking Tom!" she said, stopping short and emphasizing each adjective with a stamp of her foot, as if she were trampling upon the offending Tom. "I wish I had heard him. I'd have scratched his eyes out; talking of you as if you were dirt! I hate him, and I told him so the other day, and spit at him when he tried to kiss me!"

"Kiss you! Tom Tracy kiss you!" Harold exclaimed, forgetting his own grief in this insult to Jerry; for it seemed to him little less than profanity for lips like Tom Tracy's to touch his little Jerry,

"No he didn't, but he tried, right before that boy from Kentucky; but I wriggled away from him, and bit him, too, and he called me a cat, and said he guessed I wouldn't mind if *you* or Dick St. Claire tried to kiss me, and I shouldn't; but I'll fight *him* and Bill Peterkin every time. I wonder why all the boys want to kiss me so much!"

"I expect it is because you have just the sweetest mouth in the world," Harold said, stooping down and kissing the lips which seemed made for that use alone.

This little episode had helped somewhat to quiet Harold's state of mind, but did not change his resolve to speak to Mr. Tracy, and tell him that he could not receive any more favors from his hands. He would, however, wait until the morrow, as Jerry bade him do.

"You will worry him so that he will be crazier than a loon at the party," she said, and so Harold waited, but started for the park the next morning as soon as he thought Mr. Tracy would see him.

He had rung at the door of the rear hall, but as no one heard him he ventured in, as he had sometimes done before, when sent for Jerry if it rained, and ascending the stairs to the upper hall, knocked two or three times at Arthur's door, first gently, and then louder as there came no response.

"He cannot be there, and I must come again," he thought, as he retraced his steps, reaching the door at the lower end of the hall just as Mrs. Tracy came up the broad staircase, on her way to her room.

As that day wore on, and the next, and the next, Harold began to care less for Tom's insult, and to think that possibly he had been hasty in his determination to decline Arthur's assistance, especially as he meant to pay back every dollar when he was a man. He would at all events wait a little, he thought, and so had made no further effort to see Mr. Tracy, when Charles, found him, and told him he was wanted at the park house.

CHAPTER XXII.

SEARCHING FOR THE DIAMONDS.

THEY went directly to Mrs. Tracy's room, where they found that lady in a much higher fever of excitement than when she first discovered her loss. All the household had assembled in the hall and in her room, except Arthur, who sat in his library, occasionally stopping to listen to the sound of the many voices, and to wonder why there was so much noise.

Tom was there with his friend, Fred Raymond, anxiously awaiting the arrival of Harold, whose face wore a look of wonder and perplexity which deepened into utter amazement as Mrs. Tracy angrily demanded of him what his business was in the hall on Tuesday morning when she saw him sneaking through the door.

"Where had you been, and did you see my diamonds? Somebody has stolen them," she said, while Harold stared at her in utter astonishment.

"Somebody stolen your diamonds?" he repeated, without the shadow of an idea that she could in any way connect him with a theft; nor would the idea have come to him at all, if Tom had not said, with a sneer :

"Better own up, Hal, and restore the property. It is your easiest way out of it."

Then he comprehended, and had Tom knocked him senseless the effect could not have been greater. With lips as white as ashes, and fists tightly clenched, he stood, shaking like a leaf, unable to speak until his eyes fell upon Jerry, whose face was a study. She had thrown her head forward and on one side, and was looking intently at Tom Tracy, while her blue eyes flashed fire, and her whole atti-

tude was like that of a tiger ready to pounce upon its prey.
And when Harold said faintly, "ask Jerry ; she knows,"
she did pounce upon Tom, not bodily, but with her tongue,
pouring out her words so rapidly, and mingling with them
so much German that it was almost impossible to understand all she said.

"You miserable, good for nothing, nasty fellow," she
began. "Do you dare accuse Harold of stealing ! You,
who are not fit to tie his shoes ! And do you want to know
why he was here that morning ? I can tell you ; but no,
I won't tell *you !* I won't speak to you ! I'll never speak
to you again ; and if you try to kiss me as you did the
other day, I'll—I'll scratch out every single one of your
eyes ! *You* twit Harold of being poor, and call him a
charity ! What are you but a charity yourself, I'd like to
know. Is this your house ? No, *sir !* It is Mr. Arthur's.
Everything is Mr. Arthur's, and if you don't quit being so
mean to Harold, I'll tell him every single nasty thing I
know about you. Then see what he will do !"

As Jerry warmed with her subject, every look, every
gesture, and every tone of her voice was like Arthur's, and
Frank watched her with a fascination which made him forget everything else, until she turned suddenly to him, and
in her own peculiar style and language told him why Harold
had come to the park house that morning when the diamonds were missing.

"I advised him to come," she said, with the air of a
grown woman, "and I said I'd stand by him, and I will,
forever and ever, amen !"

The words dropped from her lips the more naturally
perhaps, because she had used them once before with reference to the humiliated boy, to whose pale, set face there
came a smile as he heard them again, and stretching out
his hand he laid it on Jerry's head with a caressing motion
which told plainer than words could have done of his affection for and trust in her.

What more Jerry might have said was prevented by the
appearance of a new actor upon the scene in the person of
Arthur himself. He had borne the noise and confusion as
long as he could, and then had rung for Charles to inquire
what it meant. But Charles was too much absorbed with
other matters to heed the bell, though it rang three times

sharply and loudly. At last, as no one came, and the bustle outside grew louder, and Jerry's voice was distinctly heard, excited and angry, Arthur started to see for himself what had happened.

"Oh, Mr. Arthur," Jerry cried, as she caught sight of him coming down the hall, "I was just going after you, to come and turn Tom out of doors, and everybody else who says that Harold took Mrs. Tracy's diamonds. She has lost them, and Tom——"

But here she was interrupted by Tom himself, who, always afraid of his uncle, and now more afraid than ever because of the peculiar look in his eyes, stammered out that he had not accused Harold, nor any one ; that he only knew the diamonds were gone and could not have gone without help.

"Do you mean those stones your mother flashed in my eyes last night ? Serves her right if she has lost them," Arthur said, without manifesting the slightest interest or concern in the matter.

But when Jerry began her story, which she told rapidly in German, he became excited at once, and his manner was that of a maniac, as he turned fiercely upon Tom, denouncing him as a coward and a liar, and threatening to turn him from the house if he dared harbor such a suspicion against Harold Hastings.

"I'll turn you all into the street," he continued, "if you are not careful, and bring Harold and Jerry here to live ; then see if I can have peace. Diamonds, indeed ! Gretchen's diamonds, too ! If they are lost, search the house, but never accuse Harold again."

At this point Arthur wandered off into German, which no one present could understand except Jerry, who stood, holding fast to his arm, her face flushed and triumphant at Harold's victory and Tom's defeat ; but as the tirade in German went on, she started suddenly forward, and with clasped hands and staring eyes stood confronting Arthur until he ceased speaking, and with a wave of his hand signified that he was through and his audience dismissed. Jerry, however, did not move, but stood regarding him with a frightened, questioning expression on her face, which was lost upon the spectators, who were too much interested in the all-absorbing topic to notice any one particularly.

Tom was the first to go away, and his example was followed by all the servants except Charles, who succeeded in getting his master back to his room and quieting him somewhat, though he kept talking to himself of diamonds, and Paris, and Gretchen, who, he said, should not be wronged.

"I am sorry this thing has happened. I have no idea that you know anything of the matter. I would as soon suspect my own son," Frank said to Harold, as he was leaving the house.

With this grain of comfort, the boy went slowly home, humiliated and cut to the heart with the indignity put upon him; while Jerry walked silently at his side until they were nearly home, when she said, suddenly:

"I b'leve I know where the diamonds are." It was a habit of Jerry's to know something about everything, and as Harold had no idea that she could know anything of the diamonds, he scarcely noticed her remark, which recurred to him years after when the diamonds came up to confront him again.

It did not take long for the whole town to know of Mrs. Tracy's loss. The papers were full of it. The neighbors talked of it constantly, and two detectives were employed to work the matter up and discover the thief, if possible. A thorough search was also made at the park house. Every servant was examined and cross-examined, and all their trunks and boxes searched; every nook and corner and room was gone through in the most systematic order, even to Arthur's apartments. This last was merely done as a matter of form, and to let the indignant servants see that no partiality was shown the officers explained to Arthur, who at first refused to let them in, but who finally opened the door himself, and bade them go where they liked.

Half hidden among the cushions of the sofa from which Arthur had risen when he let the officers in, and to which he returned again, was Jerry, her face pale to her lips and her eyes like the eyes of some hunted animal, when she saw the policemen cross the threshold.

After her return home the previous day she had been

unusually taciturn and had taken no part in the conversation relative to the missing diamonds, but just before going to bed she said to Harold :

"What will they do with the one who took the diamonds, if they find him ?"

"Send him to State's prison," Harold answered.

"And what do they do to them in State's prison ?" Jerry continued.

"Cut their hair off ; make them eat bread and water and mush, and sleep on a board, and work awful hard," was Harold's reply, given at random and without the least suspicion why the question had been asked.

Jerry said no more, but the next morning she started for the park house, which she knew was to be searched, and going to Mr. Arthur's room looked him wistfully in the face as she asked in a whisper :

"Are they found ?"

"Found ! What found ?" he said, as if all recollection of the missing jewels had passed entirely from his mind.

"Mrs. Tracy's diamonds which you gave her," was Jerry's answer.

For a moment Arthur looked perplexed and bewildered and confused, and seemed trying to recall something which would not come at his bidding.

"I don't know anything about it," he said at last. "I don't seem to think of anything, my head is so thick with all the noise there was here yesterday and the tumult this morning. Search-warrants, Charles says, and two strange men driving up so early. Who are they, Jerry ?"

"Police come to search everybody and everything. Ain't you afraid?" Jerry said.

"Afraid? No ; why should I be afraid? Why, child, how white you are, and what makes you tremble so ? You didn't take the diamonds," was Arthur's response, as he drew the little girl close to him and looked into her pallid face.

"Mr. Arthur," Jerry began, very low, as if afraid of being heard, "if I should give Maude something for her own, and she should keep it a good while, and then some day I should take it from her, when she did not know it, and hide it, and not give it up, would that be stealing?"

"Certainly. Why do you ask ?"

Jerry did not say why she asked, but put the same question to him she had put to Harold :

" If they find the one who took the diamonds will they send him to State's prison ?"

" Undoubtedly. They ought to."

" And cut off his hair ?"

She was threading Arthur's luxuriant locks caressingly, and almost pityingly, with her fingers as she asked the last question, to which he replied, shortly :

" Yes."

" And make him eat bread and water and mush?"

" Yes ; I believe so."

" And sleep on a board ?"

" Yes, or something as bad."

" And make him work awful hard until his hands are blistered?"

Now she had in hers Arthur's hands, soft and white as a woman's, and seemed to be calculating how much hard work it would take to blister hands like these.

" Yes, work till his hands drop off," Arthur said.

With a shudder, she continued :

" I could not bear it; could you?"

" Bear it? No ; I should die in a week. Why, what does ail you ? You are shaking like a leaf. What are you afraid of?"

" I don't know ; only State's prison seems so terrible, and they are looking everywhere. What if they should come in here?"

" Come in here ? Impossible, unless they break the door down," Arthur replied ; and then Jerry said to him :

" If they do, suppose you lie down and let me cover you with the afghan and cushions ?"

" But I don't want to lie down and be smothered with cushions," Arthur returned, puzzled, and wondering at the excitement of the child, who nestled close to his side, and held fast to his hand, as if she were guarding him, or expected him to guard her, while the examination went on outside, and the frightened and angry servants submitted to having their boxes and trunks examined.

At last footsteps were heard on the stairs, and the sound of strange voices, mingled with that of Frank, who was protesting against his brother's rooms being entered.

"You will lose every servant you have if we do not serve all alike," was the answer.

Then Frank knocked at his brother's door and asked admittance.

"We must do it to pacify the servants," he said, as Arthur refused, bidding him go about his business.

After a little further expostulation Arthur arose, and, unlocking the door, bade them enter and look as long as they pleased and where they pleased.

It was a mere matter of form, for not a drawer or box was disturbed ; but Jerry's breath came in gasps, and her eyes were like saucers, as she watched the men moving from place to place, and then looked timidly at Arthur to see how he was taking it. He took it very coolly, and when it was over and the men were about to leave, he bade them come again as often as they liked ; "they would always find him there ready to receive them, but the diamonds—*nix.*"

This last he said to Jerry, who, the moment they were alone and he had seated himself beside her, put her head on his arm and burst into a hysterical fit of crying.

"Why, Cherry, what is it ? Why are you crying so ?" he asked, in much concern.

"Oh, I don't know," she sobbed ; "only I was so scared all the time they were in the room. What if they had found them ! What if they should think that—that—*I* took them, and should send me to prison, and cut off my hair, and make me eat bread and water and mush, which I hate !"

Arthur looked at her a moment, and then, with a view to comfort her, said, laughingly :

"They would not send you to prison, for I would go in your stead."

"Would you ? Could you ? I mean, could somebody go for another somebody, if they wanted to ever so much ?" Jerry asked, eagerly, as she lifted her tear-stained face to Arthur's.

Without clearly understanding her meaning, and with only a wish to quiet her, Arthur answered, at random :

"Certainly. Have you never heard of people who gave their life for another's ? So, why not be a substitute, and go to prison, if necessary ?"

" Yes," Jerry answered, with a long-drawn breath, and the cloud lifted a little from her face.

After a moment, however, she asked, abruptly :

" Suppose the one who took the diamonds will not give them up, and somebody else knows where they are, ought that somebody else tell ?"

" Certainly, or be an accessory to the crime," was Arthur's reply.

Jerry did not at all know what an accessory was, but it had an awful sound to her, and she asked :

" What do they do to an accessory ? Punish her—him, I mean—just the same ?"

" Yes, of course," Arthur said, never dreaming of the wild fancy which had taken possession of her.

That one could go to prison in another's stead, and that an accessory would be punished equally with the criminal, were the two ideas distinct in her mind when she at last arose to go, saying to Arthur, as she stood in the door :

" You are sure you are not afraid to have them come here again, if they take it into their heads to do so ?"

" Not in the least ; they can search my rooms every day and welcome, if they like," was Arthur's reply.

" Well, that beats me !" Jerry said aloud to herself, with a nod for every word, as she went down the stairs and started for home, taking the Tramp House on her way. " I guess I'll go in there and think about it," she said, and entering the deserted building, she sat down upon the bench and began to wonder if she *could do it*, if worst came to worst, as it might.

" Yes, I could, for him, and I'll never tell ; I'll be that thing he said, and a substitute, too, if I can," she thought, " though I guess it would kill me. Oh, I hope I sha'n't have to do it ! I mean to say a prayer about it, anyway."

And kneeling down in the damp, dark room, Jerry prayed first, that it might never be found out, and second, that if it were she might not be called to account as an accessory, but might have the courage to be the substitute, and stand by him " forever and ever, amen !"

" I may as well begin to practice, and see if I can bear it," she thought, as she walked slowly home, where she astonished Mrs. Crawford by asking her to make some mush for dinner.

"Mush! Why, child, I thought you hated it," Mrs. Crawford exclaimed.

"I did hate it," Jerry replied, "but I want it now real bad. Make it for me, please. Harold likes it, don't you, Hally ?"

Harold did like it very much; and so the mush was made, and Jerry forced herself to swallow it in great gulps, and made up her mind that she could not stand that any way. She preferred bread and water. So, for supper she took bread and water and nothing else, and went up to bed as unhappy and nervous as a healthy, growing child well could be.

She had tried the mush, and the bread and water, and now she meant to try the shorn head, which was the hardest of all, for she had a pride in her hair, which so many had told her was beautiful.

Standing before her little glass, with the lamp beside her, she looked at it admiringly for a while, turning her head from side to side to see the bright ringlets glisten; then, with an unsteady hand she severed, one by one, the shining tresses, on which her tears fell like rain as she gathered them in a paper and put them away, wondering if the prison shears would cut closer or shorter, and wondering if it would make any difference that she was only a substitute, or at most an accessory.

It was a strange idea which had taken possession of her, and a senseless one, but it was terribly real to her, and that little shorn head represented as noble and complete a sacrifice as was ever made by older and wiser people. There was no hard board to sleep upon, and so she took the floor, with a pillow under her head and a blanket over her, wondering the while if this were not a more luxurious couch than convicts, who had stolen diamonds, were accustomed to have.

"Why, Jerry, what have you done ?" and "Oh, Jerry, how you look!" were the ejaculatory remarks which greeted her next morning, when she went down to her breakfast of bread and water, for she would take nothing else.

"Why did you do it ?" Mrs. Crawford asked, a little angry and a good deal astonished; but Jerry only answered at first with her tears, as Harold jeered at her forlorn appearance and called her a picked chicken.

"Maude's hair is short, and all the girls', and mine was always in my eyes and snarled awfully," she said at last, and this was all the excuse she would give for what she had done : while for her persisting in a bread and water diet she would give no reason for three or four days. Then she said to Harold :

"You told me that the one who stole the diamonds would have to eat bread and water and have his head shaved, and I am trying to see how it would seem—am playing that I am the man, and in prison ; but I find it very hard. I don't believe I can stand it. I am so tired and hungry, and the blackberry pie we had for dinner did look so good !"

She put her hands to her head, and looked so white and faint that Harold was alarmed, and took her at once to his grandmother, who, scarcely less frightened than himself, made her lie down, and brought her a piece of toast and a cup of milk, which revived her a little. But the strain upon her nerves for the last few days, and the fasting on bread and water proved too much for the child, who, for a week or more lay up in her little room, burning with fever, and talking at intervals, of diamonds, and State's prison, and accessories, and substitutes.

Every day Arthur came and sat for an hour by her bed, and held her hot hands in his, and listened to her talk, and wondered at her shorn head, which he did not like. As he always talked to her in German, while she answered in the same tongue, no one knew what they said to each other, though Harold, who understood a few German words, knew that she was talking of the diamonds, and the prison, and the substitute.

"I shall *never* tell !" she said to Arthur : "and I shall go ! I can bear it better than you. It is not that which makes my head ache so. It's—oh, Mr. Arthur, I thought you so good, and I am so sorry about the diamonds—Mrs. Tracy was so proud of them. Can't you contrive to get them back to her ? I could, if you would let me. I am thinking all the time how to do it, and never let her know, and the back of my head aches so when I think."

Arthur could not guess what she meant, except that the lost diamonds troubled her, and that she wished Mrs. Tracy to have them. Occasionally his brows would knit

9

together, and he seemed trying to recall something which perplexed him, and which her words had evidently suggested to his mind.

"Cherry," he said to her one day when he came as usual, and her first eager question was, "Have they found them?" "Cherry, try and understand me. Do you know who took the diamonds?"

Instantly into Jerry's eyes there came a scared look, but she answered, unhesitatingly:

"Yes, don't you?"

"No," was the prompt reply; "though it seems to me I did know, but there has been so much talk about them, and you are so sick, that everything has gone from my head, and the bees are stinging me frightfully. Where are the diamonds?"

But by this time Jerry was in the prison, sleeping on a board and eating bread and mush, and Arthur failed to get any satisfaction from her. Indeed, they were two crazy ones talking together, with little or no meaning in what they said. Only this Arthur gathered—that Jerry would be happy if Mrs. Tracy had her diamond's again and did not know how they came to her. When this dawned upon him he laughed aloud, and kissing her hot cheeks, said to her:

"I see; I know, and I'll do it. Wait till I come again."

It was ten o'clock in the morning when he left Mrs. Crawford's house; there was a train which passed the station at half past ten, bound for New York, and without returning to the park, Arthur took the train, sending word to his brother not to expect him home until the next day, and not to be alarmed on his account, as he was going to New York and would take care of himself,

Why he had gone Frank could not guess, and he waited in much anxiety for his return. It was evening when he came home seeming perfectly composed and well, but giving no reason for his sudden journey to the city. His first inquiry was for Jerry, and his second, if anything had been heard of the diamonds. On being answered in the negative, he remarked:

"Those rascally detectives are bunglers, and often-times would rather let the culprit escape than catch him. I doubt if you ever see the jewels again. But no matter; it will all come right. Tell your wife not to fret."

The next morning when Mrs. Tracy went to her room after breakfast she was astonished to find upon her dressing bureau a velvet box with Tiffany's name upon it, and inside an exquisite set of diamonds ; not as fine as those she had lost, or quite as large, but white, and clear, and sparkling as she took them in her hand with a cry of delight, and ran to her husband. Both knew from whom they came, and both went at once to Arthur, who, to his sister-in-law's profuse expressions of gratitude, replied indifferently:

"Don't bother me with thanks; it worries me. I bought them to please the little girl, who talks about them all the time. She will get well now. I am going to tell her."

Jerry was better and perfectly sane, and when she awoke that morning her first rational question had been for Arthur, and her second for the diamonds; were they found, and if not, were they still looking for them.

"No, they have not found them," Harold had said, "and the officers are still hunting for the thief, while the papers are full of the reward offered to any one who will return them. Five hundred dollars now, for Mr. Arthur has added two hundred to the first sum. He has quite waked up to the matter. You know he seemed very indifferent at first."

"Mr. Arthur offered two hundred more !" Jerry exclaimed. "Well, that beats me ! He must be crazy."

"Of course he is. He don't know what he does or says half the time, and especially since you have been sick," Harold said.

"Sick !" Jerry repeated, quickly. "Have I been sick, and is that why I am in bed so late ? I thought you had come in to wake me up, and I was glad, for I have had horrid dreams."

Harold told her how long she had been sick.

"And you've been crazy, too, as a loon," he continued, "and talked the queerest things about State's prison, and hard boards, and bread and water, and accessories, and substitutes, and so on. Mr. Arthur was here every day, and sometimes twice a day, but he did not come yesterday

at all. There, hark ! I do believe he is coming now.
Don't you know who is said to be near when you are talking about him ?"

And, with a laugh, Harold left the room just as Arthur
entered it.

"Well, Cherry," he said, "Mrs. Crawford tells me the
bees are out of your head this morning, and I am glad. I
have some good news for you. Mrs. Tracy has some diamonds, and is the happiest woman in town."

Jerry had not noticed his exact words, and only understood that Mrs. Tracy had found her diamonds.

"Oh Mr. Arthur, I am so glad !" she cried ; and springing up in bed, she threw both arms around his neck and
held him fast, while she sobbed hysterically.

"There, there, child ! Cherry, let go. You throttle me.
You are pulling my neck-tie all askew, and my head spins
like a top," Arthur said, as he unclasped the clinging arms
and put the little girl back upon her pillow, where she lay
for a moment, pale and exhausted, with the light of a great
joy shining in her eyes.

"Did she know where they came from ? How did you
manage it ? Are you sure she did not suspect ?" she
asked.

"I put them on her dressing-bureau while she was at
breakfast," he replied, "and when she came up there they
were—large solitaire ear-rings and a bar with five stones,
not quite as large or as fine as the ones she lost, but the
best I could find at Tiffany's. Why, Jerry, what is the
matter ? You do not look glad a bit. I thought you wanted
me to give them to her surreptitiously, and I did," he added,
as the expression of Jerry's face changed to one of dismay
and disappointment.

"I did—I do," she said ; "but I meant her very own—
the ones you gave her."

For a moment Arthur sat looking at her with a perplexed and troubled expression, as if wondering what she
could mean, and why he had so utterly failed to please her ;
then he said, slowly :

"The ones I gave her ? What do you mean ? You
make my head swim trying to remember, and the bumble-
bees are black-faced, instead of white, and stinging me
dreadfully. I wish you would say nothing more of the dia-

monds. It worries me, and makes me feel as if I were in a nightmare, and I know nothing of them."

Raising herself on her elbow and pointing her finger toward him in a half beseeching, half threatening way, Jerry said:

"As true as you live and breathe, and hope not to be hung and choked to death, don't you know where they are?"

This was the oath which Jerry's companions were in the habit of administering to each other in matters of doubt, and she now put it to Arthur as the strongest she knew.

"Of course not," he answered, with a little irritation in his tone. "What ails you Cherry? Are you crazy, like myself? Struggle against it. Don't let the bees get into your brain and swarm and buzz until you forget everything which you ought to remember; and do things you ought not to do. It is terrible to be crazy and half conscious of it all the time—conscious that no one believes what you say or holds you responsible for what you do."

"Don't they?" Jerry asked, eagerly, for she knew the meaning of the word "responsible." "If a crazy man or woman took the diamonds, and then forgot, and did not tell, and it was ever found out, wouldn't they be punished?"

"Certainly not," was the re-assuring reply. "Don't you know how many murders are committed and the murderer is not hung, because they say he is crazy?"

In a moment the cloud lifted from Jerry's face, which grew so bright that Arthur noticed the change, and said to her:

"You are better now, I see, and I must go before I undo it all. Good-by, and never say diamonds to me again; it gets me all in a—in a—well, a French pickle—mixed, you know."

He kissed her, and, promising to take her for a drive as soon as she was able, went out and left her alone, wondering why it was that his having given the diamonds to his sister-in-law had failed in its effect upon her, and upon himself, too.

For a long time after he was gone Jerry lay thinking with her eyes closed, so that if Harold or her grandmother came in they would think her asleep. Mr. Arthur was

certainly crazy at times—very crazy. She could swear to
that, and so could many others.   And if a crazy man was
not responsible for his acts, then he was not, and the law
would not touch him; but with regard to the accessory,
she was not sure.   If that individual were not crazy, why,
then he or she might be punished ; and as the taste she
had had of bread and water, and hard boards in the shape
of the floor, was not very satisfactory, and as Mrs. Tracy had
other diamonds in the place of the lost ones, she finally
determined to keep her own counsel and never tell what
she had heard Arthur say that morning when the theft
was discovered and he had talked so fast in German to her
and to himself.   If she had known just where the diamonds were she might have managed to return them to
their owner.   But she did not, and her better course was
to keep quiet, hoping that in time Mr. Arthur himself
would remember and make restitution ; for that he had forgotten and was sincere in saying that he knew nothing of
them, she was certain, and her faith in him, which for a
little time had been shaken, was restored.

With this load lifted from her mind Jerry's recovery
was rapid, and when the autumnal suns were just beginning to tinge the woodbine on the Tramp House and the
maples in the park woods with scarlet she took her accustomed seat in Arthur's room and commenced her lessons
again with Maude, who had missed her sadly, and who
would have gone to see her every day during her sickness,
if her mother had permitted it.

CHAPTER XXIII.

ARTHUR'S LETTER.

TWO weeks had passed since Jerry's return to her lessons,
and people had ceased to talk of the missing diamonds, although the offered reward of $500 was still in the
weekly papers, and a detective still had the matter in
charge, without, however, achieving the slightest success.
No one had been suspected, and the thief, whoever he was,

must have been an expert, and managed the affair with the
most consummate skill. Now that she had another set,
Mrs. Tracy was content, and peace and quiet reigned in
the household, except so far as Arthur was concerned. He
was restless and nervous, and given to fits of abstraction,
which sometimes made him forget the two little girls, one
of whom watched him narrowly ; and once, when they were
alone and he seemed unusually absorbed in thought, she
asked him if he were trying to think of something.

"Yes," he said, looking up quickly and eagerly ; "that
is it. I am trying to remember something which, it seems
to me, I ought to remember ; but I cannot, and the more I
try, the farther it gets from me. Do you know what it
is ?"

Jerry hesitated a moment, and then she asked:

"Is it the diamonds ?"

"Diamonds ! No. What diamonds ? Didn't I tell
you never to say diamonds to me again ? I am tired of it,"
he said ; and in his eyes there was a gleam which Jerry had
never seen there before when they rested upon her. It
made her afraid, and she answered, meekly :

"Then I cannot help you to remember."

"Of course not. No one can," Arthur replied, in a
softened tone. "It is something long ago, and has to do
with Gretchen."

Then suddenly brightening, as if that name had been
the key to unlock his misty brain, he added:

"I have it; I know; it has come to me at last !
Gretchen always sets me right. I wrote her a letter long
ago—a year, it seems to me—and it has never been posted.
Strange that I should forget that ; but something came up
—I can't tell what—and drove it from my mind."

As he talked he was opening and looking in the drawer
which Jerry had never seen but once before, and that, when
he took from it the letter in German, a paragraph of which
he had bidden her read.

"Here it is !" he said. joyfully, as he took out a sealed
envelope and held it up to Jerry. "This is the letter
which you must post at once."

He gave her the letter, which she took with a beating
heart and a sense of shame and regret as she remembered
her pledge to Mr. Frank Tracy. She had promised to

take him any letter which Mr. Arthur might intrust to
her care, and if she took this one she must keep her
word.

"Oh, I can't do it—I can't! It would be mean to Mr.
Arthur," she thought; and returning him the letter, she
said : "Please post it yourself; then you will be sure, and
I might lose it, or forget. I am careless sometimes. Don't
ask me to take it."

She was pleading with all her might; but Arthur paid
no heed, and only laughed at her fears.

"I know you will not forget, and I'd rather trust you
than Charles. Surely, you will not refuse to do so small a
favor for me ?"

"No," she said, at last, as she put the letter in her
pocket, with the thought that she would show it to Mr.
Frank as she had promised but would not let him keep it.

She found him in the room, where the dead woman
had lain in her coffin, and where he often sat alone thinking of the day when the inquest was held, and when he
took his first step in the downward road, which had lead
him so far that now it seemed impossible to turn back.

"If I had never secreted the photograph, or the book
with the handwriting, everything would have been so different, and I should have been free," he was thinking,
when Jerry knocked timidly at the door, rousing him from
his reverie, and making him start with a nameless fear
which was always haunting him.

"Oh, Jerry, it is you," he said, as the little girl crossed
the threshold, and shutting the door, stood with her back
against it, and her hands behind her. "What is it ?" he
asked, as he saw her hesitating.

With a quick, jerky movement of the head, which set in
motion the little rings of hair, now growing so fast, and
brought his brother to his mind, Jerry replied :

"I came to tell you that Mr. Arthur has written the
letter."

"What letter ?" Frank asked, for the moment forgetting the conversation he had held with the child in the
Tramp House.

"The one I promised to bring you—the one to Germany," was Jerry's answer.

And then Frank remembered what, in the excitement of the diamond theft, had passed from his mind.

"Yes, yes, I know ; give it to me," he said, advancing rapidly toward her, and putting out his hand. "When did he write it? Let me see it, please."

Rather reluctantly Jerry handed him the bulky letter, the direction of which covered nearly the whole of one side of the envelope.

Very nervously Frank scanned the address, which might as well have been in the Hindoo language for any idea it conveyed to him.

"To whom is it directed? I cannot read German," he said.

"I don't know," Jerry replied. "I have not looked at it, and would rather not."

"Why, what a little prude you are;" and Frank laughed, uneasily. "What possible harm is there in reading an address? The postmaster has to do it, and any one who took it to the office would do it if he could."

This sounded reasonable enough, and standing beside him, Jerry read the address in German first, then, as he said to her : "I don't understand that lingo, put it into English," she read again :

"To Marguerite Heinrich, if living, and if dead to any of her friends ; or, to the Postmaster at Wiesbaden, Germany. If not delivered within two months, return to Arthur Tracy, Tracy Park, Shannondale, Mass., U. S. A."

"Marguerite—Marguerite Heinrich !" Frank repeated. "That is not Gretchen. The letter is not to her."

"I guess it is," Jerry replied. "He told me once that Gretchen was a pet name for Marguerite."

"Yes," Frank returned, with a sigh of disappointment, while to himself he said "It is not Marguerite Tracy and that makes me less a scoundrel than I should otherwise have been." Then turning to Jerry, as he put the letter in his pocket, he said, "thank you for bringing this to me. I had forgotten all about it."

"Mr. Tracy, you mustn't keep the letter. It is not yours—No harm will be done if it goes. Mr. Arthur will never let Maude be wronged. Give it to me, please." Jerry cried in a tone and manner she might have borrowed

9*

from Arthur himself, it was so like him when on his dignity.

And Frank felt it, and knew that he had more than a child to deal with, and must use duplicity if he would succeed. So he said to her quietly and naturally:

"Why, how excited you are! Do you think I intend to keep the letter? It is as safe with me as with you. It is true that when I talked with you in the Tramp House I thought it must not be sent, but I have changed my mind, and do not care. I am going to the office, and will take it myself. John is saddling my horse now, and if I hurry I shall be in time for the Western mail. Good-by, and do not look so worried. Do you take me for a villain?"

He was leaving the room as he talked, and before he had finished he was in the hall and near the outer door, leaving Jerry stupefied, and perplexed, and only half re-assured.

"If I had not sold myself to Satan before, I have now, for sure; and still I did not actually tell her that I would post it, though it amounted to that," Frank thought, as he galloped through the park toward the highway which led to the town.

Once he took the letter from his pocket and examined it again, wishing that he knew its contents.

"If I could read German, I believe I am bad enough to open it; but I can't, and I dare not take it to any one who can," he said, as he put it again in his pocket, half resolving to post it and take the chances of its ever reaching Gretchen's friends, or any one who had known her. "I'll see how I feel when I get inside," he thought, as he dismounted from his horse before the door of the post-office.

The mail was just in, and the little room was full of people waiting for it to be distributed; and Frank waited with them, leaning against the wall, with his head bent down, and beating his boot with his riding-whip.

"I must decide soon," he thought, when a voice not far from him caught his ear, and glancing from under his hat, he saw Peterkin coming in, portly and pompous, and with him a dapper little man, who, in the days of the 'Liza Ann, had been a driver for the boat, but who now, like his former employer, was a millionaire, and wore a

thousand-dollar diamond ring. To him Peterkin was saying :

"There, that's him—that's Frank Tracy, the biggest
swell in town—lives in that handsome place I was telling
you about."

Strange that words like these from a man like old
Peterkin should have inflated Frank's pride ; but he was
weak in many points, and though he detested Peterkin, it
gratified him to be pointed out to strangers as a swell who
lived in a fine house, and with the puff of vanity came the
reflection that, as Frank Tracy of some other place than
Tracy Park, and a poor man, he would not be one whom
strangers cared to see, and Jerry's chance was lost again.

"Here is your mail. Mr. Tracy," the postmistress said ;
and stepping forward, Frank took his letters from her, just
as Peterkin slapped him on the shoulder, and, with a
familiarity which made Frank want to knock him down,
called out :

"Hallo, Tracy ! Just the feller I wanted to see. Let
me introduce you to Mr. Bijah Jones, from Pennsylvany ;
use to drive hosses for me in the days I ain't ashamed of,
by a long shot. He's bought him a place out from Phila-
delphy, and wants to lay it out *a la—a la*—dumbed if I
know the word, but like them old chaps' gardens in
Europe, and I told him of Tracy Park, which beats everything holler in this part of the country. Will you let us go
over it and take a survey ?"

"Certainly ; go where you like," Frank said, struggling
to reach the door ; but Peterkin button-holed him and held
him fast, while he continued:

"I say, Tracy, heard anything from them diamonds ?"

"Nothing," was the reply.

"Didn't hunt in the right quarter," Peterkin continued ; "leastwise didn't foller it up, or you'd a found 'em
without so much advertisin'."

"What do you mean ?" Frank asked.

"Oh, nothin'," Peterkin replied ; "only them diamonds
never went off without hands, and them hands ain't a
thousand miles from the park."

"Perhaps not," Frank answered mechanically, more
intent upon getting away than upon what Peterkin was
saying.

He longed to be in the open air, and as he mounted his horse, he said, as if speaking to some one near him:

"Well, old fellow, I've done it again, and sunk myself still lower. You are bound to get me now some day, unless I have a death-bed repentance and confess everything. The thief was forgiven at the last hour, why not I?"

Frank could have sworn that he heard a chuckle in his ear as he rode on, fast and far, until his horse was tired and he was tired, too. Then he began to retrace his steps, so slowly that it was dark when he reached the village and turned down the road which led by the gate through which the woman had passed to her death on the night of the storm.

As he drew near the gate, it seemed to him that there was something on the post nearest the fence which had not been there in the afternoon when he rode by—something dark and peculiar in shape, and motionless as a stone. He was not by nature a coward, and once he had no belief in ghosts or supernatural appearances, but now he did not know what he believed, and this object, whose outline, seen against the western sky where a dim light was lingering, seemed almost like that of a human form, made his heart beat faster than its wont, and he involuntarily checked his horse, just as a clear, shrill voice called out:

"Mr. Tracy, is that you? I have waited so long, and I'm so cold sitting here. Did you post the letter?"

It was Jerry, who, after he had left her in his office, had been seized with an indefinable terror lest he might not post the letter after all. It seemed wrong to doubt him, and she did not really think that she did doubt him; still she should feel happier if she knew, and after supper was over she started along the grassy road until she reached the gate. Here she waited a long time, and then, as Mr. Tracy did not appear, she walked up and down the lane until the sun was down and the ground began to feel so damp and cold that she finally climbed up to the top of the gate-post, which was very broad, and where, on her way to town, she had frequently sat for a while. It was very cold and tiresome waiting there, and she was beginning to get impatient and to wonder if it could be possible that he had gone home by some other road, when she heard the sound of horses' hoofs and felt sure he was coming.

"Why, Jerry, how you frightened me!" Frank said, as he reined his horse close up to her. "Jump down and get up behind me. I will take you home."

She obeyed, and with the agility of a little cat got down from the gate-post and on to the horse's back, putting both arms around Frank's waist to keep herself steady, for the big horse took long steps, and she felt a little afraid.

"Did you post the letter?" she asked again, as they left the gate behind them and struck into the lane.

To lie now was easy enough, and Frank replied without hesitation:

"Of course. Did you think I would forget it?"

"No," Jerry answered. "I knew you would not. I only wanted to be sure, because he trusted it to me, and not to have sent it would have been mean, and a sneak, and a lie, and a steal. Don't you think so?"

She emphasized the "steal," and the "lie," and the "sneak," and the "mean," with a kick which made the horse jump a little and quicken his steps.

"Yes," Frank assented; it would be all she affirmed, and more, too, and the man who could do such a thing was wholly unworthy the respect of any one, and ought to be punished to the full extent of the law.

"That's so," Jerry said, with another emphatic kick and a slight tightening of her arms around the conscience-stricken man, who wondered if he should ever reach the cottage and be free from the clasp of those arms, which seemed to him like bands of fire burning to his soul. "I'd never speak to him again," Jerry continued "and Mr. Arthur wouldn't either. He is so right-up and hates a trick. I don't believe, either, that any harm will come to Maude from that letter, as you said. Is there does, and Mr. Arthur can fix it, he will, I know, for I shall ask him, and he once told me he would do anything for me, because I look as he thinks Gretchen must have looked when she was a little girl like me."

They had reached the cottage by this time, where they found Harold in the yard looking up and down the lane for Jerry, whose protracted absence at that hour had caused them some anxiety, even though they were accustomed to her long rambles by herself and frequent absences from home.

"You see, I have picked up your little girl and brought her home. Jump down, Jerry, and good-night to you," Mr. Tracy said as Harold came up to them.

She was on the ground in an instant, and he was soon galloping toward home, saying to himself :

"I don't believe I can even have a death-bed repentance. I have told too many lies for that, and worse than all, must go on lying to the end. I have sold my soul, for a life of luxury, which after all is very pleasant," he continued, as he drew near the house, which was brilliantly lighted up, while through the long windows of the dining-room he could see the table, with its silver and glass and flowers, and the cheerful blaze upon the hearth. There was company staying in the house, Mr. and Mrs. Raymond from Kentucky, father and mother to Fred ; and Mr. and Mrs. St. Claire, and Grace Atherton, and Squire Harrington had been invited to dinner and were already in the dining-room when Frank entered it after a hasty toilet.

He had been out in the country and ridden further than he intended, he said, by way of apology, as he greeted his guests, and then took Mrs. Raymond in to dinner. Dolly was very fine that evening in claret velvet, with her new diamonds, which were greatly admired, Grace Atherton declaring that she liked them quite as well as the stolen ones, whose setting was rather *passee.*

"That is just why I prized them so much; it made them look like heir-looms, and as if one had always had a family," Dolly said.

Grace Atherton shrugged her still plump shoulders just a little, and thought of the first call she ever made upon Dolly, when the lady entertained her in her working-apron.

Dolly did not look now as if she had ever seen a working-apron, and was very bright and talkative, and entertaining, and all the more so because of her husband's silence. He was given to moods, and sometimes aggravated his wife to desperation when he left all the conversation to her.

"Do talk," she would say to him when they were

alone. "Do talk to people and not sit so glum, with that great wrinkle between your eyes as if you were mad at something; and do laugh, too, when any body tells any thing worth laughing at, and not leave it all to me. Why, I actually giggle at times until I feel like a fool, while you never smile or act as if you heard a word. Look at me occasionally, and when I elevate my eye-brows—*so*—brace up and say something, if it isn't so cunning."

This *elevating of the eyebrows* and *bracing up* were matters of frequent occurrence, as Frank grew more and more silent and abstracted, and now, after he had sat through a very funny story told by Mr. St. Claire, and had not even smiled, or given any sign that he heard it, he suddenly caught Dolly's eye, and saw that both eyebrows, and nose, and chin were up as marks of unusual disapprobation, for how could she guess of what he was thinking as he sat with his head bent down, and his eyes seemingly half shut. But they came open wide enough, and his head was high enough when he saw Dolly's frown; and turning to Mrs. Raymond, he began to talk rapidly and at random. She had just returned from Germany, where she had left her daughter, Marion, in school, and Frank asked her of the country, and if she had visited Wiesbaden, and had there met or heard of any one by the name of Marguerite Heinrich.

Mrs. Raymond had spent some months in Wiesbaden, for it was there her daughter was at school, and she was very enthusiastic in her praises of the beautiful town. But she had never seen or heard of Marguerite Heinrich, or of any one by the name of Heinrich.

"Marguerite Heinrich?" Dolly repeated. "Who in the world is she—and where did you know her?"

"I never did know her. I have only heard of her," Frank replied, again lapsing into a silence from which he did not rouse again.

He was thinking of the letter and of the lies he had told since his deception began, and how sure it was that he had sinned beyond forgiveness. When he was a boy he had oftened listened, with the blood curdling in his veins, to a story his grandmother told with sundry embellishments, of a man who sold his soul to the devil in consideration that for a certain number of years he was to have every

pleasure the world could give. It had been very pleasant
listening to the recital of the fine things the man enjoyed,
for Satan kept his promise well; but the boy's hair had
stood on end as the story neared its close, and he heard
how, when the probation was ended, the devil came for his
victim down the wide-mouthed chimney, scattering bricks
and fire-brands over the floor, as he carried the trembling
soul out into the blackness of the stormy night.

Strangely enough this story came back to him now,
and notwithstanding the horror of the thing he
laughed aloud as he glanced up at the tall oak mantel,
wondering if it would be that way he would one day go
with his master, and seeing in fancy Dolly's dismay when
the tea-cups, and saucers, and vases, and plaques, came
tumbling to the floor as he disappeared from sight in a blue
flame, which smelled of brimstone.

It was a loud, unnatural laugh, but fortunately for him
it came just as Grace Atherton had set the guests in a roar
with what she was saying of Peterkin's struggle to enter
society, and so it passed unnoticed by most of them. But
that night in the privacy of his room, where Dolly delivered most of her lectures, she again upbraided him with
his taciturnity, telling him that he never laughed but once,
and then it sounded more like a groan than a laugh.

"You have hit the nail on the head this time, for it
was a groan," Frank said, as he plunged into bed; and
Dolly, as she undressed herself deliberately, and put her
diamonds carefully away, little dreamed what was passing
in the mind of the man, who, all through the long hours of
the night, lay awake, seldom stirring lest he should disturb
her, but repeating over and over to himself the words:

"Lost forever and ever, but if Maude is happy I can
bear it."

CHAPTER XXIV.

TEN YEARS LATER.

JERRIE spelled her name with an *ie* now, instead of a *y*. She was twenty years old ; she had been a student at Vassar for four years, together with Nina St. Claire and Ann Eliza Peterkin, and was with them to be graduated in June. In her childhood, when we knew her as little Jerry, she was very small, but at the age of twelve she had suddenly shot up like an arrow, and now, at twenty, her school companions called her the Princess, she was so tall and straight, and graceful in every movement, with that sweet graciousness of manner which won all hearts and made her a general favorite. But whether she spelled her name with an *ie* or a *y*, and stood five feet six or four feet five, she was the same Jerry who had defended Harold against Tom Tracy, and been ready to go to prison, if need be, for Mr. Arthur. Frank, unselfish, loving and true, she had been as a child, and she was the same now that she had grown to womanhood. Nothing could spoil her, not even the adulation of her friends or the looking-glass which told her she was beautiful, just as Nina St. Claire told her every day.

"Yes ; I am not blind, and I know that I am rather good-looking," she said to Nina one morning when the latter was praising her hair which was soft and curly and retained the golden color seldom seen except in childhood. "At all events, I am not plain and I am glad, for, as a rule, people like pretty things better than ugly ones ; but I am not an idiot to think that looks are everything, and I don't believe I am very vain. I used to be though, when a child, and I remember admiring the shadow of my curls in the sunlight, but Harold gave me so many lectures upon vanity that I should not do credit to his teachings were I now to be proud of what I did not do myself."

"But Harold thinks you are beautiful," Nina replied.

"He does ? I did not know that. When did he say so ?" Jerrie asked, with kindling eyes, and a quick, side-

ways turn of her head, of which she had a habit when
startled by some sudden emotion.

"He said so last vacation, when we were home, and I
had that little musicale, and you played and sang so
divinely, and wore that dress of baby-blue which Mr.
Arthur gave you, with the blush roses in your belt," Nina
said. "I was so proud of you, and so was mamma and
Mrs. Atherton. You remember there were some New
Yorkers there who were visiting Mrs. Grace, and I was
glad for them to know that we had some talent and some
beauty, too, in the country; and Harold was proud, too.
I don't think he took his eyes off you from the time you
sat down to the piano until you left it, and when I said to
him, 'Doesn't she sing like an angel, and isn't she lovely?'
he replied : 'I think my sister Jerrie has the loveliest face
I ever saw, and that blue dress is very becoming to her.'"

"Wasn't that rather a stiff speech to make about his
sister?" Jerrie said, with a slight emphasis upon the last
word, as she walked away, leaving Nina to wonder if she
were displeased,

Evidently not, for a few minutes later she heard her
whistling softly the air "He promised to buy me a knot
of blue ribbon to tie up my bonny brown hair," and could
she have looked into Jerrie's room she would have seen her
standing before the mirror examining the face which Harold had said was the loveliest he had ever seen. Others
had said the same. Billy Peterkin, and Tom Tracy, and
Dick St. Claire, and even Fred Raymond, from Kentucky,
who was devoted to Nina. But Jerrie cared little for the
compliments of either Fred or Dick, while those of Tom
she scorned, and those of Billy she ridiculed. One word
of commendation from Harold was worth more to her than
the praises of the whole world besides. But Harold had
always been chary of his commendations, and was rather
more given to reproof than praise, which did not altogether suit the young lady.

As Jerrie had grown older, and merged from childhood
into womanhood, a change had come over both the girl
and boy, a change which Jerrie discovered first, awaking
suddenly one day to find that the brother and sister delu-
sion was ended, and that Harold stood to her in an entirely
new relation. Just when the change commenced she could

not tell.· She only knew that it had come, and that she
was not quite so happy as she had been when she called
Harold her brother and lavished upon him all the fondness of a loving sister.

Though quite as affectionate and unselfish as Jerrie,
Harold was not demonstrative, while a natural shyness and
depreciation of himself made him afraid to tell in words
just what or how much he did feel. He would rather
show it by acts ; and never was brother tenderer or kinder
to a sister than he was to Jerrie, whose changed mood he
could not understand. And so there gradually arose
between them a little cloud, which both felt and neither
could define. Arthur had kept his promise well with
regard to Jerrie, who had passed from him to Vassar, and
he would have kept it with Harold, if the latter had permitted it. But the boy's pride and independence had
asserted themselves at last. He had accepted the course
at Andover, and one year at Harvard, on condition that he
should be allowed to pay Arthur all he had received as
soon as he was able to do it. As he entered Harvard in
advance he was a junior when he decided to care for himself, and after that he struggled on, working at whatever
he could find during the summer vacations, and teaching
school for months at a time, so that his college course was
longer than usual. But it was over at last, and he was
graduated with the highest honors of his class, exciting
thunders of applause from the multitude who listened to
his valedictory and some of whom said to each other:

"The young man has a future before him. Such elo-
quence as that could move the world, and rouse or quiet
the wildest mob that ever surged through the streets of
mad Paris."

Jerrie was there, and saw and heard. And when Harold's speech was over, and the building was shaking with
applause, and flowers were falling around him like rain,
she, too, stood up and cheered so loudly that a Boston
lady, who sat in front of her, and who thought any out-
ward show of feeling vulgar and ill-bred, turned and looked
at her wonderingly and reprovingly. But in her excitement, Jerrie did not see the disapprobation in the cold,
proud eyes. She saw only what she mistook for inquiry,
and answered, eagerly :

" That's Harold—that's my brother ! Oh, I am so proud of him !"

And leaning forward so that a curl of her hair touched the Boston woman's bonnet, she threw the bunch of pond lilies, which she had herself gathered that day on the river at home before the sun was up, and while the white petals were still folded in sleep. For Jerrie had come down on the early train to see Harold graduated, and Maude had found her in the crowd and sat beside her, almost as pleased and happy as she was to see Harold thus acquit himself.

Maude's roses which she held in her hand had been bought at a florist's in Boston at a fabulous price, for they were the choicest and rarest in market, and Harold had seen both the roses and the lilies long before they fell at his feet. It was a fancy, perhaps, but it seemed to him that a sweet perfume from the latter reached him, with the brightness of Jerrie's eyes. He knew just where the lilies came from, for he had often waded out to the green bed when the water was low to get them for Jerrie ; and all the time he was speaking there was in his heart a thought of the old home, and the woods, and the river, and the tall tree on the bank, with the bench beneath, and on it the girl, whose upturned, eager face he saw above the sea of heads confronting him.

Jerrie's approval was worth more to the young man than that of all the rest ; for he knew that, though she would be very lenient toward him, she was a keen and discriminating critic, and would detect a weakness which many an older person might fail to see. But she was satisfied—he was sure of that ; and if there had been in his mind any doubt, it would have been swept away when, after the exercises were over, and he stood receiving the congratulations of his friends, she worked her way through the crowd and threw her arms around his neck, kissing him fondly, and bursting into tears as she told him how proud she was of him.

The eyes of half his classmates were upon him, and though Harold felt a thrill of keen delight at the touch of Jerrie's lips, he would a little rather she had waited until they were alone.

" There, there, Jerrie that will do !" he whispered, as he unclasped her arms and put her gently from him, though he still held her hand. "Don't you see they are all looking at us."

With a sudden jerk Jerrie withdrew her hand from his and stepped back into the crowd, her heart beating wildly and her cheeks burning with shame, as she realized what she had done and how it must have mortified Harold.

Maude was speaking to him now—Maude, with her bright black eyes and brilliant color. But she was neither crying nor strangling him with kisses. She was shaking hands with him very decorously, and telling him how pleased and glad she was. And in his hand he held her roses, which he occasionally smelled as he listened, and smiled upon her with that peculiar smile which made him so attractive. But the lilies were nowhere to be seen ; and when, an hour later, all the baskets and bouquets bearing his name were piled together, they were not there.

"He has thrown them away! He did not care for them at all ; and I might as well have staid in bed as to have gotten up at four o'clock and risked my neck to get them. He likes Maude better than he does me," Jerrie thought, with a swelling heart, and through the journey home—for they returned that night—she was very quiet and taciturn, letting Maude do the talking, and saying, when asked why she was so still, that her head was aching, and that she was too tired and sleepy to talk.

That was the last time for years that Jerrie put her arms around Harold's neck, or touched her lips to his ; for it had come to her like a blow how much he was to her, and how little she was to him.

"He likes me well enough, but he loves Maude," she thought ; and although of all her girl friends, not even excepting Nina St. Claire, Maude was the nearest and dearest, she was half-glad when, a week or two later, Maude said good-by to her, and with her mother went to Europe, where she remained for more than a year and a half.

During her absence the two girls corresponded regularly and Jerrie never failed to write whatever she thought would please her friend to hear of Harold ; and when at last Maude returned, and wrote to Jerrie, who was then at Vassar, of failing health, and wakeful nights, and her longing for the time when Jerrie would come home, and read to her, or recite bits of poetry, as she had been wont to do, Jerrie trampled every jealous, selfish thought under her feet, and in her letters to Harold urged him to see Maude as often as possible, and read to her whenever she wished him to do so.

"You have such a splendid voice, and read so well," she wrote, "that it will rest her just to listen to you, and will keep her from being so lonely, so offer your services if she does not ask for them—that's a good boy."

Then, as she remembered how weak Maude was, mentally, she said to herself :

"He will never be happy with her as she is now. A girl who cannot do a sum in simple fractions, and who, when abroad, thought only of Rome as a good place in which to buy sashes and ribbons, and who asked me in a letter to tell her who all those Cæsars were, and what the Forum was for, is not the wife for a man like Harold, and however much he might love her at first he would be sure to tire of her after a while, unless he can bring her up. Possibly he can."

Resuming her pen, she wrote :

"Don't give her all sentimental poetry and love trash, but something solid—something historical, which she can remember and talk about with you."

In his third letter to Jerrie, after the receipt of her instructions, Harold wrote as follows :

"I have offered my services as reader, and tried the solid on Maude as you advised—have read her fifty pages of Grote's history of Greece ; but when I got as far as Homeric Theogony, she looked piteously at me, while with Hesiod and Orpheus she was hopelessly bewildered, and by the time I reached the extra Hellenic religion she was fast asleep ! I do not believe her mind is strong enough to grapple with those old Greek chaps ; at all events they worry her, and tire her more than they rest her. So I have abandoned the gods and come down to common people, and am reading to her Tennyson's poems. Have read the May Queen four times, until I do believe she knows it by heart. She has a great liking for the last portion of it, especially the lines :

> "'I shall not forget you, mother :
> I shall hear you when you pass,
> With your feet above my head
> In the long and pleasant grass.'"

"I saw her cry one day when I read that to her. Poor little Maude! She is very frail, but no one seems to think her in danger, she has so brilliant a color, and always seems so bright."

Jerrie read this letter two or three times, and each time with an increased sense of comfort. No man who really loved a girl could speak of her mental weakness to another as Harold had spoken of Maude's to her, and it might be after all that he merely thought of her as a friend, whom he had always known. So the cloud was lifted in part, and she only felt a great anxiety for Maude's health, which, as the spring advanced, grew stronger, so that it was almost certain that she would come to Vassar in the summer and see her friend graduated.

Such was the state of affairs when Nina repeated to Jerrie what Harold had said to her at the musicale the previous winter. All day long there was a note of gladness in Jerrie's heart which manifested itself in snatches of song, and low, warbling, whistled notes, which sounded more as if they came from a canary's than from a human throat.

"Whistling Jerrie," the girls sometimes called her, but she rather liked the name, and whistled on whenever she felt like it.

And it was a very joyous, happy song she trilled, as she thought of Harold's compliment, and of the approaching time when he would, of course, be there to see and hear, and as, in his valedictory of two years before there had been in every line a thought of her, so in her essay, which was peculiarly German in its method and handling, thoughts of Harold were interwoven. She knew she should receive a surfeit of applause—she always did ; but if Harold's were wanting the whole thing would be a failure. So she wrote him frequently, urging him to come, and he always replied that nothing but necessity would keep him from doing so.

CHAPTER XXV.

THE TWO FACES IN THE MIRROR.

TOWARD the last of May Arthur came to Vassar, bringing with him the graduating dress which he had bought in New York, with Maude as his adviser. He had Jerrie at the hotel to spend Saturday and Sunday with him, and took her to drive and to shop, and then in the evening asked her to put on her finery, that he might see how it looked.

"I shall not hear you spout out your erudition," he said, "for I detest crowds, with the dreadful smell of the rooms. I have gotten the park house tolerably free from odors, though the cook's drain is terrible at times, and I shall have brimstone burned in the cellar once a week. But what was I saying? Oh, I know—I shall not be here at commencement, and I wish to see if my Cherry is likely to look as well as any of them."

So Jerrie left him alone while she donned the white dress, which fitted her superb figure perfectly. She knew how well it became her, and sure of Arthur's approbation, went back to the parlor, where she had left him. He was standing with his back to the door when she came in, and going up to him, she said :

"Here I am in all my gewgaws. Do you think I shall pass muster ?"

She spoke in German, as she always did to him, and when he turned quickly, there was a startled look on his face, as he said :

"Oh, Cherry, it's you! I thought for a moment it was Gretchen speaking to me. Just so she used to come in with her light footstep and soft voice, so much like yours. Where is she, Cherry, that she never comes nor writes ? Where is Gretchen now ?"

His chin quivered as he talked, and there was a moisture in his eyes, bent so fondly upon the young girl beside him. He was worn with the fatigue and excitement of his jour-

ney and the long drive he had taken, and Jerrie knew that
whenever he was tired his mind was weaker and wandered
more than usual. So she tried to quiet and divert him by
calling his attention to her dress, and asking how he liked
it.

"It is lovely," he said, examining the lace and the soft
flounces. "It is the prettiest Maude and I could find.
You know, she was with me, and helped me select it.
Yes, it's lovely, and so are you, Cherry, with Gretchen's
eyes, and hair, and smile, and that one dimple in your
cheek. She used to wear soft, white dresses, and in this
you are enough like her to be her daughter."

They were standing side by side before a long mirror,
she taller for a woman than he was for a man, so that her
face was almost on a range with his, as he stooped a little
forward.

Glancing into the mirror at the two faces so near to
each other, Jerrie saw something which for an instant set
every nerve to quivering as she stepped suddenly back,
looking first at the man's face and then at her own in the
mirror. It was gone now, the look which had so startled
her, but it had certainly been there—a likeness between
the two faces—and she had seen it plainer than she had
ever seen any resemblance between herself and the picture.
Gretchen had blue eyes, and fair hair, and fair complexion, and so had she, and so had hundreds of German girls,
and all Arthur had ever said to her had never brought to
her mind a thought like the two faces in the mirror.
What if it were so? flashed like lightning through her
brain, making her so weak that she grasped Arthur's arm
to steady herself, as she tried to speak composedly.

"You are white as your dress," he said. "It is this
confounded hot room ; let us sit nearer the window."

They sat down together on a sofa, and taking up a
newspaper Arthur fanned Jerrie gently, while she said to
him:

"Do you really think I look like Gretchen ?"

"Yes, except that you are taller. You might be her
daughter."

"Had she—had Gretchen a daughter ?" was Jerrie's
next question, put hesitatingly.

"None that I ever heard of," Arthur replied.

10

"And her name, when a girl, was Marguerite Hein-rich, was it not?" Jerrie went on.

"Yes. Who told you?" Arthur said.

"I saw it on a letter which you gave me to post years ago, when I was a child," Jerrie went on. "You never received an answer to that letter, did you?"

"What letter did you post for me to Marguerite Hein-rich? I don't know what you mean," Arthur said, the old worried look settling upon his face, which always came there when he was trying to recall something he ought to remember.

As he grew older he seemed to be annoyed when told of things he had forgotten, and as the letter had evidently gone from his mind, Jerrie said no more of it. *She* remembered it well; and never dreaming that it had not been posted, she had watched a long time for an answer, which never came. Gretchen was dead; that was settled in her mind. But who was she? With the words, "What if it were so?" still buzzing in her brain, the answer to this question was of vital importance to her, and after a moment, she continued, as if she had all the time been talking of Gretchen:

"She was Marguerite Heinrich when a girl in Weis-baden, but she had another name afterward, when she was married."

"You are talking of something you know nothing about. Can't you let Gretchen alone?" Arthur said, petu-lantly; and springing up, he began to pace the room in a state of great excitement, while Jerrie sat motionless, with a far-off look in her eyes, as if she were seeing in a vision things she could not retain, they passed so rapidly before her, and were so hazy and indistinct.

The likeness she had seen in the glass was gone now. She was not like Arthur at all; it was madness in her to have thought so. And she was not like Gretchen either. Her mother was lying under the little pine tree which she and Harold had planted above the lonely grave. Her mother had been dark, and coarse, and bony, and a peas-ant woman—so Ann Eliza Peterkin, who had heard it from her father, had told her once, when angry with her, and Harold, when sorely pressed, had admitted as much to her.

"Dark, with large, hard hands," he had said ; and Jerrie, had answered indignantly :

"But hard and black as they were, they always touched *me* gently and tenderly, and sometimes I believe I can remember just how lovingly and carefully they wrapped the old cloak around me to keep me warm. Dear mother, what do I care how black she was, and coarse. She was mine, and gave her life for me."

This was when Jerrie was a child, and now that she was older she was seeking to put away this woman with the dark face and the coarse hands, and substitute in her place a fairer, sweeter face, with hands like wax, and features like a Madonna. But only for a few moments, and then the wild dream vanished, and the sad, pale face, the low voice, the music, the trees, the flowers, the sick-room, the death-bed, the woman who died, and the woman who served, all went out together into the darkness, and she was Jerrie Crawford again, wearing her commencement dress to please the man still pacing the floor abstractedly, and paying no heed to her when she went out to change her dress for the blue muslin she had worn through the day.

When she returned to the parlor she found him at the tea-table, which had been laid during her absence. Taking her seat opposite to him she made his tea, and buttered his toast, and chatted, and laughed until she succeeded in bringing back a quiet expression to the face which bore no likeness now to her own. He was talking of the commencement exercises, and regretting that he could not be present.

"I may not be home," he said. "And if I am, I shall not come. Crowds kill me, and smells kill me, and we are sure to have both, but Harold will be here, and he is better than forty old coves like me. It is astonishing what a fancy I have taken to that young man. I don't see a fault in him, except that he is too infernally proud. Think of his refusing to take any more money from me unless I would accept his note promising to pay it back in time—just as if he ever can or will."

"Indeed he will," Jerrie exclaimed, rousing at once in Harold's defense. "He will pay every dollar, and I shall help him."

"You!" and Arthur laughed, merrily. "How will you help him, I'd like to know."

"I shall teach school, or give music lessons, or do both, to earn something for grandmother," Jerrie answered, quickly. "And I shall help Harold, and shall pay Mr. Frank all he gave grandmother for my board. I know just how much it is. Three dollars a week from the time I was four years old until I came here to school. A big sum, I know, but I shall pay it. You will see," she went on, rapidly and earnestly, as she saw the amused look on Arthur's face, and felt that he was laughing at her.

"You are going to pay my brother to the uttermost farthing, but what of me? Am I to be left in the cold?" he asked, as he arose from the table and seated himself upon the sofa near the window.

"I expect to be your debtor all my life," Jerrie said, as she went up to him. "I can never pay you for all you have done for me, never. I can only love you, which I do so dearly, as the kindest and best of men."

She was stooping over him now; and putting up his hands, Arthur drew her close to him, so that the two faces were again plainly reflected, side by side, in the mirror opposite—the man's gentle and tender as a woman's, the girl's flushed, and eager, and excited as she caught a second time the likeness which made her faint again as she clasped her hands tightly together, and listened to what Arthur was saying.

"You owe me nothing, Cherry; the indebtedness is all on my side, and has been since the day when a little white sun-bonnet showed itself at my window, and a voice, which I can hear yet, said to me, 'Mr. Crazyman, don't you want some cherries?' You don't know how much of life and sunshine you brought me with the cherries. My sky was very black those days, and but for you I am certain that I should long ere this have been what you called me—a crazy man for sure, locked up behind bars and bolts. My little Cherry has been all the world to me; and though she is very grand, and tall, and stately now, I love to remember her as the child in the sun-bonnet, clinging to the ladder, and talking to the lunatic inside. That would make a fine picture, and if I were an artist I would paint it some day. Perhaps Maude will. Did I tell you that while she was abroad she dabbled in water-colors ? and now she has what she calls a studio, where she perpetrates the most atrocious daubs you ever saw. Poor Maude ! She is weak in the upper story, but is on the whole, a nice girl, and very pretty, too, with her black eyes, and brilliant color, and kittenish ways. We are great friends now, and she is a comfort to me in your absence. I am afraid, though, that she is not long for this world. Everything tires her, and she has grown so thin that a breath might blow her away. I think it would kill Frank to lose her. His life is bound in hers ; and he once said to me, either that he had sold, or would sell, his soul for her. What do you suppose he meant ?"

Jerrie did not reply. The likeness in the mirror had disappeared as Arthur grew more in earnest, and she listened more intently to what he was saying of Maude, every word as he went on a blow from which she shrank as from some physical pain.

"Yes," Arthur continued, "Maude is weak, mentally and physically, though I believe she is trying hard to improve her mind, or rather that young man, Harold, is trying to improve it for her. He is at the house nearly every day, or she is at the cottage. But, hold on ! I wasn't to tell, and I haven't told—only he reads to her, sometimes outside when the weather will admit, but oftener in her *studio*, where she talks to him of *art,* and where I once saw him giving her a sitting while she tried to sketch his face. A caricature, I called it, ridiculing it so much that she put it away unfinished, and is now at work upon some water lilies he brought her, and which are really very good. Mrs. Tracy is not pleased with Harold's visits, and I once overheard her saying to Maude, ' Why do you encourage the attentions of that young man ? and why do you run after him every day ?' Hold on again ! What a tattler I am ! Why don't I stick to Dolly, who said, ' You certainly do not care for him. He hasn't a cent to his name, nor any family, and has even worked in Peterkin's furnace.' What Maude replied I don't know. I only heard Dolly bang the door hard as she left the room, so I suppose the answer was not a pleasing one. Dolly is a grand lady, and would not like her daughter to marry any ordinary man like Harold,"

"No," Jerrie said, slowly, as if speaking were an effort. "N-no; and you think Harold likes Maude very much?"

"Likes her? Yes. Why shouldn't he like a girl as pretty as she, especially when she meets him more than half way?" Arthur replied, and Jerrie continued, in the same measured tone:

"Ye-es, and you think he would marry her if her mother would permit it?"

"He is not at all likely to do that," Arthur answered, quickly. "A man seldom marries a woman who throws herself at his head and lets him see how much she cares for him, and Maude is doing just that. She cannot conceal anything. I tell you Cherry, if the time ever comes when you love somebody better than all the world beside, don't let him know until he speaks for himself. Don't be lightly won. Better be shy and cold than demonstrative and gushing, like Maude. Gretchen was shy as a fawn, and after I told her I loved her she would not believe it possible. But child, you look fagged and tired. It is time you were in bed. I have talked you nearly to death.

"I am not tired," Jerrie said, "and I want to know what it is about Maude's going to the cottage which you must not tell me. Is she there very often, and is that throwing herself at Harold's head, as you call it?"

She had her arm around his neck in a coaxing kind of way, and Arthur smoothed the soft white hand resting on his coat-collar, as he answered, laughingly:

"Mother Eve herself. You would have eaten the apple too, had you been Mrs. Adam. No, no, I shall not tell any secrets. You must wait and see for yourself. And now you must go, for I am tired."

She said good-night and went to her room, but not to sleep at once, because of the tumult of emotions which had been roused by what Arthur had told her of Maude and Harold.

"I don't believe now that I really meant him to make love to her when I asked him to amuse her," she whispered to herself, as she dashed away two great tears from her cheeks.

Then, after a moment, she continued:

"But they shall never know. No one shall ever know

that I care, for I don't. Harold is my brother, and I shall
love Maude as my sister, and I will do all I can to make
her more like what Harold's wife should be. She is beautiful, and good, and sweet, and true, and with money and
position can do far more for him than I could—I, the
daughter of a peasant woman, the child of a carpet-bag;
and yet—"

Here Jerrie's hands beat the air excitedly as she recalled
the wild fancy which had twice taken possession of her
that night, and which had been born of that likeness seen
in the mirror. Many times since she had passed from
childhood to womanhood had she speculated upon the
mystery which enshrouded her, while one recollection
after another of past events flitted through her brain, only
to bewilder her awhile and then to disappear into oblivion.
But never before had she been affected as she was now
when the possibility of what might be nearly drove her
wild.

"Oh, if that were so," she said, "I could help Harold,
and I'd give everything to him and make him my king, as
he is worthy to be. There is something far back," she
continued, "something different from the woman who
died at my side. That face which haunts me so often was
a reality somewhere. It has kissed me and called me darling, and I saw the life fade out of it—saw it cold and
dead. I know I did, and sometime, I'll go to Wiesbaden,
and everywhere, and clear the mystery, if possible; and if
mother was a peasant girl, with hands coarse, and hard,
and black from labor in the field, then I, too, will be a
peasant girl, and marry a peasant lad, and draw his potatoes home in a cart, while he trudges at my side."

At this picture of herself Jerrie laughed out loud, and
while trying to think how it would seem to draw potatoes
in a cart, after having dug them, she fell asleep and
dreamed of Maude and Harold, and studios and lilies, and
a face which was a caricature, as Arthur had said, and
which, when at a late hour she awoke, proved to be that of
the chambermaid, whom Arthur had sent to rouse her, as
he was waiting for his breakfast.

CHAPTER XXVI.

MAUDE'S LETTER.

TRACY PARK, June —, 18—.

" MY DARLING JERRIE :

"I wish I could send you a whiff of the delicious air I am breathing this morning from the roses under my window and the pond-lilies which Harold brought me about an hour ago. Don't you think he was up before the sun, and went out upon the river to get them for me, because he knows how fond I am of them, and I told him yesterday that they always made me think of you, they are so sweet, and pure, and fair. I wish you could have heard his voice and seen the look in his eyes, as he said : ' Yes; Jerrie is the lily and you are the rose ; you set each other off admirably. I am glad you are so good friends.'

" Harold thinks the world of you, and were you his own sister, I am sure he could not love you better than he does. How handsome he has grown since I went away. I always thought him splendid looking, but he is more than that now ; so tall and straight, with his head set on his shoulders in such an aristocratic kind of way, and then his eyes, which look at you so—well, I don't know how they do look at you, but they are eyes you would trust and never be afraid of anything bad behind them. Uncle Arthur says his mother was lovely, and that his father was one of the handsomest men of his time, but I am certain that Harold looks better than either of them, and has inherited the good qualities of both, without a single bad one. Fred Raymond—who, you know, is so sweet on Nina St. Claire —says, that if Harold had all the blood of a hundred kings in his veins, he could not be more courtly or dignified in his manner than he is, and that is a great deal for a Kentuckian to say. Fred is now at Grassy Spring, visiting Dick St. Claire, and will stay until Nina comes home. I wish Harold was rich, and if I had money of my own, I believe I'd give it to him, only he wouldn't take it, he is so awfully proud, and afraid somebody will help him ; and yet

I respect him for the pride, which has made him teach school, and do everything he could find to do in order to go through college the last two years and pay his own way. But I did not like it a bit when I heard he had accepted a situation in Peterkin's furnace. I know he had good wages, but it is dreadful to think of Harold under such a man, even if Billy is there. When I told Uncle Arthur he laughed, and said : ' Honor and shame from no condition rise.' I wonder what he meant ? I asked Tom, and he said I was a fool.

" Harold is studying law now all the time he can get in Judge St. Claire's office, but he comes to read to me for an hour or more nearly every day. He came of his own accord, too, and sometimes I half think he is trying to drive something into my head, or was, when he began to read to me about those old Greeks, Hesiod or Herod, I don't know which and Theogony—that's rather a pretty name, don't you think so ? But I could not stand the Greeks. My mind is too weak to be impressed by anything Grecian, unless it is the Grecian bend. You tried it until you were discouraged and gave it up, telling me I was the stupidest idiot you ever saw ! That was the time we had the spelling school in the Tramp House, and you were the teacher, and Harold chose me first, and I spelled biscuit ' biskit !' Do you remember how I cried ? and when you told me nobody would ever like me unless I knew something, Harold said, ' Don't talk like that, Jerrie ; those who know the least are frequently liked the best.'"

" What a comfort those words have been to me, and especially at the time when I failed so utterly in my examination at Vassar and had to give it up. Oh, Jerrie, you do not know how mortified I was over that failure, to think I knew so little ; and the worst of it is I can't learn, or understand, or remember, and it makes my head ache so to try ; I am sorry on father's account, he is so proud of me and would like to see me take the lead in everything. Poor father ! he is growing old so fast. Why, his hair is white as snow, and he sometimes talks to himself just as Uncle Arthur does. I wonder what ails him that he never smiles or seems interested in anything except when I am smoothing his hair or sitting on his knee ; then he brightens up and calls me his pet and his darling, and talks queer

10*

kind of talk, I think. He asks me if I am glad I live at Tracy Park—if I like the pretty things he buys me, and if I should be as happy if I were poor—not real poor, you know, but as we were at Langley before I was born. I went there with him a few weeks ago for the first time; and oh, my goodness gracious! such a poky little house with the stairs going right up in the room, and such a tiny, stuffy bedroom! I tried to fancy mamma's scent-bottles, and brushes, and combs, and that box for polishing her nails, transported to that room, and her in there with Rosalie dressing her hair. It made me laugh till I cried, and I think papa did actually cry, for he sat down upon the stairs and turned his head away, and when he looked up his eyes were wet and red, with such a sorry look in them that I went straight up and kissed him, and asked him playfully if he were crying for the old days when he lived in that house and sold codfish in the store.

" 'Yes, Maude,'—he said. 'I believe I'd give the remainder of my life if I could be put back as I was when your Uncle Arthur's letter came and turned my head. Oh, if the years and everything could be blotted out!'

" What do you suppose he meant? I was frightened, and did not say a word until he asked me those questions I told you about; did I like pretty things? did I like to live at Tracy Park, and could I bear to be poor and live in the Langley house? I just told him, 'No, I should not like to live in Langley, that I did like living at Tracy Park, and did like the pretty things which money bought.'

" 'Then I ought to be content, if my beautiful Maude is so,' he said, and the tired look on his face lifted a little.

" He calls me beautiful so often. But I don't see it, do you? Of course you don't. You think me too black, and small, and thin, and so I am; but I think you have the loveliest and sweetest face I ever saw, except Gretchen's. Who was she, I wonder? Uncle Arthur does not talk much of her now, though I believe he kisses her every night and morning. How much he thinks of you, and how much he has talked of *Cherry* since his visit to you in May. Did he say any thing to you of a trip to California? He took us quite by surprise two weeks ago by telling us he was going. He wanted to see the Yosemite Valley before he died, he said, and June was the time to see it.

So he started off with Charles about ten days ago, and the house seems so dull without him.

"If I can, I shall come to see you graduate with the other Vassars, though I shall be ashamed to be seen where I failed so utterly. I might have known I should, for I haven't about me a single quality which would entitle me to be a Vassar. How learned you and Nina will be, and how you will cast me in the shade, making me seem stupider than ever. I did try very hard to learn to speak German when I was abroad with mamma, for father wished it particularly; but I could not do it, and gave it up. I have not a capacity for anything, except to love and suffer and sacrifice for those I love. Do you know, it sometimes frightens me to think how devotedly I could love some one. Not a girl, but a man—a lover—a husband, who loved me. Why, I would give my life for him, and bear any kind of torture if it would add to his happiness. But why write this nonsense to you, who never acted as if you cared an atom for any boy, not even Dick St. Claire, who used to give you sugar hearts and call you his little wife. *Entre nous* (who says I don't know two French words?) mamma would like to make a match between Dick and me, but she never will. Dick is nice, and I like him, but not that way. Poor mamma! How much she thinks of money and position! I tell her she ought to have a photograph of the old Langley house hung up in her room to keep her in mind of her former condition. Just now she has the craze to hammer brass and paint in water-colors, and goes over to Mrs. Atherton's to take lessons. Don't you think that Mrs. Peterkin—*May Jane*—had like aspirations with mamma, and wanted to join the class; but the teacher found that she had as many pupils as she could attend to, and so May Jane is left out in the cold. But Mr. Peterkin says, 'By George, my wife shall have 'complishments if money can buy 'em!' And so, I suppose she will. What strides those Peterkins have taken, to be sure, and what a big house he has built with such a funny name—'*Le Batteau*,' which, as he pronounces it, sounds like *Lubber-too!* It is just finished, and they have moved into it. I have not been there, but Tom has, and he says it fairly glitters, it is so gorgeous, and looks inside like those chariots which come with circuses.

"You ought to hear Peterkin talk about his '*Ann 'Lizy*,' who, he says, 'is to Vassar, gettin' schoolin' with the big bugs, and when she comes *hum* he is goin' to get her a hoss and cart for her own, and a maid, and a vally, too, if she wants one.' Well, there are some bigger fools in the world than I am, and that's a comfort. As for Billy, he stammers worse, if possible, than he used to when he told us we were 'pl-pl-plaguey mean to pl-pl-plague Ann Lizy so ;' but I guess I will let him burst upon you in all the magnificence of his summer attire—his light clothes, short coat, tight pants, pointed shoes, and stove-pipe hat to make him look taller. He comes here occasionally to see Tom, and always talks of you. I do believe you might be Mrs. Billy Peterkin and live at *Lubber-too*, if you wanted ; but, really, Billy is very kind to Harold, who gets twice as much wages in the office, when he writes there, as he would if it were not for Billy.

"Tom is home, doing nothing, but taking his ease and aping an English swell. You know he was with mamma and me in England, and since his return has affected everything English, and looks quite like the *dude* of the period. He, too, seems interested in your return ; and I don't know but you might be mistress of Tracy Park, if you could fancy the incumbrance. Dick St. Claire is going to Vassar, and Harold, too, if he possibly can. He is very busy just now with something he must finish, and perhaps he can't be there. Tom is going, and Fred Raymond, and Billy Peterkin—quite a turn-out from Shannondale.

"I can hardly wait to see you. Only think, it is almost two years since I said good-by ; for we went to Europe just after Harold was graduated, and your last Christmas holidays were over before we came home.

"What a long letter I have written you, and have not told you a word of my health, about which you inquired so particularly. Did Uncle Arthur tell you anything ? I wish he had not, for it worries me to have people look, and act, and talk as if I were sick, when I am not. If I had not a pain in my side, and a tickling cough, which keeps me awake nights and makes me sweat until my hair is wet, I should be perfectly strong ; and but for the pain and the weariness, I feel as well as I ever did ; and I go out nearly every day, and I don't want to die and leave my beautiful home, and father, and mother, and you, and—everybody I love. I am too young to die. I cannot die.

"Oh, Jerrie, I am glad you are coming home! You will do me good, just as Harold does. He is so strong every way, and so kind. I can't begin to tell you what he has been to me since I came home in March—more than a friend—more than a brother.

"And now I must say good-by, for I am getting tired and must rest. I was at the cottage this morning, and Harold is coming here this afternoon to read Tennyson's 'May Queen' to me. He has read it a dozen times, but I am never tired of it, although it makes me cry to think of that grave in the long grass, with little Alice in it, cold and dead, listening for those she loved to come and weep over her. You know, she says to her mother:

" ' I shall hear you when you pass,
     With your feet above me, in the long and pleasant grass.'

"Oh, Jerrie, if it should be—you know what I mean; if there should come a time when people say to each other, 'Maude Tracy is dead!' you'll come after, won't you, and think of me always as the friend, who, weak and stupid as she was, loved you dearly—dearly.

"Now, good-by again. Harold has just come in, and says, 'Remember me to Jerrie, and tell her I shall hope to see her graduated, but do not know, I am so busy.'

"Truly and lovingly,
"MAUDE TRACY."

"P. S.—Tom has come in, and says, 'Give my love to Jerrie.'

"P. S. No. 2.—Dick St. Claire and Fred Raymond are here, and both send their regards.

"P. S. No. 3.—If you will believe me, Billy Peterkin is here, nibbling his little cane, and says, 'Present my compliments to Miss Crawford.'

"Just think of it. Five, or, rather, four young men—for Tom don't count—for me to entertain. But I can do it, and rather like it, too, though they all tire me, except Harold."

Jerrie read this letter which was received a few days

before commencement, two or three times, and each time she read it, the little ache in her heart kept growing larger, until at last it was actual pain, and covering her face with her hands, she cried like a child.

"It is Maude I am crying for," she kept saying to herself. "I know she is worse than they have told me. She is going to die, and I am mean to grudge her Harold's love, if that will make her happier. Why does she go to the cottage so often, I wonder? Is it to see him? He would not like me to do that. He was chagrined when I kissed him at Harvard. But, then, he does not love me, and he does Maude; but he *must* come to commencement. I'll write and tell him so;'" and seizing her pen, Jerrie wrote, rapidly and excitedly:

"DEAR HAROLD:

"I have just heard from Maude, who says there is a possibility that you will not come to Vassar; but I shall be so disappointed if you do not. I would rather have you here than all the wise old heads in the State. So come without fail, no matter what you are doing. I can't imagine anything which should keep you. Tell grandma I am longing to be home, and keep thinking just how cool and nice the kitchen looks, with the hop-vine over the door; but she will have to raise the roof soon, for I do believe I've grown an inch since last winter, and am in danger of knocking my brains out in those low rooms.

"Good-by till I see you. "JERRIE."

CHAPTER XXVII.

"HE COMETH NOT," SHE SAID.

THE *she* was Jerrie, who, the night before commencement, was shaking hands with Dick St. Claire, Fred Raymond, Tom Tracy, and Billy Peterkin, all of whom had arrived on the evening train, and after dinner had come to pay their respects to the young ladies from Shannoudale. The *he* was Harold, for whom Jerrie asked at once.

"Where is Harold? Is he coming in the morning?" she said, as she stood, tall, and straight, and queen-like, before the four young men, who glanced at each other with a significance in their looks, which she did not understand.

It was Dick St. Claire who took it upon himself to explain.

"No, Hal is not coming," he said, "and he is awfully cut up about it. He thought he might manage it until yesterday, when he found it impossible to do so. You see, he has taken a job which must be done at a certain time."

"Taken a job!" Jerrie repeated. "What job? What do you mean?" and her blue eyes flashed upon each of the young men, falling last upon Tom Tracy, as if she expected him to answer, which he did in the half sneering, half satirical tone which made her long to box his ears.

"Why, it's a sort of carpenter's job," he said; "and I heard his hammer going this morning before sunrise, for I was up early for once and out in the park. Sounded as if he were shingling a roof, and that's work, you know, which must be done in fair weather. It might rain and spoil the plastering."

"Thank you," Jerrie answered, curtly. "Harold is shingling a roof, and cannot come. But where is Maude? Is she shingling a roof, too?"

"Yes, b-b-by Jove. You've h-hit it. Maude's sh-shingling a roof, too; the b-best joke out." Billy Peterkin chimed in, glad of an opportunity to join in the conversation, and so get some attention from Jerrie.

He was a little man, only five feet two with heels, and he wore the light clothes of which Maude had written, and a stove-pipe hat and dove colored gloves, and carried a little cane, which he constantly nibbled at, when he was not beating his little boot with it. But he was good-natured and inoffensive and kind-hearted, with nothing low or mean in his nature; and Jerrie liked him far better than she did the "elegant Tom," as she had nicknamed him, who stood six feet without heels, and who knew exactly what shade of color to choose, from his neck-tie to his hose, which were always silk of the finest quality. Tom was faultlessly gotten up, and carried himself as if he knew it, and knew, too, that he was Tom Tracy, the future heir of Tracy Park, if he were fortunate enough to outlive both his uncle and his father. Jerrie had disliked him when he was a boy and was not very fond of him now although they were seemingly good friends except when he roused her to anger with what she called his airs. Turning her back upon him she pretended to be interested in "little Billy," as she was in the habit of calling him, he was so short and she was so tall.

He was speaking of Harold, and he said :

"It's a d-dused shame he co-couldn't come, b-but he sent some money by D-Dick to b-buy you a b-b-basket in New York, and by George, we've got a st-stunner down to the h-hotel ; only I'm a-afraid it'll be w-wilted some b-before to-morrow."

"Yes," Dick said, coming forward, "I should not have told you now, it Billy had not let it out ; Hal did give me some money to buy a basket of flowers for you : the very best I could find, he said, and I got a big one ; but I'm afraid it was not very fresh, for it begins to look wilted now. You must blame Tom, though ; he pretends to be up in flowers, and advised my getting this one in New York, because it was so handsome and cheap."

"Oh, it is all right," Tom drawled, in that affected voice he had adopted since his return from Europe. "It was the best, any way, we could get for the money, Hal, you know, isn't very flush in the pocket."

It was a mean speech to make, and all Tom's audience felt it to be so, while Jerrie crimsoned with resentment and answered hotly :

"Faded or not, I shall care more for Harold's flowers than for all the rest which may be given me."

This was not very encouraging to three at least of the young men, who were intending to make the finest floral offering they could find, to the girl whom in their secret hearts they admired more than any girl they had ever seen, and who, had she made the slightest sign, might have been installed at Grassy Spring, or Tracy Park, or Le Bateau, within less than a month. But Jerrie had never made a sign and had laughed and chatted and flirted with them all, not excepting Tom, who had long ago dropped his supercilious air of superiority and patronage when talking

with her, and who treated her with a gentleness and consideration almost loverlike. Horribly jealous of Harold,
whom he still felt infinitely above, although he did not
now often openly show it, he had encouraged the visits of
the latter to Tracy Park, and by jokes and hints and
innuendoes had fed the flame which he knew was burning
in his sister's heart.

"There will be a jolly row when mother finds it out,"
he said to Maude one day ; "for you know she holds her
head a great deal higher than Hal Hastings, who isn't the
chap I'd choose for a brother-in-law. But if you like him,
all right. Stick to him, and I'll stand by you to the
death."

This was to Maude ; while to his mother, when she
complained that Harold came there quite too often, and
that Maude was running after him too much, he said:

"Nonsense, mother! let Maude alone. She knows
what she is about, and would not wipe her shoes on Hal
Hastings, much less marry him. She is lonely without
Nina and Jerrie, and not strong enough to read much herself, and Hal amuses her ; that's all. I know. I have
talked with her. I am keeping watch, and the moment I
see any indications of love-making on either side I will
give you warning, and together we will put my fine chap
in his proper place in a jiffy."

Tom was a young man now of twenty-seven, tall, and
finely formed, with all his mother's good looks, and his
Uncle Arthur's courtliness of manner when he felt that his
companions were worthy of his notice, but proud, and arrogant, and self-asserting with his inferiors, or those whom
he thought such. He had never overcome his unwarrant-
able dislike of Harold, whom he considered far beneath
him ; but Harold was too popular to be openly treated with
contempt, and so there was a show of friendship and civil-
ity between them, without any real liking on either side.
Tom could not tell just when he began to look upon Jerrie
as the loveliest girl he had ever seen, and to contemplate the
feasibility of making her Mrs. Tom Tracy. His admiration for her had been of slow growth, for she was worse
than a nobody—a child of the Tramp House, of whose
antecedents nothing was known, while he was a Tracy, of
Tracy Park, whom a duchess might be proud to wed. But

he had succumbed at last to Jerrie's beauty, and sprightliness, and originality, and now his love for her had become the absorbing passion of his life, and he would have made her his wife at any moment, in the face of his mother's opposition. By some subtle intuition he felt that Harold was his rival, and whatever he could do to lower him in Jerrie's estimation he would do without the least hesitation.

It was Tom who had insisted that Harold's basket should be bought in New York, where there was a better choice he said, and he had himself selected flowers which he knew were not fresh, and would be still worse twenty-four hours later.

"Why don't you get yours here, if it is the be-best place?" Billy Peterkin had asked him, and he replied:

"Oh, we can't be bothered with more than one basket in the train. I can find something there."

He did not say what he intended to find, or that baskets were quite too common for him, but after leaving the young ladies in the evening, he went to a florist's and ordered for Jerrie a book of white daisies, with a rack of purple pansies for it to rest upon.

"That will certainly be unique, and show her that I have taste," he thought.

For Nina a bouquet was sufficient, while for Ann Eliza Peterkin he ordered nothing. Tom could be lavish of his money where his own interest was concerned, but where he had no interest he was stingy and even mean; and so poor little red-haired Ann Eliza, who would have prized a leaf from him more than all the florist's garden from another, was to get nothing from him.

"What business has old Peterkin's daughter to graduate, any way?" he thought, and he looked on with a sneer, while Billy ordered five baskets, one of which was to be of white roses, with a heart of blue forget-me-nots in the center.

"What under heaven, are you going to do with five baskets?" he asked; but Billy was non-committal, for he would not own that three were intended for Jerrie. whom he wished to carry off the palm, so far as flowers were concerned.

And she did; for of all the young ladies who the next

day passed in review before the multitude, no one attracted
so much attention or received so much praise as Jerrie, or
half as many flowers—her room was full of them—baskets
and bouquets and Tom Tracy's book showing conspicuously
from the rest and attracting universal admiration.

But alas for poor Harold's gift! Dick had watered it
the last thing before going to bed and the first thing in the
morning, but the flowers were limp and faded, and gave
forth a sickly odor, while the leaves of the roses were dropping off, and only the size which was immense, remained to
tell what it once had been. But Jerrie singled it out from
all the rest, and that night at a reception given to the grad-
uates, she wore in her bosom two faded pink roses, the only
ones she could make hold together, and which Nina told
her smelled a little old. But Jerrie did not care. They
were Harold's roses, which he had sent to her, and she
prized them more than all the rest she had received. At
little Billy's *heart* she laughed till she cried, and then gave
it to a young girl who admired it exceedingly. Tom's book
she knew was exquisite and thanked him for it, and told
him it was lovely, and then gave it to Ann Eliza, whose
offerings had been so few. A bouquet from Dick St. Claire
and Fred Raymond and a basket from her brother, were all,
and the little red-haired girl, who, with her heavy gold chain
and locket, and diamond ear-rings, and three bracelets, and
five finger rings, had looked like a jeweler's shop, felt
aggrieved and neglected, and Jerrie found her sobbing in
her room as if her heart were broken.

"Only three snipping things," she said, "and you had
twenty-five, and mother will be so disappointed, and father,
too, when he knows just how few I got. I wish I was popular like you."

"Never mind," said Jerrie, cheerfully. "It was only
a happen so—my getting so many. You are just as nice as
I am, and I'll give you part of mine to take home, to
your mother. I can never carry them all. I should have
to charter a car," and in a few moments six of Jerrie's baskets were transferred to Ann Eliza's room, including Tom
Tracy's book.

"Oh, I can't take that," Ann Eliza said; " he didn't
mean it for me; he didn't give me anything, and I—
I—"

Here she began to sob again, and laying her hand pityingly upon the bowed head, Jerrie said:

"Yes, I know; I understand. Something from Tom Tracy would have pleased you more than from any one else; but listen to me, Annie. Tom is not worth your tears."

"Don't you care for him?" the girl asked, lifting her head suddenly.

"Not a particle, as you mean. You have nothing to fear from me," Jerrie replied.

This was a grain of comfort to the girl who had been weak enough to waste her affections upon Tom Tracy, and to hope that she might eventually succeed in bringing him to her feet, for she knew his fondness for money, and that she should in all probability be one day the heiress of a million. So great was her infatuation for the man who had never shown her the slightest attention, that even his flowers, though second-hand, and not intended for her, were everything to her, and when she packed her trunk that night she put them carefully away in many wrappings of paper, to be brought out at home in the privacy of her own room, and kept as long as the least beauty or perfume remained.

It was a very merry party which the New York train carried to Shannondale the next day, and Jerrie was the merriest and gayest of them all, bandying jokes, and jests, and coquetting pretty equally with the young men, until neither Tom, nor Dick, nor Billy, quite knew what he was doing or saying. But always, in her gayest moods, when her eyes were brightest, and her wit the keenest, there was in Jerrie's heart a thought of Harold, who had so disappointed her, and a wonder as to the nature of the *job* which had been of sufficient importance to keep him from Vassar.

"'Shingling a roof, and Maude is helping him,'" Billy said. "I wonder what he meant?" she was thinking, when she heard Ann Eliza cry out that the towers of 'Le Bateau' were visible.

As she had not seen that wonderful structure since its completion, she arose from her seat, and going to the window, looked out upon the massive pile in the distance, looking, with its turrets, and towers, and round projections, like some old castle rather than a home where people could live and be happy.

"It is very grand," she said to Ann Eliza; and Billy, who was leaning toward her, replied:

"Yes, too grand for a Pe-Peterkin. It wants you there, Jerrie, as its m-m-master-p-p-piece, and, by Jove, you can b-be there, too, if you will!"

No one heard this attempt at an offer but Jerrie, who, with a saucy toss of her head, replied, laughingly:

"Thank you, Billy. I'll think of it, and let you know when I make up my mind to come. Just now I prefer the cottage in the lane to any spot on earth. Oh, here we are at the station," she cried, as the train shot round a curve, and Shannondale was reached.

There was a scrambling for bundles, and flowers, and wraps, Fred Raymond gathering up Nina's, while Dick, and Tom, and Billy, almost fought over Jerrie's, and poor little Ann Eliza would have carried hers alone, if Jerrie had not helped her.

CHAPTER XXVIII.

IN SHANNONDALE.

TEN years of change in Shannondale, and the green hill-side, which stretched from the common down to the river, and where, when our story opened, sheep and cows were feeding in the pasture land, is thickly covered with dwellings of every kind of architecture, from the Mansard roof to the Queen Anne style, just coming into fashion, while the meadow lands are dotted over with the small houses of the men who work in the large furnace, or manufactory, which Peterkin had bought and enlarged, as a monument, he said, and where he sometimes employed as many as four hundred men, and had set up a whistle which could be heard for miles and miles, it was so loud and shrill. A screecher, Peterkin called it, and he always listened with a smile of pride and satisfaction on his face when he heard the first indications of its blowing, and knew that four hundred men were quickening their steps on account of it, lest they should be a few minutes late and have their wages docked.

Peterkin counted two millions now, and boasted the finest, or at least, the most expensive house in the county, not even excepting Tracy Park, which still held its own for solidity and old-fashioned dignity, and was the show place to the strangers visiting in Shannondale.

When Peterkin made $20,000 in one day from some speculation in stocks, he said to Mr. St. Claire, who was now a judge, and with whom he pretended to be on terms of great familiarity :

"I say, judge, I'm goin' to build a buster, and whip the crowd. I've lived about long enough in that little nine-by-ten hole, and I'll be dumbed if I don't show 'em what I can do. I'll have towers, and bay-windows, and piazzers, with checkered work all 'round 'em, and a preservatory, and all kinds of new-fangled doin's. May Jane and Ann 'Liza want that Queen Ann style, but I tell 'em no such squatty things for me. They can have all the little winder panes and stained glass, cart loads on't, if they want ; but I'll have the rooms big and high, so a feller won't bump his head. Yes, *sir !* I'm in for a smasher !"

And he built "a smasher" on the site of the old house, behind which the "Lizy Ann," or what there was left of it, was lying ; and when the house was done, and furnished with the most gaudy and expensive furniture he could find in Boston and New York, he said it had just as good a right to a name as anybody! There was Tracy Park, and Grassy Spring, and Brier Hill, and Collingwood, and he'd be dumbed if he'd be outdone by any of 'em.

"He'd like to call it Lizy Ann," he said to Arthur, whom he met one day in the park, and to whom he began to talk of his new house. "He'd like to call it Lizy Ann, arter the old boat, for that craft was the beginnin' of his bein' anybody ; but May Jane and Ann 'Liza wouldn't hear to it. They wanted some new-fangled foreign name ; could Mr. Tracy suggest something ?"

"How would '*Le Bateau*' do ? It is the French for 'the boat,' and might cover your difficulty," Arthur suggested.

"That's jest the checker. Lizy Ann with a new name,

Lub—lub—what d'ye call her?" Peterkin said, and Arthur replied :

" *Le Bateau.*"

" Yes, yes—*Lubber-toe* ; that'll suit May Jane tip-top. Beats all what high notions she's got ! Why, I don't s'pose she any more remembers that she used to wash Miss Atherton's stun steps than you remember somethin' that never happened. Do you ?"

Arthur thought very likely that she did not, and Peterkin went on :

" You say it means a boat in French ; *canal,* do you s'pose ?"

Arthur did not think it mattered what boat, and Peterkin continued :

" *Lubber-toe* ! Sounds droll, but I like it. I'll see an engraver to-day, but how do you spell the plaguy thing ?"

Arthur wrote it on a slip of paper, which he handed Peterkin, who began slowly :

" *L-e-le, b-a-t-bat* ; *le-bat.* Why, what in thunder ! That ain't *Lubber-toe.* 'Taint nothin' !"

With an amused smile Arthur explained that the pronunciation of French words had very little to do with the way they were spelled ; then, very carefully pronouncing the name several times, and making Peterkin repeat it after him, he said good-by, and walked away, thinking to himself :

" There are bigger lunatics outside the asylum than I am, but it is not possible the fool will adopt that name."

But the fool did. May Jane approved, and Billy did not care, provided his father would pronounce it right, and so in less than a week, " *Le Bateau* " was on Peterkin's door-plate, and on the two gate-posts of the entrance to his grounds, and May Jane's visiting cards bore the words :

" Mrs. Peterkin. *Le Bateau.* Fridays."

She had her *days* now, like Mrs. Atherton, and Mrs. St. Claire, and Mrs. Tracy, and had her butler, too, and her maid, and her carriage; and after the house was finished, and furnished in a style that reminded one of a theatre, it was so gorgeous and gay, Peterkin concluded to have a *coat of arms* for his carriage; and remembering how Arthur had helped him in a former dilemma he sought him again and told him his trouble.

"That *Lubbertoo*" (he called it *too*, now) "went down like hot cakes, and was just the thing," he said, "and now I want some picter for my carriage door to kinder mark me, and show who I am. You know what I mean."

Arthur thought a *puff-ball* would represent Peterkin better than any thing else, but he replied :

"Yes, I know. You want a coat of arms, which shall suggest your early days—"

"When I was a flounderin' to get up—jess so," Peterkin interrupted him. "You've hit it, square. Now I'd like a picter of the Lizy Ann, as she was, but May Jane won't hear to't. What do you say, square ?"

Arthur tingled to his finger tips at this familiarity from a man whom he detested, and whom he would like to turn from his door, but the man was in his house and in his private room, tilting back in a delicate Swiss chair, which Arthur expected every moment to see broken to pieces, and which finally did go down with a crash as the burly figure settled itself a little more firmly upon the frail thing.

"I'll be dumbed if I hain't broke it all to shivers !" the terrified Peterkin exclaimed, as he struggled to his feet, and looked with dismay upon the debris. "What's the damage ?" he continued, taking out his pocket-book and ostentatiously showing a fifty-dollar bill.

"Money cannot replace the chair which once adorned the *salon* of Madame De Stael," Arthur said. "Put up your purse, but for Heaven's sake, never again tip back in your chair. It is a vulgar trick, of which no gentleman would be guilty."

Ordinarily, Peterkin would have resented language like this, but he was just now too anxious to curry favor with Arthur to show any anger, and he answered, meekly :

"That's so, square, 'Tain't good manners, and I know it as well as the next one. I'm awful sorry about the chair, and think mebby I could git it mended. I'd like to try."

"Never mind the chair," Arthur said, with an impatient gesture. "Try another and a stronger one, and let's go back to business. You want a painted panel for your carriage. How will this do ?" and he rapidly sketched a green, pleasant meadow, with a canal running through it, and on the canal a boat, drawn by one horse, which a bare-foot, eltish-looking boy was driving.

"I swow, square, you're a trump, you be," Peterkin exclaimed, slapping him on the back. "You've hit it to a dot. That's the Lizy Ann, and that there boy is Bije Jones, drivin' the old spavin hoss. You or'to hev *me* some-where in sight, cussin' the hands as I generally was, and May Jane on deck, hangin' her clothes to dry. Could you manage that ?"

Arthur thought he could, but suggested that Mrs. Peterkin might not like to be made so conspicuous.

"Possibly she will not like this drawing at all. She may think it too suggestive of other days."

"That's so," Peterkin assented, a little sadly, "and if she don't take to it, the old Harry can't make her. She used to be the meekest of wives them days she dried her clothes on the Lizy Ann, but she don't knock under wuth a cent sense we riz in the world, and Ann Lizy is wus than her mother. But I'll show this to the old woman and let you know."

May Jane did not approve, neither did Billy. No use they said, to flaunt the canal, horse, driver, and all in peo-ple's faces ; and so the discomfited Peterkin went to Arthur again and told him "the fat was all in the fire, and May Jane on a rampage."

"Try again, square ; but give us some kind of water and craft."

So Arthur good humoredly changed the canal into a gracefully flowing river, in a bend of which, in the distance there was just visible a boat, which was a cross between a gondola and one of those little dangerous things so com-mon on the lakes of Wisconsin. Standing in the bow of the boat, with folded arms, as if calmly contemplating the scenery was the figure of a man—supposed to be Peterkin— who swore "he'd keep this picter in spite of 'em ;" and as his wife did not seriously object, the sketch was transferred in oil to a panel and inserted in the carriage, which, when drawn by two shining bays and driven by a colored man in long coat and tall hat, with Peterkin sitting back in it with all the pride and pompousness of a two-millionaire, and May Jane at his side, covered with diamonds, attracted general

11

attention and comment. Billy seldom patronized the carriage, but frequently rode beside it, talking to his mother, of whom he was very fond, and taking off his hat to every person he met, whether old or young, rich or poor.

" Billy is an idiot, but very kind-hearted," people said of him, and in truth he was popular with everybody, especially the men in his father's employ, who all went to him for favors, or for an increase of wages ; for if Billy had any business it was in his father's office, where he pretended to look after matters and keep the books straight. Such had been the growth of Peterkin during the past ten years. " He had got clean to the front," he said, " and was hob-nobbin' with Square Harrenton, and Judge St. Claire, and the Tracys," all of whom shrugged their shoulders and laughed at him in secret, but treated him civilly to his face ; for, deny it as we may, money has a mighty power, and will open many a door which nothing else could move.

" Coarse and ignorant as a horse, but not so bad after all," was what people said of him now ; and in fact Peterkin had improved and softened a good deal with the accession of wealth. Nobody gave so lavishly to everything, as he did, while to his employees he was always generous and considerate. Once he thought to join the church, thinking that would add to his respectability ; but when talked with by his clergyman he showed himself so lamentably deficient in every necessary qualification that he was advised to wait a while, which he did ; but he rented the most expensive pew and carried the largest prayer-book of any one, and read the loudest, and kept his head down the longest, so long, indeed, that he once went to sleep, and had quite a little nap before his wife nudged him and told him to get up.

" Good Lord, deliver us !" was his ejaculation, as he sprang to his feet, and, adjusting his glasses, looked fiercely round at the amused congregation.

So far as money and display were concerned, the St. Claires and Mrs. Atherton had not kept up with Peterkin. On the contrary, as he grew into society they gradually withdrew, until at last Dolly Tracy had it all her own way and looked upon herself as the lady *par excellence* of the town. She had been to Europe. She had seen the queen ; she had had some dresses made at Worth's ; she had picked up a few French words which she used on all occasions, with but little regard to their appropriateness. She had decorated a tea-set and was as unlike the Dolly Tracy whom we first knew, as a person well could be. Every thing had gone well with her, and scarcely a sorrow had touched her, for though poor, stupid Jack had slept for five years in the Tracy lot with only the woman of the Tramp House for company, he was so near an imbecile when he died, that his death was a blessing rather than otherwise. Tom, with his fine figure, his fastidious tastes, and aristocratic notions, was the apple of her eye, and *tout-a-fait au fait*, she said, when her French fever was at its height and she wished to impress her hearers with her knowledge of the language; while, except for her ill-health, and the bad taste she manifested in her liking for Harold's society, Maude was *tout-a-fait au fait*, too. She had no dread of Gretchen, now; even Arthur had ceased to talk of her, and was as a rule very quiet and contented.

Only her husband troubled her, for with the passing years his silence and abstraction had increased, until now it was nothing remarkable for him to go days without speaking to anyone unless he were first spoken to. His hair was white as snow which made him look years older than he really was, while the habit he had of always walking with his head down added to his apparent years.

During the time Maude was in Europe he grew old very fast, for Maude was all that made life endurable. To see her in her young beauty flitting about the house and grounds like a bright bird, whose nest is high up in some sheltered spot where the storms never come, was some compensation for what he had done; but when she was gone there came over him such a sense of loneliness and desolation that at times he feared lest he should become crazier than his brother, who really appeared to be improving, although the strange forgetfulness of past events still clung to and increased upon him. He did not now remember ever to have said that Gretchen was with him in the ship or on the train, or that he had sent the carriage so many times to meet her; and when he spoke of her, which he seldom did to any one except to Jerrie, it was as of one who had died years ago. Occasionally, in the winter, when a wild storm was raging like that which had shaken the house and bent the evergreens the night Jerrie came, he would tie a knot of crape upon the picture, but would give no reason for it when questioned except to say, "Can't you see it is a badge of mourning?"

For a week or more it would remain there, and then he would put it carefully away, to be again brought out when the night was wild and stormy.

It was during Maude's absence that the two brothers became more intimate than they had been before since Arthur first came home, and it happened in this wise. Every day, for months after Maude and his wife went away, Frank spent hours alone in his private room, sometimes doing nothing, but oftener looking at the photograph of Gretchen and the Bible with the marked passages and the handwriting around it. Then he would take out the letter about which Jerrie had been so anxious, and examine it carefully, studying the address, which he knew by heart, and beginning at last to arrange the letters in alphabetical order as far as he could, and to try to imitate them. It was a difficult process, but little by little, with the assistance of a German text-book of Maude's which he found, he learned the alphabet, and began to form words, then to put them together, and then to read. Gradually, the work began to have a great fascination for him, and he went to Arthur one day and asked for some assistance.

"Never too old to learn," he said, "and as the house is like a tomb without Maude, I have actually taken up German, but find it up-hill business without a teacher. Will you help me?"

"To be sure, to be sure," Arthur cried, brightening up at once, and bringing out on the instant such a pile of books as appalled Frank and made him wish to withdraw his proposition.

But Arthur was eager, and persistent, and patient, and had never respected his brother one half as much as when he was stammering over the German pronunciation, which he could not well master. But he learned to read with a tolerable degree of fluency, and to speak a little, too, while he could understand nearly all Arthur said to him.

"Do you think I could get along in Germany?" he asked his brother one day.

"Certainly, you could," Arthur replied. "Are you going

there ? If you do, go to Weisbaden, and inquire for
Gretchen—how she died, and where she is buried. I should
have gone long ago, only I dreaded the ocean voyage so
confoundedly, and then I forget so badly. When are you
going ?"

"Oh, I don't know as ever," Frank answered quickly ,
and yet in his heart there was the firm resolve to go to
Weisbaden and hunt up Marguerite Heinrich's friends, if
possible.

" And if I find them, and find my suspicions correct,
what shall I do then ?" he asked himself over and over
again ; and once made answer to his question : "I will
either make restitution, or drown myself in the Rhine."

Jerrie was a constant source of misery to Frank, and
yet when she was at home he was always managing to have
her at the park house, where he could see her, and watch
her, as she moved like a young queen through the handsome rooms, or frolicked with Maude upon the lawn.

"She is surely Gretchen's daughter, and Arthur's, too,"
he would say to himself, as he, too, detected in her face the
likeness to his brother, which had so startled Jerrie in the
mirror.

He was always exceedingly kind to her, and almost as
proud of her success at Vassar as Arthur himself ; and on
the day when she was expected home he went two or three
times to the cottage in the lane, carrying fruit and flowers,
and even offering things more substantial, which, however,
were promptly declined by Mrs. Crawford, who had signified her intention to take nothing more for Jerrie's
board.

" The girl pays for herself, or will," she said, " and it is
Harold's wish and mine to be independent."

But she accepted the fruit and the flowers, and wondered a
little to see Frank so excited, and nervous, and anxious that
everything should be done to make Jerrie's final home-
coming as pleasant as possible.

It was a lovely afternoon when the young ladies from
Vassar were expected, but the train was half an hour late,
and the carriage from Grassy Spring, and the carriage from
Le Bateau had waited so long that both coachmen were
asleep upon their respective boxes, when at last the whistle
was heard among the hills telling that the cars were com-

ing. The Tracy carriage was not there, though twenty minutes before train time Maude had come down in the Victoria and on learning of the delay had been driven rapidly to the cottage in the lane from which she had not returned when at last the cars stopped before the station and the young people alighted upon the platform, which, with their luggage, seemed at once to be full.

"Your checks, miss," the coachman from Grassy Spring said to Nina, as he touched his hat respectfully to her, and his words were repeated to Ann Eliza by the servant from Le Bateau.

But Jerrie held hers in her hand with a rueful look of disappointment on her face as she looked in vain for Harold or Maude to greet her. For a single moment the difference between her position and that of Nina and Ann Eliza struck her like a blow, and she thought to herself:

"For them, everything; for me, nothing."

Then she rallied, and passing her checks to the baggage master, said to him:

"If there is a boy here with a cart or a wheelbarrow, let him take my trunks, otherwise, send them by express, I see there is no one to meet me."

"Yes'm, but they's comin'," the man replied, with a significant nod in the direction where a cloud of dust was visible, as the Tracy Victoria came rapidly up to the station, with Maude and Harold in it.

The former was standing up and waving her parasol to the party upon the platform, while, almost before the carriage stopped, Harold sprang out, and had both of Jerrie's hands in his, and held them, as he told her how glad he was to welcome her home again. He looked tired and flurried, and did not seem quite himself, but there could be no doubt that he was glad, for the gladness shone in his eyes and in his face, and Jerrie felt it in the warm clasp of his hands, which she noticed with a pang were brown, and calloused, and bruised in some places, as if they had of late been used to harder toil than usual. But she had not much time for thought before Maude's arms were around her neck and Maude was standing on tiptoe and drawing down her face, which she covered with kisses; and, between laughing and crying, exclaimed:

"You darling old Jerrie! how glad I am to see you

again ! and how tall and grand you have grown ! Why, I
don't much more than come to your shoulder. See, Harold, how Jerrie outshines me ;" and she lifted her sparkling
face to Harold, who looked down at her as a brother might
have looked at an only sister of whom he was very fond.

How pretty and piquant she was, with her brilliant
complexion and her black eyes, and how stylish she looked
in the Paris gown of embroidered linen, which fitted her
perfectly, and the big hat, which turned up just enough
on the side to give her a saucy, coquettish air, as she flitted from one to another, kissing Nina twice, Ann Eliza
once, and shaking hands with all the young men except
Tom, who put his in his pockets, out of her way.

He could not stand Maude's gush, he said, and he
watched her with a half sneering smile as she tiptoed
around, for it always seemed as if she walked upon her toes,
courtseying as she walked.

"I meant to have been here before the train," she said
to Jerrie, "and I was here about an hour ago ; but when I
found the cars were late, I drove over to tell Harold as
time with him was everything. How we did drive, though,
when we heard the whistle. Come, jump in," she continued, as she herself stepped into the Victoria. "Jump in,
and I will take you home in a jiffy. It won't hurt Hal to
walk, although he is awful tired."

"But I would rather walk ; take Harold, if he is so
tired," Jerrie said, in a tone she did not quite intend.

"Oh, Jerrie," Harold exclaimed, in a low, pained
voice, "I am not tired ; let us both walk ;" and going to
Maude, he said something to her which Jerrie could not
hear, except the words, "Don't you think it better so ?"

"Of course I do ; it was stupid in me not to see it
before," was Maude's reply, as she laid her hand on Harold's arm, where it rested a moment, while she said her
good-bys.

And Jerrie saw the little, ungloved hand touching Harold so familiarly, and thought how small, and white, and
thin it was, with the full blue veins showing so distinctly
upon it, and then she looked more closely at Maude herself, and saw with a pang, how sick she looked in spite of
the bright color in her cheeks, which came and went so
fast. There was a pallor about her lips and about her nose,

while her ears were almost transparent, and her neck was so small that Jerrie felt she could have clasped it with one hand.

"Maude," she cried, pressing close to the young girl, as Harold stepped aside, "Maude, are you ill? You are pale everywhere except your cheeks, which are like roses."

"No, no," Maude answered, quickly, as if she did not like the question. "Not sick a bit, only a little tired. We have been at work real hard, Hal and I; but he will tell you about it, and now good-by again, for I must go. I shall be round in the morning. Good-by. Oh, Tom, I forgot! We have company to dinner to-night—a Mr. and Mrs. Hart, who are friends of Mrs. Atherton, and have just returned from Germany, bringing Fred's sister, Marian, with them. She has been abroad at school for years, and is very nice. I ought to have told Fred and Nina. How stupid in me! But they will find their invitations when they get home. Now hop in, quick, and don't tear my flounces. You are so awkward!"

"I suppose Hal never tears your flounces," Tom said, as he took his seat beside his sister, and gave Jerrie a look which sent the blood in great waves to her face and neck, for it seemed to imply that he understood the case and supposed that she did, too.

"The St. Claire carriage had driven away with Nina, and Dick, and Fred, and the carriage from Le Bateau had gone, too, when at last Jerrie and Harold started down the road and along the highway to the gate through which the strange woman had once passed with the baby Jerrie in her arms. The baby was a young woman now, tall and erect, with her head set high as she walked silently by Harold's side, until the gate was reached and they passed into the shaded lane, where they were hidden from the sight of any one upon the main road leading to the park house. Then, stopping suddenly, she faced squarely toward her companion, and said:

"Why didn't you come to commencement? Tom Tracy said you were shingling a roof, and Billy Peterkin said Maude was helping you."

CHAPTER XXIX.

WHY HAROLD DID NOT GO TO VASSAR.

THE cottage in the lane was not very pretentious, and all its rooms were small and low and upon the ground floor, except the one which Jerrie had occupied since she had grown too large for the crib by Mrs. Crawford's bed. In this room, in which there was but one window, Jerrie kept all her possessions—her playthings and her books, and the trunk and carpet-bag which had been found with her. Here she had cut off her hair and slept on the floor, to see how it would seem, and here she had enacted many a play, in which the scenes and characters were all of the past. For the cold in winter she did not care at all, and when in summer the nights were close and hot, she drew her little bed to the open window and fell asleep while thinking how warm she was. That she ought to have a better room never occurred to her, and never had she found a word of fault or repined at her humble surroundings, so different from those of her girl friends. Only, as she grew taller, she had sometimes laughingly said that if she kept on she should not much longer be able to stand upright in her den, as she called it.

"I hit my head now everywhere except in the middle," she once said. "I wonder if we can't some time manage to raise the roof."

The words were spoken thoughtlessly, and almost immediately forgotten by Jerrie; but Harold treasured them up, and began at once to devise ways and means to raise the roof and give Jerrie a room more worthy of her. This was just after he had left college, and there was hanging over him his debt to Arthur and the support of his grandmother. The first did not particularly disturb him, for he knew that Arthur would wait any length of time, while the latter seemed but a trifle to a strong, robust young man. Mrs. Crawford was naturally very economical, and could make one dollar go farther than most people

11

could two ; so that very little sufficed for their daily wants
when Jerrie was away.

"I must earn money somehow," Harold thought, "and
must seek work where I can do the best, even if it is from
Peterkin."

So, swallowing his pride, he went to Peterkin's office
and asked for work. Once before, when a boy of eighteen,
and sorely pressed, he had done the same thing, and met
with a rebuff from the foreman, who said to him, gruffly :

"No, sir ; we don't want no more boys ; leastwise, gentlemen boys. We've had enough of 'em. Try t'other furnace. Mr. Warner is allus takin' all kinds of trash, out of
pity."

But the Warner factory, where Harold had once
worked, was full of boys, whom the kind-hearted employer
had taken in, and there was no place for Harold. So he
waited awhile until Jerrie needed a new dress and his
grandmother a bonnet, and then he tried Peterkin again,
and this time with success.

"Yes, take him," Peterkin said to his foreman ; "take
him, and put him to the emery wheel ; that's the place for
such upstarts ; that'll take the starch out of him double
quick. He's a bad egg, he is, and proud as Lucifer. I
don't suppose he'd touch my Bill or my Ann Lizy with a
ten-foot pole. Put him to the wheel. Bad egg ! bad egg !"

Peterkin had a bitter prejudice against the boy, on
whose account he had once been turned from the Tracy
house ; and though he had forgiven the Tracys, and would
now have voted for Frank for Congressman if he had the
chance, he still cherished his animosity against Harold,
designating him as an upstart and a bad egg, who was to be
put to the wheel ; and Harold was "put to the wheel"
until he got a bit of steel in his eye, and his hands were cut
and blistered. But he did not mind the latter so much,
because Jerrie cried over them at night and kissed them in
the morning, and bathed them in cosmoline, and called
Peterkin a mean old thing, and offered to go herself to the
wheel.

But to this Harold only laughed. He could stand it,
he said, and a dollar a day was not to be lost. He could
wear gloves and save his hands.

But the appearance of gloves was the signal for a general hooting and jeering from the boys of his own age, who were employed there, and who had from the first looked askance at Harold, because they knew how greatly he was their superior, and fancied an affront in everything he did and every word he said, it was spoken so differently from their own dialect.

"I can't stand it," Harold said to Jerrie, after a week's trial with the gloves. "I'd rather sweep the streets than be jeered at as I am. I don't mind the work. I am getting used to it, but the boys are awful. Why, they call me 'sissy,' and 'Miss Hastings,' and all that."

So Harold left the employ of Peterkin, greatly to the chagrin of that functionary, who had found him the most faithful boy he had ever had. But this was years ago, and matters had changed somewhat since then. Harold was a man now—a graduate from Harvard, with an air and dignity about him which commanded respect even from Peterkin, who was sitting upon his high stool when Harold came in with his application. Billy, who was Harold's fast friend, was now in the business with his father, and as he chanced to be present, the thing was soon arranged, and Harold received into the office at a salary of twelve dollars per week, which was soon increased to fifteen and twenty, and at last, as the autumn advanced and Harold began to talk of taking the same school in town which he had once before taught, he was offered $1.500 a year, if he would remain, as foreman of the office, where his services were invaluable. But Harold had chosen the law for his profession, and as teaching school was more congenial to him than writing in the office, and would give him more time for reading law, he declined the salary and took the school, which he kept for two successive winters, going between times into the office whenever his services were needed, which was very often, as they knew his worth, and Billy was always glad to have him there.

In this way he managed to lay aside quite a little sum of money, besides paying his interest to Arthur, and when Maude came home from Europe in March he felt himself warranted in beginning *to raise the roof.* He was naturally a mechanic, and would have made a splendid carpenter ; he was also something of an architect, and sketched upon paper the changes he proposed making. The roof

was to be raised over Jerrie's room; there was to be a
pretty bay-window at the south, commanding a view of the
Collingwood grounds and the river. There was to be
another window on a side, but whether to the east or the
west he could not quite decide. There was to be a dressing-
room and large closet, while the main room was to be carried up in the center, after the fashion of a church, and to
be ceiled with narrow strips of wood painted alternately
with a pale blue and gray. He showed the sketch to his
grandmother, who approved it, just as she approved everything he did, but suggested that he submit it to Maude
Tracy, who, she heard, had become an artist and had a
studio; so he took the plan to Maude, explaining it to
her, and saying it was to be a surprise to Jerrie, when she
came home for good in the summer. Maude was interested
and enthusiastic at once, and entered heart and soul into
the matter, making some suggestions which Harold adopted, and deciding for him where the extra window was to
be placed.

"Put it to the east," she said, "for Jerrie is always
looking toward the rising sun, because, she says, her old
home is that way. And, besides, she can see the Tramp
House she is so fond of. For my part, I think it a poky
place, and never like to pass it after dark, lest I should see
the woman standing in the door, with the candle in her
hand, crying for help. Where was Jerrie then, I wonder!
Wouldn't that make a very effective picture? The storm,
the open door, the frantic woman in it, with the candle
held high over her head, and Jerrie clutching her dress
behind, with her great blue eyes staring out in the darkness. That is the way I have always seen it. I mean to
paint the picture, and hang it in the new room as another
surprise to Jerrie."

"Oh, don't!" Harold said with a shudder. "Jerrie
would not like it. It almost killed her when she first knew
of the cry which Mr. Arthur heard and the light I saw
that night. She insisted upon knowing everything there
was to know; and when I told her all the color left her
face, and for a moment she sat rigid as a stone, with a look
I shall never forget, and then she cried as I never saw any
body cry before. This was three years ago, and she has
never spoken to me of it since."

Harold's voice trembled as he talked, while Maude cried outright. The idea of the picture was given up, and she went back to the subject of the new room in which she seemed quite as much interested as Harold himself. When the roof was raised, and the floor laid, and the frame-work of the bay-window up, she went nearly every day to the cottage to watch the progress of the work, and to keep Harold's one hired man up to the mark, if he showed the least sign of lagging.

"She is wus than a slave-driver," the man said to Harold one day. "Why, if I ever stop to take a chaw, or rest my bones a bit, she's after me in a jiffy, and asks if I don't think I can get so much done in an hour if I work as tight as I can clip it. I was never so druv in my life."

And yet both the man and Harold liked to see the little lady there, walking through the shavings, and holding high her dainty skirts as she clambered over piles of boards and shingles, or perching herself on the work bench, superintended them both, and twice by her intervention saved a door from swinging the wrong way, and from being a little askew.

Frank, too, was almost as much interested in the work as Maude was, and once offered his services, as did Dick St. Claire and Billy Peterkin.

"That's splendid. We'll have a bee, and get a lot done," Maude said ; and she pressed into the *bee* her father, and Dick, and Billy, and Fred Raymond, and Tom, the latter of whom did nothing but find fault, saying that the ceiling ought to have been of different woods, the floor inlaid, and the tops of the windows cathedral glass.

"And I suppose you will find the money for all that elegance," Maude said, as she held one end of a board for Harold to nail. "We are cutting our garment according to the cloth, and if you don't like it you'd better go away. We do not want any drones in the hive, do we, Hally ?"

She had taken to addressing him thus familiarly since they had commenced their carpenter work together, and Harold smiled brightly upon her as upon a child as she stood on tiptoe at his side.

Tom went away, but he soon came back again ; for there was for him a peculiar fascination about this room for Jerrie, and sitting down upon a saw-horse, he looked on, and whittled, and smoked, while Dick blistered his hands, and Fred raised a blood-blister by striking his finger with the hammer, and Billy ran a huge splinter under his thumb nail.

Then they all went away, and Harold was left alone, for his man had been obliged to leave, and thus the finishing up devolved upon him. But he was equal to it. The worst was over, and all that was now required was hard and constant work if he would accomplish it in time to see Jerrie graduated, as he greatly wished to do, provided he should have money enough left for the trip when everything was paid for.

But whoever has repaired an old house does not need to be told that the cost is always greater than was anticipated, and that there are a thousand difficulties which beset the unwary workman and hinder his progress. And Harold found it so. Still he worked on, early and late, taking no rest except for an hour or so in the afternoon, when he found it a very pleasant change to walk through the leafy woods, so full of summer life and beauty, to where Maude waited for him, with her sunny face and bright smile, which always grew brighter at his coming. How could he know what was in her mind?—he, who never dreamed it possible that she, of all other girls, could fall in love with him.

That Maude liked him, he was sure; but he supposed it was mostly for the amusement he afforded her, and for the sake of Jerrie, of whom she was never tired of talking. Maude's friendship was very sweet to the young man, who had so few means of enjoyment, and whose life was one of toil and care; and he went blindly toward the pitfall in the distance, and began to look forward with a great deal of pleasure to the readings or talks with Maude, even though he did not find her very intellectual. She amused and rested him, and that was something to the tired and over-worked man.

The room was finished inside at last, and looked exceedingly cool and pretty in its dress of blue and gray, and its two rows of colored glass in each window; for Harold had carried out Tom's suggestion in that respect, and by going without a new hat and a pair of pants, which he needed, had managed to get the glass, which he set himself; for, as he said to Maude, who assisted him in the matching and arrangement, he was a kind of jack-at-all-trades. Maude had also helped him to putty up the nail-holes, and had tried her hand at painting, until it gave her a sick-head-ache, and she was obliged to quit.

When Arthur first heard of the raised roof, he went down to see it, and approving of everything which had thus far been done, insisted upon furnishing the room himself. But Harold refused, saying decidedly that it was his own surprise for Jerrie, and no one must help him. So Arthur went away, and told Maude confidentially that the young man Hastings was made of the right kind of stuff, that he liked his independence, and that, although he should allow him to pay his debt, he should deposit the money as fast as received to his credit in the savings bank, so that he would eventually get it all.

"You are the darlingest uncle in the world!" Maude said, rubbing her soft cheek against his, in that purring way many men like, and which made Arthur kiss her, and tell her she was a little simpleton, but rather nice on the whole.

"And you'll not tell Jerrie a word about the room!" Maude charged him, again and again before he went to Vassar.

"Not if I can help it," was his reply, although, as the reader knows, he came near letting it out twice, but *held on in time*, so that the raised roof was still a secret from Jerrie when she reached the station and was met by Maude and Harold.

The room was all ready, with its pretty carpet of blue and drab, and a delicate shading of pink in it ; its cottage furniture simple, but suitable ; its muslin curtains, and chintz-covered lounge, and the willow chair and round table, which Maude had insisted upon buying. She *would* have some part in furnishing the room, she said, and Harold allowed her to get the chair, which she put by the window looking toward the Tramp House, and the round table, which stood in the bay-window, with a Japanese bowl upon it filled with lilies Harold had gathered in the early morn-ing. He had found it impossible to go to Vassar, there were so many last things to be done, and so little money left in his purse with which to make the journey, and as Maude had more confidence in her own taste for the arrangement of furniture than in his, she, too, decided to remain at home and see it through. The carpet was not put down until the morning of the day when the young men started for Vassar, and it was the noise of the tack hammer which Tom had heard and likened to the shingling of a roof.

" There must be flowers everywhere, Jerrie is so fond of them," Maude said ; and she brought great baskets full from the park gardens, and a costly Dresden vase, which Arthur had left for Jerrie when he went away, together with his card and his photograph, and a note in which he had written as follows :

"My Dear Child :—

" Welcome home again. I wish I could see you when your blue eyes first look upon the room I came so near telling you about. Maude would have killed me if I had. You have no idea how Harold has worked to get it done, and where he got the money is more than I know. Pinched himself in every way, of course. He is a noble fellow, Jerrie. But you know that. I saw it in your face at Vassar, and saw something else, too, which you may think is a secret. Will talk with you about it when I come home. I am off to-morrow for California. Would like to take you with me. Maybe I shall meet with robbers in the Yosemite. I'd rather like to. God bless you !

"Arthur Tracy."

" Uncle Arthur was very queer the day he went away," Maude said to Harold, as she put the note, and the photograph, and the card upon the dressing-bureau. " I heard him talking to Gretchen, and saying, 'Gretchen, Jerrie will be here by-and-by, to keep you company while I am gone—little Jerrie when I first knew her, but a great, tall Jerrie now, with the air of a duchess. Yes, Jerrie is coming, Gretchen.' How he loves her—Jerrie, I mean ; and I do not wonder, do you ?"

Harold's mouth was full of tacks and he did not reply, but went steadily on with his work until everything was done.

" Isn't it lovely, and won't she be pleased !" Maude kept saying, as she gave the room a last look and then started

for home, charging Harold to be on time at the station and
to try and not look so tired.

Harold *was* very tired, for the constant strain of the
last few weeks had told upon him, and he felt that he
could not have gone on much longer, and that only for
Maude's constant enthusiasm and sympathy he should have
broken down before the task was done. It was not easy
work, shingling roofs, and nailing down floors, and painting ceilings, and every bone in his body ached, and his
hands were calloused like a piece of leather, and his face
looked tired and pale when he at last sat down to rest
awhile before changing his working suit for one scarcely
better, although clean and fresher, with no daubs of paint
or patches upon it.

"They don't look first-rate, that's a fact," he said to
himself, as he surveyed his pants, and boots, and hat, and
thought what a contrast he should present to the elegant
Tom and the other young men at the station. "But Jerrie won't care; she understands, or will, when she sees her
new room. How pretty it is!" he added, as he stopped a
moment to look in and admire it.

A blind had swung open, letting in a flood of hot sunshine, and as it was desirable to keep the room as cool as
possible, Harold went in to close the shutter. But something was the matter with both fastening and hinge, and
he was fixing it when Maude drove up, telling him the
train was late.

"That's lucky," he said, "for this blind is all out of
gear;" and it took so much time to fix and rehang it that
the whistle was heard among the hills a mile away, just as
he entered the Victoria with Maude and started for the
station upon a run.

CHAPTER XXX.

THE WALK HOME.

ALL the way from the station to the gate Harold was trying to think of something to say besides the merest commonplaces, and wondering at Jerrie's silence. She had seemed glad to see him, he had seen that in her eyes, and seen there something else which puzzled and troubled him, and he was about to ask her what it was when she stopped so abruptly, and said:

"Why didn't you come to commencement? Tom Tracy said you were shingling a roof, and Billy Peterkin said Maude was helping you."

"Oh, that's it, is it?" Harold said, bursting into a laugh. "That is why you have been so stiff and distant, ever since we left the depot, that I could not touch you with a ten-foot pole."

"Well, I don't care," Jerrie replied, with a sob in her voice. "Everybody had some friend there, but myself. You don't know how lonely I felt when I went on the stage and knew there was no home face looking at me in all that crowd. I think you might have come any way."

"But, Jerrie," Harold said, laying his hand upon her shoulder, as they slowly walked on, "wait a little before you condemn me utterly. I wanted to come quite as much as you wanted to have me. I remembered what a help it was to me when I was graduated to see your face in the crowd and know by its expression that you were satisfied."

"I did not suppose you saw me," Jerrie exclaimed, her voice very different in its tone from what it had been at first.

"Saw you!" and Harold's hand tightened its grasp on her shoulder. "Saw you! I scarcely saw any one else except you, and Maude, who sat beside you. I knew you would be there, and I looked the room over, missing you at first, and feeling as if something were wanting to fire me up, then, when I found you, the inspiration came, and if I began to flag ever so little, I had only to look at your blue eyes and my blood was up again."

This was a great deal for Harold to say, and he felt half frightened when he had said it ; but Jerrie's answer was reassuring.

"Oh, I didn't know that. I am so glad you told me."

They were close to the Tramp House now. The walk from the station had been hot and dusty, and Jerrie was tired, so she said to Harold :

"Let's go in a moment ; it looks so cool in there."

So they went in, and Jerrie sat down upon a bench, while Harold took a seat upon the table, and said :

"I suppose you had peals of applause and flowers by the bushel."

"Yes," Jerrie replied, "applause enough, and flowers enough—twenty bouquets and baskets in all, including yours. It was kind in you to send it."

She did not tell him of the wilted condition of his flow-ers, or that one of the faded roses was pressed between the lids of her Latin grammar.

"Billy gave me a heart of blue forget-me-nots," she continued, "and Tom a book of daisies on a standard of violets. What a prig Tom is, and what a dandy Billy has grown to be, and he stammers worse than ever."

"But he is one of the best-hearted fellows in the world ;" Harold said, "he has been very kind to me."

"Yes, I know ;" Jerrie rejoined, quickly, "he makes his father pay you big wages in the office and gives you a great many holidays ; that is kind. But, oh, Harold, how I hate it all—your being obliged to work for such a man as Peterkin. I wish I were rich ! Maybe I shall be some day. Who knows ?"

The great tears were shining in her eyes as she talked, and brushing them away she suddenly changed the conver-sation, and said :

"I never come in here that a thousand strange fancies do not begin to flit through my brain, and my memory seems stretched to the utmost tension, and I remember things away back in the past before you found me in the carpet-bag."

She was gazing up toward the rafters with a rapt look on her face, as if she were seeing the things of which she was talking ; and Harold, who had never seen her in just this way, said to her very softly :

"What do you remember, Jerrie? What do you see?"

She did not move her head or eyes, but answered him.

"I see always a sweet pale face, to which I can almost give a name—a face, which smiles upon me; and a thin white hand which is laid upon my hair—a hand not like those you have told me about, and which must have touched me so tenderly that awful night. Did you ever try to recall a name, or a dream, which seems sometimes just within your grasp, and then baffles all your efforts to retain it?"

"Yes, often," Harold said.

"Just so it is with me," she continued. "I try to keep the fancies which come and go so fast, and which always have reference to the past, and some far off country—Germany, I think. Harold, I must have been older when you found me than you supposed I was."

"Possibly," Harold replied. "You were so small that we thought you almost a baby, although you had an old head on your shoulders from the first, and could you have spoken our language, I believe you might have told us who you were and where you came from."

"Perhaps," Jerry said. "I don't know; only this, as I grow older, the things way back come to me, and the others fade away. The dark woman; my mother,"—she spoke the name very low—"is not half as real to me as the pale, sick face, on which the firelight shines. It is a small house, and a low room, with a big, white stove in the corner, and somebody is putting wood in it; a dark woman; she stoops; and from the open door the firelight falls upon the face in the chair—the woman who is always writing when she is not in bed; and I am there, a little child; and when the pale face cries, I cry, too; and when she dies— oh, Harold! but you saw me play it once, and wondered where I got the idea. I saw it. I know I did; I was there, a part of the play. I was the little child. Then, there is a blur, a darkness, with many people and a crying —two voices—the dark woman's and mine; then, a river, or the sea, or both, and noisy streets, and a storm, and cold; and *you*, taking me into the sunshine."

As she talked she had unconsciously laid her hand on

Harold's knee, and he had taken it in his, and was holding it fast, when she startled him with the question :

"Do you—did you—ever think—did any body ever think it possible, that the woman found dead in here, was not my mother ?"

"Not your mother !" Harold exclaimed, dropping her hand in his surprise. "Not your mother ! What do you mean ?"

"No disrespect to her," Jerrie replied—"the good, brave woman, who gave her life for me, and whose dear hands shielded me from the cold as long as there was power in them to do it. I love and reverence her memory as if she had been my mother ; but, Harold, do I look at all as she did ? You saw her—here, and at the park house. Think—am I like her—in any thing ?"

"No," Harold answered. "You are like her in nothing ; but you may resemble your father."

"Ye-es," Jerrie said, slowly, "I may. Oh, Harold, the spell is on me now so strong that I can almost remember. Tell me again about that night, and the morning ; what they did at the park house—Mr. Arthur, I mean. He was expecting somebody ; *Gretchen*, was it not ?"

She had grasped his hand again, and was looking into his face as if his answer would be life or death to her. And Harold, who had no idea what was in her mind, and who had never thought that the dark woman was not her mother, looked at her wonderingly, as he replied :

"Yes, I remember that he had a fancy in his mind that Gretchen was coming ; but he has had that fancy so often. He said she was in the ship with him and on the train, but she wasn't. I think Gretchen is dead."

"Yes, she is dead," Jerrie said, decidedly ; "but tell me again all you know of the time I came."

Harold told her again what he knew personally of the tragedy, and all he remembered to have heard. But the thing most real to him was Jerrie herself, the beautiful girl sitting by his side and astonishing him with her mood and her questions. He had seen her often in her spells, as he called them ; when she acted her pantomimes, and talked to people whom she said she saw ; but he had only thought of them as the vagaries of a peculiar mind—a German mind his grandmother said, and he accepted her theory as the correct one.

He had never seen Jerrie as she was now, with that look in her face and in her eyes, which shone with a strange light as she went on to speak of the things which sometimes came and went so fast, and which she tried in vain to retain. It had never occurred to him that the woman he had found dead was not her mother, and he thought her crazy when she put the question to him. But he was a man, solid and steady, with no vagaries of the brain, and not a tithe of the impetuosity and imagination of the girl, who asked him at last if he had ever seen any one whom she resembled.

He was wondering, in a vague kind of way, how long she meant to stay there, and if the tea-cakes his grandmother was going to make for supper would be spoiled, when she asked the question, to which he replied:

"No, I don't think I ever did, unless it is Gretchen. You are some like her, but I suppose many German girls have her complexion and hair."

The answer was not very reassuring, and Jerrie showed it in her face, which was still upturned to Harold, who, looking down upon it and the earnest, wistful expression which had settled there, started suddenly as if an arrow had struck him, for he saw the likeness Jerrie had seen in the glass, and taking her face between both his hands, he studied it intently, while the possibility of the thing kept growing upon him, making him colder and fainter than Jerrie herself had been when she looked into the mirror.

"What if it were so?" he said to himself, while everything seemed slipping away from him, but mostly Jerrie, who, if it were so, would be separated from him by a gulf he could not pass; for what would the daughter of Arthur Tracy care for him, the poor boy, whose life had been one fight with poverty, and whose worn, shabby clothes, on which the full western sunlight was falling, told plainer than words of the poverty which still held him in thrall.

"Jerrie!" he cried, rising to his feet, and letting the hands which had clasped her face drop down to her shoulders, which they pressed tightly, as if he thus would keep her with him—"Oh, Jerrie, you are like Arthur Tracy, or you were when you looked at me so earnestly; but it is gone now. Do you—have you thought that Gretchen was your mother?"

He was pale as a corpse, and Jerrie was the calmer of the two, as she told him frankly all she had thought and felt since Arthur's visit to her.

"I meant to tell you," she said, "though not quite so soon ; but when I came in here I could not help it, things crowded upon me .so. It may be, and probably is, all a fancy, but there is something in my babyhood different from the woman who died, and when I am able to do it, I am going to Wiesbaden, for that is where Gretchen lived, and where I believe I came from, and if there is anything I shall find it. Oh, Harold! I may not be Gretchen's daughter, but if I am more than a peasant girl—if anything good comes of my search, my greatest joy will be that I can share with you, who have been so kind to me. I will gladly give you and grandma every dollar I may ever have, and then I should not pay you."

"There is nothing owing me," Harold said, the pain in his heart and his fear of losing her growing less as she talked. "You have brought me nearly all the happiness I have ever known ; for when I was a boy and every bone ached with the hard work I had to do—the thought that Jerrie was waiting for me at home, that her face would greet me at the window, or in the door, made the labor light ; and now that I am a man—" He paused a moment, and Jerrie's head drooped a little, for his voice was very low and soft, and she waited with a beating heart for him to go on. "Now that I am a man, life would be nothing to me without you."

Was this a declaration of love? It almost seemed so, and, but for a thought of Maude, Jerrie might have believed it was such, and lead him on to something more definite. As it was, her heart gave a great bound of joy, which showed itself on her face as she replied :

"If I make your life happier, *I* am glad ; for never had a poor, unknown girl, so good and true a brother as I. But come, I have kept you here too long, and grandma must be wondering where we are."

"Yes, and supper will be spoiled," Harold said, as he followed her to the door. "We are to have it in the back porch, where it is so cool, and to have tea-cakes, with strawberries from our own vines, and cream from our own cow, or rather your cow. Did I write you that she had a splendid calf, which we call Clover-top?"

They had come back to commonplaces now. Jerrie's clairvoyant spell had passed and she was herself again, simple Jerrie Crawford, walking along the familiar path, and talking of the cow which Frank Tracy had given her when it was a sickly calf, whose mother had died. She had taken it home and nursed it so carefully that it was now a healthy little Jersey, whom she called Nannie.

"A funny name for a cow," Harold had said, and she had replied:

"Yes, but it keeps repeating itself in my brain. I have known a Nannie sometime, sure, and may as well perpetuate the name in my bossy as anywhere."

Nannie was in a little inclosure by the side of the lane, and at Harold's call she came to the fence, over which she put her face for the caress she was sure to get, while Clover-top kicked up her heels and acted as if she, too, understood and was glad Jerry had come.

"Oh, it is so pleasant everywhere, and I am so glad to be home again," Jerrie said, as her eyes went rapidly from one thing to another, until at last they fell upon the raised roof looking so new and yellow in the sunlight.

CHAPTER XXXI.

AT HOME.

"OH, Harold, what have you been doing?" Jerrie exclaimed, stopping short, while a suspicion of the truth began to dawn upon her.

"That is the roof Tom told you I was shingling," Harold replied; and taking her by the arm, he hurried her on to the cottage, where Mrs. Crawford stood in the door, in her broad white apron and the neat muslin cap which Maude had fashioned for her.

With a cry of joy, Jerrie took the old lady in her arms, and kissed and cried over her.

"It is so nice to be home, and everything is so pleasant!" she said, as her eyes swept the sitting-room, and kitchen, and back porch where the tea table was laid, with its luscious berries and pitchers of cream.

"Go right up stairs with Harold. I have just come down, and can't go up again," Mrs. Crawford said, excitedly; and, with a bound, Jerrie was up the stairs and in the lovely room.

When she saw them coming in the lane, Mrs. Crawford had gone up and opened the shutters, letting in a flood of light, so that nothing should escape Jerrie's notice. And she saw it all at a glance—the high walls, the carpet, the furniture, the curtains, and the flowers—and knew why Harold did not come to Vassar.

He was standing in the bay-window, watching her, and the light fell full upon his shabby clothes, which Jerrie noticed for the first time, knowing exactly why he must wear them, and understanding perfectly all the self-denials and sacrifices he had made for her, who had been angry because he did not come to see her graduate. Had she been younger, she would have thrown herself into his arms and cried there. Harold half thought and hoped she was going to do so now, for she made a rush toward him, then stopped suddenly, and sinking into the willow chair, began to sob aloud, while Harold stood looking at her, wondering what he ought to do.

"Don't you like it, Jerrie?" he said at last.

"Like it?" and in the eyes which she flashed upon him, he read her answer. "Like it! I never saw a room I liked better. But why did you do it? Was it because of that foolish speech of mine about knocking my brains out, the ceiling was so low?"

"Not at all," Harold replied. "I had the idea in my head long before you wrote that to me, but could not quite see my way clear until last spring. I have seen Nina's room, and Maude's, and have heard that Ann Eliza Peterkin's was finer than the queen's at Windsor, and I did not like to think of you in the cooped up place this was, with the slanting roof and low windows. I am glad you like it."

And then, knowing that she would never let him rest until he had done so, he told her all the ways and means by which he had been able to accomplish it, except, indeed, his own self-denials and sacrifices of pride, and even comfort. But this she understood, and looked at the shabby coat, and shoes, and the calloused hands, which lay upon his knees as he talked, and which she wanted so much to take in hers and kiss and pity, for the hard work they had done for her. But this would have been "throwing herself at his head," and so she only cried the more, as she told him how much she thanked him, and that she never could repay him for what he had done for her.

"But it was a pleasure," he said. "I never enjoyed anything in my life as I have working in this room, with Maude to help me. She was here nearly every day, and by her enthusiasm kept me up to fever heat. She puttied up the nail-holes and painted your dressing-room, and would have helped shingle the roof if I had permitted it. She gave the chair you sit in, and the table in the window. She would do that, and I let her; but when Mr. Arthur offered his assistance, and the other Mr. Tracy, I refused, for I wanted it all my own for you."

He was speaking rapidly and excitedly, and had Jerrie looked up she would have seen in his face all she was to him; but she did not, and at mention of Maude a cloud fell suddenly upon her. But she would not let it remain; she would be happy, and make Harold so, too. So she told him again of her delight, and what a joyous coming home it was.

She had not yet seen Arthur's card, and photograph, and note; but Harold called her attention to them; and taking up the latter, she opened it, while her heart gave a throb of something between joy and pain as she saw the words, "My dear child," and then read the note so characteristic of him.

"What a strange fancy of his to go off so suddenly to California. I wonder Mr. Frank allowed it," she said, as she put the note in her pocket, and then, at a call from Mrs. Crawford, went down to where the supper was waiting for her.

The tea-cakes were a little cold, but everything else was delicious, from the fragrant tea to the ripe berries and thick, sweet cream, and Jerrie enjoyed it with the keen relish of youth and perfect health.

After supper was over Jerrie made her grandmother sit

still while she washed and put away the dishes, singing as she worked, and whistling, too—loud, clear, ringing strains, which made a robin in the grass fly up to the porch, where, with his head turned on one side he listened to this new songster, whose notes were strange to him.

And Jerrie did seem like some joyous bird just let loose from prison, as she flitted from one thing to another, now setting her grandmother's cap a little more squarely on her head, and bending to kiss the silvery hair as she said to her, " Your working days are over, for I have come home to care for you, and in the future you have nothing to do but to sit still, with your dear old lame feet on a cushion ;" now helping Harold water the flowers in the borders, and pinning a June Pink in his button-hole ; now, going with him to milk Nannie, who, either remembering Jerrie, or recognizing a friend in her, allowed her horn to be decorated with a knot of blue ribbon, which Jerrie took from her throat, and which Harold afterward took from Nannie's horn and hid away with the withered lilies Jerrie had thrown him that day at Harvard when her face and her eyes had been his inspiration.

They kept early hours at the cottage, and the people at the Park House were little more than through the grand dinner they were giving, when Jerrie said good-night to her grandmother and Harold, and went up to her new room under the raised roof. It was a lovely summer night, and the moonlight fell softly upon the grass and shrubs outside, and shone far down the long lane where the Tramp House stood, with its thick covering of woodbine.

Leaning from the window, Jerrie looked out upon the night, while a thousand thoughts and fancies came crowding into her brain, all born of that likeness seen by her in the mirror when Arthur was with her at Vassar, and which Harold, too, had recognized when she sat with him in the Tramp House. After Arthur had left her in May she had been too busy to indulge in idle dreams, but they had come back to her again with an overwhelming force, which seemed for a few moments to lift the vail of mystery and show her the past, for which she was so eagerly longing. The pale face was more distinct in her mind, as was the room with the tall white stove and the high-backed settee beside it, and on the settee a little girl—herself, she believed—and she could hear a voice from the cushioned chair speaking to her and calling her by the name Arthur had given her in his note.

"My child," he had written; but he had only put it as a term of endearment; he had no suspicion of the truth, if it were truth; and yet why should he not know? Could anything obliterate the memory of a child, if there had been one, Jerrie asked herself.

"I *will* know some time. I will find it out," she said, as she withdrew from the window and commenced her preparations for bed.

As she stepped into her dressing-room, her eyes fell upon the foreign trunk, with the contents of which she was familiar. They had been kept intact by Mrs. Crawford, who hoped that by them Jerrie might some day be identified. Going to the old trunk Jerrie lifted the lid, and took out the articles one by one with a very different feeling from what she had ever experienced before when handling them. The alpaca dress came first, and she examined it carefully. It was coarse, and plain, and old-fashioned, and she felt untuitively that a servant had worn it. The cloak and shawl, in which she had been wrapped, were inspected next, and on these Jerrie's tears fell like rain, as she thought of the woman who had resolutely put away the covering from herself to save a life which was no part of her own.

"Oh, Mah-nee," she sobbed, laying her face upon the rough coarse garments, "I am not disloyal to you in trying to believe that you were not my mother, and could you come back to me, Mah-nee, whoever you are, I'd be to you so loving and true. Tell me, Mah-nee, who I am: give me some sign that what comes to me so often of that far-off land is true. There *was* another face than yours which kissed me, and other hands, dead now, as are the dear old hands which shielded me from the cold that awful night, have caressed me lovingly."

But to this appeal there came no response, and Jerrie would have been frightened if there had. The shawl, the cloak, and the dress were as silent and motionless as she to whom they had belonged; and Jerrie folded them reverently, and putting them aside took out her own clothes next—the little dresses which showed a mother's love and care; the handkerchief marked "J;" the aprons, and the picture

book with which she had played, and from which it seemed
to her she had learned the alphabet, standing by a cushioned
chair before a tall white stove. There was only the fine
towel left, and Jerrie looked long and thoughtfully at the
letter "M," embroidered in the corner.

"Marguerite begins with M," she said, "and Gretch-
en's name was Marguerite. If it were Gretchen who worked
this letter I can touch what her hands have touched—and
she kissed the "M" as fervently as if it had been Gretch-
en's lip, and Gretchen were her mother.

On the old brass ring the key to the trunk and carpet-
bag were still fastened, together with the small key, for
which no use had ever been found. Jerrie had never
thought much about this key before, but now she held it
a long time while the conviction grew that this was the key
to the mystery; that could she find the article which this
unlocked, she would know something definite with regard
to herself. But where to look she could not guess; and
with her brain in a whirl which threatened a violent headache, she closed the chest at last, and crept wearily to bed
just as the clock, which Peterkin had set up in one of his
towers, struck for half-past ten, and Grace Atherton's carriage was rolling down the avenue from the big dinner at
the Park House.

CHAPTER XXXII.

THE NEXT DAY.

JERRIE was astir the next morning almost as soon as
the first robin began to sing under her window. She
had left a blind open, and the red beams of the rising sun
fell upon her face and roused her from a dream of Germany and what she meant to do there. Once fairly awake,
Germany seemed far away, as did the fancies of the previous night. The spell, mesmeric, or clairvoyant, or whatever one chooses to call it, was broken, and she began
dressing rapidly and noiselessly so as not to awaken her
grandmother, who slept in the room beneath hers.

"I shall get the start of her," she said, as she donned a simple working dress which had done her service during the summer vacations for three successive years. "I heard her telling Harold last night to have the tubs and water ready early, for she had put off the Monday's washing until I came home, as I was sure to bring a pile of soiled clothes. And I have ; but, my dear grandmother, your poor old twisted hands will not touch them. What is a great strapping girl like me for, I'd like to know, if it is not to wash her own clothes, and yours, too ?" and Jerrie nodded resolutely at the fresh young face in the mirror, which nodded back with a smile of approbation of the *tout ensemble* of the figure reflected in the glass.

And truly it was a very pretty and piquant picture she made in her neat calico dress, which, as it was three years old at least, was a little too short for her, and showed plainly her red stockings and high-heeled slippers, with the strap around her instep. Her sleeves were short, for she had cut them off and arranged them in a puff above her elbows to save rolling them up, and her white bib-apron was fastened on each shoulder with a knot of blue ribbon, Harold's favorite color. She had thoroughly brushed her hair, and then twisting it into a knot, had tucked it under a coquettish muslin cap, whose narrow frill just shaded her face.

"You look like a peasant girl, and I believe you are a peasant girl, and ought to be working in the fields of Germany this minute," she said to herself with a mocking courtesy, as she left the mirror and descended to the kitchen, where, early as it was, she found Harold warming some coffee over a fire of chips, and cutting a slice of dry bread.

"What in the world !" she exclaimed, stopping short on the threshold. "I meant to be the first on the scene, and lo ! here you are before me. What are you doing ?"

"Getting my breakfast," Harold replied, turning toward her with a slight shade of annoyance on his face. "You see, I have a job. I did not tell you last night that a Mr. Allen, who lives across the river, four miles away, looked in one day when I was painting your ceiling, and liked it so much that he engaged me to paint one for him. I told him I was only an amateur, but he said he'd rather

have me than all the boss painters in Shannondale. He
offered me three dollars a day and board, which means dinner and supper, or fifteen for the job; and I took the last
offer, as I can make the most at it by beginning early and
working late, and we need——"

Here he stopped short, for how could he tell Jerrie that
the raised roof had taken all his means, and that he even
owed the grocer for the sugar she had eaten upon her berries, and the butcher for the bit of steak bought the previous night for her breakfast and his grandmother's. But
Jerrie guessed it without his telling, but with her quick
instinct and delicate perception knew that no genuine man
like Harold cares to have even his best friend know of his
poverty if he can help it. Forcing back the tears which
sprang to her eyes, she said, cheerily :

"Yes, I know ; you are a kind of second Michael
Angelo, though I doubt if that old gentleman, at your age,
could have done my room better than you did. I don't
wonder Mr. Allen wants you. But you are not going to
tramp four miles on a hot morning, on nothing but bread
and coffee, and such coffee—muddier than the Missouri
River ! You shall have a decent breakfast, if I can get it
for you. Just sit down and rest, and see what a Vassar
with a diploma can do."

As she talked she was replenishing the fire with hard
wood, putting on the kettle, pouring out the coffee dregs
saved from yesterday's breakfast, and hunting for an egg
with which to settle the fresh cup she intended to make.

"No, no, Jerrie. You must not take that ; it is all we
have in the house, and grandma must have a fresh one
every day at eleven o'clock, the doctor says—it strength-
ens her," Harold said, rising quickly, while Jerrie put the
one egg back in the box and asked what Mrs. Crawford did
settle coffee with.

"I am sure I don't know ; cold water, I guess," Harold
said, resuming his seat, while Jerrie tripped here and there
laying the cloth, bringing his cup and saucer and plate,
and at last pouncing upon the bit of steak in the refrig-
erator.

But here Harold again interfered.

"Jerrie—Jerrie, that is for your breakfast and grandma's. You must not take that."

"But I shall take half of it. I would rather have a glass of Nannie's milk any time than meat, and you are going to have my share ; so, Mr. Hastings, just mind your business and let the cook alone, or she'll be givin' ye warnin'," Jerrie answered, laughingly, as she divided the steak, which she proceeded at once to broil.

So Harold let her have her way, and felt an increase of self-respect, and that he was something more than a common day-laborer, as he ate his steak and buttered toast, and drank the coffee, which seemed to him the best he had ever tasted. Jerrie picked him a few strawberries, and laid beside his plate a beautiful half-opened rose, with the dew still upon it. It was a delicate attention, and Harold felt it more than all she had done for him.

"Thank you, Jerrie," he said, picking up the rose as he finished his breakfast. "It was so nice in you to think of it, just as if I were a king instead of a jack-at-all-trades ; but I hardly think it suits my blue checked shirt and painty pants. Keep it yourself, Jerrie," and he held it up against her white bib apron. "It is just like the pink on your cheeks. Wear it for me," and taking a pin from his collar, he fastened it rather awkwardly to the bib, while his face came in so close proximity to Jerrie's that he felt her breath stir his hair, and felt, too, a strong temptation to kiss the check so near his own. "There ; that completes your costume," he said, holding her off a little to look at her. "By the way, haven't you got yourself up uncommonly well this morning ? I never saw you as pretty as you are in this rig. If it would not be very improper, I'd like to kiss you."

He was astonished at his own boldness, and not at all surprised at Jerrie's reply, as she stepped back from him :

"No, thank you ; it would be highly improper for a man who stands six feet in his boots, to kiss a girl who stands five feet six in her slippers."

There was a flush on her cheeks, and a strange look in her eyes, for she was thinking of Harvard, where he had put her from him, ashamed that strangers should see her kiss him. Harold had forgotten that incident, which at the time had made no impression upon him, and was now thinking only of the beautiful girl whose presence seemed to brighten and ennoble everything with which she came in

contact, and to whom he at last said good-by, just as
Peterkin's tower clock struck for half-past five.

"I *must* go now," he said, taking up his basket of
brushes. "I have lost a full half-hour with you, and your
steaks, and your coddling me generally. I ought to have
been there by this time. Good-by," and offering her his
hand, he started down the lane at a rapid pace, thinking
the morning the loveliest he had ever known, and wondering why everything seemed so fresh, and bright, and sweet.

If he could have sung, he would have done so; but he
could not, and so he talked to himself, and to the birds,
and rabbits, and squirrels, which sprang up before him as
he struck into the woods as the shortest route to Mr. Allen's
farm-house—talked to them of Jerrie, and how delightful
it was to have her home again, unspoiled by flattery, sweet
and gracious as ever, and how he longed to tell her of his
love, but dared not, until he was sure of her and of what
she felt for him. He had no faith now in her fancies with
regard to herself. Of the likeness to Arthur, which he
thought he saw the previous day, there had been no trace
that morning when he pinned the rose upon her bib. She
could not be Gretchen's daughter, and was undoubtedly
the child of the woman found dead in the Tramp House—
his Jerrie, whom he had found, and claimed as his own,
and whom he meant to win some day, when he had his
profession, and was established in business.

"But that will be a long, long time, and some one else
may steal her from me," he said to himself, sadly, as he
thought of the years which must elapse before he could
venture to take a wife. "Oh, if I were sure she cared for
me as I do for her, I would ask her now, and have it settled; for Jerrie is not a girl to go back on her promise,
and the years would seem so short, and the work so easy,
with Jerrie at the end of it all," he continued; and then
he wondered how he could find out the nature of Jerrie's
feeling for him without asking her directly, and so spoiling
everything if he should happen to be premature.

Would his grandmother know? Not at all likely. She
was too old to know much of love, or its symptoms in a
girl. Would Nina St. Claire know? Possibly, for she
and Jerrie were great friends, and girls always told each
other their secrets, so Maude said, and Maude was just then

his oracle. He had seen so much of her the last few months that he felt as if he knew her even better than he did Jerrie, and he was certainly more at his ease in her presence. Then why not talk with Maude and enlist her as a partisan. He might certainly venture to make her his confidant, she had been so very communicative and familiar with him, telling him things which he had wondered at, with regard to her father, and mother, and Tom, and the family-generally. Yes, he would sound Maude, very cautiously at first, and get her opinion, and then he should know better what to do. Maude would espouse his cause, he was sure, for she worshiped Jerrie. He could trust her, and he would.

He had reached the Allen farm-house by this time, and though he was perspiring at every pore, for the morning was very hot, he scarcely felt the heat or the fatigue of his rapid four-mile walk, as he mixed his paints and prepared for his work, for there was constantly in his heart a thought of Jerrie, as she had looked in that bewitching dress, and of the bright smile she had given him when she said good-by.

Meanwhile Jerrie had watched him out of sight, whistling merrily :

> " Gin a body meet a body,
>   Comin' through the rye,
>   Gin a body kiss a body,
>   Need a body cry ?"

And whistling it so loud and clear that Nannie came to the fence and put her head over it with a faint low of approval, while Clover-top thrust his white nose through the bars, and looked at her inquiringly, as Jerrie pulled up handfuls of fresh grass and fed them from her hands, noticing that Nannie had lost her knot of ribbon, and wondering where it was. Then she returned to the house, and was busying herself with preparations for her grandmother's breakfast and her own, when the latter appeared in the kitchen, surprised to find her there, and saying :

" Why, Jerrie what made you get up till I called you ? Why didn't you lie and rest ?"

" Lie and rest !" Jerrie answered, laughingly. " It is you who are to lie and rest, and not a great overgrown girl

like me. I have given Harold his breakfast and seen him
off. I cooked him half the steak," she added, as she took
out the remaining half and put it on the gridiron. "I
don't care for steak," she continued, as she saw Mrs. Crawford about to protest. "I would rather any time have
bread and milk and strawberries. I shall never tire of
them;" and the big bowl full, which she ate with a keen
relish, proved that she spoke the truth.

"Now, grandma," she said, when breakfast was over.
"I am going to do the washing. I must do something to
work off my superfluous health, and strength, and muscle.
Look at that arm, will you?" and she threw out her bare
arm, which for whiteness and roundness and symmetry of
proportion, might have been coveted by the most fashionable lady in the land. "Go back to your rocking-chair and
rest your dear, old lame foot on your softest cushion, and
see how soon I will have everything done. It is just seven
now, and by ten we shall be all slicked up, as Ann Eliza
Peterkin says."

It was of no use to try to resist Jerrie. She would have
her own way; and so Mrs. Crawford, after skimming her
milk, and attending to the cream, went to her rocking-
chair and her cushion, and sat there quietly, while Jerrie
in the wood-shed pounded and rubbed, and boiled and
rinsed, and wrung and starched and blued, and hung upon
the line article after article, until there remained only a
few towels and aprons and stockings and socks, and a pair
of colored overalls which Harold had worn at his work.
As these last were rather soiled and had on them patches
of paint, Jerrie was attacking them with a will, when her
grandmother called out with great trepidation :

"Jerrie, Jerrie, do wipe your hands and come quick !
Here's Tom Tracy, hitching his horse to the gate."

Jerrie's first impulse was to do as her grandmother bade
her, and her second to stay where she was.

"If Tom chooses to call so early he must take me as he
finds me," she thought, while to her grandmother she said :
"Nonsense ! Who cares for Tom Tracy ? If he asks for
me, send him to the woodshed. I can't stop my work."

In a moment the elegant Tom, fresh from his perfumed
bath, the odor of which still lingered about him, and faultlessly attired in a cool summer suit, was bending his tall

figure in the door-way of the woodshed, where Jerrie, who was rubbing away on Harold's overalls, received him with a nod and a smile, as she said :

" Good-morning, Tom. You are up early, and so was I. Business before pleasure, you know ; so I hope you will excuse me if I keep right on. I have stinted myself to get through, mopping and all, by ten, and it is now nine by Peterkin's bell. Pray be seated. How is Maude ?"

And she pointed to a wooden chair near the door, where Tom sat down, wholly nonplussed, and not knowing at all what to say first.

Never before had he been received in this fashion, and it struck him that there was something incongruous between himself, in his dainty attire, with a cluster of beautiful roses in his hand, and that chair, minus a back, in the woodshed, where the smell of the soap-suds would have made him faint and sick if he had not been near the open door.

Tom had not slept well the previous night. He had joined the fine dinner-party his mother had given to the Harts, and St. Claires, and Athertons, and had sat next to Fred Raymond's sister Marian, a very pretty young girl with a good deal that was foreign in her style and in her accent for she had been in Europe nine years, and had only just come home. Everything in her manner was perfect, and Tom acknowledged to himself that she was the most highly polished and cultivated girl he had ever met ; and still she tired him, and he was constantly contrasting her with Jerrie, and thinking how much better he should enjoy himself if she were there beside him, with her ready wit and teasing remarks, which frequently amounted to ridicule. Jerrie had been very gracious to him on the train, and had laughed and joked with him quite as much as she had with Dick St. Claire.

" Perhaps she likes me more than I have supposed she did," he thought. " Any way, I'd better be on hand, now she is at home and can see Harold every day. He don't care a copper for Maude, or wouldn't if she didn't run after him so much, and that will sicken him pretty soon, now that he has Jerrie. By George, I believe I'd be as poor as he is, and paint for a living if I couldn't have Jerrie without it. But I think I can ; any way, I'm going to try. She cannot be insensible to the advantage it would be to her to be my wife, and eventually the mistress of Tracy Park. There is not a girl in the world who would not consider twice before she threw such a chance away."

Such was the nature of Tom's reflections all through the dinner, and the short summer night during which he was planning his mode of attack.

" I'll call in the morning and take her some roses : she likes flowers," he thought. " I wonder what she did with those I gave her at Vassar ? They were not with her in the car, unless she had them in that paper box she carried so carefully Yes, I guess they were there, and I shall see them standing round somewhere."

And this was the secret of Tom's early call. He had thought at first to walk, but had changed his mind, and driven down to the cottage in his light buggy, with the intention of asking Jerrie to drive with him along the river road. But she did not look much like driving as she stood by the wash tub in that working-dress, which he thought the most charming of anything he had ever seen.

" I was coming this way," he said at last, " and thought I'd stop and see how you stood the journey, and I've brought you some roses."

He held them toward her, and with a smile she came forward to receive them.

" Oh, thank you, Tom," she said, " it was so kind in you. Roses are my favorites after the white pond lilies, and these are very sweet."

She buried her face in them two or three times, and then, putting them in some water, resumed her position by the wash-tub.

" I'd like you to drive with me," Tom said, " but I see you are too busy. Must you do that work, Jerrie ? Can't somebody—can't your grandmother do it for you ?"

" Grandmother ! That old lady do my washing ! No, indeed !" Jerrie answered, scornfully, as she made a dive into the boiler with the clothes-stick and brought out a pair of Mrs. Crawford's long knit stockings, which she dropped into the rinsing water with a splash. " Grandma has worked enough," she continued, as she plunged both her arms into the water. " Harold and I shall take care of her now. He was up this morning at four o'clock, and has gone to Mr. Allen's, to paint a room for him like mine."

She said this a little defiantly, for she felt hot and resentful that Tom Tracy should be sitting there at his ease, while Harold was working for his daily bread, and also took a kind of bitter pride in letting Tom know that she was not ashamed of Harold's work.

"Yes," Tom drawled, "that new room must have cost Hal his bottom dollar. We all wondered how he could afford it. I hope you like it."

She was too angry to tell him whether she liked it or not, for she knew his speech was prompted by a mean spirit, and she kept on rubbing a towel until there was danger of its being rubbed into shreds. Then suddenly remembering that Tom had not told her of Maude, she repeated her question.

"How is Maude? She was coming to see me this morning. I hope I shall have my work done before she gets here."

"Don't hurry yourself for Maude," Tom replied. "She will not be here to-day. I had nearly forgotten that she sent her love and wants you to come there. She is sick in bed, or was when I left. She had a slight hemorrhage last night. I think it was from her stomach, though, and so does mother; but father is scared to death, as he always is if Maude has a pain in her little finger."

"Oh, Tom," Jerrie said, recalling with a pang the thin face, the blue-veined hands, and the tired look of the young girl at the station. "Oh, Tom, why didn't you tell me before, so I could hurry and go to her;" and leaning over her tub, Jerrie began to cry, while Tom looked curiously at her, wondering if she really cared so much for his sister.

"Don't cry, Jerrie," he said, at last, very tenderly for him, "Maude is not so bad; the doctor has no fear. She is only tired with all she has done lately. You know, perhaps, that she was here constantly with Harold, and I believe she actually painted for him some, and for aught I know helped shingle the roof, as Billy said."

"Yes, I know; I understand," Jerrie replied. "I saw it in her face yesterday. She has tired herself out for me, and if she dies I shall hate the room forever."

"But she will not die; that is nonsense," Tom began, when he was interrupted by Mrs. Crawford, who called out:

"Oh, Jerrie, here is Billy Peterkin, with his hands full. What shall I do with him?"

Dashing away her tears, Jerrie replied:

"Send him in here, of course."

In a few moments the dapper little man was in the wood-shed, with a large bouquet of hot-house flowers in one hand and a basket of delicious black-caps in the other. For a moment he stood staring first at Tom on the wooden chair glaring savagely at him, and then at Jerrie by the washtub with the traces of tears on her face—then, with a kind of forced laugh, he said:

"Be-beg pardon, if I in-tr-trude. Looks dusedly like l-love in a t-t-tub."

"And if it is, you have knocked the bottom out," Tom said to him.

Both jokes were atrocious, but they made Jerrie laugh, which was something. She was glad on the whole that Billy had come, and when he offered her the berries and the flowers, she accepted them graciously, and bade him sit down, if he could find a seat.

"Here is one on the wash bench," she said, "or, will be when I have emptied the tub;" and she was about to take up the latter, when Billy sprang to her assistance and emptied it himself, while Tom sat looking on, chafing with anger and disgust.

After a moment Billy stuttered out:

"Ann Eliza s-s-sent me here, and wants you to c-c-come and see her rooms. G-g-got a suite, you know; and, by Jove, they are like a b-b-bazaar, they are so f-full of things, and flowers; half Vassar is there. Got your basket of daisies, Tom, and when I asked her where she g-g-got 'em, she said it was n-n-none of my business. D-did she steal 'em?" and he turned to Jerrie, whose face was scarlet, as she replied:

"No, I gave them to her, with a lot of others; I couldn't bring them all."

Tom could have beaten the air, he was so angry. He had been vain enough to hope that his gift was carefully put away in some box or parcel; and lo! it was in the possession of that red-haired Peterkin girl, whose *penchant* for himself he suspected, and whom he despised accordingly.

"Much obliged to you for giving away my flowers," he was going to say, when Mrs. Crawford called again, and this time in real distress.

"Jerrie, Jerrie! you *must* come now, for here is Dick St. Claire."

For an instant Jerrie hesitated, and then, ashamed of the feeling which had at first prompted her not to let Dick into the wood-shed, she replied :

"If Tom and Billy can be admitted to my boudoir, Dick can. Send him in."

"By George, this is jolly!" Dick said, as he seated himself upon the inverted washtub which Billy had emptied. "Have you all been washing?"

"No," Jerrie answered, proudly. "I am the washerwoman, and all those clothes you see on the line are my handiwork."

"By George!" Dick said again. "You are a trump! Jerrie, why didn't you wear that dress when you were graduated? It's the prettiest costume I ever saw."

"Th-that's what I think, only I d-didn't d-dare t-tell her so!" Billy cried, springing to his feet and hopping about like a little sparrow.

"How is Nina?" Jerrie asked, ignoring the compliment.

"Brisk as a bee," Dick replied, "and sends an invitation for you and Hal to come over to a garden-tea to-night to meet Marian Raymond, Fred's sister. Awful pretty girl, with an accent like a foreigner; was over there several years, you know. I was going to the Park House to invite you and Maude," he continued, turning to Tom, "but as you are here, it will save me the walk. Half-past five sharp."

Then, as his eye fell upon Billy, in whose face there was a look of expectancy, his countenance clouded, for Nina had given him no instructions to invite the Peterkins, and he felt that there was nothing in common between Ann Eliza Peterkin and the refined and aristocratic Marian Raymond, who had seen the best society in Europe, and in whose veins some of Kentucky's bluest blood was flowing. But Dick was very kind-hearted, and never knowingly wounded the feelings of any one if he could help it ; and, after an awkward moment, during which he was wondering what Nina would do to him if he did it, he turned to Billy and said, as naturally as if it were what he had been expressly bidden to say :

" Why, I sha'n't have to walk over to Le Bateau either. I'm in luck this hot morning, if you will take the invitation to your sister— for half-past five."

" Th-thanks," Billy began ; " b-but am I left out ?"

" Of course not. I'm an awful blunderer," Dick said, adding, mentally, " and liar, too, though I didn't say anybody would be happy to see them. Poor Billy, he is well enough, and so is Ann Eliza, if she wouldn't pile that red hair so high on the top of her head and wear so much jewelry. Well, I am in for it, and Nina can't any more than kill me."

By this time Jerrie was putting away the washing paraphernalia and sweeping the wood-shed, thus indicating that she had no more time to lose with her three callers, two of whom Dick and Billy, took the hint and left, but not until she had explained to the former that she feared it would be impossible for Harold to be present at the garden-party, as she knew he would not be home until late, and would then be quite too tired for company.

" I am sorry that he cannot join us. I counted upon him," Dick said. " But you will come, of course, and I offer my services on the spot to see you home. Do you accept them ?"

Jerrie seemed to see, without looking, the disappointment in Billy's face, and the wrath in Tom's ; but as she greatly preferred Dick's society to theirs in a walk from Grassy Spring to the cottage, she accepted his offer, and then said, laughingly :

" Now, good-morning to you, and good riddance, too, for I am in an awful hurry. I am going over to see Maude as soon as I can get myself ready."

She had not thought that Tom would wait for her, and would greatly have preferred to walk ; but Tom was persistent, and moving his chair from the wood-shed outside into the shade where it was cooler, he sat fanning himself with his hat, and watching the long line of clothes, flopping in the wind, with a feeling of mortified pride, as if his own wife had washed them. He knew that his mother had once been familiar with tubs, and wash-boards, and soap-suds, but that was before his day. Twenty-seven years had wiped all that out, and he really felt that to be a Tracy and live at Tracy Park was an honor scarcely less than to be President of the United States, and Jerrie, he was sure, would see it as such, when once the chance was offered her. She could not be so blind to her own interest as to refuse one who was so much sought after by the belles of Saratoga and Newport, where he had spent a part of two or three seasons. He had been best man at the great —— wedding in Springfield, and groomsman at another big affair in Boston, and had scores of invitations everywhere. Taken all together, he was a most desirable *parti*, and he was rather surprised himself at his infatuation for the girl whom he had found in the suds, and who was not ashamed that he had thus seen her. This was while he was watching the clothes on the line, and scowling at three pairs of coarse, vulgar stockings which he knew belonged to Mrs. Crawford, and at the pair of blue overalls which were Harold's.

"Yes, I do wonder at my interest in that nameless girl, whose mother was a common peasant woman," he thought ; but when the nameless girl appeared, fresh, and bright, and dainty, as if she had never seen a wash-tub, with her hat on her arm, and two of his roses pinned on the bosom of her dress, he forgot the peasant woman, and the lack of a name, and thought only of the lovely girl who signified that she was ready.

It was very cool in the pine woods, where the heat of the summer morning had not yet penetrated, and Tom, who was enjoying himself immensely, suggested that they leave the park, and take a short drive on the river road. But Jerrie said, "No !" very decidedly. It would be hot, there, and she was anxious to be with Maude as soon as possible. So they drove on until they reached the grounds which surrounded the house, and where they were met by Mr. Tracy.

CHAPTER XXXIII.

AT THE PARK HOUSE.

IT was six months since Jerrie had seen Frank Tracy, and in that time he had changed so much that she looked at him wonderingly as he came toward her with a smile on his haggard face, and an eager welcome in his voice, as he gave her both his hands, and told her how glad he was to see her.

His hair was very white, and she noticed how he stooped as he walked with her to the house, and told her how anxiously Maude was waiting for her.

"But she cannot talk just yet," he said. "You must do all that. The doctor tells us there is no danger if she is kept quiet for a few days. Oh, Jerrie, what if I should lose Maude after all"

They were ascending the staircase now, and Frank was holding Jerrie's hand while she tried to comfort and reassure him, and then thanked him for the fruit and the flowers he had sent to the cottage for her the day before.

"You are so good to me," she said, "you and Mr. Arthur. How lonely the house seems without him."

"Yes," Frank replied, though in his heart he felt his brother's absence as a relief, for his presence was a constant reproach to him, and helped to keep alive the remorse which was always tormenting him.

The sight of Jerrie was a pain, but she held a nameless fascination for him, and he was constantly wondering what she would say and do when she knew, as he was morally sure she would sometime know what he had done. He was thinking of this now, and saying to himself, "She will not be as hard upon me as Arthur," as he lead her up the stairs and stopped at the door of Arthur's rooms.

"Would you like to go in?" he asked. "I have the keys," and he proceeded to unlock the door.

But Jerrie held back.

"No," she said, "it is like a grave. The ruling spirit is gone."

"But you forget Gretchen. She is here, and one of Arthur's last injunctions was that I should visit her every day, and tell her he was coming back. I have not seen her this morning. Come."

He was leading her now by the wrist through the front parlor, where the furniture in its white shrouds looked like ghosts, and the pictures were covered with tarleton. It was dark, too, in the Gretchen room, but Frank threw open the blinds and let in a flood of light upon the picture, before which Jerrie stood with feelings such as she had never experienced before, when she looked upon that lovely face.

A new idea had taken possession of Jerrie since she had last seen that picture, and while, unsuspected by her, Frank was studying first her features and then those of Gretchen, she was struggling frantically with memories of the past.

"Oh, I can almost remember," she whispered, just as Frank's voice broke the spell by saying :

"Good-morning, Gretchen. Arthur is in California, but he is coming back ; he bade me tell you so."

"Is he crazy as well as Mr. Arthur ? Are we all crazy together ?" Jerrie asked herself, as she watched him closing the blinds and shutting out the sunlight from the room, so that the picture was in shadow.

"I have kept my promise to Arthur ; and now for Maude," Frank said, as he accompanied Jerrie to Maude's room.

On the threshold they met Mrs. Frank, just coming out, elegantly attired in a muslin wrapper, with more lace and embroidery upon it than Jerrie had ever worn in her life ; her hair was carefully dressed, her face was powdered, and her manner was one of languor and fineladyism, which she had cultivated so assiduously and achieved so successfully. Not a muscle of her face changed when she saw Jerrie, but she closed Maude's door quickly, and stepping into the hall, offered the tips of her fingers, as she said, in a fretful, rather than a welcoming tone :

"Good-morning. You are very late. Maude expected you two hours ago, almost immediately after Tom went out. She has worked herself into a great state of feverish nervousness."

"I am so sorry," Jerrie replied. "But 1 could not come sooner. I had a large washing to do, and that takes time, you know."

Jerrie meant no reflection upon the days when Dolly had done her own washing, and knew that it took time, but the lady thought she did, and a frown settled upon her face, as she replied :

"Surely your grandmother might have helped you, or Harold ; and Maude is so impatient and weak this morning. The doctor says there is no danger if she is kept quiet. She is only tired out, with that room of yours. Why, I am told she has actually puttied up nail holes, and painted walls, and sawed boards ! I hope you like it. You ought to, for a part of Maude's life and strength is in it."

"Oh, Mrs. Tracy," Jerrie cried, "I am so sorry. Of course I like the room, or did ; but if it has injured Maude, I shall hate it."

Dolly had given her a little stab and was satisfied, so she said, in a softer tone :

"Maude may recover—I think she will ; but everything must be done to please her, and she cannot talk to you this morning—remember that, and you must not stay too long."

"Mamma—mamma, let Jerrie in," came faintly from the closed room ; and then Mrs. Tracy stood aside and let Jerrie pass into the luxurious apartment, where Maude lay upon a silken couch, with a soft, rose-colored shawl thrown over her shoulders, her eyes large and bright, and her face as white almost as a corpse.

One looking at her needed not to be told of the peril there was in exciting her ; and Jerrie felt a cold chill creep over her as she went to the couch, and, kneeling beside it, kissed the quivering lips and smoothed the dark hair, while she tried to speak naturally and cheerfully, as if in her mind there was no thought of danger to the beautiful girl, who smiled so lovingly upon her and kept caressing her hands and her face, as if she would thus express her gladness to see her.

"I know all about it, Maude," Jerrie said. "Tom told me, and your mother. You tired yourself out for me. Hush ! Don't speak, or I shall go away," she continued, as she saw Maude's lips move. "You are not to talk.

You are to listen, just for a day or two, and then you will be better, and come to the cottage and see my lovely room. It is so pretty, and I like it so much, and thank you and Harold so much. He has gone to the Allen farm to-day to paint," she said, in answer to an eager, questioning look in Maude's eyes. "He does not know you are sick. He will come when he can see you—to-morrow, maybe. Would you like to have him ?"

A pressure of the hand was Maude's reply, as the moisture gathered upon her heavy eyelashes. But Jerrie kissed it away, and then talked to her of whatever she thought would please her. Once she made her laugh, as she took off little Billy, imitating his voice so perfectly that a person outside would have said he was in the room. Jerrie's talent for imitation and ventriloquism had not deserted her, although she did not so often practice it as when a child ; but she brought it into full play now to amuse Maude, and imitated every individual of whom she spoke, except Arthur. He was the one person whose peculiarities she could not take off.

"I have been to Mr. Arthur's room," she said, "but it seemed so desolate without him. Do you hear from him often ? I have only had one letter, and then he was in Salt Lake City, at the Continental, in a room which he said was big enough for three rooms, and had not a single bad smell in it, except the curtains, which were new, and in which he did detect a little odor."

Here Maude laughed again, while there came into her face a faint color and a look which made Jerrie's breath come quickly as, for the first time, the thought flashed across her mind that if what she had been foolish enough to dream of were true, Maude was her cousin—her own flesh and blood.

"Maude," she said, suddenly, with a strong desire to fold the frail little body in her arms and tell her what she had thought.

But when Maude looked up inquiringly at her, she only put her head down upon the shawl and began to cry. Then, regardless of consequences, Maude raised herself upon her elbow and laying her face on Jerrie's head, began herself to cry piteously.

"Jerrie, Jerrie," she sobbed, "you think I am going

to die, I know you do, and so does everybody, but I am not; I cannot die when there is so much to live for, and my home is so beautiful, and I love everybody so much, and—"

Terrified beyond measure, Jerrie put her hand over Maude's mouth and said, almost sharply:

"If you want to live you must not talk. Be careful and you will get well, the doctor says so."

But Jerrie's fears belied her words when she saw the pallor in Maude's face as she sank back upon her pillow exhausted, while, with her handkerchief she wiped a faint coloring of blood from her lips.

"I have staid too long," Jerrie said, as she arose from her seat by the couch. Then Maude spoke again in a whisper:

"Send Harold soon."

"I will," Jerrie replied, and kissing the death-like face she went softly from the room, thinking to herself, as she descended the stairs, "I believe I could give Harold to her now."

CHAPTER XXXIV.

UNDER THE PINES WITH TOM.

JERRIE found Tom just where she had left him, on the piazza outside, waiting for her, it would seem, for the moment she appeared he arose, and going with her down the steps walked by her side along the avenue toward the point where she would turn aside into the road which led to the cottage.

"How did you find Maude?" he asked.

"Weaker than I supposed," Jerrie replied, "and so tired. Oh, Tom, I know she hurt herself worrying about my room as she did, and what if she should die?"

"Nonsense," Tom answered, carelessly. "Maude won't die. She's got the Tracy constitution, which nothing can kill. Don't fret about your room. Maude liked being there. Nothing could keep her away. And don't flatter yourself that it was all love for you which took her there so much, for it wasn't. She is just mashed with Harold, while he—well, what can a young man do when a pretty girl—and Maude is pretty—when she gushes at him all the time? It is a regular flirtation, and everybody knows about it except mother and the Gov."

"Who is the Gov.?" Jerrie asked, sharply

"Why, you Vassars must be very innocent," Tom replied, with a laugh, "not to know that Gov. is one's respected sire; the old man, some call him, but I am more respectful. My gracious, though! isn't it sweltering? I'm nearly baked, you make me walk so fast!" and he wiped the great drops of sweat from his forehead.

"Why don't you go back, then?" Jerrie asked.

"I am going home with you," he replied. "Do you think I'd let you go alone?"

"Go alone?" Jerrie repeated, stopping short and fixing her blue eyes upon him. "You have let me go alone a hundred times, and after dark, too, when I was much smaller than I am now, and less able to defend myself, supposing there was anything to fear, which there is not. Pray go back, and not trouble yourself for me."

"I shall not go back," Tom said. "I waited on purpose to come with you. There is something I must say to you, and I may as well say it now as any other time."

Jerrie was tall, but Tom was six inches taller, and he was looking down into her eyes with an expression in his before which hers fell, for she guessed what it was he wished to say to her, and her heart beat painfully as, without another word, she walked rapidly on until they were in the woods near a place where four tall pines formed a kind of oblong square. Here an iron seat had been placed years before, when the Tracy children were young, and held what they called their picnics under the thick boughs of the pines which shaded them from both heat and cold. Laying his hand on Jerrie's shoulder, Tom said to her:

"Sit here with me under the pines while I tell you what for a long time I have wanted to tell you, and which may as well be told at once."

Jerrie did not speak, but she sat down upon the seat, and, taking off her hat, began to fan herself with it, while with the end of her parasol she tried to trace letters in the thick carpet of dead pine needles at her feet.

Her attitude was not encouraging, and a less conceited man than Tom would have felt disheartened, but he was not. No girl would be insane enough to refuse Tom Tracy, of Tracy Park; and at last he made the plunge and told her of his love for her and his desire to make her his wife.

"I know I was a mean little scamp when I was a boy," he said, "and did a lot of things for which I am ashamed; but I always thought you the prettiest little girl I ever saw, and now I think you the prettiest big one, and I have had splendid opportunities for seeing girls. You know I have traveled a great deal, and been in the very best society; and if I may say it, I think I can marry almost any one whom I choose. I used to fear lest you and Hal would hit it off together, or, rather, that he would try to get you, but, since he and Maude are so thick, my fears in that quarter have vanished, and I am constantly building castles as to what we will do. I did not mean to ask you quite so soon, but the sight of you this morning washing your clothes, with all that soapy steam in your face, decided me not to put it off. A Tracy has no business in a washtub."

"Did no Tracy ever wash her own clothes?" Jerrie asked with an upward and sidewise turn of her head, habitual with her when startled or stirred.

There was a ring in her voice which Tom did not quite like, but he answered, promptly:

"Oh, of course, years ago; but times change, and you certainly ought not to be familiar with such vulgar things, and at Tracy Park you will be surrounded with every possible luxury. Father, and Maude, and Uncle Arthur will be overjoyed to have you there; and if, on my part, love and money can make you happy, you certainly will be so."

"You have plenty of money of your own?" Jerrie said, with another upward toss of her golden head.

The question was full of sarcasm, but Tom did not detect it, and answered at once:

"Why, yes, or I shall have in time. Uncle Arthur, you know, is in no condition to make a will now. It would not stand a minute. All the lawyers say that."

"You have taken counsel, then?"

13

The parasol dug a great hole in the soft pines and was in danger of being broken, as Tom replied :

"Oh, yes, we are sure of that. Whatever Uncle Arthur has, and it is more than a million, will go to father, and, after him, to Maude and me ; so you are sure to be rich and to be the mistress of Tracy Park, which will naturally come to me. Think, Jerrie, what a different life you will lead at the Park House from what you do now, washing old Mrs. Crawford's stockings and Harold's overalls."

"Yes, I am thinking," Jerrie answered, very low ; and if Tom had followed the end of her parasol, he would have seen that it was forming the word Gretchen in front of him.

"Suppose **Mr. Arthur** has a wife somewhere ?" Jerrie asked.

"A wife !" Tom exclaimed. "That is impossible. We should have heard of that."

"Who was Gretchen ?" was the next query.

"Oh, some sweetheart, I suppose—some little German girl with whom he amused himself awhile and then cast off, as men usually do such incumbrances."

Tom did not quite know himself what he was saying, or what it implied, and he was not at all prepared to see the parasol stuck straight into the ground, while Jerrie sprang to her feet and confronted him fiercely.

"Tom Tracy ! If you mean to insinuate a thing which is not good and pure against Gretchen, I'll never speak to you as long as I live ! Take back what you said about Mr. Arthur's casting her off ! She was his wife and you know it ! Dead, perhaps—I think she is ; but she was his wife— his true and lawful wife ; and—I—sometimes"—

She could not add "think she was my mother," for the words stuck in her throat, where her heart seemed to be beating wildly and choking her utterance.

"Why, Jerrie," Tom said, startled at her excited appearance, and anxious to appease her, "what ails you ? I hardly know what I said, and if I have offended you, I am sorry. I know nothing of Gretchen ; her face is a good one and a pretty one, and Maude says you look like her ; though I don't see it, for I think you far prettier than she. Perhaps she was my uncle's wife ; but that does not injure **my** prospects, for of course she is dead, or she would have turned up before this time. We have nothing to fear from her."

"She may have left a child. What then?" Jerrie asked, with as steady a voice as she could command.

"Pshaw! humbug!" Tom replied, with a laugh. "That is impossible. A child would have been heard from before this time. There is no child. I'm sure I hope not, as that would seriously interfere with our prospects. Think of some one—say a young lady—walking in upon us some day and claiming to be Arthur Tracy's daughter!"

"What would you do?" Jerrie asked, in a tone of smothered excitement.

"I believe I'd kill her," Tom said, laughingly, "or marry her, if I had not already seen you. But don't worry about that. There is no child; there is nothing between us and a million, and you have only to appoint the day which will make me the happiest of men, and free you from a drudgery, which just to think of sets my teeth on edge. Will you name the day, Jerrie?"

If it had been possible for a look to have annihilated Tom, the scorn which blazed in Jerrie's eyes would have done so. To hear him talk as if the matter were settled and the money he was to inherit from his uncle could buy her made her blood boil, and seizing her poor parasol, still standing up so straight in the pine needles, she stepped backward from him and said, in a mocking voice:

"Thank you, Tom, for the honor you would confer upon me, and which I must decline, for I would rather wash grandma's stockings all my life, and Harold's overalls, too, than marry a man for money."

"Jerrie, oh, Jerrie, you don't mean it! You do not refuse me!" Tom cried, in alarm, stretching out his arm to reach her, but touching only the parasol, to which he clung desperately, as a drowning man to a straw.

"I do mean it, Tom," she said, softened a little by the pain she saw in his face. "I can never be your wife."

"But why not?" Tom demanded. "Many a girl who stands higher socially in the world than you would gladly bear my name. I might have married Governor Storey's daughter, at Saratoga, last summer, but one thought of you was enough to keep me from her. You cannot be in earnest."

"But I am. I care nothing for your money, which may or may not be yours. I do not love you Tom ; and without love I would not marry a prince."

It was very hard for Tom to believe that Jerrie really meant to refuse him, who, with all his love for her—and he did love her as well as he was capable of loving any one—still felt that he was stooping or at least was honoring her greatly when he asked her to be his wife. And she had refused him, and kept on refusing him in spite of all he could say; and worse than all, made him feel at last that she did not consider it an honor to be Mrs. Tom Tracy, of Tracy Park, and did not care either for him or his prospective fortune. She called it that finally, and then Tom grew angry and taunted her with fostering a hope that Arthur might make her his heir, or at least leave her some portion of his money.

"But I tell you he can't do it. A crazy man's will would never stand, and he is crazy and you know it. You will never touch a dollar of Uncle Arthur's money, if you live to be a hundred, unless it comes to you from me. Don't flatter yourself that you will, and don't flatter yourself either that you will ever catch Hal Hastings, who is the real obstacle in my way. He is after Maud, who ought to look higher than a painter, a carpenter, a——"

"Tom Tracy !" and Jerrie's parasol was raised so defiantly and her eyes flashed so indignantly that Tom did not finish what he was going to say, but cowered before the angry girl, who hurled her words at him with such scathing vehemence. "Tom Tracy! stop! You have said enough. When you made me believe that you really did care for me ; and I suppose you must, or you would not have thrown over a governor's daughter for me, or left so many love-lorne, high-born maidens out in the cold, I was sorry for you, for I hate to give any one pain, and I would rather have you my friend than my enemy ; but when you taunt me with expectations from your uncle——"

Here Jerrie paused, for the lump in her throat would not suffer the words to come, and there arose before her as if painted upon canvas the low room, the white stove, the firelight on the whiter face, and the little child in the far-off German city. But she would have died sooner than have told Tom of this, or that the conviction was strong upon her that she should one day stand there under the pines, herself the heiress of Tracy Park, Gretchen's memory honored, and Gretchen's wrongs wiped out.

After a moment she went on:

"I care nothing for your money, and less for you, who show the meanness there is in your nature when you speak of Harold Hastings as you have done. Suppose he is poor —suppose he is a painter and a carpenter and has been what you started to call him—is he less a man for that ? A thousand times no, and if Maude has won his love, she should be prouder of it than of a duchess' coronet ; I do not wish to wound you, but when you talk of Harold, you make me so mad. Good-morning ; it is time for me to be at my drudgery, as you call it."

She walked swiftly away, leaving her parasol, which she had again thrust into the ground, flopping in the breeze which had just sprung up, and each flop seeming to mock the discomfited Tom, who greatly astonished, but not at all out of conceit with himself, sat looking blankly after her, as with her head and shoulders more erect than usual, if possible, she went on almost upon a run until a turn in the road hid her from view. Then he arose and shook himself together, and picking up the soiled parasol, folded it carefully and put it upon the seat, saying as he did so:

"By George, did that girl know what she was about when she refused me ?"

CHAPTER XXXV.

THE GARDEN PARTY.

JERRIE walked very rapidly toward home, almost running at times, and not at all conscious of the absence of her parasol, or that the noonday sun was beating hot upon her head. She was too much excited to think of any thing clearly except of what Tom had said to her of Maude and Harold. How she hated him for it, and hated herself, for her jealousy of the poor little sick girl, whose days she feared were numbered. "If Harold is a comfort to her, shall I begrudge her that comfort! Never, no, never." she said aloud. Then as she remembered Tom's offer, which she believed had been made in good faith, she continued: "Poor Tom! I said some sharp things to him, but he deserved them, the prig! Let him marry that governor's daughter if he can. I am sure I wish him success."

She had reached home by this time and found their simple dinner waiting for her.

"Oh, grandma, why did you do it? Why didn't you wait for me?" she said, as she took her seat at the table, where the dishes were all so plain, and the cloth, though white and clean, so coarse and cheap.

Jerrie was as fond of luxury and elegance as any one, and Tracy Park would have suited her taste better than the cottage.

"But not with Tom," she kept repeating to herself, as she cleared the table and washed the dishes, and then brought in and folded the cloths for the morrow's ironing.

By this time she was very tired, and going to her room, she threw herself upon the lounge and slept soundly for two hours or more. Sleep is a wonderful tonic and Jerry rose refreshed and quite herself again. Not even a thought of Maude and Harold disturbed her as she went whistling and singing around her room, hanging up her dresses one by one, and wondering which she should wear at the garden party. Deciding at last upon a white muslin, which, although two years old, was still in fashion, and very becoming, she arranged her hair in a fluffy mass at the back of her head, brushed her bangs into short, soft curls upon her forehead, pinned a cluster of roses on the bosom of her dress, and was ready for the party.

"Tell Harold, if he is not too tired, I want him very much to come for me," she said to Mrs. Crawford, and then about five o'clock started for Grassy Spring, where she found the guests assembled in the grounds, which surrounded the house.

Tom was there in his character of a fine city dandy, and the moment he saw Jerrie he hastened to meet her, greeting her with perfect self-possession, as if nothing had happened.

"You are late," he said, going up to her. "We are waiting for you to complete our eight hand croquet, and I claim you as my partner."

"I c-c-call that mean, T-t-tom. I was g-g-going to ask J-jerrie to pl-play with m-me," Billy said, while Dick's face showed that he, too, would like the pleasure of playing with Jerrie, who was known to be an expert and seldom missed a ball.

Naturally, however, Marian Raymond as a stranger, would fall to him and they were soon paired off, Dick and Marian, Tom and Jerrie, Nina and Billy, Fred. Raymond and Ann Eliza, who wore diamonds enough for a full dress party, and whose hair was piled on the top of her head so loosely that the ends of it stuck out here and there like the streamers on a boat on gala days. This careless style of dressing her hair Ann Eliza affected, thinking it gave individuality to her appearance; and it certainly did attract general observation. Dick had stumbled and stammered dreadfully when confessing to his sister that he had invited the Peterkins, while Nina had drawn a long breath of dismay as she thought of presenting Ann Eliza and Billy to Marian Raymond, with her culture and aristocratic ideas. Then she burst into a laugh, and said, with her usual sweetness:

"Never mind, Dickie. You could not do otherwise. I'll prepare Marian, and the Peterkins will really enjoy it."

So Marian, who was a kind-hearted, sensible girl, was prepared, and received the Peterkins very graciously, and seemed really pleased with Billy, whose big, kind heart shone through his diminutive body and always won him friends. He was very happy to be there, because he liked society, and because he knew Jerrie was coming; and Ann Eliza was very glad because she felt it an honor to be invited to Grassy Spring, and because Tom was there, and when croquet was proposed she was the first to respond.

"Oh, yes, that will be nice, and I know our side will beat," she said looking at Tom as if it were a settled thing that she should play with him.

But Tom was not in a mood to be gracious. He had come to the entertainment, which he mentally called a bore, partly because he would not let Jerrie think he was taking her refusal to heart, and partly because he must see her

again, even if she never could be his wife. All the better
nature of Tom was concentrated in his love for Jerrie, and
had she married him he would probably have made her as
happy as a wholly selfish man can make happy the woman
he loves. But she had declined his offer, and wounded him
deeper than she supposed. A hundred times he had said
to himself that afternoon, that he did not care a sou, that
he was glad she had refused him, for after all it was only an
infatuation on his part ; that the girl of the carpet-bag was
not the wife for a Tracy ; but the twinge of pain in his
heart belied his words, and he knew he loved Jerrie Crawford better than he should ever again love any girl,
whether the daughter of a governor or of the President.

"And I'll go to the party too, just to show her that I
don't care, and for the sake of seeing her," he said. "She
can't help that, and it is a pleasure to look at a women so
grandly developed and perfectly formed as she is. By Jove !
Hal Hastings is a lucky dog ; but I shall hate him forever."

So Tom went to Grassy Spring in a frame of mind not
the most amiable ; and when croquet, was proposed, he
sneered at it as something quite too *passe*, citing lawn tennis
as the only decent outdoor amusement.

"Why, then, don't you set it up on your grounds,
where you have plenty of room, and ask us all over there ?"
Dick asked, good-humoredly, as he began to get out the
mallets and balls.

To this Tom did not reply, but said, instead :

"Count me out. I don't like the game, and there are
enough without me."

Just then Jerrie appeared at the gate, and he added
quickly.

"Still, I don't wish to seem ungracious ; and now Jerrie
has come, we can have an eight hand."

Hastening towards her, he met her as we have recorded,
and claimed her for his partner.

"Thank you Tom," Jerrie said with a bright smile on
her face, which made the young man's heart beat fast, as he
gave her her mallet, and told her she was to play first.

Tom was making himself master of ceremonies, and
Dick let him, and watched Jerrie admiringly as she made
the two arches, and the third, and fourth, and then sent

her ball out of harm's way. It was a long and closely contested game, for all were skillful players, except poor Ann Eliza, who was always behind and required a great deal of attention from her partner, especially when it came to croqueting a ball. She did not know exactly what to do, and kept her foot so long upon the ball that less amiable girls than Nina and Jerrie would have said she did it on purpose, to show how small and pretty it looked in her closely fitting French boot. But Jerrie's side beat, as it usually did. She had become a "rover" the second round, had rescued Tom from many a difficulty, and taken Ann Eliza through four or five wickets, besides doing good service to her other friends.

"I p-p-propose three ch-cheers for Jerrie," Billy said, standing on tiptoe and nearly splitting his throat with his own hurrah.

After the game was over they repaired to the piazza, where the little tables were laid for tea, and where Jerrie found herself *vis-a-vis* with Marian Raymond, of whom she had thought she might stand a little in awe, she had heard so much of her. But the mesmeric power which Jerrie possessed drew the Kentucky girl to her at once, and they were soon in a most animated conversation.

"You do not seem like a stranger to me," Marian said, "and I should almost say I had seen you before, you are so like a picture in Germany."

"Yes," Jerrie answered, with a gasp, and a feeling such as she always experienced when the spell was upon her and she saw things as in a dream.

"Was it in a gallery?"

"Oh, no; it was in a house we rented in Wiesbaden. You know, perhaps, that I was there at school for a long time. Then, when mamma came out, and I was through school, we staid there for months, it was so lovely, and we rented a house which an Englishman had bought and made over. Such a pretty house it was, too, with so many flowers and vines around it."

"And the picture—did it belong to the Englishman?" Jerrie asked.

"Oh, no," Marian replied; "it did not seem to belong to anybody. Mr. Carter—that was the name of our landlord—said it was there when he took the house, which

13*

was then very small and low, with only two or three rooms. He bought it because of the situation, which, though very quiet and pleasant, was so near the Kursaal that we could always hear the music without going to the garden."

"Yes." Jerrie said again, with her head on one side, and her ear turned up, as if she were listening to some forgotten strains. "Yes; and the picture was like me, you say—how like me?"

"Every way like you," Marian replied; "except that the original must have been younger when it was taken—sixteen, perhaps—and she was smaller than you, and wore a peasant's dress, and was knitting on a bench under a tree, with the sunshine falling around her, and at a little distance a gentleman stood watching her. But what is the matter, Miss Crawford? Are you sick?" Marian asked, suddenly, as she saw the bright color fade from Jerrie's face, while Tom and Dick knocked their heads together in their efforts to get her a glass of water, which they succeeded in spilling into her lap.

"It is nothing," Jerrie said, recovering herself quickly. "I have been in the hot sun a good deal to-day, and perhaps that affected me and made me faint. It has passed now;" and she looked up as brightly as ever.

"It's that confounded washing!" Tom thought; but Jerrie could have told him differently.

As Marian had talked to her of the house in Wiesbaden and the picture of the peasant girl knitting in the sunshine —she had seen, as by revelation—the picture on the wall, in its pretty Florentine frame, and knew that it resembled the face which came to her so often and was so real to her. Was it her old home Marian was describing? Had she lived there once, when the house consisted of only two or three rooms? and was that a picture of her mother, left there she knew not how or why? These were the thoughts crowding each other so fast in her brain when the faintness and pallor crept over her and the objects about her began to seem unreal. But the cold water revived her, and she was soon herself again, listening while Marian talked of heat and sun-strokes, with an evident forgetfulness of the peasant girl knitting in the sunshine; but Jerrie soon recurred to the subject and asked, abruptly:

"Was there a stove in that house—a tall, white stove,

in a corner of one of the old rooms—say the kitchen—and a high-backed settee?"

Marian looked at her a moment in surprise, and then replied:

"Oh, I know what you mean—those unwieldy things in which they sometimes put the wood from the hall. No; there was nothing of that kind, though there was an old settee by the kitchen fire-place, but not a tall stove."

"Was the picture in the kitchen?" Jerrie asked next.

"No," Marian replied, "it was in a little low apartment, which must once have been the best room."

"And was there no theory with regard to it? It seems strange that any one should leave it there if he cared for it," Jerrie said.

"Yes, it does," Marian replied; "but all Mr. Carter knew was that the people of whom he bought the house said the portrait was there when they took possession, and that it had been left to apply on the back rent; also that the original was dead. He (Mr. Carter) had bought the picture with the house, and offered to take it down, but I would not let him. It was such a sweet, sunny, happy face that it did me good to look at it, and wonder who the young girl was, and if her life were ever linked with that of the stranger watching her."

Again the faintness came upon Jerrie, for she could see so plainly the picture of the girl, with the long stocking in her lap—a very long stocking she felt sure it was, but dared not ask, lest they should think her question a strange one. Of the stranger in the back ground she had no recollection, but her heart beat wildly as she thought:

"Was that Mr. Arthur, and was the young girl Gretchen?"

How fast the lines touching her past had widened about her since she first saw the likeness in the mirror, and her confused memories began to take shape and assume a tangible form.

"I will find that house, and that picture, and Mr. Carter, and the people who lived there before him," she said to herself; and then again, addressing Marian, she asked:

"What was the street, and the number of that house?"

Marian told her the street, but could not remember the number, while Tom said laughingly:

"Why Jerrie, what makes you so much interested in an old German house? Do you expect to go there and live in it?"

"Yes," Jerrie replied, in the same light tone. "I am going to Wiesbaden sometime, and I mean to find that house and the picture which Miss Raymond says I am so much like; then I shall know how I look to others. You remember the couplet:

> "'Oh, wad some power the giftie gie us,
>   To see ourselves as others see us!'"

"Look in the glass, the best one you can find, and you'll see yourself as others see you," Dick said, gallantly.

Before Jerrie could reply, a servant appeared on the piazza, saying there was some one at the telephone asking for Mr. Peterkin.

It proved to be Billy's father, who was in the village, and had received a telegram from Springfield concerning a lawsuit which was pending between himself and a rival firm, which claimed that he had infringed upon its patents. Before replying to the telegram he wished to confer with his son, who was to come at once to the hotel, and, if necessary, go to Springfield that night.

"B-by Jove," Billy said, as he explained the matter, "it's too bad that I must g-go, when I'm enjoying m-myself t-t-tip-top. I wish that lawsuit was in Gu-Guinea."

Then turning to Ann Eliza he asked how she would get home if he did not return.

"Oh, don't trouble about me. I can take care of myself," Ann Eliza said, with a bounce up in her chair, which set every loose hair of her frowzy head to flying.

"M-m-maybe they'll send the ca-carriage," Billy went on, "and if they do-don't, m-may be you can g-go with T-Tom as far as his house, and then you wo-won't be afraid."

Tom could have killed the little man for having thus made it impossible for him not to see his sister safely home. He had fully intended to forestall Dick, and go with Jerrie if Harold did not come, for though she had refused him, he wished to keep her as a friend, hoping that in time she might be lead to consider. He liked to hear her voice—to look into her face—to be near her, and the walk in the moonlight, with her upon his arm, had been something very pleasant to contemplate, and now it was snatched from him by Billy's ill-advised speech, and old Peterkin's red-haired daughter thrust upon him. It was rather hard, and Tom's face was very gloomy and dark for the remainder of the evening, while they sat upon the piazza and laughed, and talked, and said the little nothings so pleasant to the young and so meaningless to the old who have forgotten their youth.

Jerrie was the first to speak of going. She had hoped that Harold might possibly come for her, but as the time passed on, and he did not appear, she arose to say good-night to Nina, while Dick hastened forward and announced his intention to accompany her.

"No, Dick, no; please don't," she said. "I am not a bit afraid, and I would rather you did not go."

But Dick was persistent.

"You know you accepted my service this morning," he said, and his face, as he went down the steps with Jerrie on his arm, wore a very different expression from that of poor Tom, who, with Ann Eliza coming about to his elbow, stalked moodily along the road, scarcely hearing and not always replying to the commonplace remarks of his companion, who had never been so happy in her life, because never before had she been out alone in the evening with Tom Tracy as her escort.

CHAPTER XXXVI.

OUT IN THE STORM.

FOR half an hour or more before the young people left the house a dark mass of clouds had been rolling up from the west, and by the time they were out of the grounds and in the highway, the moonlight was wholly obscured, while frequent growls of thunder and flashes of lightning in the distance told of the fast coming storm.

"Oh, I am so afraid of thunder! Aren't you?" Ann Eliza cried, in terror, as she clung closer to Tom, who did not reply until there came a gleam of lightning which showed him the white face and the loose hair blowing out from under his companion's hat.

There was a little shrick of fear and a smothered cry.

"Oh, Tom, aren't you a bit afraid?"

And then Tom answered the trembling little girl who clung so closely to him:

"Thunder and lightning, no! I'm not afraid of anything except getting wet; and if you are, you'd better run before the whole thing is upon us; the sky is blacker than midnight now. I never saw a storm come on so fast. Can you run?"

"Yes—some," Ann Eliza gasped; "only my boots are so tight and new, and the heels are so high. Do you think we shall be struck?"

"Struck? No. But don't screech and hang on to me so. We can never get along if you do," Tom growled; and taking her by the wrist, he dragged rather than led her through the woods where the great rain-drops were beginning to fall so fast, as the two showers—one from the west and one from the south—approached each other, until at last they met overhead, and then commenced a wild and fierce battle of the elements, the southern storm and the western storm each trying to outdo the other and come off conqueror.

As the thunder, and lightning, and rain increased, Tom went on faster and faster, forgetting that the slip of a girl, who scarcely came to his shoulders, could not take as long strides as a great, hulking fellow like himself.

"Oh, Tom, Tom—please not so fast. I can't keep up, my heart beats so and my boots hurt me so," came in a faint, sobbing protest more than once from the panting girl at his side; but he only answered:

"You *must* keep up, or we shall be soaked through and through. I never knew it to rain so fast. Take off your boots, if they hurt you. You've no business to wear such small ones."

He had heard from Maude that Ann Eliza was very proud of her feet, and always wore boots too small for them, and he experienced a savage satisfaction in knowing that she was paying for her foolishness. This was not very kind in Tom, but he was not a kind-hearted man, and he held the whole Peterkin tribe, as he called them, in such contempt that he would scarcely have cared if the tired little feet, boots and all, had dropped off, provided it did not add to his discomfort. They were out of the woods and park by this time, and had struck into a field as a shorter route to Le Bateau. But the way was rough and stony, and Tom had stumbled himself two or three times and almost fallen, when a sharp, loud cry came from Ann Eliza, and he felt that she was sinking to the ground.

His first impulse was to drag her on, but that would have been too brutal, and stopping short he asked what was the matter.

"Oh, I don't know. I guess I've sprained my ankle. It turned right over on a big stone, and hurts me awfully. I can't walk another step. Oh, what shall we do ?"

"I don't know," Tom answered, gloomily. "We are in an awful muss. Here it is raining great guns, and I am wet to my skin, and you can't walk, you say. What in thunder shall we do ?"

Ann Eliza was sobbing piteously, and when a glare of lightning lighted up the whole heavens, Tom caught a glimpse of her face which was distorted with pain, and this decided him. He had thought to leave her in the darkness and rain, while he went for assistance either to the Park House or La Bateau ; but the sight of her utter helplessness awoke in him a spark of pity and bending over her he said, very gently for him :

"Annie,"—this was the name by which he used to call her when they were children together, and he thought Ann Eliza too long—"Annie, I shall have to carry you in my arms ; there is no other way. It is not very far to your home. Come !" and stooping over the prostrate form he lifted her very carefully and holding her in a position the least painful for her, began again to battle with the storm, walking more carefully now and groping his way through the stony field lest he should fall and sprain his own ankle, perhaps.

"This is a jolly go," he said to himself, and then he thought of Dick and Jerrie, and wondered how they were getting through the storm, and if she had sprained her ankle and Dick was carrying her in his arms.

"He will sweat some, if he is, for Jerrie is twice as heavy as Peterkin's daughter;" and at the very idea Tom laughed out loud, thinking that he should greatly prefer having Jerrie in his arms to this little girl, who neither spoke nor moved until he laughed, and then there came in smothered tones from the region of his vest:

"Oh, Tom, how can you laugh? Do you think it such fun?"

"Fun! Thunder! Any thing but fun!" was his gruff reply, as he went on more rapidly now, for they were in the grounds of Le Bateau, and the lights from the house were distinctly visible at no great distance away. "We are here at last. Thank the Lord!" he said, as he went up the steps and pulled sharply at the bell.

"Let me down. I can stand on one foot," Ann Eliza said; and nothing loth Tom put her down, a most forlorn and dilapidated piece of humanity as she stood leaning against him with the light of the piazza lamp falling full upon her.

Her little French boots, which had partly done the mischief, were spoiled, and the heel of one of them had been nearly wrenched off when she stumbled over the stone. Her India muslin, with its sash, and ribbons, and streamers, was torn in places and bedraggled with mud. She had lost her hat in the woods, and the wind and the rain had held high carnival in her loosely arranged hair, whose color Tom so detested, and which streamed down her back in little wet tags, giving her the look of a drowned rat after it has been tortured in a trap.

Old Peterkin was reading his evening paper when Tom's loud summons sounded through the house, making him jump from his chair, as he exclaimed:

"Jiminy hoe-cakes! Who can that be in this storm?"

He had seen Billy off in the train, and had returned home just as the rain began to fall. Naturally, both he and his wife had felt some anxiety on Ann Eliza's account, but had concluded that if the storm continued she would remain at Grassy Spring, and if it cleared in time they would send the carriage for her. So neither thought of her when the loud ring came, startling them so much. It was Peterkin himself who went to the door, gorgeous in a crimson satin dressing gown which came to his feet, but which no amount of pulling could make meet together over his ponderous stomach. An oriental smoking cap was on his head, the big tassel hanging almost in his eyes, and a half burned cigar between his fingers.

"Good George of Uxbridge!" he exclaimed, as his eyes fell upon Tom, from whose soaked hat the water was dripping, and upon Ann Eliza leaning against him, her pale face quivering with pain, and her eyes full of tears. "George of Uxbridge! What's up? What ails the girl!"

"She has sprained her ankle and I had to bring her home. She can't step," Tom said.

"Jerusalem hoe-cakes! Spraint her ankle! Can't step! You brung her home! Heavens and earth! Here, May Jane, come lively! Here's a nice how-dy-do! Ann 'Liza's broke her laig, and Tom Tracy's brung her home!"

As Peterkin talked, he was carrying his daughter into the hall, hitting her lame foot against the door, and eliciting from her a cry of pain.

"Oh, father: Oh-h!—it does hurt so. Put me somewhere quick, and take off my boot."

She was dripping wet, and little puddles of water trailed along the carpet as Peterkin carried her into the sitting room, where he was about to lay her down upon the delicate satin couch, when his wife's housewifely instincts were roused, and she exclaimed:

"No father. Not there, when she's so wet, and water spots that satin so dreadfully."

"What in thunder shall I do with her? Hold her all night?" Peterkin demanded, while Tom deliberately picked up the costly Turkey hearth rug, and throwing it across the couch, said:

"Put her on that."

So Peterkin deposited her upon the rug, hitting her foot again, and sending her off in a dead faint.

"Oh, she's dead! she's dead! What shall we do?" Mrs. Peterkin cried, wringing her hands and walking about excitedly.

"Do?" Peterkin yelled. "Hold your yawp, and stop floppin' round like a hen with her head cut off! She ain't dead. She's fainted. Bring some camfire, or alcohol, or hartshorn, or Pond's Extract, or something for her to smell."

"Yes, yes; but where are they?" Mrs. Peterkin moaned, flopping around, as her husband had expressed it, while Tom rang the bell and summoned a servant, to whom he gave directions.

"Bring some camphor or hartshorn," she said. "Miss Peterkin has fainted, and get off that boot as soon as possible. Don't you see, how her foot is swelling?"

This to Peterkin, who made a dive at the boot, which resisted all his efforts, even after it was unbuttoned. The leather, which was soaked through, had shrunk so that it was impossible to remove the boot without cutting it away, and this they commenced to do.

Ann Eliza had recovered her consciousness by this time, and although the pain was terrible she bore it heroically, as piece after piece of the boot was removed, together with the silk stocking, which left her poor little swollen foot exposed and bare.

"By Jove, she's plucky!" Tom thought, as he watched the operation and saw the great drops of sweat on Ann Eliza's forehead and her efforts to quiet her mother, pretending that it did not hurt so very much. "Yes, she's plucky," and for the first time in his life Tom was conscious of a feeling of something like respect for Peterkin's red haired daughter. "She *has* a small foot, too ; the smallest I ever saw on a woman. I do believe she wears twos," he thought, while something about the little white foot made him think of poor Jack's dead feet, laid under the grass years ago.

In this softened frame of mind he at last said good-night, although pressed by Peterkin to stay and dry himself, or at least take a drink as a preventive against cold. But Tom declined both, saying a hot bath would set him all right.

"Good-by, Annie. I'm awfully sorry for the sprain," he said, offering her his hand ; and as she took it in hers, noticing about the wrist prints of his fingers which had grasped it so tightly and held it so firmly as he dragged her along over stumps, and bogs, and stones, until she sank at his feet. "I guess I was a brute to race her like that," he said to himself, as he went out into the darkness and started for home. "But I didn't want to go with her. I wanted to be with Jerrie, who, I have no doubt, went straight along, without ever thinking of spraining her ankle, as Ann Eliza did. Poor little foot! How swollen, though, it was, when they got that boot off ; but she bore it like a major ! Pity she has such all-fired red hair, and piles it up like a haystack on the top of her head, with every hair looking six ways for Sunday."

At this point in his soliloquy Tom reached home, and was soon luxuriating in a hot bath, which removed all traces of the soaking he had received. That night he dreamed of Ann Eliza, and how light she was in his arms, and how patient through it all, and that the magnificent rooms at La Bateau were all frescoed with diamonds and the floors inlaid with gold. Then the nature of his dream changed, and it was Jerrie he was carrying, bending under her weight until his back was broken. But he did not mind it in the least, and when he bent to kiss the face lying upon his bosom, where Ann Eliza had lain, he awoke suddenly to find that it was morning, and that the sun was shining brightly into his room.

CHAPTER XXXVII.

UNDER THE PINES WITH DICK.

LIKE Tom and Ann Eliza, Jerrie and Dick had run when they saw how fast the storm was coming, but it was of no use, for by the time they entered the park, the shortest route to the cottage, the rain came down in torrents, and drenched them to the skin in a few moments. Jerrie's hat was wrenched off, as Ann Eliza's had been, by the wind, which tossed her long golden hair about in a most fantastic fashion. But Dick put his hat upon her head, and would have given her his coat had she allowed it.

"No, Dick," she said, laughingly, as she saw him about to divest himself of it. "Keep your coat. I am wet enough without that. But what a storm, and how dark it grows. We shall break our necks stumbling along at this rate."

Just then a broad glare of lightning illuminated the darkness, and showed Dick the four pines close at hand. He knew the place well, for, with the Tracy children, he had often played there when a boy, and knew that the thick boughs would afford them some protection from the storm.

"By jove, we are in luck!" he said. "Here's the pine room, as we used to call it when you played you were Marie Antoinette and had your head cut off. I can remember just how I felt when your white sun-bonnet, with Mrs. Crawford's false hair pinned in it, dropped into the basket, and how awful it seemed when you played dead so long that we almost thought you were; and when you came to life, the way you imitated the cries of a French mob, I would have sworn there were a hundred voices instead of one, yelling, 'Down with the nobility!' You were a wonderful actress, Jerrie, and it is a marvel you have not gone upon the stage."

While he talked he was groping for the bench under the pines, where they sat down, Dick seating himself upon the parasol which Jerrie had left there that morning after her interview with Tom.

"Hallo! what's this?" he said, drawing the parasol from under him. "An umbrella, as I live! What good fairy do you suppose left it here for us?"

Jerrie could not tell him that she had left it there, and she said nothing; while he opened and held it so that every drop of rain which slipped from it fell upon her neck and trickled down her back.

"Great Cæsar! that was a roarer!" Dick said, as the peal of thunder which had so frightened Ann Eliza burst over their heads, and, echoing through the woods, went bellowing off in the direction of the river. "That's a stunner, but I rather like it and like being here, too. I've wanted a chance to speak to you ever since—well, ever since this morning when I saw you in that bewildering costume which showed your feet and your arms so—you know—and that thingumbob in your head, and the red stockings—and"— Here Dick became hopelessly confused and not knowing what to say next waited for Jerrie to speak.

But Jerrie did not speak, because of the sudden alarm which possessed her. She could not see Dick's face, but in

his voice she had recognized a tone heard in Tom's that
morning when she sat with him under the pines as she was
sitting now with Dick and he had asked her to be his wife.
Something told her that Dick was feeling for her hands,
which she resolutely put behind her out of his way, and as
he could not find them, he wound his arm around her and
held her fast, while he told her how much he loved her.

"I believe I have loved you," he said, "ever since the
day I first saw you at the inquest, and you flew so like a
little cat at Peterkin when he attacked Harold. I used to
be awfully jealous of Hal, for fear he would find in you
more than a sister, but that was before he and Maude got so
thick together. I guess that's a sure thing, people say so,
and it makes me bold to tell you what I have. Why are
you so silent, Jerrie? Don't you love me a little? That
is all I ask at first, for I know I can make you love me a
great deal in time. I will be so kind and true to you,
Jerrie, and father, and mother, and Nina will be so glad.
Speak to me, Jerrie, and say you will try to love me, if you
do not now."

As he talked he had drawn the girl closer to him, where
she sat rigid as a stone, wholly unmindful of the little puddles of water—and they were puddles now—running down
her back, for Dick had tilted the parasol in such a manner
that one of the points rested upon the nape of her neck.
But she did not know it, or think of anything except the
pain she must inflict upon the young man wooing her so
differently from what Tom Tracy had done. No hint had
Dick given of the honor he was conferring upon her, or of
his own and his family's superiority to herself. All the
honor and favor to be conferred were on her side ; all the
love and humility on his, and for one brief moment the
wild wish flashed upon her :

"Oh, if I could love him as a wife ought, I might be so
happy, for he is all that is noble and good and true."

But this was while she was smarting under the few
words he had said of Harold and Maude. He, too, believed
it a settled thing between the two—every body believed it
—and why should she waste her love upon one who did not
care for her as she did for him? Why not encourage a
love for Dick, who stood next in her heart to Harold ?
Thus she questioned herself until she remembered Harold's

voice as it had spoken to her that morning, and the look in
his eyes when they rested upon her, as he said good-by,
lingering a moment as if loth to leave her, and then Dick's
chance, if he had ever had any, was gone !

Turning to him, she said : " Oh, Dick, I am so sorry
you have said this to me ; sorry that you love me—in that
way—for I can't—I can't——.   I do love you as a friend,
a brother, next to Harold, but I cannot be your wife.   I
cannot."

For a moment there was perfect silence in the darkness,
and then a lurid flame of lightning showed the two faces—
that of the man, pale as ashes, with a look of bitter pain
upon it, and that of the woman, whiter than the man's and
bathed in tears, which fell almost as fast as the rain drops
were falling upon the pines.

Then Dick spoke again, but his voice sounded strange
and unnatural and a great ways off :

" If I wait a long, long time—say a year, or two, or
three—do you think you could learn to love me just a
little ?   I will not ask for much ; only, Jerrie, I do hunger
so for you that without you life would be a blank."

" No, Dick ; not if you waited twenty years.   I must
still answer no.   I cannot love you as your wife should
love you, and as some good, sweet girl will one day love
you when you have forgotten me."

This was what Jerry said to him, with much more, until
he knew she was in earnest and felt as if his heart were
breaking.

" I shall never forget you, Jerrie," he said, "or cease to
hope that you will change your mind, unless—" and here
he started so suddenly that the wet parasol, down which
streams of water were still coursing their way to Jerrie's
back, dropped from his hand and rolled off upon the bed
of pine needles at his feet, just where it had been in the
morning when Tom was there instead of himself—"unless
there is some one between us, some other man whom you
love.   I will not ask you the question, but I believe I could
bear it better if I knew it was because your love was already
given to another, and not because of anything in me."

For a moment Jerrie was silent ; then, suddenly facing
Dick, she laid her hand on his and said :

" I can trust you, I am sure of that ; there is some one

between us—some one whom I love. If I had never seen him—and if I had known you just as I do, I might not have answered as I have. I am very sorry."

Dick did not ask her who his rival was, nor did Harold come to his mind, so sure was he that an engagement existed between him and Maude. Probably it was some one whom she had met while away at school, he thought, and every nerve was quivering with pain and disappointment, when at last, as the rain began to cease, he rose at Jerrie's suggestion, and offering her his arm, walked silently and sadly with her to the door of the cottage. Here for a moment they stood side by side and hand in hand, until Jerrie said :

" Dick, your friendship has been very dear to me. I do not want to lose it."

" Nor shall you," he answered ; and winding his arms around her, he kissed her lips, saying, as he did so :

" That is the seal of our eternal friendship. The man you love would not grudge me that one kiss, but perhaps you'd better tell him. Good-by, and God bless you. When I see you again I shall try to be the same Dick you have always known."

For a little while Jerrie stood listening to the sound of his footsteps as he went splashing through the wet grass and puddles of water ; then kissing her hands to him, she whispered :

" Poor Dick ! It would not be difficult to love you if I had never known Harold."

Opening the door softly, she found, as she had expected, that both her grandmother and Harold had retired ; and taking the lamp from the table where it had been left for her, she stole quietly up to her room and crept shivering into bed, more wretched than she had ever been before in her life.

CHAPTER XXXVIII.

AT LE BATEAU.

HAROLD got his own breakfast the next morning, and was off for his work just as the sun looked into the windows of the room where Jerrie lay in a deep slumber. She had been awake a long time the previous night, thinking over the incidents of a day which had been the most eventful one of her life, but had fallen asleep at last, and dreamed that she had found the low room in Wiesbaden, with the picture of a young girl knitting in the sunshine, and the stranger watching her from a distance.

It was late when she awoke, and Peterkin's clock was striking eight when she went down to the kitchen, where she found Mrs. Crawford sewing, and a most dainty breakfast waiting for her on a little round table near an open window shaded with the hop-vines. There was a fresh egg for her, with English buns, and strawberries and cream, and chocolate served in a pretty cup which she had never seen before, while near her plate was lying a bunch of roses, and on them a strip of paper on which Harold had written:

"'The top of the mornin' to ye, Jerrie. I'd like to stay and see you, but if I work very hard to-day, I hope to finish the job on Monday and get my fifteen dollars. That's a pile of money to earn in three days, isn't it? I hope you enjoyed the garden-party. If I had not been so awfully tired I should have gone for you. Grandma will tell you that I went to bed and to sleep before that shower came up, so I knew nothing of it. I wonder how you got home; but of course Dick came with you, or Billy, or possibly Tom. I hear you entertained all three of them at the washtub! Pretty good for the first day home! Good-by till to-night. I only live till then, as they say in novels.

                                                        "HAROLD."

This note, every line of which was full of affection and thoughtfulness for her, was worth more to Jerrie than the chocolate or the bun, or the pretty cup and saucer which

Harold had bought for her the night before, going to the village, a mile out of his way, on purpose to get them and surprise her. This Mrs. Crawford told her, as she sat eating her breakfast, which she had to force down because of the lump in her throat and the tears which came so fast as she listened.

"You see," Mrs. Crawford began, " Mr. Allen paid Harold two or three dollars, and so he came home through the village, and bought the eggs, and the buns, and the chocolate, which he knew you liked, and the cup and saucer at Grady's. He has had it on his mind a long time to get it for you, but there were so many other things to pay for. Don't you think it is pretty ?"

"Yes, lovely !" Jerrie replied, taking up the delicate bit of china, through which the light shone so clearly. "It is very pretty ; but I wish he had not bought it for me," and Jerrie wiped the hot tears from both her eyes, as Mrs. Crawford continued :

"Oh, he wanted to. He is never happier than when doing something which he thinks will please you or me. Harold is the most unselfish boy I ever knew ; and I never saw him give way, or heard him complain that his lot was hard but once, and that was this summer, when he was building the room, and had to dismiss the man because he had no money to pay him. That left it all for him to do, and he was already so tired and overworked ; and then Tom Tracy was always making fun of the change, and saying it made the cottage look like a pig-sty with a steeple to it, and that you would think so, too ; and if it were his he'd tear the old hut down and start anew. Peterkin, too, made remarks and wondered where Harold got the money, and why he didn't do this and that, but supposed he couldn't afford it, adding that 'beggars couldn't be choosers.' When Harold heard all that, he was tired, and nervous, and discouraged, and his hands were blistered and bruised. His head was aching, and he just put it on that table, where you are sitting, and cried like a baby. When I tried to comfort him, he said, 'It isn't the hard work, grandmother; I don't mind that in the least ; neither do I care for what they say, or should not, if there was not some truth in it ; things are out of proportion, and the new room makes the rest of the cottage look lower than ever, and I'd like so

14

much to have everything right for Jerrie, who would not shame the queen's palace. I wish, for her sake, that I had money, and could make her home what it ought to be I do not want her to feel homesick, or long for something better, when she comes back to us.' "

Jerrie was crying outright now; but Mrs. Crawford, who was a little deaf and did not hear her, went on :

" If you were a hundred times his sister he could not love you more than he does, or wish to make you happier. He would have gone for you last night, only he was so tired, and I persuaded him to go to bed. I knew somebody would come home with you. Dick, wasn't it ? I thought I heard his voice."

" Yes, it was Dick," Jerrie answered, very low, returning again to her breakfast, while her grandmother rambled on :

" Harold slept so soundly that he never heard the storm, or knew there was one till this morning. Lucky you didn't start home until it was over. You'd have been wet to the skin."

Jerrie made no answer, for she could not tell of that interview under the pines, or that she had been wet to the skin, and felt chilly even now from the effects of it. It seemed that Mrs. Crawford would never tire of talking of Harold, for she continued :

" He was up this morning about daylight, I do believe, and had his own breakfast eaten and that table laid for you when I came down. He wanted to see you before he went, and know if you were pleased; but I told him you were probably asleep, as it was late when you came in, and so he wrote something for you, and went whistling off as merrily as if he had been in his carriage, instead of on foot in his working dress."

" And he shall have his carriage, too, some day, and a pair of the finest horses the country affords, and you shall ride beside him, in a satin gown and India shawl. You'll see !" Jerrie said, impetuously, as she rose from the table and began to clear away the dishes.

The spell was upon her strongly now, and as her grandmother talked, the objects around her gradually faded away; the cottage, so out of proportion and so humble in all its surroundings, was gone, and in its place stood a

house, grand as Tracy Park and much like it, and Harold
was the master, looking a very prince, instead of the tired,
shabbily dressed man he was now.

"And I shall be there, too," Jerrie whispered, or rather
nodded to herself. "I know I shall, and I do not believe
one word of the Maude affair, and never will until he tells
me himself, or she; and then—well, then, I will be glad
for them, until I come to be really glad myself."

She was moving rapidly around the kitchen, for there
was a great deal to be done—the Saturday's work and all
the clothes to be ironed, and then she meant to get up some
little surprise for Harold to show him that she appreciated
his thoughtfulness for her.

About half-past ten a servant from Le Bateau brought
her a note from Ann Eliza, who wrote as follows:

"DEAR JERRIE:—

"Have pity on a poor cripple, and come as soon as you can
and see me. I sprained my ankle last night in that awful
storm, and Tom had to bring me home in his arms. Think
of it, and what my feelings must have been. I am hardly
over it yet—the queer feelings, I mean—for, of course, my
ankle is dreadful, and so swollen, and pains me so that I
cannot step, but must stay in my room all day. So come as
soon as possible. You have never seen the inside of our
house or my rooms. Come to lunch, please. We will have
it up here. Good-by. "From your loving friend,
"ANN ELIZA.

"P. S.—I wonder if Tom will call to inquire for me?"

"Tell her I will be there by lunch-time," Jerrie said to
the man, while to her grandmother she continued: "The
baking and cleaning are all done, and I can finish the ironing when I get back; it will be cooler then, and I do want
to see the inside of that show-house which Harold says cost
a hundred thousand dollars. Pity somebody besides the
Peterkins did not live there."

And so, about twelve o'clock Jerrie walked up to the
grand house of gray stone, which, with its turrets, and
towers, and immense arch over the carriage drive in front
of a side door, looked like some old fuedal castle, and
flaunted upon its walls the money it had cost. Even the

loud bell which echoed through the hall like a town clock told the wealth and show, as did the colored man who answered the summons, and bowing low to Jerrie, held out a silver tray for her card.

"Nonsense, Leo!" Jerrie said, laughingly, for she had known the negro all her life and played with him, too, at times, when they both went to the district school, I have no card with me. Miss Ann Eliza has invited me to lunch, and I have come. Tell her I am here."

With another profound bow, Leo waved Jerrie into the reception-room, and then started to deliver her message.

Seated upon one of the carved chairs, Jerrie looked about her curiously, with a feeling that the half had not been told her, everything was so much more gorgeous and magnificent than she had supposed. But what impressed and at the same time oppressed her most was the height of the walls from the richly inlaid floor to the gayly decorated ceiling overhead. It made her neck ache staring up fourteen feet and a half to the costly center ornament from which the heavy chandelier depended. All the rooms of the old house had been low, and when Peterkin built the new one, he made ample amends.

"I mean to lick the crowd," he said; and a man was sent to Collingwood, and Grassy Spring, and Brier Hill, and lastly to Tracy Park, to take the height of the lower rooms. Those at Tracy Park were found to be the highest, and measured just twelve feet, so Peterkin's orders were to "run 'em up—run 'em up—run 'em up fourteen feet, for I swan I'll get ahead of 'em."

So they were run up fourteen feet, and by some mistake, half a foot higher, looking when finished so cold and cheerless and bare that the ambitious man ransacked New York and Boston and even sent to London for adornments for his walls. Books were bought by the square yard, pictures by the wholesale, mirrors by the dozen, with bronzes and brackets and sconces and tapestry and banners and screens and clocks and cabinets and statuary, together with the costliest rugs and carpets and the most exquisite inlaid tables to be found in Florence or Venice. For Peterkin sent there for them by a gentleman to whom he said:

"Git the best there is if it costs a fortune. I'm bound to lick the crowd."

This was his favorite expression; and when his house was done, and he stood, his broad, white shirt-front studded with diamonds and his coat thrown back to show them, surveying his possessions, he felt that he "had licked the crowd."

Jerrie felt so, too, as she followed the elegant Leo up the stairs and through the upper hall—handsomer, if possible, than the lower one—to the pretty room where Ann Eliza lay, or rather reclined, with her lame foot on a cushion and her well one incased in a white embroidered silk stocking and blue satin slipper. She was dressed in a delicate blue satin wrapper, trimmed with swan's-down, and there were diamonds in her ears and on the little white hands which she stretched toward Jerrie as she came in.

"Oh, Jerrie," she said, "I am so glad to see you, for it is awfully lonesome here; and if one can be homesick at home I am. I miss the girls and the lessons and the rules at Vassar; much as I hated them when I was there; and just before you came in I wanted to cry. I guess my rooms are too big and have too much in them; anyway, I have the feeling all the time that I am visiting, and every thing is strange and new. I do believe I liked the old room better, with its matting on the floor and the little mirror with the peacock feathers ornamenting the top, and that painted plastered image of Samuel on the mantel. It is very ungrateful in me, I know, when father has done it mostly to please me. Do you believe—he has hunted me up a maid, just for myself, Doris is her name; and what I am ever to do with her, or she with me, I am sure I don't know. Do you?"

Jerrie did not know either, but suggested that she might read to her while she was confined to her room.

"Yes, she might, perhaps, do that, if she can read," Ann Eliza said. "She certainly has pretension enough about her to have written several treatises on scientific subjects. She was a year with Lady Augusta Hardy, in Ireland. Don't you remember the grand wedding father and mother attended in Allington two or three years ago, when Augusta Browne was married to an Irish lord, who had been bought by her money?—for of course he did not care much for her. Well, Doris went out with her as maid, and acts as if she, too, had married a peer. She came last night, and mamma and I are already as afraid of her as we can be, she is so fine and airy. She insisted upon dressing me this morning, and I felt all the while as if she were thinking how red and ugly my hair is, or counting the freckles on my face, and contrasting me with 'my Lady Augusta,' as she calls her. I wonder if she ever saw my lady's mother, Mrs. Rossiter-Browne, who told me once that I 'had a very *petty figger*, but she presumed it would *envelope* as I grew older.' But then people who live in glass houses shouldn't throw stones," and Ann Eliza colored a little as she made this reference to her own father and mother, whose language was not much more correct than Mrs. Rossiter-Browne's.

For one brought up as she had been Ann Eliza was a rather sensible girl, and although she attached a great deal of importance to money, she knew it was not everything, and that with her father's millions there was still a wide difference between him and the men to whose society he aspired ; and knew, too, that although Jerrie had not a penny in the world, she was greatly her superior, and so considered by the world at large. She was very fond of Jerrie, who had often helped her with her lessons, and stood between her and the ridicule of her companions, and was never happier than when in her society. So now she made her bring an ottoman close beside her, and held her hand while she narrated in detail the events of the previous night, dwelling at length upon the fact that Tom had carried her in his arms, and wondering if he would call to inquire after her. Jerrie thought he would ; and, as if in answer to the thought, Doris almost immediately appeared with his card. She *was* very fine and very smart, and Jerrie herself felt awed by her dignity and manner as she delivered her message.

" The gentleman sends his compliments, and would like to know how you are this morning."

" Oh, Jerrie, it's Tom ! he has come !" Ann Eliza said, with joy in her voice. " Surely I can receive him here, for this is my parlor."

Jerrie thought she might, but the toss of the fine maid's head showed that she thought differently, as she left the room with her mistress' message.

" Thunderation ! I didn't want to see her. It's enough

to have to call," was Tom's mental comment as he followed
Doris to her mistress' room.

"What, Jerrie! You here?" he exclaimed, his face clear-
ing, and the whole aspect of matters changing at once, as
she arose to meet him.

With Jerrie there the place seemed different, and he did
not feel as if he were lowering himself, as he sat down and
joined in the dainty lunch which was brought up and served
from Dresden china, and cut glass, and was as delicate
and dainty in its way as anything he had ever found at the
Brunswick or Delmonico's. Mrs. Peterkin prided herself
upon her *cuisine*, which she superintended herself, and as
Peterkin was something of an epicure and gourmand, the
table was always supplied with every possible delicacy.

Tom enjoyed it all, and praised the chocolate, and the
broiled chicken, and the jellies, and thought Ann Eliza not
so very bad-looking in her blue satin wrapper, with the
swan'-down trimmings, and made himself generally agreeable. Maude was better, he said, and he asked Jerrie to go
home with him and see her. But Jerrie declined.

"I have a great deal of work to do yet," she said. "I
must finish ironing those clothes you saw upon the line
yesterday, and so I must be going."

Tom frowned at the mention of the clothes which Jerrie
had washed; while Ann Eliza insisted that she should stay
until the dog-cart, which had been sent to the station for
Billy, came back, when Lewis would take her home, as it
was too warm to walk. Jerrie did not mind the heat or the
walk, but she felt morally sure that Tom meant to accompany her, and greatly preferred the dog-cart and Lewis to
another *tete-a-tete* with him, for he did not act at all like a
discarded lover, but rather as one who still hoped he had a
chance. So she signified her intention to wait for the dog-
cart, which soon came, with Billy in it, anxious when he
heard of his sister's accident, delighted when he found
Jerrie there, and persistent in saying that he and not Lewis
would take her home.

"Well, if you will, you will," she said, laughingly; and
bidding Ann Eliza good-by, and telling Tom to give her
love to Maude and say to her that she did not believe she
should be at the park that day, she had so much to do, she
was soon in the dog-cart with Billy, whose face was radiant

as he gathered up the reins and started down the turnpike, driving at what Jerrie thought a very slow pace, as she was anxious to get home.

Something of Billy's thoughts must have communicated itself to Jerrie, for she became nervous and ill at ease and talked rapidly of things in which she had not the slightest interest.

" What of the lawsuit' ?" she asked.   " Are you likely to settle it ?"

" No-no," Billy answered, hurriedly.   " It will h-have to co-come into co-court in a f-few days, and I am aw-awful sorry.   I wa-wanted father to p-pay what they demanded, but he won't.   Hal is subpœnaed on the other side, as he was in our office, and is supposed to know something about it ;   b-but I ho-hope he won't da-damage us m-much, as father would n-never forgive him if he went against us."

" But he must tell the truth, no matter who is damaged," Jerrie said.

" Ye-yes," Billy replied, " of co-course he must, b-but he needn't volunteer information."

Jerrie began to think that Billy had insisted upon coming with her for the sake of persuading her to caution Harold against saying too much when he was called to testify in the great lawsuit between Peterkin & Co., manufacturers in Shannondale, and Wilson & Co., manufacturers in Truesdale, an adjoining town ;   but she was undeceived when her companion turned suddenly off upon the river road, which would take them at least two miles out of their way.

" Why are you coming here ?"   Jerrie said, in real distress.   " It is ever so much farther, and I must get home. I have piles of work to do."

" Co-confound the work," Billy replied, very energetically for him, and reining his horse up under a wide spreading butternut tree, which grew upon the river bank, he sprang out and pretended to be busy with some part of the harness, while he astonished Jerrie by bursting out, without the least stammer, he was so earnest and so excited.   " I've something to say to you, Jerrie, and I may as well say it now as any time, and know the worst, or the best.   I can't bear the suspense any longer, and I got out of the cart so

as to stand where I could look you square in the face while
I say it."

And he was looking her square in the face, while she
grew hot and cold and experienced a sensation quite different from what she had when Tom and Dick made love to
her. She had felt no fear of them, but she was afraid of
this little man, who stood up so resolutely, with his tongue
loosened, and asked her to be his wife, making his wishes
known in a very few words, and then waiting for her
answer with his eyes fixed upon her face and a firm, set
look about his mouth which puzzled and troubled her and
made her uncertain as to how she was to deal with this
third aspirant for her hand within twenty-four hours.

Billy had long had it in his mind that Jerrie Crawford
was the only girl in the world for him, but he might not
have spoken quite so soon had it not been for a conversation held with his father the previous night, when they
were alone in a private room at the hotel in Shannondale,
waiting for the train which Billy was to take, and which
was half an hour late. Peterkin had exhausted himself in
oaths and epithets with regard to the lawsuit and those
who had brought it against him, and was regaling himself
with a cigar and a glass of brandy and water, while Billy
sat by the window watching for the train and wishing himself at Grassy Spring with Jerrie. Peterkin seldom drank
to excess, but on this occasion he had taken a little too
much. When under the influence of stimulants, he was
either aggressive and quarrelsome, or jocose and talkative.
The latter mood was on him now, and as he drank his
brandy and water he held forth upon the subject of matri-
mony, wondering why his son did not marry, and saying it
was quite time that he did so and settled down.

"You can have the south wing," he said; "and if the
rooms ain't up to snuff now, why, I'll make 'em so. The
fact is, Bill, I've got money enough—three millions and
better; but somehow it doesn't seem to do the thing. It
doesn't fetch us to the quality and make us fust-cut. We
need better blood than the Peterkins or the Moshers—need
boostin'—and you must get a wife to boost us. Have you
ever thought on't?"

"Billy never had thought of it in that light," he said,

14*

although he had thought of marrying, provided the girl would have him.

"Have you! Thunderation! A girl would be a fool who wouldn't marry three millions, with Lubber-too thrown in! Who is she?" Peterkin asked.

After a little hesitancy, Billy replied:

"Jerrie Crawford."

"Jerrie Crawford! I'll be dumbed! Jerrie Crawford!" and Peterkin's big feet came down from the back of the chair on which they were resting, upsetting the chair and his brandy at the same time. "Jerrie Crawford! I swow! A gal without a cent, or name either, though I used to have a sneakin' notion that I knew who she was, but I guess I didn't. 'Twould have come out afore now. What under heavens put her into your noddle? She can't *boost!* and then she's head and shoulders taller than you be! How you would look trottin' beside her! Jerrie Crawford! Wall, I swan!" and Peterkin laughed until his big stomach shook like a bowl of jelly.

Billy was angry, and replied that he did not know what height had to do with it, or name either; and as for *boosting*, he wouldn't marry a king's daughter, if he did not love her; and for that matter Jerrie could boost, for she stood quite as high in town as any young lady.

Both Nina St. Claire and Maude Tracy worshiped her, while Mrs. Atherton paid her a great deal of attention; and so did the Mungers and Crosbys—enough sight more than they did to Ann Eliza with all her money.

"Mo-money isn't ev-everything," Billy stammered, "and Je-Jerrie would make a ve-very different pl-place of Le Bateau."

"Mebby she would—mebby she would; but I'd never thought of her for you," Peterkin said. "I'd picked out some big-bug, who perhaps wouldn't wipe her shoes on you. Jerrie is handsome as blazes and no mistake, with a kinder up and comin' way about her which takes with folks. Yes, it keeps growin' on me, and I presume Arthur Tracy would give her away, which would be a feather in your cap; but lord! you'll have to git a pair of the highest heels you ever seen to come within ten foot on her."

"Sh-she's only two inches t-taller than I am," Billy said, and his father continued:

" Wall, if your heart's set on her, go it, and quick, too. I'm goin' to have a smasher of a party in the fall, and Jerrie'll be just the one to draw. I can see her now, standin' there with the diamonds we'll give her sparklin' on her neck, and she lookin' like a queen, and the *sinecure* of all eyes. But for thunder's sake don't marry the old woman and all. Leave her to Harold, the sneak! I never did like him, and I'll be mad enough to kill him if he goes agin me in the suit, and I b'lieve he will."

At this point Peterkin wandered off to the suit entirely and forgot Jerrie, who was to boost the house of Peterkin and make it " fust-cut." But not so Billy, and all the way from Shannondale to Springfield he was thinking of Jerrie, and wondering if it were posssible that she could ever look upon him with favor. Like Tom and Dick, he could scarcely remember the time when he did not think Jerrie the loveliest girl in the world, and ever since he had grown to manhood he had meditated making her his wife, but had feared what his father might say, as he knew how much importance he attached to money. Now, however, his father signified his assent, and, resolving to lose no time, Billy, on his return next day to Le Bateau, seized the opportunity to take Jerrie home, as the occasion for declaring his love, which he did in a manly, straightforward manner, never hinting at any advantage it would be to her to be the wife of a millionaire, or offering any inducement in any way except to say that he loved her and would devote his life to making her happy. Tom Tracy Jerrie had scorned, Dick St. Claire she had pitied, but this little man she felt like ridiculing after her first emotion of fear had left her.

" Oh, Billy," she said, laughing merrily. " You can't be in earnest. Why, I'm head and shoulders taller than you are. I do believe I could pick you up and throw you into the river. Only think how we should look together ; people would think you my little boy, and that I should not like. No, I can never be your wife."

Nothing cuts a man like ridicule, and sensitive as he was with regard to his size, Billy felt it to his heart's core ; and as he stood nervously playing with the reins and looking at Jerrie sitting there so tall and erect in all the brightness of her wonderful beauty, it flashed upon him how impossible it was for that glorious creature ever to be his wife, and what a fool he had made of himself.

"For-gi-give me, Jerrie," he said, his chin beginning to quiver, and the great tears rolling down his face. "I know you ca-can't, and I ou-oughtn't to have ask-asked it, bu-but I d-did love you so much, that I f-forgot how impossible it was f-for one like you to lo-love one li-like me. I am so small and insig-insignificant, and st-stutter so. I wish I was dead," and laying his head upon the horse's neck, he sobbed aloud.

In an instant Jerrie was out of the dog-cart and at his side, talking to and trying to soothe him as she would a child.

"Oh, Billy, Billy," she said. "I am so sorry for you, and sorry I said those cruel words about your size. It was only in fun. Your size has nothing to do with my refusal. I know you have a big, kind heart, and next to Harold, and Dick, and Mr. Arthur, I like you better than any man I ever knew, but I can't be your wife. Don't cry, Billy; it hurts me so to see you and know that I have done it. Please stop and take me home as quick as possible."

With a great gulp, and a long sigh like a grieved child, Billy dried his tears, of which he was much ashamed, and helping Jerrie into the cart drove her rapidly to the door of the cottage.

"I should not like Tom, nor Dick, nor Harold to know this," he said to her, as he stood a moment with her at the gate.

"Billy!" she exclaimed, "do you know me so little as to think I would tell them, or any body? I have more honor than that," and she gave him her hand, which he held tightly as he looked into the sweet young face which could never be his, every muscle of his own quivering, and telling of the pain he was enduring.

"Good-by. I shall be more like a ma-man, and less a ba-baby when I see you again," and springing into his cart he drove rapidly away.

Jerrie found her grandmother seated at a table, and trying to iron.

"Grandma," she said, "this is too bad. I did not mean to stay so long. Put down that flat-iron this minute. I am coming there as soon as I lay off my hat."

Running up the stairs to her room, Jerrie put away her hat, and then, throwing herself upon the bed, cried for a moment as hard as she could cry. The look on Billy's face haunted her, and she pitied him now more than she had pitied Dick St. Claire.

"Dick will get over it, and marry somebody else, but Billy, never," she said.

Then, rising up, she bathed her eyes, and pushing back her tangled hair, stood for a moment before the mirror, contemplating the reflection of herself in it.

"Jerrie Crawford," she said, "you must be a mean, heartless, good-for-nothing girl, for it certainly is not your Dutch face, nor yellow hair, nor great staring eyes, which make men think that you will marry them ; so it must be your flirting, coquettish manners. I hate a flirt, I hate you, Jerrie Crawford !"

Once, when a little girl, Jerrie had said to Harold, "Why do all the boys want to kiss me so much ?" and now she might have asked, "Why do these same boys wish to marry me ?" It was a curious fact that she should have had three offers within twenty-four hours ; and she did'nt like it, and her face wore a troubled look all that hot afternoon as she stood at the ironing table, perspiring at every pore, and occasionally smiling to herself as she thought, "Grassy Spring, Le Bateau, Tracy Park. I might take my choice, if I would, but I prefer the cottage," and then at the thought of Tracy Park her thoughts went off across the sea to Germany, and the low room with the picture upon the wall, and her resolve to find it some day.

"Far in the future it may be, but find it I will, and find, too, who I am," she said to herself, little dreaming that the finding was close at hand, and that she had that day lighted the train which was so soon to bear her on to the end.

CHAPTER XXXIX.

MAUDE.

HAROLD did not finish his work at the Allen farm-house until Tuesday, so it was not until Wednesday afternoon that he started to pay his promised visit to Maude. Jerrie had seen her twice, and reported her as much better and able to be up, although still very weak.

"She is so anxious to see you. Don't you think you can go this afternoon?" she said to Harold, in the morning, as she helped him weed the garden and pick the strawberries for dinner.

"Ye-es, I guess I can—if you'll go with me," he said.

He was so loth to be away from Jerrie when it was not absolutely necessary, that even a call upon Maude without her did not seem very tempting. But Jerrie could not go, for Nina and Marian Raymond were coming to spend the afternoon, and Harold went alone to the Park House, where he found Maude in the room she called her studio, trying to finish a little water-color which she had sketched of the cottage as it was before the roof was raised.

"I mean it for Jerrie," she had said to Harold, who stood by her when she sketched it, "and I am going to put her under the tree, with her sun-bonnet hanging down her back, as she used to wear it when she was a little girl, and you are to be over there by the fence, looking at me coming up the lane."

It was the best thing Maude had ever done, for the likeness to Jerrie and to herself was perfect, while the cottage, embowered in trees and flowers, made it a most attractive picture. Harold had praised it a great deal, and told her that it would make her famous. But when the carpenter work came on Maude put it aside until now, when she brought it out again, and was just beginning to retouch it in places, as Harold was announced.

She was looking very tired, and it seemed to Harold that she had lost pounds of flesh since he saw her last.

Her face was pale and wan, but it flushed brightly as he came in, and she went forward to meet him.

"Hally, you naughty boy!" she began, as she gave him her hand. "Why didn't you come before? You don't know how I have missed you. You must not forget me now that Jerrie is at home."

She led him to a seat, and then herself sank into a large, cushioned easy-chair, against which she leaned her head wearily, while she looked at him with eyes which ought to have told how much he was to her, and so put him on his guard, and saved the misunderstanding which followed.

"No, Maude, I couldn't forget you," he said; and without really knowing that he was doing it, he put his hand upon the little, thin white one lying on the arm of the chair.

Every nerve in Maude's body thrilled to the touch of Harold's hand upon which she involuntarily laid her other one. One would have thought them lovers, sitting there together, but nothing could have been farther from Harold's mind. He was thinking only of Jerrie, and his resolve to confide in Maude, and get her opinion with regard to his chance.

"Now is as good a time as any," he thought, wondering how he should begin, and finding it harder than he had imagined it would be.

At last, after a few commonplaces, Maude told him again that he must not neglect her now that Jerrie was at home.

"Neglect you? How can I do that?" he said, "when I look upon you as one of my best friends, and in proof of it, I am going to tell you something, or, rather, ask you something, and I hope you will answer me truly. Better that I know the worst at first than learn it afterward."

Maude's face was scarlet with a great and sudden joy, and her eyes drooped beneath Harold's as he went on stammeringly, for he began to feel the awkwardness of telling one girl that he loved another, even though that other were her dearest friend.

"I hardly know how to begin," he said, "it is such a delicate matter, and perhaps I'd better say nothing at all."

"Was he going to stop? Had he changed his mind—and would he not, after all, say the words she had so longed

to hear ?   Maude asked herself, while he sat silent and unmoved, his thoughts very far from her to whom he was so
much.

Poor Maude !   She was weak and sick, and impulsive
and mistaken in the nature of Harold's feelings for her ; so
judge her not too harshly, if she at last did what Arthur
would have called "throwing herself at his head."

"I can guess what you mean," she said, after a pause,
during which he did not speak. "I have long suspected that
you cared for me, and have wondered you did not tell me
so, but supposed that you refrained because I was rich and
you were poor ; but what has that to do with those who
love each other ? I am glad you have spoken ; and you have
made me very happy; even if we can never be more to each
other than we are now, because I am going to die."

"Oh, Maude, Maude, you are mistaken. I—," came
from Harold like a cry of horror as he wrenched away his
hand lying between hers.

What could she mean ?   How had she understood him ?
he asked himself, while great drops of sweat gathered upon
his forehead and in the palms of his hands, as the past came
back to him, and he could see that what he had thought
mere friendship for himself was a far different and deeper
feeling, while he unwittingly had fanned the flame, and was
now reaping the result.

"What can I do ?" he said aloud, unconsciously, while
from the chair in which Maude was leaning back so wearily
came a weak voice like that of a child :

"Ring the bell, and give me my handkerchief."

He was at her side in a moment, bending over her, and
looking anxiously into the pallid face from which the bright
color had faded, leaving it gray, and pinched, and drawn.
Had he killed her by blurting out so roughly that she was
mistaken, and thus filling her with mortification and shame?
No, that could not be, for as he brought her handkerchief,
she whispered to him :

"I am not mistaken, Hally. I am going to die, but you
have made the last days of my life very, very happy."

She thought he was referring to herself and her situation
when he told her she was mistaken, and with a smothered
groan he was starting for the camphor, as she bade him do,
when the door opened, and Mrs. Tracy herself appeared.

" What is it ?" she asked, sharply; then, as she saw Maude's face, she knew what it was, and going to her, said to Harold :

" Why did you allow her to talk and get excited ? What were you saying to her ?"

Instantly Maude's eyes went up to Harold's with an appealing look, as if asking him not to tell her mother then —a precaution which was needless, as he had no intention to tell Mrs. Tracy, or any one, of the terrible blunder he had made ; and with a hope that the reality might dawn upon Maude, he answered, truthfully:

" I was talking to her of Jerrie. I am very sorry."

If Maude heard she did not understand, for drops of pinkish blood were oozing from her lips, and she looked as if she were already dead, as in obedience to Mrs. Tracy's command Harold took her in his arms and carried her to the couch near the open window, where he laid her down as tenderly as if she were indeed his affianced wife.

" Thanks," she sighed, softly, and her eyes looked up at him with an expression which half tempted him to kiss the lips from which he was wiping the stains so carefully, while Mrs. Tracy, at the door, gave some orders to a servant.

" You can go now," she said, returning to the couch, and dismissing him with her usual hauteur of manner ; while Maude put up her hand and whispered :

" Come soon—and Jerrie."

Had Harold been convicted of theft or murder he could scarcely have felt worse than he did as he walked slowly through the park, reviewing the situation and wondering what he ought to do.

" If it almost killed her when she thought I loved her, it would surely kill her to know that I do not," he thought. " I cannot undeceive her now, while she is so weak ; but when she is better and able to bear it, I will tell her the truth.

" And if she dies ?" came to him like the stab of a knife, as he remembered how white she looked as he held her in his arms. " If she does," he said, " no one shall ever know of the mistake she made. In this I will be true to Maude, even should the world believe I loved her and told her so. But, oh Heaven ! spare me that, and spare

Maude's life for many years. She is too young, too sweet, too good to die."

This was Harold's prayer, and that of many others during the week which followed, when Maude's life hung on a thread, and every bell at the Park House was muffled, and the servants spoke only in whispers; while Frank Tracy sat day and night in the room where his daughter lay, perfectly quiet, except as she sometimes put up her hand to stroke his white hair or wipe away the tears constantly rolling down his cheeks.

In Frank's heart there was a feeling worse than death itself, for keen remorse and bitter regret were torturing his soul as he sat beside the wreck of all his hopes and felt that he had sinned for naught. He knew Maude would die, and then what mattered it to him if he had all the money of the Rothschilds at his command?

"Oh, Gretchen, you are avenged, and Jerrie, too! Oh, Jerrie!" he said one day, unconsciously, as he sat by his daughter, who, he thought, was sleeping.

But at the mention of Jerrie's name her eyes unclosed and fixed themselves upon her father with a look in which he read an earnest desire for something.

"What is it, pet?" he asked. "Do you want anything?"

They had made her understand that she must not speak, for the slightest effort to do so always brought on a fit of coughing which threatened a hemorrhage. But they had brought her a little slate, on which she sometimes wrote her requests, though that, too, was an effort. Pointing now to the slate, she wrote, while her father held it:

"I want Jerrie."

"I thought so; and you shall have her for just as long as she will stay," Frank said; and a servant was dispatched to the cottage with the message that Jerrie must come at once, and come prepared to pass the night, if possible.

It had been very dreary for Maude during the time she had been shut up in her room, to which no one was admitted except her father and mother, the doctor, and the nurse. Many messages of inquiry and sympathy, however, had come to her from the cottage, and Grassy Spring, and Le Bateau, where Ann Eliza was still kept a prisoner with her sprained ankle; and once Jerrie had written a note full of love and solicitude and a desire to see her. As a postscript she added :

"Harold sends his love, and hopes you will soon be better. You don't know how anxious he is about you. Why, I believe he has lost ten pounds since your attack, for which he seems to blame himself, thinking he excited you too much by talking to you."

Frank read this to Maude, who, when he came to the postscript laughed aloud, as a child laughs at the return of its mother, for whom it has been hungering. This was the first word she had had from Harold, except that he had called to inquire for her, and she had so longed for something which should assure her that he remembered her as she did him. She had nó distrust of him, and would as soon have doubted that the sun would rise again as to have doubted his sinceri y ; but she wanted to hear again that he loved her, and now she had heard it, and, folding her hands upon her breast, she fell into the most refreshing sleep she had had since her illness. Could Maude have talked and seen people, or if she had been less anxious to live, she would probably have told Jerrie and Nina, and possibly Ann Eliza Peterkin, of what had passed between herself and Harold, but she had not seen them ; while life, with Harold to love her, looked so bright and sweet, that if by keeping silence she could prolong it, she would do so for months, if necessary. To live for Harold was all she wished or thought about ; and often when they hoped she was sleeping, she lay so still, with her eyes closed and her hands folded upon her breast, she was praying for life and length of days, with strength to make Harold as happy as he ought to be, and was thinking of and planning all she meant to do for him if she lived and they were married. First to Europe, where she would be so proud to show him the places she had seen, and where Jerrie would be with them, for in all her plans Jerrie had almost as prominent a place as herself.

"I am nothing without Jerrie," she thought. "She keeps me up, and Jerrie will live with us, and Mrs. Crawford ; but not here, for Harold could never get along with mother and Tom ; we will build a house together, Hally and I, with Jerrie to help and plan—build one where the cottage stands, or near it, so Jerrie can still see the old Tramp

House she is so fond of. Not a house like this, with such big rooms, but a pretty, modern Queen Ann house, with every room a corner room, and a bay-window in it. And Harold will have an office in town, and I shall drive down for him every afternoon and take him home to dinner and to Jerrie."

Such was the nature of Maude's thoughts, as she lay day after day upon the couch, too weak to do more than lift her hands or raise her head when the dreadful paroxysms of coughing seized her and racked her fragile frame. Still she was very happy, and the happiness showed itself upon her face, where there rested a look of perfect content and peace, which her father and mother had noticed and commented upon, and which Jerrie saw the moment she entered the room.

Sitting down beside her, she told her how lovely she looked in her pretty rose-colored wrapper, and how sorry every one was for her, and that both she and Nina would have been there every day, only they knew they could not see her. Then, as Maude's eyes fixed themselves steadily upon her, with a look of inquiry, she set her teeth hard, and began :

" I don't think any one has been more sorry than Harold. Why, for the first few days after you were taken so ill he just walked the floor all the time he was in the house, and when grandma asked what ailed him, he said, ' I am thinking of Maude, and am afraid my call upon her was the cause of the attack.' "

" N-n—" Maude began, but checked herself in time, and taking up her slate, wrote, " Tell him it was not his call. I am glad he came."

All day and all night Jerrie sat by her, sometimes talking to her and answering the questions she wrote upon the slate, but oftener in perfect silence, when Maude seemed to be asleep. Then Jerrie's tears fell like rain, the face upon the pillow looked so much like death, and she kept repeating to herself the lines :

> " We thought her dying when she slept,
>   And sleeping when she died."

When the warm July morning looked in at the windows of the sick-room, bringing with it the perfume of hundreds

of flowers blooming on the lawn, and the scent of the hay
cut the previous day, it found Jerrie still watching by
Maude, her own face tired and pale, with dark rings about
her eyes, which were heavy with tears and wakefulness.
She had not slept at all, and her head was beginning to
ache frightfully when the nurse came in and relieved her,
telling her breakfast was ready. Maude was awake, and
wrote eagerly upon the slate :

" You'll come back ? You'll stay all day ? You do me
so much good, and I am a great deal better for your being
here."

Jerrie hesitated a moment ; her head was aching so
hard that she longed to get away. But selfishness was not
one of Jerrie's faults, and putting her own wishes aside,
she said :

" Yes, I will stay until afternoon, and then I must go
home. I did not tell you that Harold was going away to-
night, did I ?"

Maude shook her head, and Jerrie went on :

" You know, perhaps, that some time ago a Mr. Wilson,
of Truesdale, sued Peterkin for some infringement on a
patent, or something of that sort."

Maude nodded, and Jerrie continued :

" The suit comes off to-morrow, and Harold is subpœnaed as a witness, as he was in Peterkin's office a while and
knows something about the arrangement between them. I
am sorry he has got to swear against Peterkin ; it will make
him so angry, and he hates Harold now. The suit is to be
called in the morning and Judge St. Claire and Harold are
going to-night on the five o'clock train ; and as he may be
gone a day or two I must be home to see to packing his bag.
But I will stay with you just as long as I can."

She said nothing of her head which throbbed in a most
peculiar way, making her dizzy and half blind as she went
down to breakfast, which she took alone with Mrs. Tracy.
Frank had eaten his long before, and was now pacing up
and down the piazza with his head bent forward and his
hands locked together behind him.

Tom seldom appeared until after ten, and when Jerrie
went for a few moments into the grounds, to see if the fresh
air would do her good, she found him seated in an arm-

chair under a horse chestnut tree, stretching himself and yawning as if he were just out of bed.

"Jerrie, you here? Did you stay all night? If I'd known that, I'd have made an effort to come down to breakfast, though I think getting up in the morning a bore. Why, what's the matter? You look as if you were going to faint. Sit down here," he continued, as he saw Jerrie reel forward as if she were about to fall.

He put her into the chair and stood over her, fanning her with his hat and wondering what he should do, while for a moment she lost consciousness of the things about her, and her mind went floating off after the picture on the wall in Wiesbaden, which was haunting her that morning.

When she came to herself, Tom and Dick and Billy were all three hovering around, and so close to her that without opening her eyes she could have told exactly where each one was standing, Tom by the smell of tobacco, with which his clothes were saturated, Billy by the powerful scent of white rose with which he always perfumed his handkerchief, and Dick, because, as she had once said to Nina when a child, he was so clean and looked as if he had just been scrubbed. The two young men had come to inquire for Maude, and had found Jerrie half swooning under the tree, with Tom fanning her frantically and acting like a wild man.

Jerrie had seen Dick twice since her refusal of him, and both times her manner, exactly like what it had always been to him, had put him at his ease, so that a looker-on would never have dreamed of that episode under the pines when she nearly broke his heart. Billy, however, was more conscious. He had not seen Jerrie since he took her home in his dog-cart, and his face was scarlet and his manner nervous and constrained as he stood before her, longing and yet not daring to fan her with his hat just as Tom was doing.

Of the three young men who had sought her hand, Billy's wound was the deepest, and Billy would remember it the longest; for, mingled with his defeat, was a sense of mortification and hatred of his own personal appearance, which he could not help thinking had influenced Jerrie's decision.

"And I don't blame her, by Jove !" he said to himself a hundred times. "She could not marry a pigmy, and I was a fool to hope it; but I shall love her just the same as long as I live; and if I can ever help her I will."

And when at last Jerrie was better, and assured him so with her own sweet graciousness of manner, and put her hand upon his shoulder to steady herself as she stood up, he felt that paradise was opening to him again, and that although he had lost Jerrie as a wife, he still had her as a friend, which was more than he had dared expect.

"Are you better now ? Can you walk to the house ?" Tom asked.

"Oh, yes ; the giddiness is gone," Jerrie replied. "I don't know what ails me this morning."

Never before could she remember having felt as she did now, with that sharp pain in her head, that buzzing in her ears, and, more than all, that peculiar state of mind which she called her "spells," and which seemed to hold her now, body and soul. Even when she returned to Maude's room her thoughts were far away, and everything which had ever come to her concerning her babyhood came to her again, crowding upon her so fast that once it seemed to her that the top of her head was lifting, and she put up her hand to hold it in its place. And still she staid on with Maude, although two or three times she arose to go, but something kept her there—chance, if one chooses to call by that name the something which at times molds us to its will and influences our whole lives. Something kept her there until the morning was merged into noon and the noon into the middle of the afternoon, and then she could stay no longer. The hour had come when she must go, for the other force which was to be the instrument in changing all her future was astir, and she must keep her unconscious appointment with it.

CHAPTER XL.

"DO YOU KNOW WHAT YOU HAVE DONE ?"

JUDGING from the result, this question might far better have been put to rather than by Peterkin, as he stood puffing, and hot, and indignant in the Tramp House, looking down upon Jerrie, who was sitting upon the wooden bench, with her aching head resting upon a corner of the old table standing against the wall just where it stood that stormy night years ago, when death claimed the woman beside her, but left her unharmed.

After saying good-by to Maude, Jerrie had walked very slowly through the park, stopping more than once to rest upon the seats scattered here and there, and wondering more and more at the feeling which oppressed her and the terrible pain in her head, which grew constantly worse.

"I'm afraid I'm going to be sick," she said to herself, "I never felt this way before ; and no wonder, with all I have gone through the last few weeks. The getting ready for the commencement, the coming home, and all the excitement which followed, with three men, one after another, offering themselves to me, and the drenching that night in the rain, and then watching by Maude without a wink of sleep, it is enough to make a behemoth sick, and I am so dizzy and hot—"

She had reached the Tramp House by this time, and feeling that she could go no farther without resting, she went in, and seating herself upon the bench, laid her aching head upon the table, and felt again for a few moments that strange sensation as if the top of her head were rising up and up until she could not reach it with her hand, for she tried, and thought of Ann Eliza, with her hair piled so high on her head.

"The loss of an inch or two might improve me," she said, "though I'd rather keep my scalp."

Then she seemed to be drifting away into the realms of sleep, and all around her was confusion and bewilderment.

The window, across which the woodbine was growing,

changed places with the door ; the floor rose up and bowed to her, while the room was full of faces, beckoning to and smiling upon her. Faces like the one she knew so well, the pale face in the chair; faces like her own, as she remembered it when a child ; faces like the dark woman dead so long ago and buried in the Tracy lot, and faces like Arthur's as she had seen him oftenest, when he spoke so lovingly, and called her little Cherry. Then the scene changed, and the old Tramp House was full of wondrous music, which came floating in at every crevice and through the open door and windows, while she listened intently in her dreams as the grand chorus went on. It was as if Arthur, from the top of the highest peak beyond the Rocky Mountains, and Gretchen, from her lonely grave in far-off Germany, were calling to each other across two continents, their voices meeting and mingling together in the Tramp House in a jubilistic strain, now wild and weird like the cry of the dying woman looking out into the stormy night, now soft and low as the lullaby a fond mother sings to her sleeping child, and now swelling louder and louder, and higher and higher, until the rafters rang with the joyous music, and the whole world outside was filled with the song of gladness.

Wake up, Jerrie ! Wake from the dream of rapture to a reality far more rapturous, for the time is at hand, the hour has come, heralded by the shadow which falls over the floor as Peterkin's burly figure crosses the threshold and enters the silent room.

After Peterkin's conversation with his son concerning his future wife, Jerrie had grown rapidly in the old man's favor. It is true she had neither name nor money, the latter of which was scarcely necessary in this case, but he was not insensible to the fact that she possessed other qualities and advantages which would be a help to the house of Peterkin in its efforts to rise. No girl in the neighborhood was more popular or more sought after than Jerrie, or more intimate with the big-bugs, as he styled the St. Claires, and Athertons, and Tracys. Jerrie would *draw ;* Jerrie would *boost ;* and he found himself forming many plans for the young couple, who were to occupy the south wing ; and in fancy he saw Arthur at Le Bateau half the time at least, while the rest of the time the carriages from Grassy Spring,

15

and Brier Hill, and Tracy Park were standing under the stone arch in front of the door. How then was he disappointed, and enraged, too, when told by Billy that Jerrie had refused him ?

Peterkin had been in Springfield nearly a week, and after his return home had waited a little before broaching the subject to his son ; so that it was not until the morning before the day of the lawsuit that he learned the truth by closely questioning Billy, who shielded and defended Jerrie as far as possible.

"Not have you ! Refused you ! Don't love you ! Don't care for money ! Thunderation ! What does the girl mean ! Is she crazy ? Is she a fool ? Is she in love with some other idiot ? "

"I th-think so, yes ; th-though it did not occur to me then," Billy answered, very meekly ; "and if so she ca-can't care for me any mo-more than I ca-can care for any other girl."

"And you are a fool, too," was the affectionate rejoinder. "I'll be dummed if you ain't a pair ! Who is the lucky man ? Not that dog, Harold, who is goin' to swear agin us to-morrow ? If it is, I b'lieve I'll shoot him."

"Father," Billy cried, in alarm, " b-be quiet ; if I can st-stand it, you can."

But Peterkin swore he wouldn't stand it. He'd do something, he didn't know what ; and all the morning he went about the house like a madman, swearing at his wife, because she wasn't *up to snuff*, and couldn't hoe her own with the 'ristocrats ; swearing at Billy because he was a fool, and so small that 'twas no wonder a bean-pole like Jerrie wouldn't look at him, and swearing at Ann Eliza because her hair was so red, and because she had sprained her ankle for the sake of having Tom Tracy bring her home, hoping he would keep calling to see her, and thus give her a chance to rope him in, which she never could as long as the world stood.

"Neither you nor Bill will ever marry, with all your money, unless you take up with a cobbler, and he with a washwoman," was his farewell remark as he finally left the house about three o'clock and started for the village, where he had some of his own witnesses to see before taking the train for Springfield at five.

His wife had ventured to suggest that he go in the carriage, as it was so warm; but he had answered savagely:

"Go to thunder with your carriage and coat-of-arms! What good have they ever done us only to make folks laugh at us for a pack of fools? Nothing under heaven gives us a h'ist, and I'm just goin' to quit the folderol and pad it on foot, as I used to when I was cap'n of the 'Liza Ann—dum it!"

And so, with his bag in his hand, he started rapidly down the road in the direction of Shannondale. But the sun was hot, and he was hot, and his bag was heavy, and, cursing himself for a fool that he had not taken the carriage, he finally struck into the park as a cooler, if longer, route to the station.

As he came near the Tramp House, which gave no sign of its sleeping occupant, something impelled him to look in at the door. And this he did with a thought of Jerrie in his heart, though with no suspicion that she was there; and when he saw her he started suddenly and uttered an exclamation of surprise, which roused her from her heavy slumber.

"Oh!" she exclaimed, but whatever else she might have said was prevented by his outburst of passion, which began with the question:

"Do you know what you have done?"

Jerrie looked at him wonderingly, but made no reply, and he went on:

"Yes, do you know what you have done?—you, a poor, unknown girl, who, but for the Tracys, would have gone to the poor-house, sure as guns, where you orter have gone! Yes, you orter. You refuse my Bill! you, who hadn't a cent to your name; and all for that sneak of a Harold, who will swear agin me to-morrer. I know he's at the root on't, though Bill didn't say so, and I hate him wuss than pizen; he, who has been at the wheel in my shop! he to be settin' up for a gentleman and a cuttin' out my Bill, who will be wuth more'n a million—yes, two millions, probably, and you have refused him! Do you hear me, gal?"

"Yes, I hear you," she said. "You are talking of Harold, and saying things you shall not repeat in my presence."

"Hoity-toity, miss! What's to hinder me repeatin' in

your presence that Harold Hastings is a sneak and a snob, a hewer of wood, a drawer of water, and a——"

Jerry had risen to her feet, and stood up so tall and straight that it seemed to Peterkin as if she towered even above himself, while something in the flash of her blue eyes made him think of Arthur when he turned him from the house for accusing Harold of theft, and also of the little child who had attacked him so fiercely on that wintry morning when the dead woman lay stretched upon the table at the Park House, with her dark face upturned to the ceiling above.

"I shall hinder you," she said, her voice ringing clear and distinct ; "and if you breathe another word against Harold, I'll turn you from this room. The Tramp House is mine ; Mr. Arthur gave it to me, and you cannot stay in it with me."

"Heavens and earth ! hear the girl ! One would s'pose she was the Queen of Sheby to hear her go on, instead of a beggar, whose father was the Lord only knows who, and whose mother was found in rags on this 'ere table. Drat the dum thing !" Peterkin roared, bringing his fist down with such force upon the poor old rickety table that it fell to pieces under the blow and went crashing to the floor.

Jerrie's face was a face to fear then, and Peterkin was afraid, and backed himself from the room, with Jerrie close to him, never speaking a word, but motioning him to the door, through which he passed swiftly, and, picking up his bag, walked rapidly away, growling to himself :

"There's the very old Harry in that gal's eye. Bill did well to get shet of her ; and yit, if she'd married him, how she would have rid over all their heads ! Well, to be sure, what a dum fool she is !"

CHAPTER XLI.

WHAT JERRIE FOUND UNDER THE FLOOR.

MEANTIME Jerrie had gone back to the wreck of the table, which she handled as carefully and reverently as if it had been her mother's coffin she was touching. One of the legs had been broken before, and she and Harold had fastened it on and turned it to the side of the house where it would be more out of the way of harm, and it was this leg which had succumbed first to the force of Peterkin's fist, and as the entire pressure of the table was brought to bear upon it in falling, it had been precipitated through a hole in the base board, which had been there as long as she could remember the place, not so large at first, but growing larger each year, as the decaying boards crumbled or were eaten away by rats.

Jerrie called it a rat-hole, and had several times put a trap there to catch the marauders, who sometimes scampered across her very feet, so accustomed were they to her presence. But the rats would not go into the trap, and then she pasted a newspaper over the hole, but this had been torn, and hung in shreds, while the hole grew gradually larger.

Taking up the top of the table, Jerrie dragged it to the center of the room, and putting three of the legs upon it, went to search for the fourth, one end of which was just visible at the aperture in the wall. As she stooped to take it out, a bit of the decayed floor under her feet gave way, making the opening so large, that the table-leg disappeared from view entirely. Then Jerrie went down upon her knees, and, thrusting her hand under the floor, felt for the missing leg, striking against stones, and bits of mortar, and finally touching something from which she recoiled for an instant, it was so cold and slimy.

But she struck it again in her search, this time more squarely, and grasping it hard in her hand, brought it out to the light, while an undefinable thrill, half of terror, half of joy, ran through her frame, as she held it up and examined it carefully.

It was a small hand-bag of Russia leather, covered with mold and stained with the damp of its long hiding-place, while a corner of it showed that the rats had tested its properties, but, disliking either the taste or the smell, had left it in quiet. And there under the floor, not two feet from where Jerrie had often played, it had lain ever since the wintry night years before, when it had probably fallen from the table. Then the rats, attracted by this novel appearance in their midst, had investigated and dragged it so far from the opening that it could not be seen unless one went down upon the floor to look for it.

This was the conviction that flashed upon Jerrie as she stood, without the power at first to speak or move.

In her ears there was a roaring sound like the rushing of distant waters falling heavily, while the objects in the room swam around her, and she experienced again that ringing sensation as if the top of her head were leaving her. She was so sure that here at last was a message from the dead—that she had the mystery of her babyhood in her grasp—and yet, for full two minutes she hesitated and held back, until at last the face which had haunted her so often seemed almost to touch her own with a caress which brought the hot tears to her eyes, and the spell which had bound her hands and feet was broken.

The bag was clasped, but not locked, although there was a lock, and Jerrie thought involuntarily of the key found with the other articles on the dead woman's person. To unclasp the bag required a little strength, for the steel was covered with rust; but it yielded at last to Jerrie's strong fingers, and the bag came open, disclosing first some hard object carefully wrapped in a silk handkerchief which had been white in its day, but now was yellow and soiled by time. At this, however, Jerrie scarcely looked, for her eye had fallen upon a package of papers beneath it, folded with care, and securely tied with a bit of faded blue ribbon.

Seating herself upon the bench where she had been sleeping when Peterkin's voice aroused her, Jerrie untied the package, and then began to read, first slowly, as if weighing every word and sentence, then faster and faster, until at last it seemed that her eyes fairly leaped from page to page, taking in the contents at a glance, and comprehending everything.

When she had finished, she sat for a moment rigid as a corpse, and then, with a loud, glad cry, which went floating out upon the summer air, "Thank Heaven, I have found my mother!" she fell upon her face, insensible to everything.

How long she lay thus she did not know, but when she came back to consciousness the sunlight had changed its position in the room, and she felt it was growing late.

Starting up, and wiping from her face a drop of blood which had oozed from a cut in her forehead caused by her striking it against some hard substance when she fell, she looked about her for a moment in a bewildered kind of way, not realizing at first what had happened ; and even when she remembered, she was too much stunned and astonished to realize it all as she would afterward when she was calmer and could think more clearly.

Taking up the papers one by one, in the order in which she had found them, she tied them again with the blue ribbon, and put them into the bag.

"There was something more," she whispered, trying to think what it was.

Then, as her eye fell upon the first package she had taken out, and which was wrapped in a silk handkerchief, she took it up, and removing the covering, started as suddenly as if a blow had been dealt her, for there was a tortoise-shell box, with its blue satin lining, and its diamonds, which seemed to her like so many sparks of fire flashing in her eyes and dazzling her with their brilliancy.

Just such a box as this, and just such diamonds as these, Mrs. Frank Tracy had lost years ago, and as Jerrie held them in her hand and turned them to the light, till they showed all the hues of the rainbow, she experienced a feeling of terror as if she were a thief and had been convicted of the theft. Then, as she remembered what she had read, she burst into a hysterical fit of laughing and crying together, and whispered to herself :

"I believe I am going mad like him."

After a time she arose, and with the bag on her arm and the diamonds in her hand, she started for home, with only one thought in her mind :

"I must tell Harold, and ask him what to do."

She had forgotten that he was to leave that afternoon

on the train—forgotten everything, except the one subject which affected her so strongly, so that in one sense she might be said to be thinking of nothing, when, as she was walking with her head bent down, she came suddenly face to face with Harold, who, with his satchel in his hand, was starting for the train due now in a few minutes.

"Jerrie," he exclaimed, "how late you are! I waited until the last minute to say good-by. Why, what ails you, and where have you been?" he continued, as she raised her head and he saw the strange palor of her face.

"In the Tramp House," she answered, in a voice which was not hers at all, and made Harold look more curiously at her.

As he did so he saw peeping from a fold of the silk handkerchief the corner of the tortoise-shell box which he remembered so well, and the sight of which brought back all the shame and humiliation and pain of that morning when he had been suspected of taking it.

"What is it? What have you in your hand?" he asked.

Then Jerrie's face, so pale before, turned scarlet, and her eyes had in them a wild look which Harold construed into fear, as, without a word, she laid the box in his hand, and stood watching him as he opened it.

Harold's face was whiter than Jerrie's had been, and his voice trembled as he said, in a whisper:

"Mrs. Tracy's diamonds!"

"Yes, Mrs. Tracy's diamonds," Jerrie replied, with a marked emphasis on the *Mrs. Tracy.*

"How came you by them, and where did you find them," Harold asked next, shrinking a little from the glittering stones which seemed like fiery eyes confronting him.

"I can't tell you now. Put them up quick. Don't let any one see them. Somebody is coming," Jerrie said, hurriedly, as her ear caught a sound and her eye an object which Harold neither saw nor heard as he mechanically put the box into his side pocket and then turned just as Tom Tracy came up on horseback.

"Hallo, Jerrie! hallo, Hal!" he cried, dismounting quickly and throwing the bridle-rein over his arm. "And so you are off to that suit?" he continued, addressing him-

self to Harold. "By George, I wish I were a witness, I'd
swear the old man's head off; for I believe he is an old
liar!" Then turning to Jerrie, he continued: "Are you
better than you were this morning? Upon my word, you
look worse. It's that infernal watching last night that ails
you. I told mother you ought not to have done it."

Just then a whistle was heard in the distance; the
train was at Truesdale, four miles away.

"You will never catch it," Tom said, as Harold
snatched up his bag and started to run. "Here, jump on
to Beaver, and leave him at the station. I can go there
for him."

Harold knew it was impossible for him to make time
against the train, and, accepting Tom's offer, he vaulted
into the saddle and galloped rapidly away, reaching the
station just in time to give his horse to the care of a boy
and to leap upon the train as it was moving away.

Meanwhile Tom walked on with Jerrie to the cottage,
where he would have stopped if she had not said to him:

"I would ask you to come in, but my head is aching
so badly that I must go straight to bed. Good-by, Tom,"
and she offered him her hand, a most unusual thing for her
to do on an ordinary occasion like this.

What ailed her, Tom wondered, that she spoke so kindly to him and looked at him so curiously? Was she sorry
for her decision, and did she wish to revoke it?

"Then, by Jove, I'll give her a chance, for every time
I see her I find myself more and more in love," Tom
thought, as he left her and started for the station after
Beaver, whom he found hitched to a post and pawing the
ground impatiently.

Mrs. Crawford was in the garden when Jerrie entered
the house, and thus there was no one to see her as she hurried up stairs and hid the leather bag away upon a shelf in
her dressing-room. First, however, she took out two of the
papers and read them again, as if to make assurance doubly
sure; then she tried the little key to the lock, which it
fitted perfectly.

"There is no mistake," she whispered; "but I can't
think about it now, for this terrible pain in my head. I
must wait, till Harold comes home; he will tell me what to
do, and be so glad for me. Dear Harold, his days of labor

are over, and grandmother's, too. Those diamonds are a fortune in themselves, and they are *mine!* my own! she said so! Oh, mother, I have found you at last, but I can't make it real; my head is so strange. What if I should be crazy? What if that dreadful taint should be in my blood, or what if I should die just as I have found my mother! Oh, Heaven, don't let me die; don't let me lose my reason, and I will try to do right; only show me what right is."

She was praying now upon her knees with her throbbing head upon the side of the bed, into which she finally crept with her clothes on, even to her boots, for Jerrie was herself no longer. The fever with which for days she had been threatened, and which had been induced by over-study at Vassar, and the excitement which had followed her return home, could be kept at bay no longer, and when Mrs. Crawford, who had seen her enter the house, went up after a while to see why she did not come down to tea, she found her sleeping heavily, with spots of crimson upon her cheeks, while her hands, which moved incessantly, were burning with fever. Occasionally she moaned and talked of the Tramp House, and rats, and Peterkin, who had struck the blow and knocked something or somebody down, Mrs. Crawford could not tell what, unless it were Jerrie herself, on whose forehead there was a bunch the size now of a walnut.

"Jerrie, Jerrie," Mrs. Crawford said in alarm, as she tried to remove the girl's clothes. "What is it, Jerrie? What has happened? Who hurt you? Who struck the blow?"

"Peterkin," was the faint response, as for an instant Jerrie opened her eyelids only to close them again and sink away into a heavier sleep or stupefaction.

It seemed the latter, and as Mrs. Crawford could not herself go for a physician, and as no one came down the lane that evening she sat all night by Jerrie's bed, bathing the feverish hands and trying to lessen the lump on the forehead, which, in spite of all her efforts, continued to swell until it seemed to her it was as large as a hen's egg.

"Did Peterkin strike you, and what for?" she kept asking; but Jerrie only moaned and muttered something she could not understand, except once, when she said, distinctly:

" Yes, Peterkin. Such a blow ; it was like a black-smith's hammer, and knocked the table to pieces. I am glad he did it."

Mrs. Crawford asked herself in vain what she meant, and when at least the early summer morning broke, she was almost as crazy as Jerrie, who was steadily growing worse, and who was saying the strangest things about arrests and blows, and Peterkin, and Harold, and Mr. Arthur, whose name she always mentioned with a sob and a stretching out of her hands, as to some invisible presence. Help must be had, and for two hours Mrs. Crawford watched for the coming of some one, until at last she saw Tom Tracy galloping up on Beaver.

" Tom, Tom," she screamed from the window, " don't get off, but ride for your life and fetch the doctor, quick. Jerrie is very sick ; has been crazy all night, and has a bunch on her head as big as a bowl, where she says Peterkin struck her."

" Peterkin struck Jerrie ! I'll kill him !" Tom said, as he tore down the lane and out upon the highway in quest of the physician, who was soon found and at Jerrie's side, where Tom stood with him ; gazing awestruck upon the fever-stricken girl, who was tossing and talking all the time, and whose bright eyes unclosed once and fixed themselves on him, as he spoke her name and laid his hand on one of hers.

" Oh, Tom, Tom," she said, " you told me you'd kill her. Will you kill her ? Will you kill her ?" And a wild, hysterical laugh echoed through the room, as she kept repeating the words, " Will you kill her ? Will you kill her ?" which conveyed no meaning to Tom, who had forgotten what he had said he would do if a claimant to Tracy Park should appear in the shape of a lady.

Whatever Jerrie took up she repeated rapidly until something else came into her mind, and when Mrs. Crawford referring to the bunch on her head, said to the physician, " Peterkin struck the blow, she says," she began at once like a parrot, " Peterkin struck the blow ! Peterkin struck the blow !" until another idea suggested itself, and she began to ring changes on the sentence, " In the rat-hole ; in the Tramp House ; in the Tramp House ; in the rat-hole," talking so fast that sometimes it was impossible to follow her.

The blow on her head alone could not have produced this state of things; it was rather over-excitement, added to some great mental shock, the nature of which he could not divine, the doctor said to Tom, who in his wrath at Peterkin was ready to flay him alive, or at least to ride him on a rail the instant he entered town.

It was a puzzling case, though not a dangerous one as yet, the physician said. Jerrie's strong constitution could stand an attack much more severe than this one; and prescribing perfect quiet, with strict orders that she should see no more people than was necessary, he left, promising to return in the afternoon, when he hoped to find her better. Tom lingered a while after the doctor had left, and showed himself so thoughtful and kind that Mrs. Crawford forgave him much which she had harbored against him for his treatment of Harold.

All night Tom's dreams had been haunted with Jerrie's voice and Jerrie's look as she gave him her hand and said, "Good-by, Tom," and he had ridden over early to see if the look and tone were still there, and if they were, and he had a chance, he meant to renew his offer. But words of love would have been sadly out of place to this restless, feverish girl, whose incoherent babblings puzzled and bewildered him.

One fact, however, was distinct in his mind—Peterkin had struck her a terrible blow in the Tramp House. Of that he was sure, though why he should have done so he could not guess; and vowing vengeance upon the man, he left the cottage at last and rode down to the Tramp House, where he found the table in a state of ruin upon the floor, three of the legs upon it and the other one nowhere to be seen.

"He struck her with it and then threw it away, I'll bet," he said to himself, as he hunted for the missing leg; "and it was some quarrel he picked with her about Hal, who is going to swear against him. Jerrie would never hear Hal abused, and I've no doubt she aggravated the wretch until he forgot himself and dealt her that blow. I'll have him arrested for assault and battery, as sure as I am born."

Hurrying home, he told the story to his mother, who smiled incredulously and said she did not believe it, bidding him say nothing of it to Maude, who was not as well as usual that day. Then he told his father, who started at once for the cottage, where Mrs. Crawford refused to let him see Jerrie, saying that the doctor's orders were that she should be kept perfectly quiet, and that she did seem a little better and more rational. But as they stood talking together near the open door, Jerrie's voice was heard calling:

"Let Mr. Frank come up."

So Frank went up, and, notwithstanding all he had heard from Tom, he was surprised at Jerrie's flushed face and the unnatural expression of her eyes, which turned so eagerly toward him as he came in.

For a moment her mind was tolerably clear, and she said to him abruptly, while she held his gaze steadily with her bright eyes:

"You posted that letter?"

Frank knew perfectly well that she meant the letter whose superscription he had studied so many times, and which had seldom been absent from his thoughts an hour since that night when, from her perch on the gate-post, Jerrie had startled him with the question she was asking him now. But he affected ignorance and said, as indifferently as he could:

"What letter do you mean?"

"Why, the one Mr. Arthur wrote to Gretchen, or her friends, in Wiesbaden, and gave me to post. You took it for me to the office, and I sat on the gate so long waiting for you to come and tell me you had posted it sure."

"Oh, yes, I remember it, and how you frightened me sitting up there so high like a goblin," Frank answered, falteringly, his face as crimson now as Jerrie's, and his eyes dropping beneath her gaze.

"Gretchen's friends never got that letter," Jerrie continued.

"No, they never got it," Frank answered mechanically.

"If they had," Jerrie went on, "they would have answered it, for she had friends there."

Frank looked up quickly at the girl talking so strangely to him. What had she heard? What did she know? or was this only an outburst of insanity? She certainly looked crazy as she lay there talking to him. He was sure of it a moment after when she said to him as he arose to go :

"You have been kind to me, you and Maude—you and Maude—and I shan't forget it. Tell her I shan't forget it—I shan't forget it. Kiss me, Mr. Tracy, please."

Had he been struck by lightning, Frank could hardly have been more astonished than he was at this singular request, and for a moment he stared blankly at the girl who had made it, not because he was at all adverse to granting it, but because he doubted the propriety of the act, even if she were crazy. But something in Jerrie's face, like Arthur's, mastered him, and, stooping down, he kissed the parched lips through which the breath came so hotly, wondering as he did so what Dolly would say if she could see him, a white-haired man of forty-five, kissing a young girl of twenty, and that girl Jerrie Crawford.

"Thanks," Jerrie said, wiping her mouth with the back of her hand. "I think you have been chewing tobacco, haven't you ? But I shant forget it; I shall do right; I shall do right."

She was certainly growing worse, Frank thought, as he went down to confer with Mrs. Crawford as to what ought to be done, and to offer his services. He would remain there that afternoon, he said, and send a servant over to be in the house during the night.

"She is very sick," he said ; "but it does not seem as if her sickness could be caused wholly by that bruise on her head. Do you think Peterkin struck her ?"

"She says so," was Mrs. Crawford's reply, "though why he should do it, I cannot guess."

Then she added that a servant would not be necessary, as Harold would be home by seven.

"But he may not," Frank replied. "Squire Harrington came at two, and reported that the suit was not called until so late that they would not probably get through with the witnesses to-day, so Hal may not be here, and I will send Rob anyway."

On his way home Frank, too, looked in at the Tramp House, and saw the broken-down table, and hunted for the missing leg, and with Tom concluded that something unusual had taken place there, though he could not guess what.

That evening, as Jerrie grew more and more restless and talkative, Mrs. Crawford listened anxiously for the train, and when it came, waited and watched for Harold, but watched in vain, for Harold did not come. Several of her neighbors, however, did come; those who had gone to the city out of curiosity to attend the law-suit, and "see old Peterkin squirm and hear him swear;" and could she have looked into the houses in the village that night, she would have heard some startling news, for almost before the train rolled away from the platform, everybody at or near the station had been told that Mrs. Tracy's diamonds had been found in Harold Hastings' pocket, and that he was under arrest.

Such news travels fast, and it reached the Park House just as the family were finishing their late dinner.

"I told you so! I always thought he was guilty, or knew something about them," Mrs. Frank exclaimed, with a look of exultation on her face as she turned to her husband. "What do you think now of your fine young man, who has been hanging around here after your daughter until she is half-betwaddled after him?"

Frank's face was very grave as he answered, decidedly:

"I do not believe it. Harold Hastings never took your diamonds."

"How came he by them, then?" she asked, in a loud, angry voice.

"I don't know," her husband replied; there is some mistake; it will be cleared in time. But keep it from Maude; I think the news would kill her."

Meantime Tom had sat with his brows knit together, as if intently thinking; and when at last he spoke, he said to his father:

"I shall go to Springfield on the ten o'clock train, and you'd better go with me."

To this Frank made no objections. If his wife's diamonds were really found, he ought to be there to receive them; and, besides, he might say a word in Harold's defense, if necessary. So ten o'clock found him and Tom at the station, where was also Dick St. Claire, with several other young men, pacing up and down the platform and excitedly discussing the news, of which they did not believe a word.

"I almost feel as if they were hurting me when they touch Hal, he's such a noble fellow," Dick said to Mr. Tracy and Tom. "We are all as mad as we can be, and so a lot of us fellows, who have always known him, are going over to speak a good word for him, and go his bail if necessary. I don't believe, though, they can do anything after all these years; but father will know. He is there with him."

And so the night train to Springfield carried ten men from Shannondale, nine of whom were going to stand by Harold, while the tenth, hardly knew why he was going or what he believed. Arrived in the city, their first inquiry was for Harold, who, instead of being in the charge of an officer as they had feared, was quietly sleeping in his room at the hotel, while Judge St. Claire had the diamonds in his possession.

CHAPTER XLII.

HAROLD AND THE DIAMONDS.

WHEN Harold sprang upon the train as it was moving from the station and entered the rear car, he found Billy and Peterkin near the door, the latter button-holing Judge St. Claire, to whom he was talking loudly and angrily of Wilson, who had brought the suit against him.

"Yes, yes, I see ; I know ; but all that will come out on the trial," the judge said, trying to silence him.

But Peterkin held on, until his eye caught Harold, when he at once let the judge go, and seating himself by the young man, began in a soft, coaxing tone for him :

"I don't see why in thunder you are goin' agin me, who have allus been your friend, and gin you work when you couldn't git it any wheres else ; and I can't imagine what you're goin' to say, or what you know."

Harold's face was very red, but his manner was respectful as he replied :

" You cannot be more sorry than I am that I am subpœnaed as a witness against you. I did not seek it. I could not help it ; but, being a witness, I must answer the questions truthfully."

" 'Thunder and lightning, man ! Of course you must ! Don't I know that ?" the irascible Peterkin growled, getting angry at once. "Of course you must answer questions, but you needn't blab out stuff they don't ask you, so as to lead 'em on. I know 'em, the blood-hounds ; they'll squeeze you dry, once let 'em get an inkling you know sunthin' more. Now, if this goes agin me, I'm out at least thirty thousand dollars ; and between you and I, I don't mind givin' a cool two thousand, or three, or mebby five, right out of pocket, cash down, to anybody whose testimony, without bein' a lie—I don't want nobody to swear false, remember—but, heavens and earth, can't a body forgit a little, and keep back a lot if they want to ?"

" What are you trying to say to me ?" Harold asked, his face pale with resentment, as he suspected the man's motive.

" Say to you ? Nothin', only that I'll give five thousand dollars down to the chap whose testimony gets me off and flings Wilson."

" Mr. Peterkin," Harold said, looking the old wretch fully in the face, " if you are trying to bribe me, let me tell you at once that I am not to be bought. I shall not volunteer information, but shall answer truthfully whatever is asked me."

" Go to thunder, then ! I always knew you were a bad aig," Peterkin roared ; and as there was nothing to be made from Harold, he changed his seat to the one his son was occupying.

Left to himself, Harold had time to think of the diamonds, which, indeed, had not been absent from his thoughts a moment since Jerrie gave them to him. They were closely buttoned in his coat pocket, where they burned like fire, as he wondered where and how Jerrie had found them.

" In the Tramp House it must have been," he said to himself ; " but who put them there, and how did she chance to find them, and why did she look so wild and excited, so like a crazy person, when she gave them to me, bidding me let no one see them ?"

These questions he could not answer, and his brain was all in a whirl when the train reached Springfield, and with the others, he registered himself at the hotel. Suddenly, there came back to him, with horrible distinctness, the words Jerrie had spoken to him years ago, when he walked homeward with her from the Park House, where he had been questioned so closely by Mrs. Tracy with regard to her diamonds and what he had been doing in the house on the morning of their disappearance.

"I believe I know where the diamonds are," she had said, and in his excitement he had scarcely noticed it; but it came back to him now with fearful significance, as, after the gas was lighted, he sat alone in a little reception-room opening from one of the parlors. Did Jerrie know where they were, and had not spoken? And, if so, was she not guilty in trying to shield another? For that she took them herself he never for a moment dreamed. It was some one else, and she knew and did not tell. He was certain of it now, as every incident connected with her strange sickness came back to him, when she seemed to be doing penance for another's fault. She had called herself an accessory, and that was what she was, or rather what the world would call her, if it knew. To him she was Jerrie, the girl he loved, and he would defend her to the bitter end, no matter how culpable she had been in keeping silence so long.

But who took them? That was the question puzzling him so much as he sat thinking, with his head bent down, and so absorbed that he did not hear a step in the adjoining room, or know that Peterkin had seated himself just where a large mirror showed him distinctly the young man in the next room, whom he recognized at once, though Harold never moved for a few moments or lifted his head.

At last, however, he unbottoned his coat, and after glancing cautiously around to make sure no one was near, he took the box from his pocket, and holding the stones to the light examined them carefully, taking in his hand first the earrings and then the pin, and holding them in such a way that two or three times they flashed directly in the eyes of the cruel man watching him.

"Yes, they are Mrs. Tracy's diamonds: there can be no mistake," he whispered, just as he became conscious that there was some one in the door looking at him,

Quick as thought he put the box out of sight while Peterkin's voice, exultant and hateful called out :

" Hallo, Mr. Prayer-book, your piety won't let you keep back a darned thing you know agin me, but it lets you have in your possession diamonds which I'd eenamost swear was them stones Miss Tracy lost years ago and suspected you of takin'.   I know the box any way, I heard it described so often, and I b'lieve I know them diamonds.   I seen 'em in the looking-glass settin' in t'other room, and seen you look all round like a thief afore you opened 'em.   So fork over, and mebby you can give me back May Jane's pin you stole at the party the night Mr. Arthur came home. Fork over I say !"

Too much astonished at first to speak, Harold looked at the man who had attacked him so brutally, while his hand closed tightly over the diamonds in his pocket, as if fearing they might be wrenched from him by force.

" Will you fork over, or shall I call the perlice ?" Peterkin asked.

" Call the police as soon as you like," Harold replied, " but I shall not give you the diamonds."

" Then you own that you've got 'em !   That's half the battle !" Peterkin said, coming close up to him, and looking at him with a meaning smile more detestable than any menace could have been.   " I know you have got 'em, and I can ruin you if I try, and then what'll your doxie think of you !   Will she refuse my Bill for a thief, and treat me as if I was dirt ?"

" What do you mean, sir ?" Harold demanded, feeling intuitively that by his *doxie* Jerrie was meant, and feeling a great horror, too, lest by some means her name should be mixed up with the affair before she had a chance to explain.

The reference to Billy was a puzzle, but Peterkin did not long leave him in doubt.

" I mean that you think yourself very fine, and always have, and that are gal of the carpet-bag thinks herself fine, too, and refused my Bill for you, who hain't a cent in the world.   I seen it in her face when I twitted her on it, and she riz up agin' me like a catamount.   But I'll be even with you both yit.   I've got you in my power, young man, but——" and here he came a step or two nearer to Harold and dropping his voice to a whisper, said : "I shan'n't do nothin', nor say nothin' till you've gin your evidence, and if you can hold your tongue I will. You tickle me, and I'll tickle you! See?"

Harold was too indignant to reply, and feeling that he was degrading himself every moment he spent in the presence of such a man, he left the room without a word, and went to his own apartment, but not to sleep, for never had he spent so wretched a night as that which followed his interview with Peterkin. Of what the man could do to him, he had no fear. His anxiety was all for Jerrie. Where did she find the diamonds, and for whom had she kept silence so long? and what would be said of the act when it was known, as it might be, though not from him?

Two or three times he arose and lighting the gas, examined the diamonds carefully to see if there were not some mistake. But there could be none. He had seen them on the lady's person and had heard them described so accurately that he could not be mistaken; and then the box was the same he had once seen when Jack took him to his mother's room to show him what Uncle Arthur had brought. That was a tortoise shell of an oval shape, and lined with blue satin, and this was a tortoise shell, oval-shaped, and lined with blue satin. Harold felt, when at last the daylight shone into his room, that if it had tarried a moment longer he must have gone mad. He was very white and haggard, and there were dark rings under his eyes when he went down to the office, where the first person he met was Billy, who also looked pale and worn, with a different expression upon his face from anything Harold had ever seen before. It was as if all life and hope had gone, leaving him nothing now to care for. In his anxiety and worry about the diamonds Harold had scarcely given a thought to what Peterkin had said of Jerrie's refusal of Billy, for it seemed so improbable that the latter would presume to offer himself to her; but at sight of Billy's face it came back to him with a throb of pity for the man, and a thrill of joy for himself for whom Peterkin had said his son was rejected.

"Does Billy know of the diamonds, I wonder?" he thought.

As if to answer the question in the negative, Billy came

quickly forward, and, offering his hand, bade Harold good-morning, and then motioning him to a seat, took one beside him, and began :

"I'm awful sorry, Hal, th-that you are mix-mixed up in th-this, but I sup-suppose you m-must t-tell the truth."

"Yes, I must tell the truth," Harold said.

"Fa-father will be so m-mad," Billy continued. "I wi-wish I could t-t-testify f-for you, bu-but I can't. You were th-there, I wa-wan't, and all I know fa-father told me ; bu-but d-dont volunteer information."

"No," Haro'd said, slowly, wishing that the ocean were rolling between him and this detes'able suit.

Once he resolved to go to Judge St. Claire, deliver up the diamonds, and tell him all he knew about them, but this would be bringing Jerrie into the matter, and so he changed his mind and wandered aimlessly about the town until it was time for him to appear at the court-house, where a crowd was gathering. It was late before the suit known as *Wilson vs. Peterkin* was called, and later still when Harold took the stand.

"White and trembling, so that both his hands and his knees were shaking visibly, he looked more like a criminal than a witness, and he was so agitated and pre-occupied, too, that at first his answers were given at random, as if he hardly knew what he was saying ; nor did he, for over and beyond the sea of faces confronting him, Judge St. Claire's wondering and curious—Billy's wondering, too —Wilson's disappointed and surprised, and Peterkin's threatening and exultant by turns—he saw only Jerrie coming to him in the lane and asking him to keep the diamonds for her—saw her, too, away back years ago in the little room, with her fever-stained cheeks and shorn head, talking the strangest things of prisons, and substitutes, and accessories, and assuring some one that she would never tell, and was going for him, if necessary.

Who was that man ? Where was he now ? and why had he imposed this terrible secret upon Jerrie ?

These were the thoughts crowding through his brain while he was being questioned as to what he knew of the agreement between the plaintiff and defendant while in the office of the latter. Once a thought of Maude crossed his mind with a keen pang of regret, as he remembered the lovely face which had smiled so fondly upon him, mistaking his meaning utterly, and appropriating to herself the love he was trying to tell her was another's. And with thoughts of Maude there came a thought of Arthur, the very first which Harold had given him. Arthur, the crazy man, who himself had hidden the diamonds, and for whom Jerrie was ready to sacrifice so much. It was clear as daylight to him now, the anxiety and strain were over, and those who were watching him so intently as he gave his answers at random, with the sweat pouring down his face, were electrified at the start he gave as he came to himself and realized for the first time where he was, and why he was there. Arthur would never see Jerrie wronged. *She* was safe, and with this load lifted from him, he gave his whole attention to the business on hand, answering the questions now clearly and distinctly.

When at last the lawyer said to him, " Repeat what you can remember of the conversation which took place between the plaintiff and defendant on the morning of——, 18—," he gave one sorry look at poor Billy, who was the picture of shame and confusion, and then, in a clear, distinct voice, which filled every corner of the room, told what he had heard said in his presence, and what he knew of the transaction, proving conclusively that the plaintiff was right and Peterkin a rascal, and this in the face of the man who had ask him not to *blab,* and who shook his fist at him threateningly as the narrative went on.

" Would you believe the defendant under oath ?" was asked at the close, and Harold answered, promptly :

" Under oath—yes."

" Would you, if not under oath ?"

" If an untruth would be to his advantage, no," and then Harold was through.

As he stepped down from the witness stand old Peterkin arose, so angry, that at first he could scarcely articulate his words.

" You dog ! you liar ! you thief !" he screamed ; " to stand there and lie so about me ! I'll teach you—I'll show 'em what you are. If there's a perlice, I call on 'em to arrest this feller for them diamonds of Miss Tracy's ! They are in his pocket—or was last night. I seen 'em myself, and he dassent deny it."

By this time the court-house was in wild confusion, as
the spectators arose from their seats and pressed forward to
where Peterkin stood denouncing Harold, who looked as if
he were going to faint, as Billy hastened to his side, whis
pering :

"Le-lean on me, and I will get you out of this. Fa-father
is mad."

But order was soon restored, though not until Peterkin
had yelled again, as Harold was leaving the room :

"Search him, I tell you ! Don't let him escape ! He's
got 'em in his pocket—Miss Tracy's diamonds ! Lord of
heavens ! don't you remember the row there was about 'em
years ago ?"

Of what followed during the next hour Harold knew very
little. There was a crowd around him, and cries of "He
is going to faint !" while Billy's stammering voice called,
pleadingly, "St-stand back, ca-can't you, and gi-give him
air."

Then a deluge of water in his face ; then a great darkness, and the voices sounded a long way off, and he felt so
tired and sleepy, and thought of Jerrie, and Maude, and
lived over again the scene in the Tramp House, when he
found the former in the bag, and felt her arms around his
neck as he staggered with her through the snow, wondering
why she was so heavy, and why her feet were dragging on
the ground. When he came more fully to himself, he was
in a little room in the court-house, and Billy's arm was lying
protectingly across his shoulder, while Billy's father was
bellowing like a bull :

"Be you goin' to let him go ? Ain't you goin' to git a
writ and arrest him ? Why don't you handcuff him, somebody ? And you, Bill, be you a fool to stan' there huggin'
him as if he was a gal ! What do you mean ?"

"Ha-Hal is my fr-friend, father. He never to-took
the diamonds," Billy answered, sadly, while Judge St.
Claire, who had the box of jewels in his hand and was looking very anxious, turned to the angry man, clamoring so
loudly for a *writ*, and said, sternly :

"Even if Harold took the diamonds—which he did
not, I am certain of that—there is some mistake which he
will explain ; but if he took them, it is too late to arrest him.
A theft committed ten years ago cannot be punished now."

"May the Lord give you sense," Peterkin rejoined, with a derisive laugh. "Don't tell me that a body can't be punished for stealin' diamonds cf 'twas done a hundred years ago."

"But it is true, nevertheless," the judge replied.

Turning to another lawyer, who was standing near, Peterkin asked :

"Is that so, square ? Is it so writ ? Is that the law?"

"That is the law," was the response.

"Wall, I'll be condumbed, if that don't beat all !" Peterkin exclaimed. "Can't be sent to prison ! I swow ! There ain't no law nor justice for nobody but *me*, and I must be kicked to the wall ! I'll give up and won't try to be nobody. I vum !" And as he talked he walked away to ruminate upon the injustice of the law which could not touch Harold Hastings, but could throw its broad arms tightly around himself.

Meanwhile the judge had ordered a carriage and taken Harold with him to his private room in the hotel, where the hardest part for Hal was yet to come.

"Now, my boy," the judge said, after he had made Harold lie down upon the couch and had locked the door, "now tell me all about it. How came you by the diamonds ?"

It was such a pitiful, pleading, agonized face which lifted itself from the cushion and looked at Judge St. Clair, as Harold began :

"I cannot tell you now—I must not ; but by and by perhaps I can. They were handed to me to keep by some one, just for a little while. I cannot tell you who it was. I think I would die sooner than do it. Certainly I would rather go to prison, as Peterkin wishes me to."

There was a thoughtful, perplexed look in the judge's face as he said :

"This is very strange, Harold, that you cannot tell who gave them to you, and with some people will be construed against you."

"I know it ; but I would rather bear it than have that person's name brought in question," was Harold's reply.

"Do you think that person took them ?" the judge asked.

"No, a thousand times, no !" and Harold leaped to his

feet and began to pace the floor hurriedly. "They never took them, never; I'd swear to that with my life. Don't talk any more about it, please; I can't bear it. I have gone through so much to-day, and last night I never slept a wink. Oh, I am so tired!" and with a groan he threw himself again upon the couch, and, closing his eyes, dropped almost instantly into a heavy slumber, from which the judge did not rouse him until after dinner, when he ordered some refreshments sent to his room, and himself awoke the young man, who could only swallow a cup of coffee and a part of a biscuit.

"I am so tired," he kept repeating; "but I shall be better in the morning;" and long before the night train had come he was in bed sleeping off the effects of the day's excitement.

The next morning when he went down to the office he was surprised and bewildered at the crowd which gathered around him—the friends who had come on the train to stand by and defend him, if necessary; and as the home faces he had known all his life looked kindly into his, and the familiar voices of his boyhood told him of sympathy for and faith in him, while hand after hand took his in a friendly clasp, that of Dick St. Claire clinging to his with a grasp which said plainer than words could have done, "I believe in you, Hal, and am so sorry for you," the tension of his nerves gave way entirely, and, sinking down in their midst, he cried like a child when freed from some terrible danger.

He had not thought before that he cared for himself what people said, but he knew now that he did, and this assurance of confidence from his friends unnerved him for a time; then, dashing away his tears and lifting up his face, on which his old winning smile was breaking, he said:

"Excuse me for this weakness; only girls should cry, but I have borne so much, and your coming was such a surprise. Thank you all. I cannot say what I feel. I should cry again if I did."

"Never mind, old boy," Dick's cheery voice called out. "We know what you would say. We came to help you, just a few of us; but if anything had really happened to you, why, all Shannondale would have turned out to the rescue."

16

"Thank you, Dick," Harold said, then, as his eye fell for the first time upon Tom, he exclaimed with a glad ring in his voice, "and you, too, Tom!"

"Yes, I thought I'd come with the crowd and see the fun," Tom answered, indifferently, as he walked away by himself.

Tom had said very little on the train, or after he reached the hotel, but no one had listened with more eagerness to every detail of the matter than he had done, and all that morning he was busy gathering up every item of information, and listening to the guesses as to who the person could be who gave the diamonds to Harold.

The jewels had been identified by his father and by himself, although an identification was scarcely necessary as Harold had distinctly said:

"They are the Tracy diamonds; the person who gave them to me said so."

But who was the person? That was the question puzzling the heads of all the Shannondale people as the morning wore on, and each went where he liked. At last, toward noon, Tom found himself near Harold in front of the court-house, and going up to him, said:

"Hal, I want to talk to you a little while."

"Yes," Hal said, and selecting a retired corner, Tom began:

"Hal, I've never shown any great liking for you, and I don't s'pose I have any, but I don't like to see a man kicked for nothing, and so I came over with the rest."

"Thank you, Tom," Harold replied, "I don't think you ever did like me, and I don't think I cared if you didn't, but I'm glad you came. Is that all you wished to say to me?"

"No," Tom answered. "Jerrie is very sick—"

"Jerrie! Jerrie sick! Oh, Tom!"

It was a cry of almost despair as Harold thought, "What if she should die and the people never know."

"She had an awful headache when you left her in the lane, and the next morning she was raving mad—kind of a brain fever, I guess."

Harold was stupefied, but he managed to ask:

"Does she talk much? What does she say?"

There was alarm in his voice, which the sagacious Tom detected, and, strengthened in his suspicion, he replied :

"Nothing about the diamonds, and the Lord knows I hope she won't."

"What do you mean ?" Harold asked, in a frightened tone.

"Don't you worry," Tom replied. "I wouldn't harm Jerrie any more than you would, but— Well, Hall, you are a trump ! Yes, you are, to hold your tongue and let some think you are the culprit. Hal, Jerrie gave you the diamonds. I saw her do it in the lane as I came up to you. I did not think of it at the time, but afterward it came to me that you took something from her and slipped it into your pocket, and that you both looked scared when you saw me. Jerrie was abstracted and queer all the way to the house, and had a bruise on her head, and she keeps talking of the Tramp House and Peterkin, who, she says, dealt the blow. I went to the Tramp House, and found the old table on the floor, with three of the legs on it ; the fourth I couldn't find. I thought at first that the old wretch had quarreled with her about you on account of the suit, and she had squared up to him, and he had struck her ; but now I believe *he* had the diamonds, and she got them from him in some way, and he struck her with the missing table leg. If you say so, I'll have him arrested."

Tom had told his story rapidly, while Harold listened, until he suggested the arrest of Peterkin, when he exclaimed :

"No, no, Tom. No ; don't you see that would mix Jerrie's name up with the diamonds, and that must not be. She must not be mentioned in connection with them until she speaks for herself ; and, besides, I do not believe it was Peterkin who took them. It might have been your uncle Arthur."

"Uncle Arthur ?" Tom said, indignantly. "Why, he gave them to mother."

"I know he did," Harold continued ; "but in a crazy fit he might have taken them away and secreted them and then forgotten it, and Jerrie might have known it, and not been able to find them till now. Many things go to prove that ;" and very briefly Harold repeated some incidents connected with Jerrie's illness when she was a child.

"That looks like it, certainly," Tom said ; but I am awfully loth to give up arresting the brute, and believe I shall do it yet for assault and battery. He certainly struck her. You will see for yourself the lump on her head."

So saying Tom arose to go away, but before he went he made a remark quite characteristic of him and his feeling for Harold, to whom he said, with a laugh :

"Don't, for thunder's sake, think us a kind of Damon and Pythias twins, because I've joined hands with you against Peterkin and for Jerrie. Herod and Pilate, you know, became friends, but I guess at heart they were Pilate and Herod still.

"No danger of my presuming at all upon your friendship for myself, though I thank you for your interest in Jerrie," Harold replied.

Then the two separated, Tom going his way and Harold his, until it was time for the afternoon train which was to take them home."

The suit had gone against Peterkin, and it was in a towering rage that he stood in the depot, denouncing everybody, and swearing he would sell out Lubertoo and every dumbed thing he owned in Shannondale and take his money away, "and then see how they'd git along without his capital to boost 'em." At Harold he would not even look, for his testimony had been the most damaging of all, and he frowned savagely when on entering the car he saw his son in the same seat with him, talking in low, earnest tones, while Harold was evidently listening to him with interest. The suit had been a pain and trouble to Billy, from beginning to end, for he knew his father was in the wrong, and he bore no malice toward Harold for his part in it, and when the diamonds came up, and his father was clamoring for a writ, he was the first to declare Harold's innocence and to say he would go his bail. Now, there was in his mind another plan by which to benefit his friend, and rival, too—for Billy knew he was that ; and the heart of the little man ached with a bitter pain and sense of loss whenever he thought of Jerrie, and lived over again the scene under the butternut tree by the river, when her blue eyes had smiled so kindly upon him and her hands had touched his, even while she was breaking his heart. When Billy reached his majority his father had given him

$100,000, and thus he had business of his own to transact, and a part of this was just now centered in Washington Territory, where, in Tacoma, on Puget Sound, he owned real estate and had dealings with several parties. To attend to this an agent was needed for a while, and he said to himself :

"I'll offer it to Hal, with such a salary that he cannot refuse it ; that will get him out of the way until this thing blows over."

Billy knew perfectly well that although everybody said Harold was innocent and that nine-tenths believed it, there would still be a few in Shannondale—whose opinions his father's money controlled—who, without exactly saying they doubted him, would make it unpleasant for him in many ways; and from this he would save him by sending him to Tacoma at once, and thus getting him out of the way of any unpleasantness which might arise from his father's persecutions or those of his clan. It was this which he was proposing to Harold, who at once thought favorably of it—not because he wished to escape from the public, he said, but because of the pay offered, and which seemed to him far more than his services would be worth.

"You are a noble fellow, Billy," he said. "I'll think of the plan, and let you know after I've seen Jerrie and Judge St. Claire."

"A-all ri-right ; he'll a-advise you to go," Billy said, as they arose to leave the car, followed by Peterkin, who had been engaged in a fierce altercation with Tom, that young man having accused him of striking Jerrie, and threatening to have him arrested for assault and battery the moment they reached Shannondale.

"Thunder, and lightning, and guns !" old Peterkin exclaimed, while the spittle flew from his mouth like the spray from Niagara. "I assault and batter Jerrie Crawford !—a gal ! What do you take me for, young man ? I'm a gentleman, I be, if I ain't a Tracy ; and I never salted nor battered nobody, and she'll tell you so herself. Heavens and earth ! this is the way 'twas," and Peterkin shook from his head to his feet—for, like most men who clamor so loudly for the law, he had a mortal terror of it for himself, and Tom's threatening looks and words made him afraid. "This is how 'twas : I found her in the Tramp

House, and I was allfired mad at her about somethin'—I shan't tell what, for Bill would kill me; but I pitched in to her right and left; and, by gum, she pitched into me, so that for a spell it was nip-and-tuck betwixt us; and, by George, if she did'nt order me out of the Tramp House, and said it was her'n; and I'll be dumbed if I don't believe she'd of put me out, too, body and bones, if I hadn't gone. She was just like a tiger; and, I swan, I was feared on her, and backed out with a kind of flourish of my fist on that darned old rotten table, which went all to smash; and that's all I know. You don't call that 'sault and batter, do you?"

Tom could not say that he did, but he replied:

"That's your version of it. Jerrie may have another, and her friends ain't going to have her abused by a chap like you; and my advice is that you hold your tongue, both about her and Harold. It will be better for you. Do you understand?"

"You bet!" Peterkin said, with a meaning nod, breathing a little more freely as he caught sight of the highest tower of *Lubbertoo*, and more freely still when he arrived at the station, where he was met by his coat-of-arms carriage, instead of a writ, and was suffered to go peaceably home, a disappointed, if not a better man.

CHAPTER XLIII.

HAROLD AND JERRIE.

THE news which so electrified all Shannondale was slow in reaching Mrs. Crawford, but it did reach her at last, crushing and overwhelming her with a sense of shame and anguish, until as the day wore on, Grace Atherton, and Mrs. St. Claire, and Nina, and many others, came to reassure her, and to say that it was all a mistake, which would soon be cleared up.

Thus comforted and consoled, she tried to be calm, and wait patiently for the train. But there was a great pity for her boy in her heart, as she sat by Jerrie's bedside and watched her in all her varying moods, now perfectly quiet, while her wide-open eyes stared up at the ceiling as if she

were seeing something there, now talking of Peterkin, and
the Tramp House, and the table, and the blow, and again
of the bag, which she said was lost, and which her grandmother must find.

Thinking she meant the carpet-bag, Mrs. Crawford
brought that to her; but she tossed it aside impatiently,
saying:

"No, no; the other one, which tells it all. Where is it!
I must have lost it. Find it, find it. To be so near, and
yet, so far. What did it say? Why can't I think? Am I
like Mr. Arthur—crazy, like him?"

Mrs. Crawford thought her crazier than Arthur, and
waited still more impatiently for Harold, until she heard
his step outside, and knew that he had come.

"Harold!"

"Grandma!" was all they said for a moment, while the
poor old lady was sobbing on his neck, and then he comforted her as best he could, telling her that it was all over
now—that no one but Peterkin had accused him—that every
body was ready to defend him, and that after a little he
could explain everything.

"And now I must see Jerrie," he continued, starting
for the stairs, and glad that his grandmother did not attempt to follow him.

Jerrie had heard his voice, and had raised herself in bed,
and as he came in, met him with the question:

"Have you brought them? Has any one seen them?"

The strange light in her eyes should have told Harold
how utterly incapable she was of giving any rational answers
to his questions, but he did not think of that, and instead
of trying to quiet her, he plunged at once into the subject
she had broached:

"Do you mean the diamonds?" he asked.

"Yes," she replied, "the diamonds! the diamonds!
Where are they!"

"Mrs. Tracy has them by this time," Harold replied.

"Mrs. Tracy!" Jerrie exclaimed. "What has she to do
with them. They are not hers. They are mine—they are
mine! Bring them to me—bring them to me."

She was terribly excited, and for a time Harold bent all
his energies to soothe her, and at last when from sheer
exhaustion she became quiet he said to her,

" Jerrie, where did you find the diamonds ?"

She looked at him curiously, but made no reply, and he went on.

" You must tell me where you found them ; it is necessary I should know."

Still she did not reply, and he continued :

" Those diamonds have caused me a great deal of trouble, and will cause me more unless you tell me where you found them. Try and think. Was it in the Tramp House ?"

That started her at once, and she began to rave of the Tramp House, and the rat-hole, and the table, and Peterkin, who dealt the blow. The bruise on her head had not proved so serious as was at first feared, and with her tangled hair falling over her face Harold had not noticed it. But he looked at it now and questioned her about it, asking if Peterkin struck her there.

" No," she said, and began again to babble of rat-holes, and table-legs, and bags, and diamonds, until Harold was convinced that there was nothing to be learned from her in her present condition, and started for the Tramp House to see what that would tell him. The table was still upon the floor, with the three legs upon it, while the fourth one was missing. But Harold found it at last, for, remembering what Jerrie had said of the rat-hole, he investigated that spot and from its enlarged appearance drew his own conclusion. Jerrie had found the diamonds there ; he had no doubt of it, and he said so to Tom Tracy who appeared in the door-way just as he was leaving it. Sitting down upon the bench inside the two young men, who had been enemies all their lives, but who were now drawn together by a common sympathy and love for Jerrie talked the matter over again, each arriving at the same theory as the most probable one they could accept.

Arthur, in a crazy fit, had secreted the diamonds, and Jerrie knew it, though possibly not where he had put them. This accounted for her strange sickness when a child, while her finding them later on, added to other causes, would account for her sickness now. " Peterkin owns that he was blowing her up for something, and that he knocked the table down with his fist, but he swears he didn't touch her,"

Tom said, repeating in substance all Peterkin had said to him in the train when shaking with fear of a *writ*.

"And do you still mean to keep silent with regard to Jerrie?" he asked.

"Yes," Harold replied. "Her name must not be mentioned in connection with the diamonds. I can't have the slightest breath of suspicion touching Jerrie, *my sister*."

"Sister be hanged!" Tom began, savagely, then checked himself, and added, with a laugh: "Don't try to deceive me, Hal, with your sister business. You love Jerrie, and she loves you, and that is one reason why I hate you, or shall, when this miserable business is cleared up. Just now we must pull together and find out where she found the diamonds, and who put them there. To write to Uncle Arthur would do no good, though seeing him might; the last we heard he was thinking of taking the coast voyage from San Francisco to Tacoma."

"Tom," Harold exclaimed, with great energy, as he sprang to his feet, "that decides me;" and then he told of the offer Billy had made him on the car. "When I saw how sick Jerrie was, I made up my mind not to accept it, although I need the money badly. But now, if she gets no worse, I shall start for Tacoma in a few days and shall find your Uncle Arthur, if he is to be found."

It was growing dark when the two young men finally emerged from the house and stood for a moment outside, while Harold inquired for Maude.

"She is not very well, that's a fact," Tom said, gloomily; "and no wonder when mother keeps her cooped up in one room, without enough fresh air, and let's nobody see her except the family and the doctor, for fear they will excite her. She knows nothing about the diamonds, or that Jerrie is sick. I did tell her, though, that you had come home; and, by Jove! I pretty near forgot it. She wants to see you bad; but, Lord! mother won't let you in. No use to try. She's like a she wolf guarding its cub. Good-night."

And Tom walked away, while Harold went back to the cottage, where he found Jerrie sleeping very quietly, with a look on her face so like that it had worn in her babyhood, when he called her his little girl, that he involuntarily

16*

stooped down and kissed it as one would kiss a beautiful baby.

The next morning Jerrie was very restless and wild, and Harold began to doubt as to whether he ought to take the Western trip or not.

If he went he must go at once, and to leave Jerrie in her present state seemed impossible. He would consult the physician first, and Judge St. Claire next. The doctor gave it as his opinion that Jerrie was in no danger, if she were only kept quiet. She had taken a severe cold and overtaxed her strength, but he had no fear for the result, and he thought Harold might venture to leave her.

"Yes, I'd go if I were you," he added, for, like Billy, he too thought it might be pleasanter for Harold to be out of the way for a time, although he did not say so.

And this was the view the Judge took of it, after a few moments' conversation. His first question had been :

"Well, my boy, can you tell me now who gave them to you ?"

"No, I can't," was Harold's reply, and then, acting upon a sudden impulse, he burst out impetuously : "Yes, I will, for I can trust you, and I want your advice so badly."

So he repeated rapidly all he knew, and his theory with regard to Arthur, whom he wished to find, and of Billy's proposition that he should go on his business to Tacoma.

For a few moments the Judge seemed perplexed and undecided. If Harold stayed he might have some unpleasant things to bear and hear, for there were those who would talk, in spite of their protestations of his innocence ; while to go might look like running away from the storm, with the matter unexplained. On the whole, however, he thought it was better to go.

"Jerrie's interests are safe with me," he said, "and by the time you return everything will be explained ; but find Mr. Tracy as soon as possible. I am inclined to think your theory with regard to him correct."

So it was decided that Harold should go, and the next night was appointed for him to start. Had he known that Peterkin, and even Mrs. Tracy, were each in her and his own way insinuating that he was running from public opinion, nothing could have induced him to leave. But he did not know it, and went about his preparations with as brave a heart as he could command under the circumstances. Jerrie was more quiet now, though every effort on his part to learn anything from her concerning the diamonds brought on a fit of raving, when she would insist that the jewels were hers, and must be brought to her.

"But you told me they were Mrs. Tracy's," he said to her once.

And she replied :

"So they are, or were ; but oh, how little you know !"

And this was all he could get from her.

He told her he was going away, but that did not affect her, and she began to talk of Maude, who, she said, must not be harmed.

"Have you seen her ?" she asked him.

"Not yet," he replied, "but I am going to say good-by ;" and on the day of his departure he went to the Park House and asked if he could see Maude.

"Of course not," was Mrs. Tracy's prompt reply, when the request was taken to her. "No one sees her, and I certainly shall not allow him to enter her room."

"But, Dolly," Frank began, protestingly, but was cut short by the lady, who said :

"You needn't 'Dolly' me, or try to take his part, either. I have my opinion, and always shall. He cannot see Maude, and you may tell him so," turning now to the servant who had brought Harold's message, and who softened it as much as possible.

Harold had half expected a refusal, and was prepared for it. Taking a card from his pocket, he wrote upon it :

"DEAR MAUDE :—I am going away for a few weeks, and am very sorry that I cannot see you ; but your mother knows best, of course, and I must not do anything to make you worse. I shall think of you very often, and hope to find you much better when I return.   "HAROLD."

"Will you give this to her ?" he said to the girl, who answered that she would, and who took it to her young mistress late in the afternoon, while the family were at dinner, and she was left in charge of the invalid.

"Mr. Hastings sent you this," she said, handing the card to Maude, into whose face the bright color rushed, but left it instantly as she read the few hurried lines.

"Going away! Gone! and I didn't see him!" she exclaimed, regardless of consequences. "And mother did it. I know she did. I *will* talk," she continued, as the frightened girl tried to stop her, and then ran for Mrs. Tracy, who came in much alarm, asking what was the matter.

"You sent Harold away. You didn't let him see me, and he is—" Maude gasped, but could get no farther, for the paroxysm of coughing which came on, together with a hemorrhage which made her so weak that they thought her dying all night, she lay so white and still, and insensible, save at times when her lips moved, and her mother heard her whisper:

"Send for Harold."

CHAPTER XLIV.

JERRIE CLEARS HAROLD.

THE next day two items of news went like wildfire through the little town of Shannondale—the first, set afloat by Peterkin and helped on by Mrs. Tracy, that Harold had run away from public opinion, which was fast turning against him, since he could not explain where he found the diamonds; and the second, that both Maude Tracy and Jerrie Crawford were much worse, which made Harold's sudden departure all the more heinous in the eyes of his enemies; for what but conscious guilt could have prompted him to leave his sister, who, it was said, was calling for him with every breath, and charging him with having taken the diamonds? This was false; for although Jerrie's fever had increased rapidly during the night, and her babbling was something terrible to hear, there was in it no accusation of Harold, although she was constantly talking to him, and asking for the diamonds and the bag.

"It is a pity he ever told her about them," the doctor said, as twice each day, for four successive days, he came and looked upon her fever-stained cheeks, and counted her rapid pulse, and took her temperature, and listened to her strange talk; and then, with a shake of his head, drove over to Tracy Park and stood by poor little Maude's couch, and looked into her death-white face, and counted her faint heart beats, and tried in vain to find some word of encouragement for the stricken man, who looked about as much like death as the young girl so dear to him. And every morning, on his way from the cottage to Tracy Park, the doctor saw under the pines two young men, Tom and Dick, seated upon the iron bench each whittling a bit of pine, which one was unconsciously fashioning into a cross and the other into a grave-stone.

Tom had found Dick there working at his cross, and, after a simple good-morning, had sat down beside him and whittled in silence upon another bit of wood until the doctor appeared on his way to Tracy Park. Then the whittling ceased, and both young men arose, and, going forward, asked how Jerrie was.

"Pretty bad. Hal oughtn't to have gone, though I told him there was no danger. We must telegraph if she gets worse," was the reply, as the doctor rode on.

Then Tom and Dick separated and saw no more of each other until the next morning, when they went again, and whittled in silence under the pines until the doctor came in sight, when the same question was asked and answered as on the previous day.

Billy never joined them, but sat for hours and hours under the butternut tree where Jerrie had refused him, watching the sluggish river, and wondering what the world would be to him if Jerrie were not in it. Had Billy been with Tom and Dick, he could not have whittled as they did, for all the nerve power had left his hands, which lay helplessly in his lap, and when he walked he looked more like a withered old man than a young one of twenty-seven.

Maude was the first to rally—her first question for Harold, her second for Jerrie—and her father, who was with her, answered truthfully that Harold had not returned, and that Jerrie was sick and could not come to her. He did not say how sick, and Maude felt no alarm, and waited patiently as the days went by and Jerrie did not appear, but grew worse so fast that the whole town was moved with sympathy for and interest in her.   Jerrie was a general favorite and flowers and fruit and delicacies of every kind were sent to the cottage.   Carriage after carriage stopped before the door, offer after offer of assistance was made to Mrs. Crawford, while Nina and Marian Raymond were there constantly ; and Billy went to Springfield for a chair in which to wheel his sister to the cottage, for she could not yet mount into the dog-cart; and Tom and Dick whittled on until the cross and the grave-stone were finished, and, with a sickly smile, Tom said to Dick :

"Would you cut Jerrie's name upon it ?"

"No ; oh, no !" Dick answered with a gasp.   "She may be better to-morrow."   And when the crisis was past, and Jerrie's strong constitution triumphed over the disease which had grappled with it, the village wore a holiday air, as the people said to each other, gladly :   "Jerrie is better ; Jerrie will live !"

Her recovery was rapid, and within a week after she awoke to perfect consciousness, she was able to sit up a part of every day, and had walked across the floor and read a letter from Harold, full of solicitude for herself and enthusiasm for his trip over the wild mountains and across the vast plains to the lovely little city of Tacoma, built upon a cliff and looking seaward over the sound.

"Dear Harold," Jerrie whispered.   "I shall be so glad when he comes home.   Nothing can be done till then ; I am so bewildered when I try to think."

In her weak state, everything seemed unreal to Jerrie, except the fact that she had found her mother, and many times each day she thanked her God who had brought her this unspeakable joy, and asked that she might do right when the time came to act.   She knew the bag was safe, for she found it just where she had put it.   But where were the diamonds ?   Had Harold taken them with him ?   Had he told any one ?   Did his grandmother know anything about them, she wondered, and she tried in many ways to draw Mrs. Crawford out, but was unsuccessful, for there was now too much pain and bitterness connected with the diamonds for Mrs. Crawford to speak to her of them.   But the poisonous breath of gossip had been at work ever since

Harold went away, quietly aided and abetted by Mrs. Tracy, and openly pushed on by Peterkin, until Tom Tracy went to him one day and threatened to have him tarred and feathered and ridden on a rail, if he ever breathed Harold's name again in connection with the diamonds.

"Wall, I swow!" was all Peterkin said, as he put an enormous quid of tobacco in his mouth, and walked away, thinking to himself, "T'would take an all-fired while to scrape them tar and feathers off of me, I'm so big, and I b'lieve the feller meant it. Them high bucks, wouldn't like no better fun than to make a spectacle of me; so I guess I'll dry up a spell."

But the trouble did not stop with Peterkin's talk, for a neighboring Sunday paper, which fed its readers with all the choicest bits of gossip, came out with an article headed "The Tracy Diamonds," and after narrating the story in a most garbled and sensational manner, went on to comment upon the young man's having run away, rather than face public opinion, and to comment also upon the law which could not touch him because the offense was committed so long ago.

One after another, and without either knowing that the other had done so, Tom, and Dick, and Billy, waited upon the editor of the Sunday *News*, threatening to sue him for libel if he did not retract every word of the offensive article in his next issue, which he did. But the mischief was done, and the paper found its way at last to Jerrie, sent unwittingly by Ann Eliza, who covered it over a basket of fruit and flowers which was carried one afternoon to the cottage.

Jerrie had been down stairs several times and had walked a little way in the lane but was in her room when the basket was brought to her. Raising the paper, she was about to throw it on the floor, when her eye caught the words, "The Tracy Diamonds," and with bloodless lips and wildly beating heart she read the article through, understanding the situation perfectly, and resolving at once how to act. It seemed to her that she was lifted above and out of herself, she felt so strong, and light, and well, as she put on her bonnet and shawl, and taking the leather bag in her hand, hurried down stairs in quest of Mrs. Crawford.

"Grandma!" she exclaimed, "why haven't you told me

about Harold, and the suspicion resting on him, and why did you let him go until I was better, and what are the people saying? Tell me every thing."

Jerrie would not be put off, and Mrs. Crawford told her every thing she knew, and that she herself had added to the mystery by the strange things she had said in her delirium about the diamonds, which she insisted were hers.

"And they are mine!" Jerrie said, while Mrs. Crawford looked at her in alarm, lest her madness had returned.

"Where are you going?" she gasped, as Jerrie turned toward the door.

"To Tracy Park, to claim my own and clear Harold!" was the reply. "When I come back I will tell you all, but now I can't wait."

"But, Jerrie, you are not strong enough to walk there, and besides, they have company this afternoon, some kind of a new-fangled card party, and you must not go," Mrs. Crawford said.

"I have the strength of twenty horses," Jerrie replied, "and if they have company, so much the better, for there will be more to hear my story. Good-by."

She was off like an arrow, and went almost upon a run through the woods until the house was reached, and then she stopped a moment to take breath and look about her. How fair and beautiful was every thing, and Jerrie's heart beat so hard that she felt for a moment as if she were choking to death as she sat under a maple tree and tried to think it all over, to make sure there was no mistake. Opening the box she took out two papers and read them again as she had the night she was taken sick. One was a certificate of marriage, the other of a birth and baptism; there was no mistake.

Holding the papers in one hand and the bag in the other, she went on to the house, from which shouts of laughter were issuing, Nina's voice, and Marian's, and Tom's, and Dick's, and Mrs. Tracy's. She could hear that distinctly, and she shuddered a little at the sound, for it brought back to her mind all the slights she had received from that woman who was so cruel to Harold, and the pity which had been springing up in her heart ever since she looked at the windows of Maude's room and thought of the white-faced girl lying there, died out, and it was more a

Nemesis than a gentle, forgiving woman who walked boldly into the hall and stood in the drawing-room door.

Mrs. Tracy was having a progressive euchre party that afternoon. A friend in Boston had written her about it, and, proud to be the first to introduce it in Shannondale, she stood, flushed and triumphant, with the restored diamonds in her ears and at her throat, laughing merrily at Judge St. Claire, who had won the booby prize—a little drum, as something he could *beat*—and who looked as if he did not quite see the joke.

Apart from the rest, Frank Tracy sat looking on, though with no apparent interest in the matter. He had joined in the game because his wife told him he must, and had borne meekly her sarcastic remarks when he trumped her ace and ordered up on nothing. His thoughts were not with the cards, but up stairs with Maude, who seemed to be better, and for whom there was constantly a prayer in his heart.

"Spare her, and I will make reparation; I will tell the truth."

He was trying to bribe the Lord to hear him, when he saw Jerrie in the door—tall, thin, and white from her recent sickness, with eyes which rolled and shone, and flashed as Arthur's did sometimes, and which fell at last upon Mrs. Tracy, where they rested with an intensity which must have drawn that lady's notice to her, if Frank had not exclaimed, as he rose to his feet:

"Jerrie! How did you get here?"

Then all turned and looked at her, and crowded around her with exclamations of surprise and wonder.

For a moment Jerrie stood like one in a catalepsy, with no power to move or speak, but when Mrs. Tracy came forward, and in her iciest tones said to her: "Good-afternoon, Miss Crawford. To what am I indebted for this unexpected pleasure?" her faculties came back, her tongue was loosened, and she replied in a clear voice, which rang through the room like a bell, and was, indeed, the knell to all the lady's greatness:

"I am here to claim my own, and to clear Harold from the foul suspicion heaped upon him. I have seen the paper, have heard the whole from grandma, and am here to defend him. It was I who gave him the diamonds! It was for me he kept silent, and let you think what you would."

"You gave him the diamonds?" Mrs. Tracy repeated, "you gave him the diamonds! and have come to confess yourself a—"

She never finished the sentence, for something in Jerrie's face frightened her, while her husband, who had come forward, laid his hand warningly upon her arm.

So absorbed were they all that no one saw the little girl, who at the sound of Jerrie's voice had, in her eagerness to see her, crept down the stairs, and now stood in the doorway opposite to Jerrie, her large, bright eyes looking in wonder upon the scene, and her ears listening intently to what was as new to her as it had been to Jerrie an hour ago.

"Don't give me the name you have more than once given to Harold," Jerrie said, as with a gesture she silenced Mrs. Tracy. "The diamonds are mine, not yours. Can one steal his own?"

"Yours! Your diamonds! What do you mean?" Mrs. Tracy asked.

"They were my mother's," Jerrie replied, "and she sent them to me."

They all thought her crazy except Frank, to whom there had come a horrid presentiment of the truth, and who clutched his wife's arm hard, as she said in a mocking, aggravating tone :

"And your mother was—?"

Then Jerrie stepped into the room, and stood in their midst like a queen among her subjects, as she answered :

"My mother was Marguerite Heinrich, of Wiesbaden, better known to you as Gretchen ; and my father is Arthur Tracy, and I am their lawful child. It is so written here," and she held up the papers and the bag; "I am Jerrie Tracy !"

CHAPTER XLV.

WHAT FOLLOWED.

"THANK God that it is out! I couldn't have borne it much longer," came involuntarily from Frank's lips.

But no one heard it; for with one bound, as it seemed to the petrified spectators, who divided right and left to let her pass, Jerrie reached the opposite door-way, and stooping over the little figure lying there so still, lifted it tenderly, and carrying it up stairs, laid it down in the room it would never leave again until other hands than hers carried it out and laid it away in the Tracy lot, where only Jack and the dark woman were lying now.

Maude had heard all Jerrie was saying, and understood it, too; and at the words, "I am Jerry Tracy," she felt an electric thrill pass over her, like what she had experienced when watching the acting in some great tragedy; then all was darkness, and she knew no more until Jerrie was bending over her and she heard her mother saying:

"Leave her to me, Miss Crawford. You have done harm enough for one day. You have killed my daughter!"

"No," Maude cried, exerting all her strength "She has not hurt me. She must not go. I want her; for if what she said is true, she is my own cousin. Oh, Jerrie, I am so glad!" and throwing her arms around Jerrie's neck, Maude sobbed convulsively, and clung tightly to Jerrie, who, nearly distraught herself, did not know what to do. She knew that Mrs. Tracy looked upon her as an intruder, and possibly a a liar; but she cared little for that lady's opinion. She only thought of Frank and what he would say.

Lifting up her head at last from the pillow where she had lain it for a moment, she saw him standing at the foot of the bed, taller, straighter than she had seen him in years, with a look on his face which she knew was not adverse to herself.

"Jerrie," he said, slowly and thickly, for something choked his speech, "I can't tell you now all I feel, only I am glad for you and Arthur, but gladder for myself."

What did he mean? Jerrie wondered; while Maude's eyes sought his questioningly, and his wife said, sharply:

"You are talking like a lunatic! Do you propose to give up so easily to a girl's bare word? Let Jerrie prove it before she is mistress here."

Then Maude whispered: "There were papers in your hand, Jerrie, and you said, 'It is so written here.' Bring the papers and read them to us. I can bear it. I must hear them. I must know."

"Better let her have her way," Frank said; and Dolly could have knocked him down, he spoke so cheerfully; while Jerrie answered:

"I can't read them myself aloud. I couldn't bear it."

"But Marian can. She understands German. Let them all come up; they will have to know," Maude persisted.

After a moment, during which a powerful tonic had been given to his daughter, Frank went down to his guests, who were eagerly discussing the strange story, which not one of them doubted in the least.

In her haste to reach Maude, Jerrie had dropped the bag and the two papers, which Judge St. Claire picked up and held for a moment in his hand; then passing the papers to Marian, he said:

"It can be no secret now, and Jerrie will not care. What do the papers contain?"

Running her eyes rapidly over them, Marian said:

"The first is a certificate of marriage between Arthur Tracy and Marguerite Heinrich, who were married October 20th, 18—, in the English church at Wiesbaden, by the Rev. Mr. Eaton, then the officiating clergyman. The second is a certificate of the birth and baptism of Jerrine, daughter of Arthur and Marguerite Tracy, who was born at Wiesbaden, January 1st, 18—, and christened January 8th, 18—, by the Rev. Mr. Eaton."

Then a deep silence fell upon the group, while Tom stood like one paralyzed. He understood the situation perfectly, and knew that Jerrie was mistress of Tracy Park.

"May as well vacate at once," he said at last, with an attempt to smile, as he walked slowly out of the house.

Just then Frank came down, saying that Maude insisted upon knowing what was in the papers which Marian was to

read, while the others were to come up and listen. He did
not seem at all like a man who had lost anything, but
bustled about cheerily ; and when the judge said to him
apologetically, "We know the contents of two of the
papers. They are certificates of the marriage of Arthur
with Gretchen, and of Jerrie's birth. I hope you don't
mind if we read them," he answered, briskly.

"Not at all—not in the least. Arthur and Gretchen !
I thought so. Where is Tom ? He must hear the papers."

He found his son sitting under the tree where he had
been sitting the morning when Jerrie came near fainting
there, and in his hand was a bit of wood finished like a
grave-stone—the same he had whittled under the pines,
and on which he was now carving, "Euchred, August —,
18—."

"This is the monument to our downfall," he said, as
his father came up to him with something so pitiful in his
face and voice that Frank gave way suddenly, and, sitting
down beside him, laid his hand upon his tall son's head
and cried for a moment like a child, while Tom's chin
quivered, and he was mortally afraid there was something
like tears in his own eyes, and he meant to be so brave and
not show that he was hurt.

" I am sorry for you, my boy," Frank said at last, "but
glad for Jerrie—so glad—and she will not be hard upon
us."

" I shall ask no favors of her. I can stand it if you
can, though money is a good thing to have."

And then, without in the least knowing why, he thought
of Ann Eliza, and wondered how her ankle was getting
along, and if he ought not to have called upon her again.

" Marian is going to read the papers in Maude's room,
and I have come for you," Frank said.

" I don't care to hear them," Tom replied. " I am
satisfied that we are beggers, and Jerrie the heiress."

But Frank insisted, and Tom went with him to his
sister's room, followed by their friends, for whom the
dinner was waiting and spoiling in the kitchen, where as
yet no hint of what was transpiring had reached, save the
fact that Maude had been down stairs and fainted. She
was propped upon pillows, and her eyes were fixed upon

Jerrie, who sat by her side, holding her hands, which she occasionally kissed, and caressed.

" Where did you find the bag ?" the Judge asked ; and then Jerrie narrated the particulars of her interview with Peterkin, whose destruction of the table had resulted in her finding the bag with the diamonds in it.

" They were mother's," she said, the last word almost a sob, as she turned her eyes upon Mrs. Tracy, who stood like a block of stone, with no sympathy or credulity upon her face. " Father bought them for her at the same time with Mrs. Tracy's, which they are exactly like. It is so written in her letter. And she sent them for me. They are mine, and I gave them to Harold to keep until I could think what to do. The diamonds are mine."

She was still looking at Mrs. Tracy, on whom all eyes were resting as the precious stones flashed and glittered, and shone in the sunlight.

For an instant the proud woman hesitated, then quickly unclasping the ear-rings and the pin, she laid them in Jerrie's lap.

" You are welcome to your property if it is yours, I am sure," she said, and was about to leave the room.

But her husband kept her back.

" No, Dolly," he said. " You must stay, and hear, and know. It concerns us all."

As he had closed the door and stood against it, she had no alternative except to stay, but she walked to the window and stood with her back to them all, while Marian put into English and read, that message from the dead.

CHAPTER XLVI.

THE LETTERS.

THERE were four of them—two in Arthur's handwriting ; one directed to Mrs. Arthur Tracy, Wiesbaden, postmarked Liverpool ; one to Marguerite Heinrich, Wiesbaden, postmarked Shannondale ; one in a strange handwriting to Arthur Tracy, if living, and one to Arthur

Tracy's friends, if he were dead, or incapable of understanding it.

And it was this last which Marian read ; for as Arthur was living, she felt that with his letters strangers had nothing to do. The letter to the friends, which had evidently been written at intervals, as the writer's strength would permit, was as follows :

WIESBADEN, December —, 18—.

"To the friends of Mr. Arthur Tracy, if he is dead, or incapable of understanding this letter, from his wife, who was Marguerite Heinrich, and whom he always called Gretchen.

"I want to tell you about it, for the sake of my little Jerrie, whom, if her father is dead, I give to your care, praying God to deal with you as you are good and just to her. And I want you to forgive my husband, and not be angry with him for marrying me, a poor, obscure girl, with neither money nor name. I was seventeen when I first saw Mr. Tracy. My father was dead. I was an only child, and my mother kept a little fancy shop in Wiesbaden. I went to school and learned what other girls like me learned —to read and write, and knit and sew, and fear God and keep His commandments. People called me pretty. I don't know that I was, but he told me so when he came to me one day as I was knitting under a tree in the park. He had a picture made of me as I was then, and it is on the wall, but I have pawned it for the rent, as I have almost everything."

"Oh, Jerrie !" Marian exclaimed at this point.

But Jerrie's face was buried in Maude's pillow, and she made no response. So Marian read on :

"He came many times, for I was always there waiting for him, I am afraid ; but when he said he loved me and wanted me for his wife, I could not believe it, he was so grand, so like nobility, and I so poor and plain. Then mother died suddenly—well to-day, dead to-morrow—with cholera, and I was left alone.

"'Gretchen, we must be married now,' he said to me, the night after the funeral ; and I answered him, 'Yes, we must be married ;' and we were, the next day, in the little English church, by Mr. Eaton, the pastor. You will find the certificate with the other papers. Do you ever remember a beautiful moonlight night, when the air was soft, and warm, and sweet with many summer flowers, and there was music in the distance, and heaven seemed so near that you could almost touch the blue lining which separates it from us? Well, just like that was my life with Arthur for a few months. Oh, how I loved him, and how he loved me! It frightened me sometimes, he was so fierce and—I don't know what the word is—so something in his love. He never left me a moment. He couldn't, he said, for I was his balance-wheel, and without me he was lost. I think now he was crazy then. I know he was afterward, when he did such queer things, and forgot so often—sometimes the house we lived in, sometimes his own name, and at last, me, his Gretchen! That was so sad, when he went away, and staid away for weeks, and said he had forgotten. But he was sorry, too, and made it up, and for ten days heaven came down again so I could touch it; then he went away, and I have never seen him since.

"You must excuse me, his friends—if I stopped a little while to cry; it makes me so lonesome to think of the long years—four and more—which have been buried with the yesterday's, under the flowers, and under the snow, since Arthur went away and left me all alone. If I had told him, he might have come back, he was so fond of children; but I was not sure, and would not tell a lie, and let him go without a hint. I wrote him once I had something to tell him when he came which would make him glad, as it did me, and he never replied to it, though he wrote two or three times more, and sent me money, but did not tell where he was, only he was being cured, he said—that was all. In January my baby was born, and I had her christened Jerrine, by Mr. Eaton. You will find it with the papers. Then, how I longed for him, and waited, and watched; but he never came, and I knew he had forgotten; but I did not doubt his love for a moment, or that he would one day come back; and I tried to improve myself, and learn what was in books, so I could mate with him better when he came home, which he never did; and the years went on, and my little Jerrie grew more lovely every day. She is standing by me now, and says, 'Are you writing to him?'

"Darling Jerrie, you will be kind to her, won't you,

for his sake, and for me, too, who will be dead when you read this?"

Jerrie was sobbing now, and Maude's arm was around her neck, while Frank had walked to a window, and, like his wife, was looking out upon the lawn, which he did not see for the tears which filled his eyes.

"When the money stopped," the letter went on, "we grew so poor, Jerrie and I and Nannine—that is the French woman who lives with me and whom Jerrie calls Mah-nee. She will bring my child to you when I am dead; and oh, be kind to her, for a truer, more faithful woman never lived. She is such a comfort to me, except when she scolds about Arthur and calls him a *bete noir*, which he is not, as you will see. He was shut up, I don't know where, but think it was where they put people with bad heads, and he forgot everything till he was out, and as far as Paris on his way to America. Then he remembered, and wrote me from Liverpool such a letter—full of love and sorrow for the past, and sent me such lovely diamonds, just like those he had bought for his sister in America, he said—and he was going home at such a date on the Scotia, and he wished me to join him in Liverpool. I send the letter with this to prove that I write true. But it was too late, for I was too weak to travel; neither could I write to him in America for he gave me no address.

"That was last September, and I have been dying ever since, for my heart broke when I thought of what was and what might have been, could I have found him. The money he sent me then I am saving for Nannine and Jerrie to take them to America when I am dead. All the days and nights I prayed that Arthur might remember and write me again, and God heard, and he did; and five days ago I received his letter. So crazy it was, but just as full of love and tenderness and a desire to see me. He told me of his lovely home and the Gretchen room, where my picture is in the window; and in case there should be no one to meet me at the station when I arrived he sent me directions how to find Tracy Park, and told me just what to do when I reached New York. He would come for me himself, he said, only the sea made him so sick, and he was afraid he should forget everything if he did. But you will see in his letter what he wrote and how fond he was of me; and if he is

17

alive and too crazy to understand now, tell him, when he is better, how I loved him, and prayed for him every hour that God would bring him, at last, where I am going so soon. Nannine will take him my Bible, with passages marked by me, and a photograph, which I had taken a year ago, and which will tell you how I looked then. Now I am so thin and pale that Arthur would hardly know me. I send, too, a lock of Jerrie's hair, cut when she was three weeks old. She is such a comfort to me, and so old and womanly for her years! She will remember much of our life here for she notices everything and understands it, too, and goes over, as in a play, what she sees and hears.

"We have been cold and hungry sometimes, but not often, the neighbors are so kind; and when I am dead they will see that Nannine is made ready for America, with Jerrie, and the papers, and the diamonds, which I might have pawned when our need was greatest, but I could not. I must save them for Jerrie, and may she wear them many days in years to come, when her mother is dust and ashes in the ground, but a glorified spirit in Paradise, where I shall watch over her, and, if I can, be with her often, and keep myself in her mind, so that she will never forget my face, or the old home in Germany.

"God bless my little daughter, and make her a true, noble woman; and God bless you, Arthur's friends, who read this, and incline you to be kind and just to Jerrie, and see that she has her own; for there must be money at Tracy Park; and if you are poor and Jerrie comes rich, tell her from her mother to be kind to you, and give as you have given to her. Now I must stop, I am so tired and it is growing so dark that Nannine has opened the stove door to let the light fall on the paper in my lap, and Jerrie is standing by me and says, 'Are you going to God pretty soon?'

"Yes, darling, very soon—to-night, perhaps, or to-morrow, or when He will. The air grows cold, the night is coming on, my eyes are dim, my head is tired. I think, yes, I think it will be to-morrow. Good-by.

"GRETCHEN TRACY."

As she finished reading, Marian arose, and going up to Jerrie kissed her lovingly and said to her in German:

"That was your mother's picture in our old home in Wiesbaden. I am so glad for you."

A low sob was Jerrie's reply, and then Judge St. Claire asked :

"Is that all ?"

"Yes," Marian said. "All except Mr. Tracy's letters to Gretchen. Oh, no," she added ; "there is something more ;" and feeling in the bag, she drew out two small papers, one crumpled and worn, as if it had often been referred to, the other folded neatly and tied with a white ribbon.

This Marian opened first, and found it to be a certificate, written in English, to the effect that Mrs. Arthur Tracy, *nee* Marguerite Heinrich, died at such a date and was buried by the Rev. Dr. Bellows, the resident rector of the English church ; the other was in Arthur's handwriting, and the directions he had written to his wife, as to what she was to do and how to find Tracy Park.

"Yes," Judge St. Claire said, coming forward and taking the paper from her hand, "this is what the station-master saw the poor woman examining that night in the storm. She probably dropped it into the bag without stopping to fold it. There can be no doubt."

Then a deep silence reigned for a moment in the room, until Mrs. Tracy, who, all through the reading had stood like a block of granite by the window, turned and walking up to Jerrie, said, in a bitter tone :

"Of course there is no mistake. I do not doubt that you are mistress here, and am ready to leave at once. Shall we pack up and quit to-night ?"

"Dolly ! Mother !" came angrily and sternly from both Tom and Frank, and "Oh, mamma, please," came faintly from Maude, while Jerrie lifted up her head, and looking steadily at the cruel woman, said :

"Why are you so hard with me ? I cannot help it. I am not to blame. I mean to do right ; only wait—a little. I am so sick now—so dizzy and blind. Will somebody lead me out where I can breathe. I am choking here."

It was Tom who took her into the open air and to a seat under the tree where once before she had almost fainted, as she did now, with her head upon his shoulder, for he put it there, and then pushed her hair back from her face, as he said, lightly :

" Don't take it so hard ; if we can stand it, you can !"
Then Jerrie straightened up and said :

" Tom, do you want to kill me now ?"

" What do you mean ?" he asked, and she replied :

"Don't you know you said under the pines that you
would kill any claimant to Tracy Park who might appear
against you !"

" I remember it," Tom said, "but I didn't think then
that the claimant would be you," and he put his arm around
her as he continued : "I can't say that I am not awfully
cut up to be turned neck and heels out of what I believed
would be my own, but if I must be, I am glad it is you who
do it, for I know you'll not be hard upon us, or let Uncle
Arthur be, even if mother is so mean. Remember, Jerrie,
that I loved you and asked you to be my wife when I believed you poor and unknown."

Tom was very politic, but all the good there was in him
seemed now to be on the surface, and while inwardly rebelling at his misfortune, he felt a thrill of joy in knowing
that Jerrie was his cousin, and would not be hard upon him.

" Shall we go back to the house ?" he said at last, and
they went back, meeting the people upon the piazza, where
they stopped for a moment while Jerrie's hands were shaken,
and she was congratulated that at last the mystery was
cleared, and her rights restored to her.

"Mr. Arthur Tracy ought to be here," Judge St. Claire
said.

" Yes, I'd thought of that," Tom replied, "and shall
telegraph him to-morrow."

Then they said good-night, and without going in to see
either Mr. or Mrs. Tracy again, Tom and Jerrie walked
toward the cottage, through the woods where the trees met
in graceful arches over head, and the moonlight fell in
silver flecks upon the grass, and the summer air was odor-
ous and sweet with the smell of the pines and the balm of
Gilead trees scattered here and there. It was a lovely
place, and Tom thought so with a keen sense of pain, as,
after leaving Jerrie at her gate, he walked slowly back,
until he reached the four pines, where he sat down to think
and wonder what he should do as a poor man, with neither
business or prospects.

" I don't suppose father has laid up much," he said,

"for since Uncle Arthur came home he has done very little business, and has spent what really was his own recklessly and without a thought of saving, he was so sure to have enough at last, and Uncle Arthur was so free to give us what we asked for. But that will end when he knows he has a daughter, and as he never fancied me much, I shall either have to beg, or work, or starve, or marry a rich wife, which is not so easy for a poor dog to do. I don't suppose that governor's daughter would look at me now, nor any one else who is anybody. By George, I ought to have called on Ann Eliza again. I wonder if it's too late. I believe I'll walk around there any way, and if I see a light, I'll go in, and if old *paterfamilias*—how I'd like to kick him—is there, I'll tell him the news, and that I know now he did not strike Jerrie with the table-leg, and perhaps I'll apologize for what I said in the car. Tom Tracy, you are a scoundrel, and no mistake," he added, with energy, as he arose and struck into the field, through which he had dragged Ann Eliza the night of the storm.

There were lights at Le Bateau, and Tom was soon shaking hands with old *paterfamilias*, and with Ann Eliza, who was now able to come down stairs.

CHAPTER XLVII.

ARTHUR.

HE had enjoyed himself immensely, from the moment he first caught sight of grand old Pike's Peak on the distant plains until he entered the city of the Golden Gate, and, standing on the terrace of the Cliff House, looked out upon the blue Pacific, with the sea lions disporting on the rocks below. For he went there first, and then to Chinatown, and explored every nook and corner, and opium den in it, and drank tea at twenty dollars a pound in a high-toned restaurant, and visited the theater and the Joss-house, and patronized the push-cars, as he called them, every day, and experienced a wonderful exhilaration of spirits, as he sat upon the front seat, with the fresh air blowing upon his face, and only the broad, steep street, lined with palaces, before him.

"This is heaven! this clears the cobwebs!" he said to Charles, who sat beside him with chattering teeth and his coat-collar pulled high about his ears, for the winds of San Francisco are cold even in the summer.

Arthur's first trip was to the Yosemite, taking the Milton route, and meeting with the adventure he so much desired; for in the early morning, between Chinese Camp and Priest's, the stage was suddenly stopped by two masked marauders, one of whom stood at the horses' heads, while the other confronted the terrified passengers with the blood-curdling words:

"Hands up, every soul of you!"

And the hands went up from timid women and strong men, until click-click came in rapid succession from the driver's box, where Arthur sat, and shot after shot followed each other, one bullet grazing the ear of the highwayman at the horses' heads, and another cutting through the slouched hat of his comrade near the stage.

"Leave, or I'll shoot you dead! I've five more shots in this one, and two more revolvers in my pockets, and I'm not afraid!" Arthur yelled, jumping about like a maniac, and so startling the robbers that they fled precipitately, followed for a little distance by Arthur, who had leaped from the stage and who started in pursuit, with a revolver in each hand, and ball after ball flying ahead of him as he ran.

When at last he came back, the passengers flocked around him, grasping his hands and blessing him as the preserver of their money, if not of their lives. After that Arthur was a lion whom all the people in the valley wished to see and talk with, and with whom the landlord bore as he had never borne with a guest before, for Arthur found fault with the rooms, which he likened to bath-tubs, and fault with the smells which came from the river, and fault with the smoke in the parlor, but made ample amends by the money he spent so lavishly, the scores of photographs he bought, and the puffs he wrote for the San Francisco papers, extolling the valley as the very gate of heaven, and the hotel as second only to the Palace, and signing himself "Bumble Bees."

He went on every trail, and climbed the highest possible peak, and when he stood on the top of old Capitan and looked down upon the world below, he capered and shouted like a madman, singing at the top of his voice, "Mine eyes have seen the coming of the glory of the Lord, glory, glory, hallelujah!" until the rocky gorges rang with the wild echoes which went floating down the valley below, where the sun was shining so brightly and the grass was growing so green.

On his return to San Francisco after an absence of several weeks, he took up his abode at the Palace Hotel, which he turned topsy-turvy with his vagaries; but the landlord could afford to bear much from one who spent his money so freely; and so he was allowed to change rooms every day if he liked, and half the plumbers in the city were called in to see what caused the smells which he declared worse than any thing he had ever met in his life, and which were caused in part by the disinfectants which he bought by the wholesale and kept in his bathroom, his wash-room, and under his bed, until the chambermaid tied up her nose in camphor when she went in to do her work.

But his career was brought to a close suddenly one morning, when, just as he was taking his coffee and rolls in his room, Charles brought him the following telegram:

"Come immediately. There's the devil to pay.
"TOM TRACY."

Arthur read the message two or three times, not at all disturbed by it, but vastly amused at its wording; then, putting it down, he went on with his breakfast until it was finished, when he took a card from his pocket and wrote upon it:

"Pay him then, for I sha'nt come.
"ARTHUR TRACY."

This was handed to Charles with instructions to forward it to Tracy Park. This done, he gave no further thought to the message so full of such import to himself, but began to talk of and plan his contemplated trip to Tacoma by the next steamer which sailed. It was six o'clock when he had his dinner in his own private parlor, where he was served by both Charles and a waiter, and where a second telegram was brought him.

"Confound it," he said, "have they nothing to do at home but to torment me with telegrams? Didn't I tell them to pay the old Harry and done with it? What do they mean?" and putting the envelope down by his plate he went quietly on with his dinner until he was through, when he took it up, and, breaking the seal, read:

"Come at once. I need you.

"JERRIE."

That changed everything, and with a bound he was in the next room, gesticulating fiercely, and ordering Charles to step lively and get everything in readiness to start home on the first eastward bound train which left San Francisco.

"'That rascally Tom is a liar," he said. "It's not the devil to pay. It's Jerrie. Do you hear, it's Jerrie. Bring me some paper, quick, and don't stand staring at me as if I were a lunatic. It's Jerrie, who needs me."

Charles brought the paper, on which his master wrote:

"Coming on the wings of the wind.
"Yours respectfully,
"ARTHUR TRACY."

In less than half an hour this singular message was flying along the wires across the continent, and within a few hours Arthur was following it as fast as the steam horse could take him.

CHAPTER XLVIII.

WHAT THEY WERE DOING AND HAD DONE IN SHANNON-DALE.

IF the earth had opened suddenly and swallowed up half the inhabitants of Shannondale the other half could not have been more astonished than they were at the news which Peterkin was the first to tell them, and which he had risen very early to do, before some one else should be before him. Irascible and quick tempered as he was, he was easily appeased and the fact that Jerrie was Arthur Tracy's daughter changed his opinion of her at once.

"The biggest heiress in the county except my Ann 'Liza, and, by gum, I'm glad on't for her and Arthur. I allus said she was hisen, and by George, to think I helped her into her fortin, for if I hadn't of knocked that rotten old table down she'd of never found them memoirs," he said to the first person to whom he communicated the news, and then hurried off to enlighten others, until every body knew and was discussing the strange story.

Before noon scores of people had found it in their way to walk past the cottage hoping to catch sight of Jerrie, while a few went in to tell her how glad they were for her and Mr. Arthur. But Jerrie was in her room too sick and tired to see them, and they could only question Mrs. Crawford who was herself half crazed.

When Mrs. Crawford heard the story Jerrie told her after her return from the Park House, she had been for a few moments stupefied with amazement, and had sat motionless until she heard Jerrie say to her:

"Dear grandma, I told you your working days were over, and they are, for what is mine is yours and Harold's, and my home is your home always, so long as you live."

Then the poor old lady put her head upon Jerrie's arm and cried hysterically for a moment, then she rallied, and kissed the young girl who had been so much to her, and whom for a brief, moment she feared she might have lost. For a long time they talked of the past and the future, and

17*

of Harold, who was in Tacoma, where he might have to remain for three or four weeks longer. He had written several times to his grandmother and once to Jerrie, but had made no mention of the diamonds, while in her letters to him Mrs. Crawford had refrained from telling him what some of the people were saying, and the construction they were putting upon his absence. Jerrie had not yet written to him, but, "I shall to-morrow," she said, "and tell him to come home, for I need him now, if ever."

Jerrie was very tired when she went at last to bed, but the dreamless sleep which came upon her, and which lasted until a late hour in the morning, did her good, and probably saved her from a relapse, which might have proved fatal. Still she was very weak and too sick to go down stairs, for the excitement of the previous night was telling upon her, and when Tom came asking to see her, she received him in her room. He had been up since sunrise, strolling through the park, with a troubled look on his face, for he was extremely sorry for himself, though very glad for Jerrie, whose sworn ally he was and would be to the end. In a way he had tried to comfort his mother by telling her that neither his uncle or Jerrie would be unjust to her, if she'd only behave herself, and treat the latter as she ought, and not keep up such a high and mighty and injured air, as if Jerrie had done something wrong in finding out who she was.

But Dolly would not be comforted, and her face wore a sullen, defiant expression, as she moved about the house where she had queened it so long that she really looked upon it as her own, resenting bitterly the thought that another was to be mistress there. She had talked with her husband, and made him tell her exactly how much he was worth in his own right, and when he told her how little it was, she had exclaimed, angrily :

"We are beggars, and may as well go back to Langley and sell codfish again."

She had seen Tom that morning, and when to her question, "Why are you up so early?" he replied, "To attend to Jerrie's affairs," she tossed her head scornfully, and said :

"Before I'd crawl after any girl, much less Jerrie Crawford ! You'd better be attending to your own sister.

She's worse this morning, and looks as if she might die at any minute."

Then Tom went to Maude, who, since the shock of the night before, had lain as if she were dead, except for her eyes, in which there was a new and wondrous light, and which looked up lovingly at Tom as he came in and kissed her, a most unusual thing for him to do.

"Dear Tom," she whispered, "come closer to me," and as he bent down to her, she continued, "is every thing Jerrie's?"

"Yes, or will be. She is Uncle Arthur's daughter."

"Shall we be very poor?"

"Yes, poor as a church mouse."

Then there was a pause, and when Maude spoke again, she said, slowly:

"For me, no matter—sorry for you, and father, and mother; but glad for Jerrie. Stand by her, Tom; tell mother not to be so bitter—it hurts me. Tell Harold, when he comes, I meant to do so much for him, but Jerrie will do it instead. Tell her I must see her, and send for Uncle Arthur."

There was a lump in Tom's throat as he left his sister's room, and going to the village, telegraphed to his uncle's headquarters at the Palace Hotel in San Francisco.

At least a hundred people stopped him on his way to the office, asking if what they had heard was true, and to all he replied:

"True as the gospel; we are floored, as Peterkin would say."

And then he hurried to the cottage to see Jerrie, and tell her of the message sent to Arthur, though not how it was worded. After a moment he continued, hesitatingly, as if half ashamed of it:

"I called at *Lubbertoo* last night to inquire after Ann Eliza's foot, and you ought to have seen Peterkin when I told him the news. At first he could not find any word in his vocabulary big enough to swear by, but after a while one came to him, and what do you think it was?"

Jerrie could not guess, and Tom continued:

"He said, 'By the great Peterkin!' and then he swowed and vowed, and snummed, and vummed, and dummed, and finally said he was glad of it, and had always known you were a Tracy. Ann Eliza was so glad she cried, and I think Billy cried, too, for he left the room suddenly, with very suspicious looking eyes. Why, everybody is glad for you, Jerrie, and nobody seems to think how mean it is for us; but I'm not going to whine. I'm glad it's you, and so is Maude, and she wants to see you. I believe she's going to die, and—and—Jerrie—"

Something choked Tom for a moment, then he went on :

"If Uncle Arthur should get high, and order us out at once, as father seems to think he will, you'll—you'll—let us stay while Maude lives, won't you?"

"Tom," Jerrie said, reproachfully, "what do you take me for, and why does your father think his brother will order him out?"

"I don't know," Tom replied, "but he seems awfully afraid to meet him. Mother says he was up all night walking the floor and talking to himself, and yet he says he is glad, and he is coming this morning to see you and talk it over. I believe I hear him now speaking to Mrs. Crawford. Yes, 'tis he; so I guess I'll go; and when I hear from my telegram I'll let you know. Good-by."

A moment after Tom left the room his father entered it, looking haggard and old, and frightened, too, it seemed to Jerrie, as she met him with a cheery "good-morning, Uncle Frank."

It was the first time she had addressed him by that name, and her smile was so bright and her manner so cordial that for an instant the cloud lifted from his face, but soon came back darker than ever as he declined the seat she offered him and stood tremblingly before her.

Frank had not slept the previous night, but had walked his room until his wife said to him, angrily :

"I thought you were glad; seems to me you don't act like it; but for pity's sake stop walking, or go somewhere else to do it and not keep me awake."

Then he went into the hall outside, and there he walked the livelong night, trying to think what he should say to Jerrie, and wondering what she would say to him, for he meant to tell her everything. Nothing could prevent his doing that; and as soon as he thought she would see him he started for the cottage, taking with him the Bible, the photograph and the letter he had secreted so long. All the way there he was repeating to himself the form of speech with which he should commence, but when Jerrie said to him, so graciously, "good-morning, Uncle Frank," the words left him, and he began, impetuously :

"Don't call me uncle. Don't speak to me, Jerrie, until you have heard what I have come to confess on my knees, with my white head upon the floor, if you will it so, and that would not half express the shame and remorse with which I stand before you and tell you I am a cheat, a liar, a villain, and have been since the day when I first saw you and that dead woman we thought your mother."

Jerrie was dumb with surprise, and did not speak or move as he went on rapidly, telling her the whole, with no attempt at an excuse for himself, except so far as to repeat what he had done in a business point of view, making provision for her in case of his death and enjoining it upon his children to see that his wishes were carried out.

"Here is the Bible," he said, laying the book in her lap. "Here is the photograph, and here the letter which you gave me to post, and which, had it been sent, might have cleared the mystery sooner."

He had made his confession, and he stood before her with clasped hands, and an expression upon his face such as a criminal might wear when awaiting the jury's decision. But Jerrie neither looked at him nor spoke, for through a rain of tears she was gazing upon the sweet face, sadder and thinner than the face of Gretchen in the window, but so like it that there could be no mistaking it, and so like to the face which had haunted her so often and seemed so near to her.

"Mother, mother ! I remember you as you are here, sick and sorry, but oh, so lovely !" she said, as she pressed her lips again and again to the picture, with no thought or care for the wretched man who had come a step nearer to her, and who said, at last :

"Will you never speak to me Jerrie ? Never tell me how much you despise me ?"

Then she looked up at the face quivering with anguish and entreaty, and the sight melted her at once. Indeed, as he had talked she had scarcely felt any resentment toward him, for she was sure that though his error had been great, his contrition and remorse had been greater, and she thought of him only as Maude's father and the man who had always been kind to her. And she made him believe at last that she forgave him for Maude's sake, if not for his own.

"Had my life been a wretched one because of your conduct," she said, "I might have found it harder to forgive you, but it has not. I have not been the daughter of Tracy Park, it is true, but I have been the petted child of the cottage, and I would rather have lived with Harold in poverty all these years than to have been rich without him. And do you know, I think it was noble in you to tell me when you might have kept it to yourself."

"No, no. I couldn't have done that much longer," he exclaimed, energetically, as he began to walk up and down the room. "I could not bear it. And the shadow which for years has been with me night and day, counseling me for bad, was growing so black, and huge, and unendurable, that I must have confessed or died. But it is gone now, or will be when I have told my brother."

"Told your brother! You don't mean to do that?" Jerrie exclaimed.

"But I do mean to do it," Frank replied, "as a part of my punishment, and he will not forgive as you have done. He will turn me out at once, as he ought to do."

Jerrie thought this very likely, and with all her powers she strove to dissuade Frank from making a confession which could do no possible good, and might result in untold harm.

"Remember Maude," she said, "and the effect this thing would have upon her if your brother should resort to immediate and violent means, as he might in his first frenzy."

"But I mean to tell Maude, too," Frank replied.

Then Jerrie looked upon him as madder than Arthur himself, and talked so rapidly and argued so well that he consented at last to keep his own counsel, for the present at least, unless the shadow still haunted him, in which case he must tell as an act of contrition or penance.

"He will think the photograph came with the other papers in the bag," Jerrie said, as she again kissed the sweet face, which looked so much like life that it was hard

to think there was not real love and tenderness in the eyes
which looked into hers so steadfastly.

It was the hardest to forgive the letter hidden so
long, and Jerrie did feel a pang of resentment, or
something like it, as she took it in her hand and thought
of the day when Arthur had confided it to her, saying he
could trust her when he could not another. And she had
trusted Frank, who had not been true to her trust, and
here, after the lapse of years, was the letter, with its singular superscription covering the whole side, and its seal
unbroken. But she would break it now. She surely
might do that, if Arthur was never to see it ; and, after a
moment's hesitancy, she opened it and read, first, wild,
crazy sentences, full of love and tenderness for the little
Gretchen to whom they were addressed, and whom the
writer sometimes spoke to as living, and again as dead.
There was a strong desire expressed to see her, a wish for
her to come and get her diamonds before they were taken
from her a second time. Here Jerrie started with an exclamation of surprise, and involuntarily read aloud :

" The most exquisite diamonds you ever saw, and I long
to see them on you. They are safe, too—from her—Mrs.
Frank Tracy—who had the boldness to flaunt them in my
face at a party the other night. How she came by them I
can't guess ; but I know how she lost them. I found them
on her dressing-table, where she left them when she went
to breakfast, and took possession at once. That was no
theft, for they are mine, or rather yours, and are waiting
for you in my private drawer, where no one has ever looked,
except a young girl called Jerrie, who interests me greatly,
she is so much like what you must have been when a child.
There has been some trouble about the diamonds—I hardly
know what, my head is in such a buzzing most of the time
that everything goes from me, but you. Oh, if I had
remembered you years ago as I do now—"

Jerrie could read no further, for the letter dropped
from her hands, as she cried, joyfully :

" I knew he had them. I was sure of it, though I did
not know where they were."

Then very briefly she explained to Frank that on the
morning when the diamonds were missed, Arthur was so
excited because Harold had been in a way accused, that he

had rambled off into German, and said things which made her think he had taken them himself and secreted them.

"You remember my sickness," she said, "and how strangely I talked of going to prison as an accessory or a substitute? Well, it was for your brother I was ready to go; and when he told me, as he did one day, that he knew nothing of the diamonds, I was never more astonished in my life; but afterward, as I grew older, I believed that he had forgotten them, as he did other things, and that some time he would remember and make restitution. I am glad we know where they are, but we cannot get them until he returns. When do you think that will be?"

Frank did not know. It would depend, he said, upon whether he was in San Francisco when Tom's telegram was received. If he were, and started at once, traveling day and night, he would be home in a week.

It seemed a long time to wait in Jerrie's state of mind, and very, very short to the repentant man, who shrank from his brother's return as from an impending evil, although it was a relief to think that he need not tell him what a hypocrite he had been.

"Thank you, Jerrie," he said at last, as he arose to go. "Thank you for being so kind to me. I did not deserve it. I did not expect it. Heaven bless you. I am glad for you, and so is Maude. Oh, Jerrie, Heaven is dealing hard with me to take her from me, and yet it is just. I sinned for her; sinned to see her in the place I was sure was yours, for I knew you were Arthur's child, and I meant to go to Germany some day, when I had the language a little better, and clear it up, and then I had promised myself to tell you. Will you say again that you forgive me before I go back to Maude?"

He was standing before her with his white head dropped upon his hat, the very picture of misery and remorse, and Jerrie laid her hand upon his head, and said:

"I do forgive you, Uncle Frank, fully and freely, for Maude's sake if no other; and if she lives what is mine shall be hers. Tell her so, and tell her I am coming to see her as soon as I am able. I am so tired and sick to-day, and everything is so strange. Oh, if Harold were here."

Jerrie was indeed so tired and exhausted that for the

remainder of the day she saw no one but Judge St. Claire and Tom, both of whom came up together, the latter bringing the answer to his telegram, and asking what to do next.

"Why, Tom," Jerrie said, as she read Arthur's reply, "'Pay him then, for I shan't come,' what does he mean? What did you say to him, and whom are you to pay?"

With a half comical smile Tom replied, "I told him the old Nick was to pay, though I am afraid I used a stronger name for his Satanic majesty than that. I guess you'll have to try what you can do."

And so Jerrie's message, "I need you," went across the continent, and brought the ready response, "Coming on the wings of the wind." It was Judge St. Claire who wrote to Harold, for Jerrie, who said: "Tell him everything, and how much I want him here; and tell him, too, of Maude, whose life hangs on a thread. That may bring him sooner."

It was three days before Jerrie was able to go to the Park House, and then Tom came for her, saying Maude was failing very fast. The news which had come upon her so suddenly with regard to Jerrie's birth and the suspicions resting upon Harold shortened the life nearing its close, and the moment Jerrie entered the room she knew the worst, and with a storm of sobs and tears knelt by the sick girl's coach and cried:

"Oh, I can't bear it. I'd give up everything to save you. Oh, Maude, you don't know how much I love you."

Maude was very calm, though her lips quivered a little and the tears filled her eyes as she put her hand in Jerrie's. A great change had come over Maude since the night when she heard Jerrie's story—a change for the better some might have thought, although the physician who attended her gave no hope. She neither coughed nor suffered pain, and could talk all she liked, although often in a whisper, she was so very weak.

"Yes, Jerrie," she said, "I know you love me, and it makes me very glad, and dying seems easier, for I know you will be cared for—Once, when I first thought I must die, I wrote something on paper for father and uncle Arthur to see when I was dead, and it was that they should take you in my place, you and Harold,"

Maude's voice shook a little here, but she soon steadied it and went on :

" I wanted them to give you what I thought would be mine had I lived, and what all the time was yours. Oh, Jerrie, how can you help hating me, who have stood so long where you ought to have stood, and enjoyed what you ought to have enjoyed ?"

" Maude," Jerrie cried, " don't talk like that ; as if I, or any one, could ever have hated you. Why, I worshiped you as some little empress when I used to see you in your bright sashes and yellow kid boots, with the amber beads around your neck ; and if the contrast between your finery and my high-necked gingham apron and white sun-bonnet sometimes struck me painfully, I had no wish to take the boots and sashes from you, whom they fitted so admirably ; and as we grew older and you did not shrink from or slight Jerrie Crawford, I cannot tell you how great was the love which grew in my heart for you, the dearest girl friend I ever had, and a thousand times dearer now I know you are my cousin."

Maude was silent for a moment, and then she asked, abruptly :

" Jerrie, why did you never fall in love with Harold ?"

" Oh, Maude !" and Jerrie started as if Maude had struck her, while the tell-tale blood rushed to her face, and into her eyes there came a look which even Maude could understand.

" Jerrie," she exclaimed, " forgive me. I didn't know, I never guessed, I was so stupid ; but I have been thinking so much since Harold went away. Does he know about you ? who you are, I mean ? and how long before he will come home ?"

" Judge St. Claire wrote him everything three days ago," Jerrie replied, " and told him how sick you were. That will surely bring him at once, if it is possible for him to leave ; but it will be three or four days now before the letter will reach him, and it will take a week for him to come. Would you like to see him very much ?"

" Yes," Maude answered, " but I never shall. Jerrie, did Harold ever—did he—does he—love you ?"

" He never told me so," Jerrie said, frankly ; " but I have thought that he loved you,"

"N—no," Maude answered, piteously. "It was all a mistake, and when I am dead and Harold comes, promise to tell him something from me, will you?"

"Yes," Jerrie replied, and Maude continued:

"Tell him the very first time you and he are alone together, and speak of me, that I have been thinking and thinking until it came to me clear as day that it was all a mistake, a stupid blunder on my part. I was always stupid, you know; but I believe my brain is clearer now. Will you tell him, Jerrie?"

"Mistake about what?" Jerrie asked, with a vague apprehension that the task imposed upon her might not be a pleasant one if she knew all it involved.

"Harold will tell you what," Maude answered. "He will understand what I mean, but I shall not be here when he comes. I am sure of it. I hope to live till Uncle Arthur comes, for I must see him and ask him not to be hard on poor father, and tell him I am sorry that I have been so long in the place where you should have been. You will stay here and be with me to the last. I want you to hold my hand when I say good-by forever. You are so strong that I shall not be afraid with you to see and hear as long as I hear and see anything."

"And are you afraid?" Jerrie asked, and Maude replied:

"Of the death struggle, yes; but not what lies beyond where He is, the Saviour, for I know I am going to Him; and when they think me asleep I am often praying silently for more faith and love, and for you all, that you may one day come where I soon shall be. Heaven is very, very beautiful, for I have seen it in my dreams—a material heaven some would say, for there are trees, and flowers, and grass; and on a golden bench, beneath a tree whose leaves are like emeralds, and whose blossoms are like pearls, I am sitting, on the bank of a shining river, resting, and waiting, as little Pilgrim waited for the coming of the Master, and for you all."

Maude was very tired, and her voice was so low that Jerrie could scarcely hear it, while the eyelids drooped heavily, and in a few moments she fell asleep, with a rapt look on her face as if she were already resting on the golden seat beneath the tree whose leaves were emeralds and whose blossoms were like pearls.

That night Jerrie wrote as follows :

"DEAR HAROLD: Maude is very low, and, unless you come soon, you will never see her again. The judge has written you of me, but I must tell you myself that nothing can ever change me from the Jerrie of old ; and the fact which makes me the happiest is that now I can help you who have been so kind to me. How I long to see you and talk it all over. We expect Mr. Arthur in a few days. I cannot call him father yet, until he has himself given me the right to do so by calling me daughter first ; but to myself I am calling Gretchen mother all the time, my darling little mother ! Oh, Harold, you must come home and share my happiness which will not be complete till you are here." "JERRIE."

During the next few days Jerrie staid with Maude waiting anxiously for tidings from Arthur until one lovely September morning, a telegram was brought to Frank from Charles, which said they would be home that afternoon.

CHAPTER XLIX.

TELLING ARTHUR.

WHO should do the telling was the question which for some time was discussed by Frank and Judge St. Claire and Jerrie. Naturally the task fell upon the latter, who went over and over again in her mind what she should say and how she should commence.

But when at last the announcement came that Arthur was in Albany, it seemed to her that she had suddenly turned into stone, for every thought and feeling left her, and she had no plan of action or speech as she moved mechanically about Arthur's rooms, making them bright with flowers, especially the Gretchen room, which was a bower of beauty when her skillful hands had finished it.

Slowly the day wore on, every minute seeming an hour, and every hour a day, until Jerrie heard the carriage driv-

ing down the avenue, and not long after the whistle of the
engine in the distance. Then, bending over Maude and
kissing her fondly, she said :

"Pray for me, darling, I am going to meet my father."

Arthur had been very quiet during the first part of the
journey from San Francisco, and it was with difficulty that
Charles could get a word from him.

"Let me alone," he said once, when spoken to. "I am
with Gretchen. She is on the train with me, and I'm trying to make out what it is she is telling me."

But after Albany was left behind, his mood changed
and he became as wild and excitable as he had before been
abstracted and silent, and when at last Shannondale was
reached, he bounded from the car before the train stopped,
and was collaring Rob, the coachman, and demanding of
him what was the matter with Jerrie and why he had been
sent for. Rob, who had received his instructions to be
wholly non-committal, answered stolidly that nothing was
the matter with Jerrie, but that Miss Maude was very sick
and probably would not live many days.

"Is that all ?" Arthur said, gloomily, as he entered the
carriage. "I don't see what the old Harry has to do with
Maude's dying, and certainly Tom's telegram said something about that chap. I have it in my pocket. Yes, here
it is. 'Come immediately. The devil is to pay.' That
doesn't mean Maude. There is something else Rob has not
told me. Here you rascal, you are keeping something from
me ! What is it ? Out with it ?" he shouted to the driver,
as he thrust his head from the carriage window, where he
kept it, and in this way was driven to the door of the Park
House, where Frank was waiting for him outside, and
where, inside, Jerrie stood, holding fast to the banisters of
the stairs, her heart throbbing wildly one moment, and the
next seeming to lie pulseless as a piece of lead.

She heard Arthur's voice as he came up the steps, speaking to Frank, and asking why he had been sent for ; and
the next moment she saw him entering the hall, tall and
erect, but with the wild look in his eyes which she knew so
well, but which changed at once to a softer expression as
they fell upon her.

"Cherry, you here !" he cried, as he sprang to her side
and kissed her forehead and lips, while Jerrie could scarcely

restrain herself from falling upon his neck and sobbing out, "Oh, my father! I am your daughter, Jerrie!" But the time for this had not come, and when he questioned her eagerly as to why she had sent for him, she only replied:

"Maude is very sick. But come with me to your rooms, and I will tell you everything."

"Then there is something to pay; I thought so," he said, as he followed her up stairs into the Gretchen room, where he stood for a moment amazed at the effect produced by the flowers and vines which Jerrie had arranged so skillfully. "It is like Eden," he said, "and Gretchen is here with me. Darling Gretchen!" he continued, as he walked up to the picture and kissed the lovely face which, it seemed to Jerrie, smiled in benediction upon them both, as they stood there side by side, her hands resting on his shoulder, which she pressed hard, as if to steady herself, while he talked to the inanimate face before him.

"Have you been lonesome, Gretchen, and are you glad to have me back again? Poor little Gretchen!" And now he turned to Jerrie, and said: "It all came to me on the top of those mountains, about Gretchen—who she was, and how I forgot her so long—that is the strangest of all; and, Cherry," here his voice dropped to a whisper, "I know for sure that Gretchen is dead—that came to me, too."

"Yes, Gretchen is dead," Jerrie answered him, while her hands tightened their grasp on his shoulder, as she went on: "I have had a message from her, and that is why we sent for you."

Jerrie's hands were not strong enough to hold him then, and, wrenching himself from her, he stood confronting her with a look more like that of a maniac than any she had seen in him before, and which might have frightened one with nerves less strong than her's. But she was not afraid, and a strange calmness fell upon her, now that she had actually reached a point, where she must act, and her eyes, which looked so steadily into Arthur's, held them fast, even while he interrogated her rapidly.

"A message from Gretchen! Where is it? Give it to me quick, or tell me about it! Where is she, and when is she coming?"

"Never!" Jerry answered, sadly. "I told you she was

dead. But sit here," and she motioned him to a large, arm chair. "Sit here, and let me tell you what I know of Gretchen."

Something in the girl's manner mastered him and made him a child in her hands.

Sinking into the chair, pale and panting with excitement, he leaned his head back wearily, and closing his eyes, said to her:

"Begin. What did Gretchen write?"

Jerrie felt that she could not stand through the interview, and, bringing a low ottoman to Arthur's side, seated herself upon it just where she could look into his face and detect every change in it.

"Let me tell you of Gretchen as she was when you first knew her," she said, "and then you will be better able to judge of the truth of all I know."

He did not reply, and she went on:

"Gretchen was very young—sixteen or seventeen—when you first saw her knitting in the sunshine under the trees in Wiesbaden, and very beautiful, too—so beautiful that you went again and again to look at her and talk to her, until you came to love her very much, and told her so at last; but you seemed so much above her that she could not believe you at first. At last, however, you made her understand, and when her mother died suddenly——"

"Her mother was Mrs. Heinrich, and kept a kind of fancy store," Arthur interposed, as if anxious that nothing should be omitted.

"Yes, she kept a fancy store," Jerrie rejoined; "and when she died suddenly and left Gretchen alone, you said to her, 'We must be married at once,' and you were, in the little English chapel, by the Rev. Mr. Eaton, who was then rector."

Here Arthur's eyes opened wide and fixed themselves wonderingly upon Jerrie, as he said:

"Are you the old Harry that you know all this? But go on; don't stop; it all comes back to me so plain when I hear you tell it. She wore a straw bonnet trimmed with blue, and a white dress, but took it off directly for a black one because her mother was dead. Did she tell you that?"

"No," Jerrie replied. "She told me nothing of the dress, only how happy she was with you, whom she loved so much, and who loved her and made her so happy for a time that earth seemed like heaven to her, and then——"

Here Jerrie faltered a little, but Arthur's sharp " What then ?" kept her up, and she continued :

" Then something came to you, and you began to forget everything, even poor little Gretchen, and went away for weeks and left her very sad and lonely, not knowing where you were ; and then, after some months, you went away and never came back again to the little wife who waited, and watched, and prayed, and wanted you so badly."

" Oh, Cherry ! oh, Gretchen ! I'm so sorry ! I didn't mean to do it ; I surely didn't. May God forgive me for forgetting the little wife ! Was it long ? Was it months, or was it years ? I can't remember, only that there was a Gretchen, and I left her," Arthur said.

" It was years, four or more and—and—"—Jerrie's breath came heavily now, for she was nearing the point relating to herself and wondering what the effect would be upon him. " After awhile there came into Gretchen's life the dawning of a great hope, which she felt would make you glad, and wishing to keep it a secret till you came home, she only gave you a hint of it. She wrote : " I have something to tell you which will make you as happy as it does me——"

" Stop !" and Arthur put out both his hands as if groping for something which he could not find ; then he said. " Go on," and Jerrie went on, slowly now, for every word was an effort, and spoken so low that Arthur bent forward to listen to her.

" I don't know just where Gretchen's home was when she lived alone waiting for you. I only know that after awhile there came to it a little baby—a girl baby—Gretchen's and yours——"

She did not get any further, for with a bound Arthur was on his feet, every faculty alert, every nerve strung to its utmost pitch, and every muscle of his face quivering with wild excitement, as he exclaimed :

" A baby ! Gretchen's baby and mine ! A little girl ! Oh, Cherry, if you are deceiving me now !"

Jerrie too, had risen, and was standing before him with her hands upon his arm and her eyes, so like Gretchen's, looking into his, as she said :

" I am not deceiving you. There was a baby born to

you and Gretchen some time in January, 18—, and it was christened in the little church where you were married, by the Rev. Mr. Eaton. Oh, Mr. Arthur how can I tell you; the baby, is living yet—grown to womanhood now, for this happened more than twenty years ago, and the girl is twenty now, and is waiting and longing so much for her father to recognize and claim her. Oh, don't you understand me? Look at *me* and then at Gretchen's picture!"

For an instant Arthur stood like one stricken with paralysis, his eyes leaping from Jerrie's face to Gretchen's, and from Gretchen's back to Jerrie's, and then, with a motion of his hands as if fanning the air furiously, he gasped:

"Twenty years ago—twenty years ago? How old are you, Cherry?"

"Twenty," she answered, but her voice was a whisper, and her head fell forward a little, though she kept her eyes upon Arthur, who went on:

"And they christened my baby and Gretchen's you say? What name did they give her? Speak quick, for I believe I am dying."

"They called her Jerrine, but you know her as Jerrie, for—for I am Gretchen's daughter," Jerrie said.

With a wild, glad cry, "My daughter! oh, my daughter! Thank God! thank God!" Arthur sank back into the chair fainting and insensible.

For hours he lay in a state so nearly resembling death that but for the physician's reassurance that there was no danger, Jerrie would have believed the great joy given her was to be taken from her at once. But just as the twilight shadows began to gather in the room he came to himself, waking as from some quiet dream, and looking around him until his eyes fell upon Jerrie sitting by his side; then over his white face there came a look of ineffable joy and tenderness and love, as he said, with a smile the most winning and sweet Jerrie had ever seen:

"My daughter, my little Cherry, who came to me up the ladder, with Gretchen's eyes and Gretchen's voice, and I did not know her—have not known her all these years, although she has so puzzled and bewildered me at times. My daughter! oh, my daughter!"

He accepted her unquestioningly, and Jerrie threw herself into the arms he stretched toward her, and on her

18

father's bosom gave vent to the feelings she had restrained
so long, sobbing passionately as she felt Arthur's kisses
upon her face, and his caressing hands upon her hair, as he
kept repeating :

" My daughter ! Gretchen's baby and mine !"

" There is more to tell. I have not heard it all, or how
you came by the information," he said, when Jerrie was a
little composed, and could look at and speak to him without a burst of tears.

" Yes, there is much more. There is a letter for you,
with those you wrote to her," Jerrie said, " but you must
not have them to-night. To-morrow you will be stronger,
now you must rest."

She spoke like one with authority, and he did just what
she bade him do—took the food she brought him, went to
bed when she said he must go, and, with her hand locked
in his, fell into a heavy slumber, which lasted all through
the night, and late into the next morning. It almost seemed as if he would never waken, the sleep was so like death ;
but the doctor who watched him carefully quieted Jerrie's
fears and told her it would do her father good, and that in
all probability he would awake with a clearer mind than
he had had in years, for as a great and sudden shock sometimes produced insanity, so, contrarywise, it sometimes restored a shattered mind to its equilibrium.

And the doctor was partially correct, for when at last
Arthur awoke he seemed natural and bright, with a recollection of all which had happened the day before, and an
earnest desire for the letters and the rest of the story,
which Jerrie told him, with her arm across his neck, and
her cheek laid occasionally against his, as she read him the
letter directed to his friends, and then showed him the
certificate of her birth and her mother's death.

" Born, January 1st, 18—, to Arthur Tracy and Marguerite, his wife, a daughter," Arthur repeated, again and
again, and as often as he did so, he kissed the bright face
which smiled at him through tears, for there was almost as
much sadness as joy mingled with the reading of that message from the dead.

Just what Gretchen's letter to Arthur contained Jerrie
never knew, except that it was full of love and tenderness,

with no word of complaint for the neglect and forgetfulness which must have hastened her death.

"Oh, Gretchen, I can't bear it, I can't," Arthur moaned, as he laid his hand upon Jerrie's shoulder and sobbed like a child. "To think I could forget her, and she so sweet and good."

Everything came back to him for a time, and he repeated to Jerrie much which was of interest to her concerning her mother, but with which the reader has nothing to do; while Jerrie, in her turn, told him all she could remember of her life in the old house where Gretchen had died. Then she asked him why he had never told them that she was his wife. "It might have helped to clear up the mystery with regard to Mah-nee and myself," she said, and he replied: "Yes, yes, it might, and I don't know why I didn't. When we were first married I was going to write Frank about it, but Gretchen persuaded me not to. She had an idea that I was as much above her as a king is above his subjects, and that my friends would be very angry with me and perhaps win my love from her. I think this idea so strong with her must have found a place in my maddened brain and kept me from telling who she was. I remember having a feeling that I must not tell until she came, when I knew her sweetness and beauty would disarm all prejudice there might exist against her. I was sane enough always to know that my wife would not be acceptable to either Frank or Dolly. But oh, I wish I had told them the truth at once! Poor Gretchen, poor Gretchen!" He began to pace the room rapidly and to beat the air with his hands, as he always did when roused and excited. But Jerrie quieted him at last and then gave him his own letters addressed to Gretchen; but at these he barely glanced, muttering, as he did so, "How could I have written such crazy bosh as that?" and then suddenly recollecting himself, he asked for the photograph mentioned in Gretchen's letter to his friends, and which he seemed to think had come with the other papers. Taking it from the bag, Jerrie handed it to him, while his tears fell like rain as he gazed upon the face which was far too young to wear the sad, wan look it did.

"That is as I remember her," Jerrie said, referring again to the strange ideas which had filled her brain and made her sure that not the dark woman found dead at her side was her mother, but another and far different person, whose face haunted her so continually and whose voice she sometimes seemed to hear speaking to her from the dim shadows of the far-off past when they lived in the little house in Wiesbaden, where the picture hung on the wall.

Arthur remembered the picture well and when it was taken, though that, too, had faded from his mind until Jerrie told him of it.

"We will go there together, Cherry," he said, "and find the house and the picture, and Gretchen's grave, and bring them home with us. There is room for them at Tracy Park."

He was beginning to talk wildly again, but Jerrie succeeded in pacifying him, and taking up the box of diamonds opened it suddenly and held it before his eyes. In reading the letters he had not seemed to pay any attention to the diamonds, but when Jerrie said to him : "These were mother's. You sent them to her from England," he replied : "Yes, I remember, I bought them in Paris with other things—dresses, I think—for her," while into his face there came a troubled look as if he were trying to think of something.

Jerrie, who could read him so well, saw the look, and, guessing at once its cause, hastened to say :

"Father, do you remember that you gave Mrs. Tracy some diamonds like these, and that some one took them from her ? Try and think," she continued, as she saw the troubled look deepen and the fire beginning to kindle in his eyes. "It was years ago, just after a party Mrs. Tracy gave, and at which she wore them. You were there and thought they were Gretchen's, did you not ?"

"Ye-es," he answered, slowly, "I believe I did. What did I do with them ? Do you know ?"

"I think you put them in your private drawer. Suppose you look and see."

"Obedient to her as a child, Arthur opened his private drawer, bringing out one thing after another, all mementoes of the old Gretchen days, and finally the diamonds, at which he looked with wonder and fear, as he said to Jerrie :

"Did I take them ? Will they call it a steal ? I thought they were Gretchen's. I remember now."

Jerrie did not tell him then of the trouble the secreting of the diamonds had brought to her and Harold, but she said :

"No one will think it a steal, and Mrs. Tracy will be glad to get her jewels back. May I take them to her now ?"

"Take them to her?—no," Arthur said, decidedly. "She has another set—I bought them for her, and she wears them all day long. Ha, ha ! diamonds in the morning, with a cotton gown ;" and he laughed immoderately at what he thought Dolly's bad taste. "Take them to her ? No! They are yours."

"But I have mother's," Jerrie pleaded ; "and I cannot wear two sets."

"Yes, you can—one to-day, one to-morrow. I mean you shall have seven—one for every day in the week. What has Dolly to do with diamonds. They are for ladies, and she is only a whitewashed one."

He was very much excited, and it took all Jerrie's tact to soothe and quiet him.

"Father," she began, and he stopped at once, for the sound of that name spoken by Jerrie had a mighty power over him—"Father, listen to me a moment."

And then she told him of the suspicions cast upon Harold, and said :

"You do not wish him to suffer any more ?"

"Harold ? The boy who found you in the carpet-bag —Amy's boy! No, never ! Where is he that I have not seen him yet ? Does he know you are my daughter ?"

Jerrie had not mentioned Harold before, but she told her father now where he was, and why he had gone, and that she had written him to come home, on Maude's account, if on no other."

"Yes--Maude—I remember ; but Harold did not care for Maude. Still, he had better come. I want him here with you and me ; and you must stay here now day and night. Select any room you please ; all is yours, my daughter."

"But I cannot leave grandma," Jerrie said.

"Let her come, too," Arthur replied, "There's room for her,"

"No," Jerrie persisted; "that would not be best. Grandma could not live with Mrs. Tracy."

"Then let Dolly go at once. I'll give the order now," and Arthur put out his hand to the bell-cord.

But Jerrie stopped him instantly, saying to him:

"Remember Maude. While she lives her mother, must stay here."

"Yes, I forgot Maude. I have not seen her yet," Arthur replied, subdued at once, and willing that Jerrie should take the jewels to Dolly, who deserved but little forbearance from her.

Up to the very last Mrs. Tracy had, unconsciously perhaps, clung to a shadowy hope that Arthur might repudiate his daughter and call it a trumped-up affair; but when she heard how joyfully he had acknowledged and claimed her, she lost all hope, and her face wore a gloomy expression when Jerrie entered her room, and told her in a few words that her own diamonds had been found, and where they had been secreted, and that she had come to return them.

"Then your father was the thief," Dolly said, with that rasping, aggravating tone so hard to hear unmoved.

"Call him what you please. A crazy man is not responsible for his acts," Jerrie answered calmly, as she walked from the room, leaving Dolly to her own morbid and angry thoughts.

Not even the restored diamonds had power to conciliate her.

"I'll never wear them, because she has some like them," she said to herself; and then the thought came to her that she could sell them, and add to the sum which her husband had invested in his own name.

"Yes, I'll do it," she continued, "but even that will hardly keep the wolf from the door, for Frank is growing more and more imbecile every day, and Tom is good for nothing. He'll have to scratch for himself, though, I can tell him."

Here her very characteristic soliloquy was brought to an end by a faint call, which had the power to drive every other thought from her heart, for the mother-love was strong even with her, and going to Maude, she asked what she wanted.

"Uncle Arthur," Maude replied; "I have not seen him yet. And Jerrie, too; she has scarcely been here to-day."

Maude's request was made known to Arthur, who, two or three hours later, went to her room, and told her how sorry he was to find her so sick, and that he hoped she would soon be better.

Frank was with Maude, sitting upon the side of her bed, near the head, with his arm across her pillow, and his eyes fixed anxiously upon her as she held her conference with his brother.

"No, uncle," she said, "I shall never be any better in this world; but, pretty soon, I shall be well in the other. And I want to tell you how glad I am for you and Jerrie, and to thank you for your kindness to us all these years, when Jerrie should have been here in our place."

"Yes, yes," Arthur said, with a wave of his hand. "Only I didn't know. If I had—"

"It would have been so different," Maude interrupted him. "I know that, but I want you to be kind to poor father still, and forgive him, he is so sorry, and—"

"Oh, Maude, Maude," came like a groan from Frank, as he laid his hand on Maude's lips, while Arthur replied:

"Forgive him for what? He couldn't help being here. I sent for him. He did not keep Jerrie from her rightful position as my daughter. If he had, I could never forgive him. Why, I believe I'd kill him, or any other one who, knowing that Jerrie was my daughter, kept it from me."

He was gesticulating with both hands, and Jerrie, who had come in with him, took hold of them as they were swaying in the air and said to him softly:

"Father!"

The word quieted him, and with a gasp his mood seemed to change at once.

"Maude is very tired," Jerrie went on; "perhaps we'd better go now, and come again to-morrow."

"Yes, yes, that's best, child. I'm not fond of sick rooms, though I must say this is very free from smells," Arthur replied; then stooping down he kissed Maude and said to her as he arose to go:

"Don't worry about your father; he is my brother, and he was kind to Jerrie. I shan't forget that. Come, my daughter."

And putting his arm around Jerrie he left the room.

CHAPTER L.

THE FLOWER FADETH.

IT was some days after Arthur's return before the household settled down into any thing like order and quiet for Arthur was so restless and so happy, and so anxious for every one to recognize Jerrie as his daughter—Miss Tracy, he called her when presenting her to the people who had known her all her life—the St. Claires, and Athertons, and Crosbys, and Warners—who came to call upon and congratulate him. Even Peterkin came with a card as big as the back of Webster's spelling book, and himself gotten up in a dress coat, with lavender kids on his burly hands, which nearly crushed Arthur's as he expressed himself "tickleder than he ever was before in his life."

"And to think I was the means on't," he said, "for if I hadn't of kicked that darned old table into slivers when I was givin' on't to Jerrie, she'd never of knowd what was in that dumbed rat-hole. I was a little too upstrupulous, I s'spose, but I'll be darned if she didn't square up to me like a catamount, till my hair riz right up, and I concluded the Tramp House was no place for me. But I respect her for it ; yes, I do, and by George, old chap, I congratulate you with my whole soul, and so does May Jane, and so does Ann 'Lizy, and so does Bill, and so does the whole coboodle on us."

This was Peterkin's speech, which Arthur received more graciously than Jerrie, who, remembering Harold, could not be very polite to the man who had injured him so deeply. As if divining her thoughts, Peterkin turned to her and said :

"Now, one word, Miss Tracy, about Hal. I hain't one to go halves in any thing, and I was meaner to him than pussly ; but you'll see what I'll do. I've met with a change. I swow, I have," and he laid his lavender kid on his stomach. "He never took them diamonds, nor May Jane's pin, nor nothin', and I've blaated it all over town that he didn't, and I've got a kerridge hired, and some chaps, and a brass

band, and a percession, and when Hal comes, there's to be
an oblation to the depot, with the bugle a playin' 'Hail to
the Chief,' and them hired chaps a histen' him inter the
kerridge, with the star spangled banner a floatin' over it,
and a drawin' him home without horses! What do you think
of that for high?" and he chuckled merrily as he repeated
the programme he had prepared for Harold's reception.

Jerrie shuddered, mentally hoping that Harold's coming
might be at night, and unheralded, so as to save him from
what she knew would fill him with disgust.

That call of Peterkin's was the last of a congratulatory
nature made at Tracy Park for weeks, for the shadow of
death had entered the grand old house, the doors and windows of which stood wide open, one lovely September
morning, about a week after Arthur's return. But there
was no stir or sign of life, except in the upper hall, near
the door, and in the room where Maude Tracy was dying.
Jerrie had been with her constantly for two or three days,
and the conversation the two had held together would never
be forgotten. Maude was very peaceful and happy and sure
of the home beyond, where she was going, and very lovely
and sweet to those around her, thinking of everything, and
planning everything, even whose hands were to lower her
into the grave.

"Dick, and Fred, and Billy, and Harold," she said to
Jerrie, one day. "Something tells me Harold will be here
in time for that; and if he is, I want those four to put me
in the grave. They can lift me, for I shall not be very
heavy," and, with a smile, she held up her wasted arms and
hands, not as large now as a child's. "And, Jerrie," she
went on, "I want the grave lined with boughs from our
old playing-place—the four pines, you know—and many
flowers, for I shudder at the thought of the cold earth
which would chill me in my coffin. So, heap the grave with
flowers, and come often to it, and think lovingly of me,
lying there alone. I am thinking so much of that poem
Harold read to me long ago of poor little Alice, the May
queen, who said she should hear them as they passed, with
their feet above her in the long and silent grass. Maybe
the dead can't do that, I don't know, but if they can, I
shall listen for you, and be glad when you are near me,
and I know I shall wait on the golden seat by the river.

18*

Remember your promise to tell Harold that it was all a mistake. My mind gets clearer toward the end, and I see things differently from what I did once, and I know how I blundered. You will tell him?"

Again Jerrie made the promise, with a sinking heart, not knowing to what it bound her; and as Maude was becoming tired, she bade her try to rest while she sat by and watched her.

The next day, at the same hour, when the balmy September air was everywhere, and the mid-afternoon sun was filling the house with golden light, and the crickets' chirp was heard in the long grass, and the robins were singing in the tree-tops, another scene was presented in the sick room, where Frank Tracy knelt at his dying daughter's side, with his face bowed on his hands, while her fingers played feebly with his white hair as she spoke to Arthur, who had just come in. They had told him she was dying and had asked for him, and with his nervous horror of everything painful and exciting, he had shrunk from the ordeal; but Jerrie's will prevailed, and he went with her to the room, where Frank and his wife and Tom were waiting—Tom standing, with folded arms, at the foot of the bed, and looking, with hot, dry eyes, into the face on the pillow, where death was setting his seal; the mother, half fainting upon the lounge, with the nurse beside her; and Frank oblivious of everything except the fact that Maude was dying.

" Kiss me good-by, Uncle Arthur," she said, when he came in, "and come this side where father is." Then, as he went round and stood by Frank, she reached her hand for his, and putting it on her father's head, said to him: "Forgive him, Uncle Arthur; he is so sorry, poor father —the dearest, the best man in the world. It was for me; say that you forgive him."

Only Frank and one other knew just what she meant, although a sudden suspicion darted through Jerrie's mind, and, when Arthur looked helplessly at her, she whispered to him:

" Never mind what she means—her mind may be wandering; but say that you forgive him, no matter what it is."

Thus adjured, Arthur said to the grief-stricken man, who shook like an aspen :·

" I know of nothing to forgive, except your old disbelief

in Gretchen, and deceiving me about sending the carriage the night Jerrie came; but if there is anything else, no matter what it is, I do forgive you freely."

"Thanks," came faintly from Maude, who whispered: "Remember it is a vow made at my death-bed."

She had done all she could, this little girl, whose life had been so short, and who, as she once said, had been capable of nothing but loving and being loved; and now, turning her dim eyes upon Jerrie, she went on:

"Remember the promise, and the flowers, and the golden seat where you will find me resting by the river whose shores I am now looking upon, for I am almost there, almost to the golden seat, and the tree whose leaves are like emeralds, and where the grass and flowers are like the flowers and grass of summer just after a rain. I am glad for you, Jerrie. Good-by; and you, dear father, good-by."

That was the last, for Maude was dead; and the servants, who had been standing about the door, stole noiselessly back to their work, with wet eyes and a sense of pain and loss in their hearts, for not one of them but had loved the gentle girl now gone forever from their midst.

It was Jerrie who led Frank from the room to his own, where she left him by himself, knowing it would be better so, and it was Arthur who took Dolly out, for Tom had disappeared, and no one saw him again until the next day, when he came down to breakfast, with a worn, haggard look upon his face, which told that he did care, though his mother thought he did not, and taunted him with his indifference. He had gone directly to his room and locked the door, and smoked and smoked, and thought and thought, and then, when it was dark, he had stolen out into the park as far as the four pines, and smoked, and looked up at the stars and wondered if Maude were there with Jack, sitting on the golden seat by the river. Then, going back to the house when no one saw him, he went into the room where Maude was lying, and looked long and earnestly upon her white, still face, and wondered in a vague kind of way if she knew he was there, and why he had never thought before what a nice kind of girl she was, and why he had not made more of her as her brother.

"Maude," he whispered, with a lump in his throat, "if you can hear me, I'd like to tell you I am sorry that I was ever mean to you, and I guess I did like you more than I supposed."

Then he kissed her pale forehead and went to his room, where he smoked the night through, and in the morning felt as if he had lived a hundred years since the previous night, and wondered how he should get through the day. It occurred to him that it might be the proper thing to see his mother ; and after breakfast he went to her room, and was received by her with a burst of tears and reproaches for his indifference and lack of feeling in keeping himself away from everybody, as if it were nothing to him that Maude was dead, or that there was nothing for him to do.

"Thunderation, mother !" Tom exclaimed, "would you have me yell and scream, and make a fool of myself ? I sat up all night long, which was more than you did, and I've been meditating in the woods, and have seen Maude and made it square with her. What more can I do ?"

"You can see to things," Mrs. Tracy replied. "Your father is all broken up and has gone to bed, and it is not becoming in me to be around. Somebody must take the helm."

"And somebody has," Tom answered her. "Uncle Arthur is master of ceremonies now. He is running the ranch, and running it well, too."

And Tom was right, for Arthur had taken the helm, and aided and abetted by Jerrie, was quietly attending to matters and arranging for the funeral, which Dolly said must be in the house, as she would not go to the church with a gaping crowd to stare at her. So it was to take place at the house on Friday afternoon, and Arthur ordered a costly coffin from New York, and nearly a car-load of flowers and floral designs, for Jerrie had explained to him Maude's wishes with regard to her grave, which they lined first with the freshest of the boughs from the four pines, filling these again with flowers up to the very top, so that the grave when finished seemed like one mass of flowers, in which it would not be hard to lie.

Dolly had objected to Billy as one of the pall-bearers. He was too short, she said, and not at all in harmony with Dick, and Fred, and Paul Crosby, the young man who, in Harold's absence, had been asked to take his place. But

Arthur overruled her with the words, "It was Maude's wish," and Billy kept his post.

The day arrived, and the hour, and the people came in greater crowds than they had done when poor Jack was buried, or the dark woman, Nannine, with only Jerrie as chief mourner, and the procession was the longest ever seen in Shannondale ; and Dolly, even while her heart was aching with bitter pain, felt a thrill of pride that so many were following her daughter to the grave.

Arrived at the cemetery, there was a halt for the mourners to alight and the bearers to take the coffin from the hearse—a halt longer than necessary, it seemed to Jerrie, who did not see the young man making his way through the ranks of people crowding the road, and straining every nerve to reach the hearse, which he did just as the bearers were taking the coffin from it.

With a quick movement he put Paul Crosby aside, saying, apologetically :

"Excuse me, Paul. I must carry Maude to her grave. She wished it."

Even then Jerrie did not see him or dream that he was there, but when toward the close of the service she took a step or two forward to look into the grave before it was filled up, and he put a hand upon her shoulder and said, "Not too near, Jerrie," she started suddenly, with a suppressed cry, and turning, saw him standing by her, tall, and erect, and self-possessed, as he faced the multitude, some of whom had suspected him of crime, but all of whom were ready now to do him justice and bid him welcome home.

"Oh, Harold," Jerrie said, as she grasped his arm, "I am so glad you are here. I wish you had come before."

Harold could not reply, for they were now leaving the spot, and many gathered around him ; first and foremost Peterkin, who came tramping through the grass, puffing like an engine, and, unmindful of the time or place, slapping him upon the shoulder, as he said :

"Well, my boy, glad to see you back, 'pon my soul, I be ; but you've flustrated all my plans. I was meanin' to give you an oblation ; got it all arranged, and you spiled it by takin' us onawares, like a thief in the night. I beg your pardon," he continued, as he met a curious look in

Harold's eyes. "I'm a blunderin' cuss, I be. I didn't mean nothin'. I've never meant nothin' and if I hev I'm sorry for it."

Harold did not hear the last, for he was handing Jerrie into the carriage with her father, who bade him enter, too, saying they would leave him at the cottage where he wished to go as soon as possible. There was no time for much conversation before the cottage was reached, and Harold alighted at the gate, and no allusion whatever was made to Jerrie's changed relations until Harold stood looking at her as she kept her seat by her father, and made no sign of an intention to stop. Then he said, as calmly as he could:

"Do you stay at the Park House altogether now?"

"Oh, no," she answered, quickly. "I have been there a great deal with Maude, but am coming home to-night. I could not leave grandma alone, you know."

She acknowledged the home and the relationship still, and Harold's face flushed with a look of pleasure, which deepened in intensity when Arthur, with a wave of the hand habitual to him, said:

"I must keep her now that you are here to see to the grandmother, but will let you have her to-night. Come up later, if you like, and walk home with her."

"I shall be most happy to do so," Harold said, and then the carriage drove away, while he went in to his grandmother, who had not attended the funeral, but who knew that he had returned, and was waiting for him.

CHAPTER LI.

UNDER THE PINES WITH HAROLD.

IT seemed to Harold that it had been a thousand years since he left Shannondale, so much had come into and so much had gone out of his life since he said good-by to the girl he loved and to the girl who loved him. One was dead, and he had only come in time to help lay her in her grave; while the other, was, some might think, farther removed from him than death itself could have removed her.

But Harold did not feel so. He had faith in Jerrie—that she would not change, and when he read the Judge's letter in the privacy of his room at the Tacoma, he rejoiced with an exceeding great joy that her home and birthright had been so strangely restored. He never doubted the story for a moment, but felt rather as if he had known it always, and wondered how any one could have imagined for a moment that blue-eyed, golden-haired Jerrie was the child of the dark, coarse looking woman found dead beside her. " I am so glad for Jerrie," he said, without a thought that her relations to himself would in any way be changed.

Once when she had told him of the fancies which haunted her so often, he had put them from him with a fear that, were they true, Jerrie would be lost to him forever. But he had no such misgivings now ; and when Jerrie's letter came, urging his return, both for her own sake and Maude's, he wrote a few hurried lines telling her how glad he was for her, and of his intention to start for the East as soon as possible. " To-morrow, perhaps," he wrote, " in which case I may be there before this letter reaches you, for the mails are sometimes slow, and the Judge's communication was overdue three or four days."

Starting the second day after his letter, Harold traveled day and night, while something seemed beckoning him on ; and when, between St. Paul and Chicago, there came a detention from a freight car off the track, he felt that he must fly, so sure was he that he was wanted and anxiously looked for at Tracy Park, where at that very time Maude was dying. The next afternoon he left Chicago, and with no further accident reached Shannondale just as the long procession was winding its way to the cemetery.

He had heard from an acquaintance in Springfield that Maude was dead, and of her request that he should be one of the pall-bearers, together with Dick, and Fred, and Billy. " And I will do it yet," he said, with a throb of pain, as he thought of the little girl who had died believing that he loved her. Once or twice he had resolved to write and tell her as carefully as possible of her mistake, but as often had changed his mind, thinking to wait until she was better ; and now she was dead, and the chance for explanation gone forever; but he would, if possible, carry out the wish she had expressed with regard to himself.

Striking into the fields from the station, he reached the cemetery in time to take his place by Billy; and then he looked for Jerrie, and felt an indefinable thrill when he saw her on her father's arm, and began to realize that she was Jerrie Tracy. But all that was over now; he had talked with her face to face, and had found her the same Jerrie he had always known, and he was going to see her in her own home at Tracy Park—the daughter of the house, the heiress of Arthur Tracy, and of more than two millions, it was said—for, despite Frank's extravagance, all of which Arthur had met without a protest, his money had accumulated rapidly, so that he was a much richer man now than when he first came home from Europe.

Harold found the family at dinner, Mr. and Mrs. Tracy and Tom in the dining-room, and Arthur and Jerrie in the Gretchen room, to which he was taken at once.

"Come in—come in, my boy. You are just in time for dessert," Arthur said, rising with alacrity and going forward to meet him; while Jerrie, too, arose and took his hand, and made him sit by her, and questioned him of his journey, and helped him to the fairest peach and the finest bunch of grapes, and felt so proud of him, and of her father, too, as they talked together; and Harold showed no sign of any inequality, even if he felt it, which he did not.

"A fine young man, with the best of manners, and carries himself as if he were the lord high chancellor," Arthur said, when, after dinner, Harold left them to pay his respects to the other inmates of the family, whom he found just leaving the dining-room.

Dolly bowed to him coldly at first, and was about to pass on, when, with a burst of tears, she offered him her hand, and said:

"Oh, Harold, why didn't you come before? Maude wanted to see you so badly."

This was a great deal for Dolly, and Tom stared at her in amazement, while Harold explained that he had come as soon as he possibly could, and tried to say something of Maude, but could not, for the tears which choked him. Frank was unfeignedly glad to see him, and told him so.

"Our dear little girl was fond of you, Hal. I am sure

she was, and I shall always like you for that. Heaven bless you, my boy," he said, as he wrung Harold's hand and then hurried away after his wife, leaving Harold alone with Tom, who, awfully afraid he should break down, said, indifferently:

"Glad to see you Hal. Wish you had come before Maude died. She was in a tearin' way to see you. Have a cigar? Got a prime lot in my room. Will you go there?"

Harold was in no mood for cigars, and, declining Tom's offer, sauntered awhile around the grounds, where he found himself constantly expecting to find the dead girl sitting under a tree waiting for him with the light whose meaning he now knew kindling in her beautiful eyes as she bade him welcome. He was glad now that he had not written and told her of her mistake, and he felt in his heart a greater tenderness for the Maude dead than he ever could have felt for the Maude living.

It was beginning to grow dark when he returned to the house, where he found Jerrie in the hall ready to go home. Arthur was at her side, with his arm thrown lovingly around her, and as he passed her over to Harold, he said:

"Make the most of her to-night, my boy, for to-morrow she comes home to stay."

For a time Harold and Jerrie walked on in silence, but when they reached the four pines, Jerrie halted suddenly and said:

"Let us sit down, Harold. I have a message from Maude, which I promised to deliver the first time we were alone together after you came home."

Jerrie's voice trembled a little, and after they were seated she was silent until Harold said to her:

"You were going to tell me of Maude;" then she started and replied:

"Yes; she wanted so much to see you and tell you herself. I don't know what she meant, but she said she had made a mistake, and I must tell you so, and that you would understand it. She had been thinking and thinking, she said, and knew it was a stupid blunder of hers; that was what she called it—a stupid blunder; and she was sorry for you that she had made it, and bade me say so, and tell you no one knew but herself and you. Dear little Maude! I wish she had not died."

Jerrie was crying, and perhaps that was the reason she did not mind when Harold put his arm around her and drew her so close to him that his brown hair touched her golden curls, while the pines moaned and sighed above them for a moment, and then grew still, as if listening for what Harold would say.

"Yes," he began slowly, "I think I know what Maude meant by the mistake. Did she say I must tell you what it was?"

"She said you would tell me, but perhaps you'd better not," Jerrie replied.

"Yes, I must tell you," he continued, "as a preliminary to what I have to say to you afterward, and what I did not mean to say quite so soon; but this decides me," and he drew Jerrie closer to him as he went on: "Did you ever think that I loved Maude?"

"Yes, I have thought so," was Jerrie's answer.

"She thought so, too," Harold continued, "and it was all my fault, not hers. She was so sweet and good, and so interested in you and all I wanted to do for you, that I regarded her as a very dear friend, nothing more. And because I looked upon her this way, I foolishly went to her once to confess my love for another, and ask if she thought I had a chance for success. I must have bungled strangely, for she mistook my meaning and thought I was speaking of herself, and in a way she accepted me; and before I had time to explain, her mother came in and I have never seen her since. That is what Maude meant. She saw the mistake and wished to rectify it by giving me the chance to tell you myself what I wanted to tell you then and dared not."

Jerrie trembled violently, but made no answer, and Harold went on:

"It may seem strange that I, who used to be so much afraid of Jerrie Crawford that I dared not tell her of my love, have the courage to do it now that she is Jerrie Tracy, and I do not understand it myself. Once, when you told me your fancies concerning your birth, a great fear took possession of me, lest I should lose you, if they were true; but when I heard that they were true, I felt so sure of you that I could scarcely wait for the time when I could ask you, as I now do, to be my wife, poor as I am, with nothing but love to give you. Will you, Jerrie?"

His face was so close to hers now that her hot cheeks touched his, but she made no reply for a moment, and then she said :

"Oh, Harold, it seems so soon, with Maude only buried to-day.　What shall I say ?　What ought I to say ?"

"Shall I tell you ?" he answered.　"Say the first English word you ever spoke, and which I taught you.　Do you remember it ?"

"*Ess !*" came involuntarily from Jerrie, in the quick lisping accent of her babyhoood, when that was all the English she could master ; and almost before it had escaped her, Harold smothered it with the kisses he pressed upon her lips as he claimed her for his own.

"But, Harold," she tried to explain between his kisses, "I meant that I *did* remember.　You must not—you must not kiss me so fast.　You take my breath away.　There !　I won't stand it any longer.　I'm going straight home to tell grandma how you act !"

"And so am I," Harold said, rising as she did, but keeping his arm around her as they went slowly along in the soft September night, with the stars, which were shining for the first time on Maude's grave, looking down upon them, and a thought of Maude in their hearts, and her dear name often upon their lips, as they talked of the past, trying to recall just when it was that friendship ceased and love began, and deciding finally that neither knew nor cared when it was, so great was their present joy and anticipation of the future.

CHAPTER LII.

"FOR BETTER, FOR WORSE."

"GRANDMA, Jerrie has promised to be my wife !" Harold said to his grandmother that night, and "Father, I have promised to marry Harold," Jerrie said to Arthur the next morning as she stood before him, with Harold's hand in hers, and a look in her face something like what Gretchen's had worn when Arthur first called her his wife,

"Lord bless you, I knew it was coming, but didn't think it would be quite so soon. You shock my nerves dreadfully," Arthur exclaimed, springing up and walking two or three times across the room. Then, confronting the young couple, he said, "Going to marry Harold? I knew you would all the time. Well, he will do as well as any one to look after the business. Frank is no good, and Colvin is too old. So, get married at once, within a week if you like. I'm off for Germany next month, to find Gretchen's grave, and the house, and the picture, and everything, and as I shall take you with me I shall need some one with brains to look after things while I am gone."

"But father," Jerrie began, "if I go to Germany, Harold will go, too, and if he stays here, I shall stay."

Arthur looked at her inquiringly a moment, and then, as he began to understand, replied:

"Ah, yes, I see; 'where thou goest, I go, and where thou—and so forth, and so forth. Well, all right; but you must be married here in your father's house, and soon too. I'll engage passage at once in the Germanic, which sails the 15th of October, and you shall be married the 10th. That's three weeks from to-day, and will give you a few days in New York. I'll leave Frank here till we return, and then he must go, of course, and the new mistress step in with Mrs. Crawford to superintend. We will get some nice man and woman to stay with her while we are gone."

He had settled everything rapidly, but Jerrie had something to say upon the subject. She did not wish to come to Tracy Park altogether while Mrs. Tracy was there, she said, and preferred to be married in the cottage, the only home she had ever known.

"I shall stay with you all day," she continued, "but go home at night."

"And so have a long walk with Harold. Yes, I see," Arthur said, laughingly, but assenting finally to her proposal.

It was Jerrie now who planned everything, with Harold's assistance, and who broached the subject of Frank's future to her father, asking what provision he intended to make for him when he left Tracy Park.

"What provision?" Arthur said. "I guess he has made provision for himself all these years, when my purse

has been as free to him as myself. Colvin tells me there
has been an awful lot of money spent somewhere."

" Yes," Jerrie replied, "but you gave him permission
to spend it, and it would hardly be fair now to leave him
with little or nothing, and he so broken down. When
Maude thought she was going to die, and before she knew
who I was, she wrote a letter for her father and you, asking
him to give me what he would have given her, and you to
do the same. So, now, I want you to give Maude's father
what you would have given me for Maude's sake."

" Bless my soul, Jerrie !" Arthur said. " What a beggar you are ! I don't know what I should have given you ;
all I am worth, perhaps. How much will satisfy you for
Frank ? Tell me, and it is done."

Jerrie thought one hundred thousand dollars would not
be any too much, nor did it seem so to Arthur, who placed
but little value upon his money, and Jerrie was deputed to
tell her uncle what provision was to be made for him, and
that, if he wished, he was to remain at the park until his
brother's return from Europe.

Frank was not in his own room, but Mrs. Tracy was,
and to her Jerrie first communicated the intelligence that
she was to be married and go with her father to Germany.
The look which the highly scandalized lady gave her was
wonderful, as she said :

" Married ! almost before the crape is off the door, or
the flowers wilted on Maude's grave ! Well, that shows
how little we are missed ; and I am not surprised, though
I think Maude would be, at Harold, certainly. I suppose
you know there was something between them ; but a man
will do anything for money. I wish you joy of your husband."

Jerrie was too indignant to explain anything, and hurried off in quest of her uncle, whom she found in Maude's
room, where he spent the most of his time, walking up and
down and examining the different articles which had belonged to his daughter, and which, at his request, remained
untouched as she had left them. Her brushes, her comb,
her bottle of perfumery, her work-box, her Bible, a little
half-finished sketch, and the soft bed-slippers she had worn
when she died, and one of which he held in his hand when
Jerried went in to him.

"It is so like Maude," he said, with quivering lips, "and when I hold it in my hand I can almost hear the dear little feet, which I know are cold and dead, coming along the hall as she used to come, and will never come again. I think I should like to die here in this room and go where Maude has gone, and I believe I should go there. I am sure God has forgiven me, and Maude forgave me, too, for I told her."

"You did! I thought so," Jerrie said.

"Yes, I had to tell her," he continued, "and I am glad I did, and she loved me just the same. You saw her die. You heard what she said to me. She must have believed in me, and that keeps me from going mad. I told Dolly, too, and she said she'd never speak to me again as long as she lived, and she didn't either until last night, when I was alone in here, crying on Maude's bed; then she came to me and called me Frank, and said she was sorry she had been so hard, and asked me what we were going to do. I'm sure I don't know; do you?"

He was so like a child in his appeal to her, that Jerrie's tears came fast as she told him of her approaching marriage and what her father intended doing for him. Then Frank broke down entirely.

"I don't deserve it, and I know I owe it to you, whom I have injured so much," he said, while Jerrie tried to comfort him.

"I must go back now to father," she said at last; and she went out into the hall, where she encountered Tom just coming from his mother's room.

"Hallo!" Tom cried, with an attempt at a smile; "and so you are going to marry Harold?"

"Yes, Tom; I'm going to marry Harold," Jerrie replied, unhesitatingly, as she laid her hand on Tom's arm and walked with him down the stairs.

It seemed to her the most natural thing in the world that she should marry Harold, and she was not at all abashed in speaking of it to Tom; and when they saw Harold coming up the walk, the color rushed to her cheeks, and her eyes grew wondrously bright with the love-light which shone in them, as she dropped Tom's arm and hurried to Harold's side.

"By George, I b'lieve I'll go and hang myself!" Tom

said, under his breath, as he stalked moodily away; but
instead of that he went across the fields to Le Bateau,
where he sat for an hour, talking with old Peterkin and
waiting for Ann Eliza, who had gone to Springfield, her
father said, after a new gown, for which he was to pay two
hundred dollars.

"Think on't!" he continued. "When we was fust
married and run the 'Liza Ann, the best gown May Jane
had to her back was a mercener or balzarine—dummed if I
know what you call it—at one and ninepence a yard; but
now, lord land, what's a two hundred dollar gownd to me!
Ann Eliza can have forty on 'em, if she wants to. There
she is; there's the kerridge! By gosh, though, ain't she a
neat little filly!" and the father's face glowed with pride as
he watched his daughter alighting from the carriage, to
which Tom had hastened in order to assist her, for she was
still a little lame and limped as she walked.

He saw the two hundred dollar gown, for Peterkin would
have it displayed, and admired it, of course, and wished
that he had half the sum it cost in his own right, and wondered if he could stand it, as he walked slowly home, where
he heard from his mother that they were still to remain at
Tracy Park for a while, and that his father was to have one
hundred thousand dollars settled upon him.

"I guess now I'll wait a spell, and let old Peterkin go
to thunder," he decided, and for two weeks and more Ann
Eliza watched in vain for his coming, while Peterkin remarked to his wife that if Tom Tracy was goin' to play fast
and loose with his gal, he'd find himself brought up standin'
mighty lively.

The news that Harold and Jerrie were soon to be married, and go with Arthur to Germany, created some surprise
and some talk, too, in town, where many of the people had
believed that there had been an understanding, if not an
engagement, between Harold and Maude. But Tom put
that right with a few decided words. There had never
been an engagement, he said. Maude had liked Harold
very much, and he had liked her, but had always preferred
Jerrie; in short, matters had been as good as settled
between them long ago.

This last was a little fiction of Tom's brain, but the
people accepted it as true, and began to look eagerly for-

ward to the approaching marriage, which took place in Mrs. Crawford's parlor, with only a few intimate friends present—Grace Atherton, the St. Claires, Ann Eliza Peterkin, and the Tracys, with the exception of Dolly, who could not do so great violence to her feelings as to attend a wedding. Billy was not there, but he sent a magnificent emerald ring to Jerrie, with the following note :

"DEAR JERRIE: I can't see you married, although I am glad for you, and glad for Hal. God bless you both. I shall never forget you as long as I live ; and when you come back, maybe I can bear to see you as Hal's wife, but now it would kill me. Good-by."

Jerrie read this note with wet eyes, and then passed it to Harold, to whom she told of that episode under the butternut tree, when Billy asked her to be his wife.

"I am awful sorry for him, but I can't let him have you, Jerrie," Harold said, passing the note back to her, and kissing her tenderly, as he added : "That is my last for Jerry Tracy, my little girl of the carpet-bag. When I kiss you again, you will be my wife."

"Come children, we are waiting," came with startling distinctness from Arthur at the foot of the stairs, and then Harold and Jerrie went down to the parlor, where they were soon made one, Arthur giving the bride away, and behaving pretty well under the circumstances.

He had been very flighty the day before, insisting that Jerrie should be married in white, with a blue ribbon on her bonnet, just as Gretchen had been, and when she reminded him of Maude's recent death, he replied :

"Well, Gretchen will wear colors if you don't." And he brought out and laid upon his bed the dress, which had been waiting for Gretchen on that stormy night when he heard the wild cry of the dying woman above the wintry gale. She was with him again in fancy, and when he went out to the carriage which was to take him to the cottage, he stepped back and stood a moment by the door as if to let some one enter before him, and during the ceremony those nearest to him heard him whispering to himself, "I, Arthur, take thee, Gretchen," and so forth ; but when it was over he seemed perfectly rational, as he kissed his daughter and shook hands with his son-in-law, to whom he

gave a check for ten thousand dollars, saying as he did so
that young men must have a little spending money.

It was a very pleasant wedding, and every one seemed
happy, even to Dick, whose spirits, however, were rather
too gay to be quite natural, and whose voice shook a little
as he called Jerrie Mrs. Hastings and told her he hoped to
see her in Paris in the spring as he thought of going over
there with Nina to join the Raymonds.

"Oh, I hope you will! Nothing could make me so
happy as to meet you there," Jerrie said, looking at him
with an expression which told him she was thinking of the
pines and was sorry for him.

The newly married pair were going directly to New
York, where Arthur was to join them on the 14th, as the
Germanic sailed the 15th.

All the wedding guests accompanied them to the
station, Tom accepting a seat in the coupe with Ann Eliza,
who wore her two hundred dollar gown, and was, of course,
overdressed. But Tom did not think much about that. He
was ill at ease that morning, though trying to seem natural ;
and when the train which took Jerrie away disappeared
from view, he felt as if every thing which had made life desirable had left him forever, and he cared but little now
what he did, or with whom his lot was cast.

So when Ann Eliza said to him, "It is such a fine day ;
suppose we drive along the river ; it may dispel the blues,"
he assented, and soon found himself bowling along the
smooth turnpike with Ann Eliza, whom he thought rather
interesting, with the tears shed for Jerrie on her long, light
eyelashes.

"I shall miss her so much, and be so lonely without
her. I hope you'll call often," she said to him, when at
last the drive was over, and Tom promised that he would,
and kept his promise, too ; for after Arthur left, he found
Tracy Park so insupportably dull, with his father always
in Maude's room, and his mother always in tears, that it
was a relief to go to Le Bateau and be made much of as if
he were a prince, and treated to nice little lunches and
suppers, even if old Peterkin did make one of the party
and disgust him so at times that he felt as if he must
snatch up his hat and fly.

And one night, when the old man had been more than

19

usually disagreeable and pompous, he did start up abruptly and leave the house, mentally vowing never to enter it again.

"I'd rather saw wood than listen to that infernal old brag," he was saying to himself, when he heard a wheezy sound behind him, and looking around saw the old brag in full pursuit, and beckoning him to stop.

"I'm goin' to walk a spell with you," he said, locking his arm in Tom's as he came up. "I want to have a talk."

"Yes," Tom faltered, with a dreadful sinking of the heart, while Peterkin went on:

"You see you've been a comin' to Lubbertoo off and on for mighty nigh a month, and as the parent of a family it's time I as't your intentions."

"Intentions!" Tom stammered, trying to draw his arm from Peterkin's.

But he might as well have tried to wrench it from a vise, for Peterkin held it fast and went on:

"Yes, intentions! Thunderation, hain't a chap 'sposed to have intentions when he hangs round a gal who has money, like my Ann 'Liza? I tell you what, Thomas," and his manner became very insinuating and frank, "as nigh as I can calkerlate I'm worth three millions, fair and square, and there's three on 'em to divide it amongst—May Jane, Bill, and Ann 'Liza. Now, s'posin' we say, threes into three million, don't it leave a million?"

Tom acknowledged that it did, and Peterkin continued:

"Jess so. Now I aint one of them mean skunks that wants his folks to wait till he's dead afore they enjoys themselves; and the day my Ann 'Liza is married, I plank down a million in hard cash for her and her husband to do what they darned please with; cut a dash in Europe as Hal is doin', if they like, or cut a splurge to hum, it's all one to me. I call that square, don't you?

Tom admitted that he did, and Peterkin went on:

"Now, then, I ain't a goin' to have Ann 'Liza's affections trifled with, and if I catch a feller a doin' on't d'ye know what I'll do?"

Tom could not guess, and Peterkin continued:

"I'll lick him within an inch of his life, and then set the dogs on him, and heave him inter the river! See?"

It was not a warm day, but Tom was perspiring at every

pore as he saw presented to him the choice between a million or to be " licked within an inch of his life and then dogged into the river." Naturally he chose the first as the lesser evil of the two, and began to lie as he had never lied in his life before. He was very glad, he said, that Peterkin had broached the subject, as it made matters easier for him by showing him that his suit would not be rejected, as he had feared it might be.

"You know, of course, Mr. Peterkin," he said, "that I am now a poor young man, with no expectations whatever, for though Uncle Arthur has settled something upon father, I cannot depend upon that, and how could I dare to look as high as your daughter without some encouragement?"

"Encouragement, boy? Great Scott!" and releasing Tom's arm, Peterkin hit him a friendly slap, which nearly knocked him down. "Great Scott! What do you call encouragement? When a gal is so flustified at seein' you, that she teters right up and down, while her mother hunts heaven and earth for tit-bits to tickle your palate with—quail on toast, mushrooms, sweet breads, and the Lord knows what—ain't that a sign they are willin'? Thunder and guns! what would you have? Ann 'Liza can't up and say, 'Marry me, Tom;' nor I can't up and say, 'Thomas, marry my daughter,' can I? But if you want to marry her, say so like a man, and I swan I'll meet you like a man, and a father!"

Alas for Tom! he had nothing left him to do except to say that he wished to marry Ann Eliza, and that he would come the next evening and tell her so.

It was Peterkin who answered his ring when he presented himself at the door of Le Bateau, Peterkin more inflated and pompous than ever as he shook the young man's hand, calling him Thomas, and telling him to go right into the parlor, where he would find Ann 'Liza waitin' for him. and where they could bill and coo as much as they liked, for he and May Jane would keep out of the way and give 'em a chance.

Even then Tom cast one despairing glance toward the door, with a half resolve to bolt; but Peterkin was behind him, pushing him on to his fate, which, after all, was not so very bad when he came to face it. There was nothing low, or mean, or coarse about Ann Eliza, who was by no means ill looking, as she stood up to receive her lover, with a droop in her eyes, and a flush on her cheeks; for she knew the object of his visit, into which he plunged at once. He did not say that he loved her, but he asked her in a straightforward way to be his wife, and then waited for her answer, which was not long in coming, for Ann Eliza was no dissembler. She loved Tom Tracy with her whole soul, and felt herself honored in being sought by him.

"Oh, Tom!" she said, "it does not seem possible for you to love me, but, if you really do, I will be your wife and try to make you happy, and—and—"

She hesitated a moment, and then went on:

"Save you as much as possible from father. We cannot live here; you and he would not get on; he means well and is the kindest of fathers to me, but he is not like you, and we must go away."

She was really a very sensible girl, Tom thought, and in his joy at finding her so sensible he stooped and kissed her forehead as the proper thing for him to do, while she, the poor little mistaken girl, threw herself into his arms and began to cry, she was so glad and happy.

Tom did not know exactly what he ought to do. It was a novel situation for him to be in, with a girl sobbing on his bosom, and his first impulse was to push her off; but when he remembered that she represented a million of dollars, he did what half the men in the world would have done in his place: he held her close and tried to quiet her, and told her he was not half good enough for her, and knew in his heart he was telling the truth, and felt within him the stirring of a resolve that she should never know he did not love her, and that he would make her happy, if he could.

And so they were betrothed, and Peterkin came in with May Jane and made a speech half an hour long to his future son-in-law, and settled just when they were to be married and what they were to do.

Christmas week was the time, and he vowed he'd give 'em a wedding which should take the starch entirely out of Gusty Browne, whose mother, Mrs. Rossiter-Browne, would think Gusty was never married at all when she saw what he could do. Greatly he lamented that Harold and Jerrie could not be present. "But they'll see it in the papers,"

he said, "for I'll have a four-column notice, if I write it
myself and pay for it, too! And when you meet 'em in
Europe you can tell 'em what they missed."

To all this Tom listened with great drops of cold sweat
running down his back as he thought of the ridicule he
should incur if Peterkin carried out his intentions to "take
the rag off the bush," as he expressed it. The trip to Europe pleased him, but the party filled him with horror from
which he saw no escape, and he was anything but a happy
man, when he at last said good-by to Peterkin, who slipped
into his hand a check for $2,000, saying, when he protested
against taking it:

"Don't be a fool, Thomas. I'm to be your dad, so take
it; you'll need it. I know your circumstances; they ain't
what they was, and I don't s'pose you've got enough to buy
the engagement ring. I want a big one. A solitary—no
cluster for me. I know what 'tis to be poor. Take it,
Thomas."

So Tom took it with a sense of shame which prompted
him several times to tear it in shreds and throw them to
the winds. But this he did not do, for he knew he should
need money, as he had none of his own; and when, a few
days before, he had asked Colvin for some, that worthy man,
who had never taken kindly to him, had bidden him go to
a very warm place for money, as he had no orders to give
him any.

"Your uncle," he said, "settled one hundred thousand
dollars on your father—the more fool he—and expects
him to live on it. So my advice to you is that you go to
work."

Now, Tom couldn't work, and after a little, Peterkin's
gift did not seem so very humiliating to him, although he
could not bring himself to tell his mother of it when he
announced his engagement to her, which he did bluntly,
and with nothing apologetic in his manner or speech.

"I am going to marry Ann Eliza Peterkin some time
during the holidays, and start at once for Europe," he said,
and then brought some water and dashed it in her face, for
she immediately went into hysterics and declared herself
dying.

When she grew calm, Tom swore a little, and talked a
good deal, and told her about the million, which he said

was not to be sneezed at, and told her what Colvin had said to him, and asked what the old Harry he was to do if he didn't marry Ann Eliza, and told her of the proposed party, asking her to save him from it if she could.

When she found she could not help herself, Dolly rose to the situation, and said she would see her daughter-in-law elect, whom Tom was to bring to her, as she could not think of calling at La Bateau in her present state of affliction. So Ann Eliza came over, and her mother came with her. But the latter Dolly declined to see. She could not endure everything, she said to Tom, and was only equal to Ann Eliza, whom she met with a bow and the tips of her fingers, without rising from her chair. Still, as the representative of a million, Ann Eliza was entitled to some consideration, and Dolly motioned her to a seat beside her, and with her black-bordered handkerchief to her eyes, said to her :

"Tom tells me you are going to marry him, and I trust you will try to make him happy. He is a most estimable young man now, and if he should develop any bad habits, I shall think it owing to some new and bad influence brought to bear upon him."

"Yes'm," Ann Eliza answered, timidly ; and the great lady went on to talk of family, and blood, and position, as something for which money could not make amends, and to impress upon the girl a sense of the great honor it was to be a member of the Tracy family.

Then she spoke of the wedding party, which she trusted Ann Eliza would prevent, as nothing could be in worse taste when they were in such affliction, adding, that neither herself nor Mr. Tracy could think of being present.

"Be married quietly, without any display, if you wish to please me," she said ; and with a wave of her handkerchief she signified that the conference was ended.

"Well, Annie, how did you and my lady hit it ?" Tom asked, meeting Ann Eliza in the hall as she came out, flushed and hot from the interview.

"We didn't hit it at all," Ann Eliza replied, with a gleam in her eye which Tom had never seen before. "She just talked as 'f I were dirt, and that you were only marrying me for my money. She don't like me, and I don't like her, there !" and the indignant little girl began to cry,

Tom laughed immoderately, and, passing his arm around her as they went down the stairs, he said :

"Of course you don't like her. Who ever did like her mother-in-law? But you are marrying me, not my mother, so don't cry, *petite.*"

Tom was making an effort to be very kind, and even lover-like to his fiancée, who was easily comforted, and who, on her return to Le Bateau told her father plainly that the party must be given up, as it would be out of place and deeply offend the Tracys. Very unwillingly Peterkin gave it up, and sent word to that effect to Mrs. Rossiter-Browne, who had already been apprised of the coming event and was having a wonderful gown made for the occasion.

"I find," he wrote, "that it wouldn't be at all *rachel-shay* to have a blow out whilst the family is in deep black; but when they git into lavender, and the young folks is home from their tower, I'll have a tearer."

Peterkin tried two or three times to see Mrs. Tracy, but she put him off with one excuse after another, until Tom took the matter in hand and told her she was acting like a fool and putting on quite too many airs. Then she appointed an interview, and, bracing herself with a tonic, went down to the darkened, cheerless room, and by her manner so managed to impress him with her superiority over him and his that he forgot entirely the speech he had prepared with infinite pains, and which had in it a good deal about family *bonds*, and family *units*, and *Aaron's beard*, and brotherly love. This he had rehearsed many times to May Jane, with wonderful gestures and flourishes; "but, I'll be bumped," he said to her on his return from the Park House, "if I didn't forget every blessed word, she was so high and mighty. Lord! as if I didn't know what she sprung from; but that's the way with them as was born to nothin'. May Jane, if I ever catch you puttin' on airs 'cause you're a Peterkin, I b'lieve I'll kill you!"

After this, anything like familiar intercourse ceased between the heads of the two families until the morning after Christmas Day, when Frank and Dolly drove over to Le Bateau, where were assembled the same people who had been present at Jerrie's wedding, and where Peterkin insisted upon darkening the rooms and lighting the gas, as something a little out of the usual order of things in Shannondale. Peterkin was very happy, and very proud of this alliance with the Tracys, and his pride and happiness shone in his face all through the ceremony ; and when the clergyman asked, "Who giveth this woman to be married to this man ?" his manner was something grand to see as he stepped forward and responded, "I do, sir," in a voice so loud and full of importance that Dolly involuntarily groaned, while Tom found it hard to refrain from laughing.

Tom behaved very well, and kissed his bride before any one else had a chance to do so, and called May Jane mother and Peterkin father, after he saw the papers which made Ann Eliza possessor in her own right of a million dollars ; and when, an hour later, she handed over to him as his own, a deed of property valued at one hundred thousand dollars, he took her in his arms and kissed her again, telling her what was very true, that she was worth her weight in gold. Tom had felt his poverty keenly, and all the more so that Ann Eliza's engagement-ring, a superb solitaire, had been bought with her father's gift, as had their passage tickets to Europe. But now he was a rich man, made so by his wife's thoughtful generosity, and he was conscious of a new set of feelings and emotions with regard to her, and inwardly vowed that he would make her happy.

They took the train for New York that afternoon, accompanied by Peterkin, who, when the ship sailed away next day, stood upon the wharf waving his hands and calling out as long as they could hear him, "God bless you, my children, ! God bless you, my children !" Then he went back to Shannondale and called at Tracy Park, and reported to Frank, that the youngsters had gone, and that Mrs. Thomas Tracy looked as well as the best on 'em in the ship, and a darned sight better than some !

After this the great houses of La Bateau and Tracy Park settled down into perfect quiet, especially that of Tracy Park, where Dolly shut herself up in her mourning and crape, and Frank spent most of his time in Maude's room, with her photograph in his hand, and his thoughts busy with memories of the dear little girl lying in her grave of flowers under the winter snow.

CHAPTER LIII.

AFTER TWO YEARS.

TWO years since Harold and Jerrie went away, and it was October again, and the doors and windows of the Park House were all open to the warm sunshine which filled the rooms, where the servants were flitting in and out with an air of importance and pleased expectancy, for that afternoon the master was coming home, with Harold and Jerrie; and what was more wonderful and exciting still, there was in the party a little boy, born in Wiesbaden six months before, and christened Frank Tracy. They had gone directly to Germany—Arthur, Harold, and Jerrie— for the former would not stop a day until Wiesbaden was reached; and there, overcome with fatigue and the recollections of the past which crowded upon him so fast, Arthur fell sick and was confined to his room at the hotel for a week, during which time Jerrie explored the city with Harold and a guide, finding every spot connected with Gretchen and her life, even to the shop where Frau Heinrich had sold her small wares.

As soon as her father was able, she took him to them one by one. Hand in hand, for he seemed weak as a little child, they went to the bench under the trees where he had first seen Gretchen knitting in the sunshine, with the halo on her hair, and here Arthur took off his hat as if on consecrated ground, and whispered, " May God forgive me !" then to the little shop once kept by Frau Heinrich, where Arthur astonished the woman by buying out half her stock, which he ordered sent to his hotel, and afterward gave away ; then to the English church, where he knelt before the altar and seemed to be praying, though the words he said were spoken more to Gretchen than to God ; then to the house where he had lived with his bride, when heaven came down so close that she could touch it, or, rather, to the site of the house, for fire had done its work there and they could only stand before the ruins, while Arthur said again and again, " May God forgive me !" then to the house where Jerrie had lived and Gretchen had died, and where the picture still hung upon the wall, a wonder and delight to all who had rented the place since Marian's parents lived there. Jerrie recognized it in a moment, and so did Arthur, but he could only wring his hands before it and sob, "Oh, Gretchen, my darling, my darling!" Changed as the house was Jerrie found the room, where she had played and her mother had died.

"The big stove stood here," she said, indicating the spot, "and mother sat there writing to you, when Nannine opened the door and let the firelight shine upon the paper. I can see it all so distinctly; and over there in the corner was the bed where she died."

Then Arthur knelt down upon the spot, and as if the oft-repeated ejaculation, "May God forgive me!" were wholly inadequate now, he said the Lord's Prayer, with folded hands and streaming eyes, while Jerrie stood over him, with her arm around his neck.

"Oh, Gretchen!" he cried, "do you know I am here after so many years?—Arthur, your husband, who loved you through all? Come back to me, Gretchen, and I'll be so tender and true—tender and true! My heart is breaking, Gretchen, and only for Cherry, our little girl baby, I should wish I were dead, like you. Oh, Gretchen! Gretchen! sweetest wife a man ever called his! and yet I forgot you, darling—forgot that you had ever lived! May Heaven forgive me, I could not help it; I forgot everything. Where are you, Cherry? It's getting so dark and cold, and Gretchen is not here—I think you must take me home."

Jerrie took him back to the hotel, where he kept his room for three days, and then they went to Gretchen's grave beside her mother, which Jerrie had found after some little search and inquiry. Here Arthur stood like a statue, holding fast to Jerrie, and gazing down upon the neglected grave, on which clumps of withered grass were growing and blowing in the November wind.

"Gretchen is not in this place," he said, mournfully, with a shake of his head. "She couldn't rest here a moment, for she liked everything beautiful and bright, and this is like the Potter's Field. But we'll put up a monument for her, and make the place attractive; and by and by, when she is tired of wandering about, she may come back and rest when she sees what we have done, and knows that we have been here. We will buy that house, too," he said, as he walked away from the lonely grave; and the next day Harold found the owner and commenced negotiations for the house, which soon changed hands and became the property of Arthur.

Just what he meant to do with it he did not know, until Jerrie suggested that he make it an asylum for homeless children, who should receive the kindest and tenderest care from competent and trustworthy nurses, hired for the purpose.

"Yes, I'll do it," Arthur said, "and will call it 'The Gretchen Home.' Maybe she will come there some time, and know what I have done."

This idea once in his mind, Arthur never let go of it until the house was fitted up with school-rooms and dormitories, and filled with little ones rescued from want and misery. The general supervision of this home was placed in the hands of the English rector, the Rev. James Hart, whose many acts of kindness and humanity among the poor had won for him the sobriquet of St. James, and with whom the interests of the children were safe as with a loving father.

"There is money enough," Arthur said, when giving his instructions to the matron, a good-natured woman who, he knew, would never abuse a child. "Money enough; so give them something beside bread and water for breakfast and mush and molasses for supper. Children like cookies and custard pie, and if there comes a circus to town let them go once in a while; it won't hurt them to see a little of the world."

Frau Hirch looked at him in some surprise, but promised compliance with his wishes; and when in the middle of December he left Wiesbaden for Italy he had the satisfaction of knowing that the inmates of the Gretchen Home were enjoying a bill of fare not common in institutions of the kind.

It was not difficult to find in Wiesbaden people who remembered Gretchen and the grand marriage she had made with the rich American, who afterward abandoned her. That was the way they worded it, and they remembered, too, the little girl, Jerrine, whom, after her mother's

death, the nurse, Nannine, took to her father's friends, since
which nothing had been heard from her. Thus had there
been in Arthur's mind any doubt as to Jerrie's identity it
would have been swept away; but there was none. He had
accepted her from the first as his daughter, and he always
looked up to her as a child to its mother whom it fears to
lose sight of.

The winter was mostly spent in Rome, where Harold
and Jerrie visited every part of the city, while Arthur
staid in his room talking to an unseen Gretchen, who
afforded him almost as much satisfaction as the real one
might have done. In May they went to the lakes and in
June drifted to Paris, where Jerrie was overjoyed to meet
Nina and Dick, who were staying with the Raymonds at a
charming chateau just outside the city. Here she and
Harold passed a most enjoyable week, and before she left
she was made happy by something which she saw and which
told her that Dick was forgetting that night under the pines,
and that some day not far in the future he would find in
Marian all he had once hoped to find in her. In Paris, too,
she came upon Ann Eliza at the Bon Marche, with silks
and satins piled high around her, and two or three obsequious
clerks in attendance, for La Petite Americaine, was well
known to the trades people, who eagerly sought her patronage and that of my lord monsieur, who impressed them
greatly with his air of importance and dignity. Tom was
enjoying himself immensely, and was really a good deal improved and very kind to his little wife, whom he always
addressed as Petite or Madame, and who was quite a belle
and a general favorite in the American colony. Following
a fashion, which Tom was sure had been made for his benefit,
she had cut off her obnoxious red hair and substituted in
its place a wig of reddish brown, which for naturalness and
beauty was a marvel of art and skill, and became her so well
that Tom really thought her handsome, or at least very
stylish and stunning, which was better than mere beauty.
They had a suite of rooms at the Continental, and there
Harold and Jerrie dined with them in their private parlor,
for Tom was too fine a gentleman to go to _table d' hote_
with the common herd. Ann Eliza's grand maid, Doris,
was with her still, and had come to look upon her young
mistress as quite as great a personage as the Lady Augusta

Hardy, whom she had ceased to quote, and who, with her mother, Mrs. Rossiter-Browne, was now in the city, attended, it was said, by a Polish count, who had an eye upon her money. Once, when they were alone, Jerrie asked Tom when he was going home, and, with a comical twinkle in his eye, he replied, "When I hear that my respected father-in-law has gone off with apoplexy, and not before." Jerrie thought this a shocking speech, but she was glad to see him so happy, and, as she told Harold, "so much more of a man than she had ever supposed he could be."

That summer Harold and Jerrie spent in Switzerland, with the Raymonds and St. Claires and Tracys, while Arthur went to Wiesbaden to see to the Gretchen Home, which he found so much to his taste that he remained there until Harold and Jerrie, after a trip through Austria and Germany, joined him in November, when they went again for the winter to Italy, coming back in the Spring to Wiesbaden, and because Arthur would have it so, taking up their abode for awhile in the Gretchen Home, which had been greatly enlarged and improved, and now held thirty deserted and homeless children. Here, in April, Jerrie's little boy was born, in the same room and corner where Gretchen had died, and where Arthur again went down upon his knees and said the Lord's Prayer, to which he added a fervent thanksgiving for Jerrie spared and a baby given to him.

"I hoped it would be a girl," he said, "for then we should have called it Gretchen, but as it is a boy, suppose we name it Heinrich?"

"No, father," Jerrie said, decidedly. "Baby is not to be Heinrich, or Arthur, or Harold, although I think the last the dearest name in the world," and she put up her hand caressingly to the brown beard of the tall young man bending over to kiss her pale face and look at his son. "We will call the baby Frank Tracy."

And so Frank Tracy was the name given to the child, who was more like its father than its mother, and whom Arthur called Tracy, which he liked better, he said, than he did Frank.

They remained in Wiesbaden until June, then went to Switzerland and Paris, and in October sailed for home, where the Park House was ready for them, with no mistress to dispute Jerrie's rights and no master except the lawful one. Just out of town on a grassy ridge overlooking the river, a gentleman from New York had built a pretty little cottage, which, as his wife died suddenly, he never occupied, but offered for sale, with all its furniture and appointments.

"Let's buy it," Dolly said to her husband. "We must go somewhere before Arthur comes home, and we can live there very respectably and economically, too."

She was beginning to count the cost of everything, and was almost penurious in her efforts to make their income go as far as possible. So they bought the pretty place, which she called Ridge Cottage, but Frank did not live to occupy it. After Tom went away and left him alone with his wife, who was not the most agreeable of companions, he failed rapidly, both in body and mind, and those who saw him walking about the house, with his white hair and bent form, would have said he was seventy rather than fifty years old. Every day, when the weather permitted, he visited Maude's grave, where he sometimes staid for hours, looking down upon the mound and talking to the insensible clay beneath.

"I am coming, Maude, very soon, to be here beside you," he would say. "Everybody has gone, even to Tom, and your mother is sometimes hard upon me because of what I did ; and I am tired, and cold, and old, and the world is dark and dreary, and I am coming very soon."

Then he would walk slowly back, taking the post-office on his way, to inquire for letters from the folks, as he designated the absent ones. These letters were a great comfort to him, especially those from Jerrie, who wrote him very often and told him all they were doing and seeing, and tried to make him understand how much she loved and sympathized with him. Not a hint had been given him of the baby ; and when, in June, he received a letter from her containing a photograph of the little boy named for him, he seemed childish in his joy, and started with the picture at once for Maude's grave. Kneeling down, with his face in the long grass, he whispered :

"Look, Maude !—Jerrie's baby boy, named for me— Frank Tracy ! Do you hear me, Maude ? Frank Tracy,

for me—who wronged her so. God bless Jerrie, and give
her many years of happiness when I'm dead and gone,
which will not now be long. I am coming very soon,
Maude ; sooner than you think, and shall never see Jerrie's
little boy, God bless him !"

That night Frank seemed brighter than usual, and
talked a great deal with his wife, who, to the last day of
her life, will be glad that she was kind to him and humored
all his fancies ; and once, when he lay upon the couch, with
the baby's picture in his hand, she went and sat by him
and ran her fingers caressingly through his white hair, and
asked if he were not better.

"Yes, Dolly," he said, taking her fingers in his hand
and holding them fast. "A great deal better. Jerrie's
baby has done me good, and you, too, Dolly You don't
know how nice it seems to have you smooth my hair ; it is
like the old days at Langley, when we sang in the choir together, and you were fond of me."

"I am fond of you now, Frank," Dolly replied, as she
stooped to kiss the face in which there was a look she had
never seen before, and which haunted her long after he had
said good-night and gone to Maude's room, where he said
he would sleep, as he was likely to be restless and might
keep her awake.

The next morning Dolly took her breakfast alone, for
Frank did not join her.

"Let him sleep," she said to the servant, who suggested calling him ; but when some time later, he did not
appear, she went herself to Maude's room, into which the
noonday sun was shining, for every blind and window was
open and the light was so dazzling that for a moment she
did not see the still figure stretched upon the bed, where,
with Maude's picture in one hand and Jerrie's baby's in
the other, her husband lay, calmly sleeping the sleep which
knows no waking.

On his face there was a look of rapturous joy, and on
his lips a smile as if they were framing the loved name of
Maude when death came and sealed them forever. Around
him was no sign of struggle or pain, for the covering was
not disturbed ; and the physician when he came said he
must have died quietly and possibly instantly without a
note of warning. They buried him beside his daughter and

then Doily was alone in the house, which became so intolerable to her that she left it early in August and took possession of the cottage on the Ridge, which, did not seem haunted with the ghosts of the dead.

And so it happened that Mrs. Crawford alone stood in the door-way to welcome the travelers when, late in the bright October afternoon they came, tired and dusty, but so glad to be home once more and to feel that now it really was home to all intents and purposes.

"I was never so glad in my life, and if Uncle Frank were here I should be perfectly happy," Jerrie cried, as she threw herself upon Mrs. Crawford's neck, hugging and kissing her awhile, and then taking her baby from the nurse she put it into the old lady's arms, saying as she did so:

"Another grandson for you—Harold's baby. Isn't he a beauty?"

And little Tracy was a beautiful child, with his father's features and complexion, but Jerrie's expression and ways, and Mrs. Crawford felt, as she folded him to her bosom, that he would be the crowning joy of her old age. At first Harold puzzled and perplexed her, he was so changed from the Harold who had shingled roofs and painted barns and worked in Peterkin's furnace. Foreign travel and prosperity set well upon him, and one could scarcely have found a more refined or polished young man than Harold as he moved about the premises, with a smile and pleasant word for every one, whether of high or low degree. He had known what poverty meant, with slights on account of it, and had risen above it all, and remembering the days when he worked in the Tracy fields and envied his companions their leisure and freedom from toil, he had resolved that, if possible, some portion of mankind should be happier because of him.

All Shannondale hastened to call upon the travelers, and no one was louder or more demonstrative in his welcome than Peterkin, who called himself their *kin*, and was very proud of the connection and of his son *Thomas*, for whom he made many inquiries. It did not take long for the family to settle down into every-day quiet, Jerrie proving herself a competent and thorough housekeeper, while Harold was to all intents and purposes the head to whom every one

deferred and went for directions. Arthur, who had half
died from seasickness, had at once taken to his rooms and
his old mode of life, telling Harold and Jerrie to do what
they liked and not bother him. One change, however, he
made ; he put Harold into the office in the place of Colvin,
who had done his business for so many years, and who was
glad to give it up, while Harold was glad to take it, as it
gave him something to do and did not greatly interfere
with his law studies, which he immediately resumed,
applying himself so closely that he was admitted to practice
within the year, and in time became one of the ablest lawyers in the State.

For another year the Raymonds and St. Claires remained
abroad, and then, just before they sailed for home, there
was a double wedding one morning in London, when Fred
and Dick were the bridegrooms, and Marian and Nina were
the brides. Dick had not forgotten the night under the
pines, but he had ceased to remember it with pain ; and
when he asked Marian to be his wife he told her of it, and
of his old love for Jerrie, while she in turn told him of a
grave among the Alps by which she had stood with an
aching heart while strangers buried from her sight a young
artist from Boston, who, had he lived, would have made it
impossible for her to be the wife of Dick St. Claire. But
Allan was dead, and Jerrie was a wife and mother, and so
across the graves of a living and a dead love the two grasped
hands, and forgetting the past as far as possible, were content with the new happiness offered to them. Nina's home
was to be in Kentucky, but Marian staid at Grassy Spring,
and became Jerrie's most intimate friend, and a constant
visitor at Tracy Park, where she is always welcome.

.   .   .   .   .

It is five years now since Harold and Jerrie came home,
and toddling about the house is a little girl whom they call
Gretchen, and who has all the soft beauty of the Gretchen
in the picture, together with Jerrie's stronger and more
marked features. This little girl is Arthur's idol, and has
succeeded in luring him from his room, in which, until she
came, he was staying closer than ever. Now, however, he
is with her constantly, either in the house, or in the grounds,
or sitting under a tree holding her in his lap, while he talks

his strange talk to the other Gretchen, and the child listens wonderingly, with her great blue eyes fixed upon him.

"This is our grandchild," he will say. nodding to the space beside him, while little Gretchen nods, too, as if she also saw a figure sitting there. "Our grandchild, and Jerrie's baby, and you are its grandmother. Grandma Gretchen! That's funny;" and then he laughs, and baby laughs, and says after him, lispingly, "Danma Detchen, dat's funny."

Then Tracy comes up with his whip and his cart, and his straw hat hanging down his back, and Arthur points him out to the spirit Gretchen as her grandson, who, he says, is all Hastings, with a very little Tracy and not a grain of German in him, "but very nice, very nice, and you are his grandmother, too, and I am his grandfather, whom he once called an old crazy man, because I wouldn't let him play in my room with a little alligator which his Aunt Dolly—that's Mrs. Frank Tracy—sent him from Florida."

"Well, you be crazy, ain't you?" the boy says, seating himself upon the bench and nestling his brown head against the arm of the man, who replies:

"I don't know whether I am or not, but if to be very happy in the companionship of the living and of the dead, and to have one as real as the other is craziness, then I am crazy. But God is good, and when he took Gretchen from me he sent me your mother in the carpet-bag. Praised be God."

And then, for the hundredth time, he tells to the boy and to the baby, too, the story of the carpet-bag and the little girl, their mother, whom the boy, their father, found in the Tramp House one wintry morning years ago, and carried through the snow. And Tracy, who is very chivalrous and very brave, and old for his years, starts to his feet with dilating eyes and says:

"I just wish I'd been there. I'd carried mamma, and wouldn't let her drop in the snow as papa did. Where was I then, grandpa?"

But grandpa does not answer, and begins the story of the cherries and the ladder, which Tracy likes even better than that of the carpet-bag, particularly the part where the white sun-bonnet appears in the window and the shrill voice calls out : "Mr. Crazyman, Mr. Crazyman, don't you want some cherries?"

This Arthur makes very dramatic and real, and Tracy holds his breath; and sometimes, when the question is more real than usual, little Gretchen puts out her hand, and says:

"*Ess*, div me some."

Then the boy and the old man laugh and Tracy runs after a passing butterfly, and Arthur goes on with his talk to the baby, until she falls asleep, and he takes her to the crib he has had put in the bay-window under the picture which smiles down upon the sleeping infant whose guardian angel it seems to be.

The Tramp House has been repaired and renovated, the table mended, and the rat hole stopped up; and the trio frequently go there together, for it is the children's play-house, where Arthur is sometimes a horse, sometimes a bear, and sometimes a whole menagerie of animals, just as the fancy takes the restless, active Tracy. Once or twice Arthur has been the dead woman on the table, with little Gretchen beside him in the carpet-bag, and Tracy tugging with all his might to lift her out; but after the day when he let her fall, and gave her a big bump upon her forehead, that kind of play ceased, and the boy, who had inherited his mother's talent for acting was compelled to try some other make-believe than that of the tragedy on the wintry night many years before.

Billy Peterkin has never married, and never will, but he and Jerrie are the best of friends, and he is very fond of her children, whom he often takes out in his dog cart, holding Gretchen in his lap, while Tracy sits beside him with the lines, pretending to drive.

Tom is still abroad, waiting for that fit of apoplexy which is to be the signal of his return; but the probabilities are that he will wait a long time, for Peterkin, who is himself afraid of apoplexy, has gone through the Banting process, which has reduced his weight from fifty to seventy-five pounds, and as he is very careful in his diet Tom may stay abroad longer than he cares to do, unless Ann Eliza's persuasions bring him home to his dreaded father-in-law. There was a little girl born to them in Rome, whom they called Maude, but she only lived a few weeks, and then they buried her under the daisies in the Protestant burying-ground, where so many English and Americans are lying. And Eliza sent a lock of the little one's hair to her father, who had it framed and hung in his bedroom, and wore on his hat a band of crape which nearly covered it, while his wife was draped in black from head to foot, and looked, as Peterkin said, about as genteel as the widder Tracy herself.

Dolly still calls the Ridge Cottage her home, but she is not often there, for a mania for traveling has seized her, and she is always upon the move, in search of some new place, where she hopes to find rest and quiet. She still dresses in black, relieved at times with something white, but she has laid aside crape and sports her diamonds, which she did not find it necessary to sell, and which attract a great deal of attention, they are so clear and large. One year she spent in Europe with Tom and Ann Eliza, the latter of whom she made so uncomfortable with her constant dictation and assumption of superiority that Tom at last came to the rescue, and told her either to mind her business and let his wife alone, or go home. As she could not do the former she came home and joined a Raymond party to California, but soon separated herself from it, as the members were not to her taste, she said, and were constantly doing something to offend her aristocratic ideas. Every summer she goes either to Saratoga or the sea-side or the mountains, and every winter she drifts southward to Florida, where, at certain hotels, she is as well known as the oldest habitue. She has a maid, and as far as possible keeps herself aloof from the common herd, consorting only with those who she knows have money and position at home. Poor foolish Dolly, who has forgotten Langley and its humble surroundings. There are many like her in real life, but only one in our story, to which we now write

THE END.

Mary J. Holmes' Novels.

Tempest and Sunshine	$1 50	Darkness and Daylight........$1 50
English Orphans	1 50	Hugh Worthington... .... 1 50
Homestead on the Hillside....	1 50	Cameron Pride................. 1 50
'Lena Rivers	1 50	Rose Mather.................... 1 50
Meadow Brook	1 50	Ethelyn's Mistake............. 1 50
Dora Deane	1 50	Millbank 1 50
Cousin Maude	1 50	Edna Browning................. 1 50
Marian Grey	1 50	West Lawn..................... 1 50
Edith Lyle	1 50	Mildred....................... 1 50
Daisy Thornton	1 50	Forrest House................. 1 50
Chateau D'Or	1 50	Madeline...................... 1 50
Queenie Hetherton	1 50	Christmas Stories............. 1 50
Bessie's Fortune	1 50	Gretchen....(New)............. 1 50

Charles Dickens—15 Vols.—"Carleton's Edition."

Pickwick and Catalogue........$1 50	David Copperfield.............$1 50
Dombey and Son................. 1 50	Nicholas Nickleby............. 1 50
Bleak House.................... 1 50	Little Dorrit. 1 50
Martin Chuzzlewit............. 1 50	Our Mutual Friend......... ... 1 50
Barnaby Rudge—Edwin Drood. 1 50	Curiosity Shop—Miscellaneous. 1 50
Child's England—Miscellaneous 1 50	Sketches by Boz—Hard Times. 1 50
Christmas Books—Two Cities.. 1 50	Great Expectations—Italy...... 1 50
Oliver Twist—Uncommercial.. 1 50	*Full Sets* in half calf bindings..... 50 00

Marion Harland's Novels.

Alone	$1 50	At Last......................$1 50
Hidden Path	1 50	Sunnybank..................... 1 50
Moss Side	1 50	Ruby's Husband............... 1 50
Nemesis	1 50	My Little Love............... 1 50
Miriam	1 50	True as Steel....(New). 1 50

Agusta J. Evans' Novels.

Beulah	$1 75	St. Elmo.....................$2 00
Macaria	1 75	Vashti 2 00
Inez	1 75	Infelice...................... 2 00
At the Mercy of Tiberius. (New) 2 00		

Captain Mayne Reid's Works.

The Scalp Hunters	$1 50	The White Chief	$1 50
The Rifle Rangers	1 50	The Tiger Hunter	1 50
The War Trail	1 50	The Hunter's Feast	1 50
The Wood Rangers	1 50	Wild Life	1 50
The Wild Huntress	1 50	Osceola, the Seminole	1 50

Hand-Books of Society.

The Habits of Good Society—The nice points of taste and good manners. .$1 00
The Art of Conversation—For those who wish to be agreeable talkers .. 1 00
The Arts of Writing, Reading and Speaking—For Self-Improvement ... 1 00
New Diamond Edition—The above three books in one volume—small type. 1 50

Josh Billings.

His Complete Writings—With Biography, Steel Portrait and 100 Illustrations.$2 00

Arsene Houssaye.

Philosophers and Actresses—Steel portraits of Voltaire and Mme. de
   Parabère. 2 vols., per set $4 00
Men and Women of the Eighteenth Century—Steel portraits of Louis
   XV. and Mme. de Pompadour. 2 vols., per set 4 00

Annie Edwardes' Novels.

Stephen Lawrence	$1 50	A Woman of Fashion	$1 50
Susan Fielding	1 50	Archie Lovell	1 50

Ernest Renan's French Works.

The Life of Jesus. Translated	$1 75	The Life of St. Paul. Translated	$1 75
Lives of the Apostles. Do.	1 75	The Bible in India—By Jacolliot.	2 00

G. W. Carleton.

Our Artist in Cuba, Peru, Spain and Algiers—150 Caricatures of Travel.....$1 00

M. M. Pomeroy (Brick).

Sense. A serious book.	$1 50	Nonsense. (A comic book)	$1 50
Gold Dust. Do.	1 50	Brick-dust. Do.	1 50
Our Saturday Nights	1 50	Home Harmonies	1 50

Miscellaneous Works.

Carleton's Hand-Book of Popular Quotations—With their authorship....$1 50
Carleton's Classical Dictionary—A Condensed Mythology for popular use. 75
Fifty Years among Authors, Books and Publishers—By J. C. Derby.... 2 00
Children's Fairy Geography—With hundreds of beautiful illustrations.... 1 00
Carleton's Popular Readings—Edited by Anna Randall Diehl. 2 vols., each 1 50
Laus Veneris, and other Poems—By Algernon Charles Swinburne......... 1 50
Sawed-off Sketches—Comic book by "Detroit Free Press Man." Illustrated 1 50
Hawk-eye Sketches—Comic book by "Burlington Hawk-eye Man." Do. 1 50
The Culprit Fay—Joseph Rodman Drake's Poem. With 100 illustrations... 2 00
Parlor Amusements—Games, Tricks, Home Amusements, by Frank Bellew. 1 00
Love [L'Amour]—English Translation from Michelet's famous French work. 1 50
Woman [La Femme]—The Sequel to "L'Amour." Do. Do. 1 50
Verdant Green—A racy English college story. With 200 comic illustrations. 1 50
Clear Light from the Spirit World—By Kate Irving...................... 1 25
Bottom Facts Concerning Spiritualism—By John W. Truesdell 1 50
Mal Moulée—A splendid Novel, by Ella Wheeler Wilcox.................. 1 00
A Northern Governess at the Sunny South—By Professor J. H. Ingraham. 1 50
Birds of a Feather Flock Together—By Edward A. Sothern, the actor ... 1 50
Yachtman's Primer—Correct Instructions for Amateur Sailors. By Warren. 50
Longfellow's Home Life—By Blanche Roosevelt Machetta. Illustrated... 1 50
Every-Day Home Advice—For Household and Domestic Economy......... 1 50
Ladies' and Gentlemen's Etiquette Book of the best Fashionable Society. 1 00
Love and Marriage—A book for unmarried people. By Frederick Saunders. 1 00
Under the Rose—A Capital book, by the author of "East Lynne". 1 00
So Dear a Dream—A novel by Miss Grant, author of "The Sun Maid.".... 1 00
Give me thine Heart—A capital new domestic Love Story by Roe......... 1 00
Meeting her Fate—A charming novel by the author of "Aurora Floyd."... 1 00
Faithful to the End—A delightful domestic novel by Roe................. 1 00
So True a Love—A novel by Miss Grant, author of "The Sun Maid.".... 1 00
True as Gold—A charming domestic story by Roe....................... 1 00

Humorous Works.

A Naughty Girl's Diary........§	50	West India Pickles.W.P.Talboys$1	00
A Good Boy's Diary............	50	The Comic Liar—By Alden......	1 50
Bad Boy's Reader—F. Bellew..	10	Store Drumming as a Fine Art.	50
Abijah Beanpole in New York.	50	Mr.Spriggins—By WidowBedott.	1 50
Never—Companion to "Don't."..	25	Phemie Frost—Ann S. Stephens.	1 50
Always—By author of "Never."..	25	That Awful Boy—N. Y. Weekly.	50
Stop—By author of "Never."....	25	That Bridget of Ours. Do. ..	50
Smart Sayings of Children—Paul	1 00	Orpheus C.Kerr—Four vols.in one.	2 00
Crazy History of the U. S......	50	Ingglish az she iz Spelt.........	25
Cats, Cooks, etc.—By E. T. Ely..	50	Man Abroad....................	25

Miscellaneous Works.

Dawn to Noon—By Violet Fane..$1	50	Gospels in Poetry—E.H.Kimball.$1	50
Constance's Fate. Do. ..	1 50	The Life of Victor Hugo.... ..	50
French Love Songs—Translated.	50	Don Quixote. Illustrated.....	1 00
Lion Jack—By P. T. Barnum....	1 50	Arabian Nights. Do.	1 00
Jack in the Jungle. Do.	1 50	Robinson Crusoe. Do.	1 00
How to Win in Wall Street....	50	Swiss Family Robinson—Illus..	1 00
The Life of Sarah Bernhardt...	25	Debatable Land—R. Dale Owen.	2 00
Arctic Travels—By Dr. Hayes..	1 50	Threading My Way. Do.	1 50
Whist for Beginners......	25	Spiritualism—By D. D. Home...	2 00
Flashes from "Ouida."..........	1 25	Fanny Fern Memorials—Parton	2 00
Lady Blake's Love Letters....	25	Northern Ballads-E. L.Anderson	1 00
Lone Ranch—By Mayne Reid..	1 50	Stories about Doctors—Jeffreson	1 50
The Train Boy—Horatio Alger..	1 25	Stories about Lawyers. Do.	1 50
Dan, The Detective. Do.	1 25		

Miscellaneous Novels.

Doctor Antonio—By Ruffini.....$1	50	Was He Successful ?—Kimball. $1	75
Beatrice Cenci—From the Italian.	1 50	Undercurrents of Wall St. Do.	1 75
The Story of Mary.	1 50	Romance of Student Life. Do.	1 75
Madame—By Frank Lee Benedict	1 50	To-day. Do.	1 75
A Late Remorse. Do.	1 50	Life in San Domingo. Do.	1 75
Hammer and Anvil. Do.	1 50	Henry Powers, Banker. Do.	1 75
Her Friend Laurence. Do.	1 50	Led Astray—By Octave Feuillet.	1 50
Mignonnette—By Sangrée.......	1 00	Boscobel, a Winter in Florida..	1 25
Jessica—By Mrs. W. H. White...	1 50	The Darling of an Empire......	1 50
Women of To-day. Do.	1 50	Confessions of Two..	1 50
The Baroness—Joaquin Miller...	1 50	Nina's Peril—By Mrs. Miller...	1 50
One Fair Woman. Do.	1 50	Marguerite's Journal—For Girls	1 50
The Burnhams—Mrs.G.E.Stewart	2 00	Rose of Memphis—W.C.Falkner	1 50
Eugene Ridgewood—Paul James	1 50	Spell-Bound—Alexandre Dumas.	75
Braxton's Bar—R. M. Daggett..	1 50	Purple and Fine Linen—Fawcett	1 50
Miss Beck—By Tilbury Holt....	1 50	Pauline's Trial—L. D. Courtney.	1 50
A Wayward Life...............	1 00	The Forgiving Kiss—M. Loth..	1 75
Winning Winds—Emerson......	1 50	Measure for Measure—Stanley..	1 50
A College Widow—C.H.Seymour	1 50	Charette—An American novel....	1 50
Me—By Mrs. Spencer W. Coe....	50	Fairfax—By John Esten Cooke...	1 50
Peace Pelican—Fannie Smith...	1 50	Hilt to Hilt. Do.	1 50
Hidden Power—T. H. Tibbles...	1 50	Out of the Foam. Do.	1 50
Two of Us—Calista Halsey......	75	Hammer and Rapier. Do.	1 50
Cupid on Crutches—A. B. Wood.	75	Kenneth—By Sallie A. Brock....	1 75
ParsonThorne—E.M.Buckingham	1 50	Heart Hungry.Mrs.Westmoreland	1 50
Errors—By Ruth Carter.........	1 50	Clifford Troupe. Do.	1 50
UnmistakableFlirtation—Garner	75	Price of a Life—R. F. Sturgis...	1 50
Wild Oats—Florence Marryatt..	1 50	Marston Hall—L. Ella Byrd.....	1 50
Widow Cherry—B. L. Farjeon..	25	Conquered—By a New Author...	1 50
Solomon Isaacs. Do.	50	Tales from the Popular Operas.	1 50
Doctor Mortimer—Fannie Bean.	1 50	Edith Murray—Joanna Mathews	1 50
Two Brides—Bernard O'Reilly..	1 50	San Miniato—Mrs.C.V.Hamilton.	1 00
Louise and I—By Chas. Dodge..	1 50	All for Her—A Tale of New York.	1 50
My Queen—By Sandette........	1 50	L'Assommoir—Zola's great novel	1 00
Fallen among Thieves—Rayne.	1 50	Vesta Vane—By L. King, R.....	1 50
Saint Leger—Richard B. Kimball	1 75	Walworth's Novels—Six vols...	1 75

www.ingramcontent.com/pod-product-compliance
Lightning Source LLC
Chambersburg PA
CBHW032026120726
47901CB00006BB/1670